**More Praise f...
of Emma...**

"A luxurious and sensual read... tenderly romantic.... I didn't want it to end!"
— *New York Times* bestselling author Celeste Bradley

"This wickedly exciting romance will draw you in and take hold of your heart."
— *USA Today* bestselling author Elizabeth Boyle

"Regency fans will thrill to this superbly sensual tale of an icy widow and two decadent rakes.... Balancing deliciously erotic encounters with compelling romantic tension and populating a convincing historical setting with a strong cast of well-developed characters, prolific romance author Wildes provides a spectacular and skillfully handled story that stands head and shoulders above the average historical romance." — *Publishers Weekly* (starred review)

"Wickedly delicious and daring, Wildes's tale tantalizes with an erotic fantasy that is also a well-crafted Regency romance. She delivers a page-turner that captures the era, the mores, and the scandalous behavior that lurks beneath the surface." — *Romantic Times* (4½ stars, top pick)

"Emma Wildes has thoroughly enchanted e-book readers with her emotionally charged story lines.... [A] gem of an author ... Ms. Wildes tells this story with plenty of compassion, humor, and even a bit of suspense to keep readers riveted to each scandalous scene—and everything in between." — Romance Junkies

continued ...

Also by Emma Wildes

The Notorious Bachelors

Our Wicked Mistake
His Sinful Secret
My Lord Scandal

Seducing the Highlander
Lessons from a Scarlet Lady
An Indecent Proposition

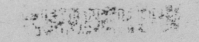

ONE WHISPER AWAY

LADIES IN WAITING

Emma Wildes

A SIGNET ECLIPSE BOOK

SIGNET ECLIPSE
Published by New American Library, a division of
Penguin Group (USA) Inc., 375 Hudson Street,
New York, New York 10014, USA
Penguin Group (Canada), 90 Eglinton Avenue East, Suite 700, Toronto,
Ontario M4P 2Y3, Canada (a division of Pearson Penguin Canada Inc.)
Penguin Books Ltd., 80 Strand, London WC2R 0RL, England
Penguin Ireland, 25 St. Stephen's Green, Dublin 2,
Ireland (a division of Penguin Books Ltd.)
Penguin Group (Australia), 250 Camberwell Road, Camberwell, Victoria 3124,
Australia (a division of Pearson Australia Group Pty. Ltd.)
Penguin Books India Pvt. Ltd., 11 Community Centre, Panchsheel Park,
New Delhi - 110 017, India
Penguin Group (NZ), 67 Apollo Drive, Rosedale, North Shore 0632,
New Zealand (a division of Pearson New Zealand Ltd.)
Penguin Books (South Africa) (Pty.) Ltd., 24 Sturdee Avenue,
Rosebank, Johannesburg 2196, South Africa

Penguin Books Ltd., Registered Offices:
80 Strand, London WC2R 0RL, England

First published by Signet Eclipse, an imprint of New American Library,
a division of Penguin Group (USA) Inc.

First Printing, May 2011
10 9 8 7 6 5 4 3 2

For my cousin Douglas.
You are one of the nicest people I know.

ACKNOWLEDGMENTS

I never embark on this journey alone, and I appreciate the efforts of all the people who help me get from the first page to the last. Thanks again to my agent, the fabulous Barbara Poelle, my wonderful editor, Laura Cifelli, and also Jesse Feldman, who is always on her "A" game.

I'd like to also mention Judie Aitken, who is not only a talented author, but who steered me in the right direction when I mentioned I had a somewhat unusual hero for this story.

Chapter 1

It was a perfectly enjoyable evening until the *incident*.

Lady Cecily Francis smiled graciously at the young man escorting her off the floor, accepted a glass of champagne from a passing footman with a tray, and excused herself, pleading the need to sit down for a few minutes. Her feet were starting to hurt, as she'd been steadily engaged for every dance. *Besieged* was a more appropriate way to put it, and while she was flattered at all the attention, she was not embracing her first season with a high level of enthusiasm.

Cecily thought the ballroom too crowded, the din of hundreds of conversations much too loud, and the air too close. But, as it had been pointed out to her time and again by well-meaning aunts, cousins, and various other members of the family, including her father, a young woman did not snare a husband by languishing in the country.

She spotted her sister standing and chatting with a group of young ladies and made her way toward them, not a particularly easy task in the milling throng. When she was only a few feet away, a small disaster occurred in the form of a rather foxed gentleman telling a story that included a wide gesture with one arm, which unfortunately jostled Cecily's elbow and resulted in a slosh of champagne across her chest. The culprit was oblivious, even when she made an inarticulate sound of dismay. This was the first time she'd worn this gown and blue silk and champagne were not a good mixture. Several droplets trickled between her breasts.

"Allow me."

Glancing up, she looked into the darkest eyes she had ever seen, belonging to a tall man tugging a linen handkerchief from his coat pocket. She recognized him at once, for all of the *haut ton* was whispering over the arrival of Jonathan Bourne, the new Earl of Augustine—partly because of his exotic background and partly due to his striking looks.

"Thank you," she said gratefully, though she was a bit off balance at having the full attention of London's current most notorious and eligible—no one denied the Bourne fortune—earl.

Except he didn't hand her the snowy white square. Instead he leaned forward and, in the middle of a fashionable crush in a London ballroom, audaciously wiped away the untimely spill himself.

Startled, Cecily felt the brush of the fine material across her throat and the upper swells of her breasts, the gesture almost an intimate caress. It was as if he'd touched her without the benefit of the thin piece of linen between her damp skin and his long fingers, and she could not help it, she blushed, the heat rising into her cheeks.

"You are welcome." He tucked the handkerchief away, his expression amused.

A very shocked part of her could not believe he'd just done something so outrageous in front of witnesses, and another wayward part of her was fascinated by the impact of his male beauty. He was sinfully dark, from his sleek ebony hair, currently constrained fashionably in a queue, to those seductive eyes, to his bronze skin. His unusual coloring aside, his bone structure was finely modeled—arched brows, straight nose, slightly square chin . . . and his lower lip a bit fuller, giving his mouth a sensual cast.

He looked foreign and his accent confirmed it.

The quirk of his smile told her he had a very good idea of his impact on her also, not quite arrogant but certainly full of male self-assurance.

That sort of flagrant masculinity was not an English trait, as if the well-cut coat and fitted breeches were part of a disguise. It didn't matter that his cravat was perfectly tied and secured with a glittering diamond stick-pin, or that his boots were obviously custom-made and polished to a high sheen.

Somehow he still managed to give the impression that he was . . . untamed. Exotic. Perhaps even *uncivilized* despite all the trappings of gentility.

Then he made matters worse by leaning forward, close enough that his breath was warm against her ear. "You have turned a very delicious shade of pink, my lady. But console yourself with the knowledge I would much rather have licked it off, so my handkerchief was actually a polite choice." He paused at her slight gasp over that audacious comment. Then he executed a formal bow. "Good evening."

He turned and walked away, past the gaping onlookers as if he didn't even see them.

In contrast, Cecily was all too conscious of the avid stares, among them her sister's. Only a few feet away in the small circle of her friends, Eleanor had an expression of scandalized censure on her face.

Surely it was best to act as if the brief moment hadn't happened? Cecily joined the now-silent group. "Such a crush," she said brightly, but she knew her cheeks were still flame bright.

Eleanor, however, was not quite as willing to ignore what had just happened. "I wasn't aware you knew Lord Augustine," she said pointedly. Two years older, Eleanor was in her second season, her first having been marked by her refusal of several offers of marriage and not exactly a success otherwise either. Her older sister was a great deal more voluptuous than Cecily, her hair an entirely different shade, though there was a family resemblance. This evening she wore a pretty yellow gown, her dark blond hair twisted into an elegant chignon.

"I *don't* know him." Her glass half empty now, Cecily took a gulp.

"He certainly acted in a familiar manner."

As if that was *her* fault. It was a pity most of her champagne had been splashed on her person, for Cecily could have used some sustenance at this moment.

"He's from the colonies," one of her friends said, as if that explained the man's *outré* behavior. "Everyone is talking about it. He's very . . . different."

"So provincial," another one murmured, languidly moving her fan, her eyes narrowed as she followed his progress through the throng, his height making him easily visible. "So unfashionably dark, as well. Is it true his mother was of mixed blood? I'm told she was half savage and half French. What a combination. Earl Savage is somewhat of a mongrel, is he not?"

If the young lady thought so, she still seemed to watch his tall form move through the crowd with feminine interest.

Cecily noticed she wasn't the only one. All the females in the ballroom—at least every one she could see—seemed to find the earl quite interesting.

"It's obvious he's not English, one merely has to look

at him. But for all that, he is intriguingly handsome," Miss Felicia Hasseleman declared. "And by all accounts quite rich. His questionable heritage aside, he isn't a bad prospect. But I hear he isn't interested in marriage. Not a first for him either. I understand he has an illegitimate child and brought her with him from America. He openly acknowledges the little girl but refused to marry her mother."

That *was* rather shocking.

"Even wealth and an earldom cannot make up for *that*," Mary Foxmoor, whose father was a baronet and owned about half of Sussex, said with a sniff. "I would never consider a man who forced me to accept his by-blow. It's . . . distasteful. No, he is not a suitable prospect."

Ah, that subject again. Cecily couldn't help but experience a surge of annoyance that overshadowed her embarrassment over what had just happened. They all had a single purpose: to find a man with a title and a fortune. It might be a romantic and idealistic way to look at it, but Cecily wished to choose a husband for reasons other than his bloodlines and wealth.

And, though she would never say so out loud because it would be repeated everywhere, she did have some admiration for him since he didn't disdain his own flesh and blood and pretend the little girl didn't exist just because she wasn't legitimate. Cecily had no idea what the circumstances were that prompted Lord Augustine to decline to play the gentleman and wed the mother of his child, but she knew that many so-called gentlemen sired children on their mistresses and tucked them away on distant estates or sometimes didn't even take *that* much responsibility.

"What did he say to you?" Eleanor asked, her gaze openly curious.

There was no help for it. Another rush of warmth infused her cheeks as Cecily recalled his scandalous comment. Worse, a traitorous part of her wondered what it would be like to feel that finely modeled mouth graze her bare skin. . . .

She shook her head in brisk refusal.

"You aren't going to tell us?" Felicity said indignantly.

"No." Cecily did her best to look bland. "It was nothing."

All of them exchanged glances. "You're *sure* you don't know Lord Augustine?" Miss Foxmoor asked with skepticism. "He actually whispered in your ear."

"We've never even been introduced," Cecily said shortly, not willing to admit how unsettled that brief encounter had left her.

"Well," Eleanor said dryly, "I think you've met each other now."

For a welcome change, Jonathan wasn't bored. Who would have thought a spilled glass of champagne would so liven up the evening?

Well, not the beverage perhaps, but certainly the lovely bosom it had graced was the reason for his improved enjoyment of the party.

He'd acknowledge that perhaps he shouldn't have been so bold—not in front of the judgmental beau monde, but in his defense, he had been on his best behavior ever since his ship had docked several months ago. The strictures of society had never mattered to him, but he was adjusting, though he found most of it frivolous and, in his eyes, unnecessary.

"Am I about to receive a lecture on propriety?" he asked over the rim of his cut-crystal glass, grateful to be out of the stuffy ballroom and on the terrace. The London sky always held a slight haze from chimney smoke, but at least this evening there were stars, due to a welcome breeze scented with the promise of rain.

James, his first cousin, son of his father's younger brother, just smiled with cynical resignation, propping one arm against the balustrade. "Is it worth it to point out you shouldn't have done it?"

From the shocked expression on the young lady's face, that was true. So Jonathan equivocated. "She's very beautiful."

James blew out a short breath. "So are many other ladies who already eye you with both curiosity and willingness. Different sorts of ladies than the innocent daughter of the Duke of Eddington."

He'd didn't have to be told she was innocent. It had been there in the slight—and very arousing—swift intake of her breath as he leaned close and whispered in her ear.

It wasn't a guess that no man had ever done that before. He'd shocked her, but then again, she hadn't reacted like an outraged innocent either.

How intriguing.

She wore a floral perfume, the provocative scent drifting from her smooth pale skin. And her eyes were an unusual clear topaz color. He'd expected blue from her golden blond hair and ivory complexion. The delicacy of her bone structure and the way her slenderness emphasized her feminine curves had struck him with a surprising impact.

Usually he didn't favor pale blondes, but the duke's daughter was lovely indeed. "What's her name?"

"Cast your interest elsewhere, Jon."

They knew each other well, courtesy of James's service in the Royal Navy, which had sent him to America, where by virtue of family connection their paths had crossed. Considering the tension between their countries—only recently resolved—their communication had been both friendly and constant despite the conflict. Jonathan liked James and would have considered him a friend, their close family tie aside. They even looked a little alike, they'd both been told, though their coloring was very different.

Jonathan arched a brow in amusement. "Are you my keeper now?"

"Thankfully, no." James's grin was rueful. "I doubt anyone could manage that task. But if you'd like some advice, keep in mind this is not the wilderness. The rules of decorum chafe, I agree, but they do exist. I know you dislike autocratic sanctions."

"Boston is hardly a wilderness."

"And how much time do you actually spend in Boston?" James sipped his whiskey and looked bland.

Too much, Jonathan wanted to answer. He disliked cities. Still, he did business in Boston often because he was a partner in a venture that owned several banks there. James was correct in that whenever he could, he resided at his country house. Long rides, early swims in the lake, the sun coming up over the trees . . .

He missed it fiercely already, and he knew his time here had barely begun.

"Tell me about her."

"Shall I begin with how she comes with a price you have expressed no interest in paying? If you wish to stand in a cathedral in front of witnesses and pledge your name and protection for her place in your bed, then go ahead and pursue her. Otherwise, I advise you to look for amusement along other avenues. Her father is a very powerful man. The Duke of Eddington is one of the richest men in Britain."

A night bird sang somewhere, the call unfamiliar. Three weeks in England now. Jonathan felt like such a stranger. Back home he could have identified the bird with unerring accuracy. "I hardly said I wished to dally with her. I'm just curious."

His cousin gave him a long, considering look that was a mixture of amusement and skepticism, and then shrugged. "She made her debut this spring and her older sister is also considered eligible, though not as popular due to her reputation as a bluestocking of the first order. The combination of beauty and dowry has had a predictable impact on society. Lady Cecily is expected to make a very superior match."

Jonathan doubted with cynical practicality that he fell into that *superior* category. For all his fortune and the title he'd never wanted, he did have his mixed blood, and while he might be a novelty to certain English ladies, he was different in a society that celebrated conformity.

Cecily. He thought it suited her. Very English, very delicate, very much reminiscent of rose blossoms in a verdant garden. Yet the very word *match* brought forth a heartfelt grimace. James was right. He wasn't even sure why he'd asked. Even if her highbrow family approved of him—and he was skeptical that they would—he wasn't in the market for a wife.

Time to change the subject away from the duke's delectable but untouchable daughter. He said coolly, "Tell me what you found out today about the mining interests."

He listened as his cousin explained that the records were sketchy and the estate manager had yet again hedged over the ineptitude in the bookkeeping. "Terminate Browne's employment," Jonathan instructed in concise decision. "It's clear he's worth nothing. We'll start looking for a new man tomorrow. I'll hire someone I trust and we can start with a fresh eye to what might have happened."

"I agree. I tried to tell your father a long time ago to reassign management of all of the properties, including the mines."

"And it took me nearly a year to come to England." Jonathan acknowledged that by the time the news of his father's death reached him and he had settled his business obligations in America enough to be able to sail for England, not to mention the length of the voyage, he hadn't arrived to take charge of his inheritance in a timely fashion.

Not to mention that there had been some legalities to handle, such as proving his parentage. To his extreme irritation, there was dissension over his right to inherit, but his father had anticipated the trouble and wisely made sure the right documents were all in place with his solicitor.

Prejudice against half-breed offspring transcended wars and oceans apparently. There were times when he feared for his daughter's future, for she had obstacles to surmount. At least he had legitimacy in his favor.

Adela was the joy of his life.

"But you came," James said with equanimity. "And I, for one, am glad you are here. I wasn't making much progress."

As next in line for the title, his cousin had not only handled affairs until Jonathan's arrival, but he had done so knowing that someone else would inherit. It was a generous gesture, and Jonathan had persuaded him to continue to manage several of his various holdings. "I appreciate all your efforts." Jonathan had to add, "I understand that my half sisters can be a challenge."

"You will find no argument here. Luckily for me," James muttered, lifting his glass to his mouth, "they are *your* problem now."

Chapter 2

By mere coincidence and through no fault of her own, she had set London on its ear.

No, Cecily corrected silently, looking at the blocks of sunlight on the rich rug of her grandmother's formal sitting room. Lord Augustine had caused this furor.

She sat perched on the edge of her embroidered Louis Quatorze chair and said as politely as possible, "Cannot we change the subject?"

Her grandmother, her spine as rigid as a spike, said in a chilly voice, "Did you know they are currently taking wagers in the gentlemen's clubs over what it was he might have said to you?"

The answer to her question was yes, she'd heard—of course, since Eleanor had warned her in a very concise way—but it was clear her grandmother was scandalized at the idea of one of her family being the subject of tawdry betting between young men with too much money and not enough entertainment.

Never mind that Cecily hadn't asked for the dubious honor. Grandmama could be horrified all she wanted, but truly, Cecily knew she'd done nothing wrong.

Other than to refuse to fuel the rumors by repeating what he'd said. Even she wasn't sure why she was being so reticent, except that she'd been more than a little struck by his dark beauty and he truly hadn't been rude in any way. Quite the contrary. A little scandalous . . . yes, that was undisputed, but frankly, Lord Augustine had piqued her interest.

None of the polite, fawning suitors of the season so far had done the same.

"What happened is certainly not worthy of all this attention," she protested. "Some clumsy gentleman bumped me and I spilled a bit of champagne. Lord Augustine came to my aid. That is *all* that happened."

"He touched your . . . your *person*, and with outrageous informality whispered something to you in a way that even a husband would not do with his wife in such a public venue."

Perhaps because most aristocratic husbands and wives can barely stand each other. She almost said it out loud, but refrained. Another lecture on the benefits of dynastic alliances and her duty as the daughter of a duke was the last conversation she wanted.

Well, maybe not the last, because the current one wasn't all that enjoyable either. If she could, she'd eschew reprimanding lectures for the rest of her life.

"I am not responsible for his lordship's behavior," Cecily said with as much calm as possible, seeing with relief the arrival of a maid with the tea trolley. "And really, all he did was come to my aid."

"Not quite the story recounted to me."

Later, she would strangle Eleanor for pleading a headache and avoiding tea with the Dowager Duchess of Eddington, leaving Cecily to face the old dragon alone. She loved her grandmother, but there was no doubt she was a formidable personage in many ways.

"It was perfectly innocent."

"If so, why not just reveal what he said?"

Now there was a valid point. "Well, it was not *completely* innocent," she admitted with reluctance. "However, I do not want everyone to keep talking about it, so I have declined to comment."

To her surprise, her grandmother paused for a moment and then nodded in approval. "If it would fuel the fire, it is best to keep it to yourself."

Through several cups of tea, currant scones, éclairs, and the chef's famous raspberry jam, the subject lapsed and Cecily almost thought she was free of it until she rose to leave, going over to give her grandmother a dutiful kiss on the cheek.

Her gray hair neatly coiffed, the lines of her patrician face as uncompromising as her posture, her grandmother said unexpectedly, "I know you will find this difficult to believe, but you are the spitting image of myself at eighteen."

Cecily straightened and smiled. "That is encouraging. You are very handsome, Grandmama."

"Humph." The sound was derisive, but there could have been a faint uncharacteristic gleam of humor in her eyes. "False flattery doesn't move me. My point is that beauty can be a commodity, child, or it can be a liability. Maybe it would be best to keep your distance from Lord Augustine."

Cecily left a bit bemused, for her grandmother rarely said anything personal. As she headed back toward her room, she happened to encounter her brother in the hallway of the family apartments. Roderick halted when he caught sight of her. "I was just looking for you."

With the same fair coloring and fine family features, he was close enough in age that they'd spent many childhood hours together, though as the heir, he had gone off to Eton, and then Cambridge, and been kept apart as they approached adulthood and he trained to become the duke someday. Only since she'd come to London had she had seen a little more of her brother.

"You just missed tea with Grandmama," she informed him.

"Thank God," he muttered.

"Are we being disrespectful?"

"It wasn't my intention, but it is still heartfelt gratitude to the powers above. I will freely admit she terrifies me most of the time. Can I have a word?"

Cecily laughed, but then it faded and she eyed him with an enlightened wariness. "Only if it isn't about Lord Augustine. I am sick unto death over the subject. Really, society needs more titillating events to keep their attention."

"I won't mention his name." Her brother scowled. "Though I am half tempted to—"

She interrupted with decisive firmness. "Don't you dare do anything to keep my name on the tongue of every gossipmonger in the *ton*."

His eyes were crystalline blue, like their father's and Eleanor's, and he hesitated and held her gaze for a moment before he nodded. "I'll leave it alone."

"I would advise it." Not just for the sake of her reputation, but she had a fair idea that Jonathan Bourne was not someone she wanted her brother facing in a duel. Not only was Roderick younger, but he lacked that highly honed edge of danger. Besides, defending her honor was not necessary. Other than that outrageous comment, no insult had been given. As it was, the whispers wouldn't last. The *ton* was notoriously fickle. "Now," she said, drawing in a breath, "what is it you wish to discuss?"

"Viscount Drury."

She didn't mean to groan out loud, but truly, she couldn't help it. "Roddy, I—"

"Hear me out," he interrupted with an impatient gesture.

The elegant hallway with its high ceilings and small polished tables was suddenly not private enough. She had a sense of what her brother was going to say. "Fine. I'd rather talk in here."

The sitting room off her bedroom was at least more secluded. Who knew when a chambermaid might come along with an armful of linens, and if they continued to argue in the hallway they might be overheard. Well, maybe not *argue*, but she knew they were about to strongly disagree.

Roderick followed her, quiet as he closed the door, and when he turned around, he said abruptly, "He is going to offer for you. He told me so this afternoon. With Father's permission in hand, he plans to propose to you. Surely you knew."

"I was afraid of it." Cecily sat down abruptly on the edge of a silk-covered chair and sighed. Elijah Winters, Lord Drury, had been very attentive. Two bouquets of flowers had arrived just that morning, and he had begun to call almost every day. It was problematic in more than just one way.

"Afraid of it? That doesn't sound very promising."

"I know he is your friend."

"But?" Roderick didn't sit but paced over to the fireplace and turned around, elegant in his dark blue coat, his hair fashionably mussed. "I hear the hedging in your voice."

She clasped her hands. "But there are two very good reasons I will refuse, the least of which is I am not interested. The first and foremost is Eleanor."

Her brother actually looked surprised. "What? What does she have to do with this?"

Are all men so dense? she wondered irritably.

Carefully, she said, "She is fond of him in a way I am not."

"I thought you liked him."

"I do." Cecily fought the urge to grind her teeth. "But not as she does. Haven't you noticed?"

"No."

"Think about it. She wears her nicest gowns when he comes here. She tries her best to be tactful, which is her downfall, for when she stifles her personality, it comes off too stilted. Lord Drury might just be as oblivious as you are. It is somewhat of a problem. As far as I can tell, she is so terrified of saying the wrong thing to him that she barely manages to string two words together coherently. If she didn't care what he thought, she would simply be herself. Then there is also the way she looks at him."

"Looks at him?" Her brother seemed truly mystified.

Explaining it looked to be a lesson in futility, so Cecily just said, "Trust me, she is infatuated with him. Surely you know that last season he had an interest in her, but something happened."

"I suppose they seemed to chat a bit more than is usual. . . . Eleanor isn't the average female and she likes to talk about politics and such. I thought that was it," he admitted. "He never said anything to me that indicated it was more than an acquaintance."

"Did it strike you that she declined to even entertain an offer of marriage from anyone else?"

"She's remarkably stubborn, you know that. What makes you think he had anything to do with it?"

It was difficult to draw the line between confidence and speculation, and Roddy might not be the most perceptive male on earth—was there even such a creature?—but he was trustworthy, so Cecily said abruptly, "At the beginning of the season she wrote me about him."

Roderick's demeanor changed. "She did?"

Eleanor was not one to write in the first place, much

less to reveal her intimate thoughts. That letter was quite telling. "Yes, she did. And described him in glowing terms, for her."

It finally sank in. Roderick muttered, "Oh, I see." Then he dropped into a delicate chair that looked insufficient to hold his tall body and rubbed his forehead. "Well, that's a damnable complication."

Lord Drury was a very nice man. He was also handsome, rich, and well mannered. Cecily was sure he would make an admirable husband. For her sister. Who she was convinced wanted him. "Isn't it?" she agreed. "The question is how are you going to deal with it?"

"Me?" Her brother's slumped form straightened in alarm. "I do not see how this is my affair."

She gazed at him, almost laughing at the surprise evident in his expression. "Yes, indeed. *You.* We just discussed how you and Drury are friends. Can't you speak to him about Eleanor? She's beautiful, accomplished, and everything else a man could want. Find out what happened to cool his interest."

"I think I can guess." Roderick ran his hand through his fair hair. "She's often too opinionated. No one says anything in front of me, but I know it is why she was so unpopular her first season."

Unfortunately their sister was also extremely outspoken, too clever by half, and did not have a flirtatious bone in her body. Cecily had the feeling men found her intimidating compared to most of the simpering debutantes. Because of Eleanor's tendency to be less than diplomatic, she made it a point to keep as quiet as possible in social situations, and that didn't help matters either. Cecily was sure people could sense the awkwardness.

"I agree. As I said, I think there was an incident between them."

"I didn't know she fancied him in a serious way."

Roderick looked chagrined. "And he's besotted with you. Does she realize it?"

Besotted was the wrong word. Maybe the viscount thought she was suitable, but that was quite different from infatuation, and Cecily rather thought her sister *did* realize it. "If she does, she has never mentioned it, but that alone speaks volumes. I now think he might be the reason she hasn't favored anyone else."

"Are you sure?"

Cecily nodded. "You could hint at her interest, but in the most delicate way possible."

"Delicate?" Roderick sounded appalled.

Maybe that was the wrong word to use with the male of the human species. She amended her comment: "Be subtle. Bring up her name and gauge his reaction. Maybe if he knew how she feels, he might assess the situation differently. I haven't received the impression he is truly fond of me—we don't know each other well enough for that. I've just had my coming out, and he has decided it is time to look for a wife. I'm flattered, but I suspect we'd end up boring each other to death. He needs someone much more like Eleanor."

Roderick eyed her dubiously and asked again, "You're sure this is true?"

She thought of the last party they'd attended and how Eleanor had watched the handsome viscount the entire evening, while feigning nonchalance. She and Eleanor might be several years apart in age, but they were very close and Cecily *knew* her sister. She nodded decisively. "I am."

It sounded distinctly like her brother said a blasphemous word under his breath. "I suppose if you are going to refuse him, I can find some diplomatic way of mentioning Eleanor." Roderick rose then, but he paused before leaving the room. His gaze was direct. "I know

I said I wouldn't bring it up, but what the devil *did* Augustine say to you the other night? I'm as curious as everyone else."

Is the whole world obsessed with this question?

If she told him the truth, he might just play the outraged brother, and maybe he even should, but once again, it would lift the gossip to new heights. The earl had been audacious, but certainly it wasn't worth the furor over it.

"It was nothing," she said firmly.

Jonathan reined in his horse and slid off, patting the neck of the sleek black with an appreciative hand. "Good afternoon, Will."

"Did you have a good ride, milord?" The young groom came forward and took the reins, his expression scrupulously polite, but there was a hint of humor in his eyes. "'Tis a lovely day."

At least the staff seemed to like his lack of formality He knew his peers were not nearly as accepting. "Riding in a park isn't exactly the same as what I am used to, but yes, it was good to enjoy a bit of sunshine." Jonathan tugged off his gloves and grinned. "And I was able to absent myself while a drove of females descended on the household. Maybe you'd better leave Seneca saddled in case I need to make a quick escape."

The boy grinned back. "I'll have him at the ready, sir."

Earl or not, there was no issue in Jonathan's mind with familiarity with servants, and the boy, probably no more than sixteen, with his shock of fair hair and ingenuous good humor, was a natural with horses, which lifted any man high in his opinion. He asked with resignation, "I take it my sisters have arrived?"

"Two hours ago."

He was doomed to having to play host and guardian,

and he knew it, so he merely inclined his head. "I suppose I had better go in."

Will coughed on a laugh. "No help for it, milord, I'm afraid."

As he strode toward the front of the house and the steps, Jonathan mentally shook his head. It was bad enough having to travel to England to assume his responsibilities as his father's only son, but to have to deal with the animosity of his family was a teeth-grinding ordeal he wished he could simply avoid. That didn't appear possible, however. The most untenable part of the whole situation was that by the technicality of English law, he was the guardian of each one of them until they married.

How ironic. Being responsible for three young ladies who disdained him. But he had done his duty in that he'd invited them to London, and though Lillian's note back had been to the point and barely polite, she had accepted for all of them with a literary sniff of ungraciousness.

James was right. They *were* his problem.

Very much so.

That was fine. He could easily endure their derision if that was how it was going to be, but he would not tolerate it if they snubbed Adela. His daughter shouldn't have to pay for his sins, and he knew firsthand what it was like to suffer for a questionable parentage, earl or not. He'd even debated leaving his daughter behind with his aunt, but both he and Adela would suffer from being apart, so he hoped he'd made the right decision. In the next few moments, he would find out if it was a mistake.

His three half sisters were in the formal drawing room, he discovered, sitting in silence as if it were some sort of penance, hands folded in their laps, their expressions reflecting varying levels of emotion. Lily, naturally, he noted as he stood in the doorway, declined to do more than simply cast a glance in his direction, her hauteur evident. Betsy was absorbed in the view out to the gardens and didn't seem to notice him standing there, but the youngest, Carole, actually offered a tentative smile.

They were different from each other in personality, but in looks they had all inherited their father's fairness and elegant bone structure. Given his dark skin and ebony hair, he could hardly believe that he and the three of them shared a common parent

There was also more that separated them. And he wasn't referring to their two very different continents. They were English ladies. He was hardly an aristocrat by any standard except that of his birth.

Yet they were irrevocably tied together. He could care less about estates and wills and monetary gain, but when he'd received the letter informing him of his father's death, he did care about his half sisters enough to cross the Atlantic to make sure he saw to their futures. He could have entrusted solicitors to deal with the details, but quite frankly, his mother's people instilled in every member of the tribe a sense of responsibility for the welfare of them all. Family was everything.

This was why he'd come to England.

It was no surprise that Lily spoke first. "We're here," she said rigidly, as if he couldn't see them clearly. At twenty-two, she was the oldest. Looking at her he wasn't sure why she hadn't married yet. Her hair was a glossy chestnut brown, her skin flawless and pale, and her eyes a clear blue. He wouldn't describe her as a raving beauty, but she was certainly very pretty, and he knew from his meetings with his father's solicitors that she had a generous dowry.

James had described her as far too independent by nature, and maybe it was true. She certainly made no secret of her lack of desire to come to London, but Jonathan had insisted, since he could hardly supervise new wardrobes and the other—to him a mystery—nuances of what it took to launch a young lady into London society on his own. They had one aunt who was a possibility as a chaperone, but she suffered from a disease of the joints and was currently still in Essex, unable to make the journey.

So it was up to him. At least Lillian had been through a launch into society before. He needed help of some kind, and if she wasn't willing to do it for him, she needed to do it for their two younger sisters.

"Your arrival is duly noted." He strolled in and headed for the brandy decanter. When dealing with three females who were virtually strangers and not necessarily friendly, a little fortitude was not a bad idea. "How was the journey?" he inquired politely.

"Tolerable."

He picked up a glass, dashed some of the amber liquid into it from the decanter, and took a healthy sip. It allowed him a moment to decide how to respond. After all, he didn't know his half sisters well, and culturally they were an ocean apart from him. "Glad to hear it."

Three pairs of blue eyes regarded him with what was probably well-deserved disparagement for such an innocuous comment.

His smile was crooked. "Let me rephrase. I am delighted that all three of you have decided to join me here in London, for without you I am uncertain that I will behave myself with the decorum associated with the earls of Augustine."

"Word has it," Lily said with frosty propriety, "you have already failed there, my lord."

Chapter 3

It was very difficult to live a lie, and more so when facing down her older brother, his dark inquiring gaze seeming to go right through her.

She was *such* a fraud.

Lily sat up so straight her spine ached and with effort controlled the inner desire to burst into tears. Jonathan, the new Earl of Augustine, looked at her in question, and truly, she wasn't even sure why she'd brought the challenge up.

She didn't hate him. How could you hate someone you didn't know? She did despise what he represented, which was their father's desire to marry a heathen in America. And always, always, in her mind was how her mother had not been the love of his life but second-best, the match arranged by their families upon his return to England after the death of his first wife, Jonathan's mother.

It was a hard task to come to terms with the fact that her mother and father had never loved each other. She hadn't ever quite mastered it. It was ironic to realize that it had always bothered Lily far more than it bothered her mother, who had enjoyed her role as countess and freely spent her husband's fortune.

They were both gone now, dead within days of each other from the same virulent fever, and she and her sisters were utterly dependent on this half brother that none of them knew. In her memory, Jonathan had come to England only once. Their father had preferred to visit his son in America.

She resented her brother for that too. Those long absences had been difficult. Though her mother hadn't seemed to care overmuch, Lily had missed her beloved father terribly as a child.

Along those same lines, Jonathan had blithely brought his bastard along, as if it wasn't going to stir up scandal. The man clearly had no sense of propriety.

At the moment, though, she'd already spoken up, so there was no use for it but to brazen it out. She cleared her throat. "You are the subject of much gossip, my lord."

As if *she* had the right to condemn him. Her sordid mistake had kept the gossip sheets full for weeks, maybe even months.

He had the nerve to look amused. "Am I?"

"Indeed."

There. It was said. His past indiscretion aside, she didn't have to point out how he'd been seen publicly touching the bosom of the Duke of Eddington's daughter. What good would that do? It was enough to level an accusing stare in his direction and wait.

After all, she was not in charge. *He* was.

A damnable truth.

They looked nothing alike. He was dark—in every way. Dark hair, dark eyes, bronze skin. Handsome . . . she supposed he was, with their father's fine bones and his mother's barbaric coloring. Tall, wide-shouldered, with his hair currently constrained neatly but obviously much too long to be fashionable. Society had already dubbed him "Earl Savage."

He took another sip of the brandy and simply

shrugged. "I cannot imagine why anyone would listen to common gossip."

She wasn't altogether surprised he dismissed society's strictures, given his general air of disregard for convention.

But, a voice in her head pointed out with annoying logic, he wasn't raised in England, and for that matter, he was wealthy and privileged and *male*, which meant he could do as he damn well pleased as long as it didn't bother him to be the target of censure and avid interest. Which, it needed to be noted, he already was.

"They do," she said acerbically.

"I see." Maybe—just maybe—there was a small flicker of reaction in his eyes. "Do I somehow owe you all an apology?"

It was Carole who said, "No. Gentlemen are allowed to behave as they wish."

Ever the peacemaker. Actually, both Betsy and Carole were remarkably even-tempered and well mannered. *She* was the impulsive one. Lily debated for a moment whether or not she should point out that he might owe the Duke of Eddington's daughter an apology, but decided not to pursue an argumentative course. Jonathan would have to handle that on his own.

She had her sisters to protect. Antagonizing the current Earl of Augustine was counterproductive to her purposes. She would have stayed in the country if possible, but as much as she might be loath to admit it, he was right. She had ruined her chances for a good match, but she wanted to see both Betsy and Carole settled with suitable gentlemen. Not just because of sisterly duty but because she truly loved them and they deserved it. In the end, she said merely, "I wasn't aware if you realized under how much scrutiny your every move will be."

Her brother propped a shoulder against the mantel

and smiled with a lazy quirk of his lips, the snifter of brandy cupped in his long fingers. "I think I'm learning. If my sisters in Essex have heard something about me, I must have committed some atrocious blunder. I don't suppose this has to do with the lovely Lady Cecily?"

Well, at least he wasn't *completely* unaware.

"Yes, it does. Perhaps you should keep your hand-kerchief to yourself," she suggested wryly, relenting a little, because truthfully, his response was surprisingly gracious.

"My intentions were chivalrous, I assure you."

"The problem seems to be with the execution." Lily was acutely aware of both Betsy and Carole listening to the exchange with rapt attention. They were young, the former nineteen and the latter eighteen . . . so elaboration in their presence was not appropriate. "That aside, and since we are here, do you have any idea of how you wish to proceed with the season, my lord?"

"You are my sister, Lillian. I am sure there is no need for you to address me in such a formal manner."

He was rather infuriatingly right, but on the other side of the coin, she had no idea of his intentions when it came to her sisters. Would he provide a proper coming out for them or would he be parsimonious about it? She didn't know him well enough to judge. Stiffly, she said, "We do not have a close acquaintance. Formality seems appropriate."

And safe. She liked safety. Forming attachments had always presented a problem. Look at the aching loss she'd suffered after what had happened to her parents. Look at what had happened with Arthur. There was no choice with her sisters—she loved them already. No one could dictate that she had to love *him* just because they had the same father.

"So fierce. It reminds me of the strong women of my people."

She flushed at the undercurrent of soft mockery in his tone. Though, to be fair, she wasn't exactly welcoming her older brother with open arms either. He sensed it, and she didn't blame him particularly if he resented her lack of enthusiasm over his presence.

"Your people?" she asked with clipped inquiry. "May I remind you that you are an Englishman as well as a member of the aristocracy? Our family has ties back to William of Normandy."

"I suppose I should have phrased it differently. The part of my heritage that I understand better. And for your information, my mother's family was in America thousands of years before William of Normandy was even born. She was the daughter of a chieftain, and I am more aristocratic through her than through our father."

That small speech, carefully modulated, stopped her, especially since he didn't seem antagonistic as much as he was simply stating a fact. Lillian sat with her hands folded in her lap and wondered if he'd often had to defend his unusual lineage. There was something about him that said he didn't usually bother.

The room was suddenly much too civilized, especially with him standing there, courteous and yet, despite how he was dressed, still less than English, with his different coloring and dark, uncompromising stare. He wasn't from her world, but now he controlled it.

Unfair.

"I'm not trying to be judgmental." She summoned a reasonable tone. "I'm merely pointing out the repercussions of committing what could be viewed as a serious lapse in etiquette by the *ton*."

He didn't care. He didn't even have to say it. It was

evident in the nonchalant pose of his lean body, and the irreverent laughter in his eyes. "And what might that be?"

Ooh, he was exasperating. It was also clear that he was a free spirit, and his disregard for social criticism—if she was willing to admit it—was something they shared with their father. Papa had married extremely unconventionally, and God alone knew she'd thumbed her nose at the gossip and taken her own road. It was hypocritical for her to fault her brother for having the same flaw.

The road to ruin.

And the cost . . . dear heavens, the cost . . .

Primly, she said, "My lord, can we discuss this alone?"

"My study?" Jonathan couldn't decide if he should be amused or annoyed as he made the suggestion. Obviously, Lily didn't want their younger sisters to hear what she wanted to say, but he was not certain he wanted to hear it either.

"I suppose Father's study would be acceptable." Lily rose immediately. There was a steely glint in her eye that gave him pause, and she walked past him in a whisper of light blue muslin.

James had been a bit evasive on the subject of Lady Lillian, other than saying she was on the independent side, and Jonathan was wondering if that might not just be the understatement of the year. She was too young to be so grave, and maybe expecting her to help oversee their sisters' debut was asking too much, but this was not familiar territory for him either. If he'd already blundered, God alone knew it just might happen again. Because he didn't care for himself, it was difficult to understand how desperately important social status might be to his family. In his world, it was insignificant, but in theirs . . . well, someone had to teach him the rules.

Adela had to be considered also. She was too young now to feel the ramifications of ostracism, but one day she might.

Both Carole and Betsy, mirror images of each other with their shining curls and blue eyes, watched them leave, neither one of them making a comment.

Of course Lillian knew the way to the study, he mused as he politely followed her decisive footsteps down the marble hallway. She had been raised between the London town house and the country estate.

He had not. *Father's study*. Maybe in truth it belonged more to her than it did to him.

It put him in his place as the usurper—never mind that he had never wanted the title in the first place. She didn't accept him as earl, and quite frankly, he wasn't sure he could blame her.

That was only one of the many differences between them.

Lily immediately took a chair by the fireplace, unlit at this time of year. The window was open to the late-afternoon breeze, and the light wind blew a loose, shining curl across her cheek. She said succinctly, "We need to speak plainly."

"My preference, always." Jonathan folded his arms across his chest and sat casually on the edge of the desk. "Please do so, for I am in the dark as to the need for this conversation."

"I didn't wish to discuss this in front of Betsy and Carole."

"That was made clear enough."

She visibly squared her shoulders. "What has Cousin James told you?"

"About what?" Quizzically, he regarded his sister.

She swallowed. He saw the convulsive ripple of the muscles in her slim throat. Her voice had an audible tremor. "Are you being deliberately obtuse? Or are you trying to spare my feelings by pretending you don't know?"

That was a tricky question if he'd ever heard one.

"Lily," he said, feeling his way through it because if there was one thing he wasn't talented at, it was reassuring uncertain young women. Well, he could do fairly well with five-year-olds, but this wasn't the same thing at all. "Perhaps you should just tell me what it is you are afraid James might have revealed."

"It is mortifying." She glanced away.

Mortifying. Yes, it was. He saw it in her posture, in the rigidity of her slender body in the blue gown that even he recognized was not in the latest fashion, in the tense set of her features.

For the first time since setting foot on English soil and realizing he was responsible for his siblings, he actually *understood* it.

This trouble does not just belong to her. It also belongs to me.

His aunt—who had raised him upon the death of his mother—would have called it a "serene sign," that phrase encompassing all the situations in which a person was guided—gently—in a direction they didn't wish to go.

Like this one.

"Enlighten me." He crossed to a small side table, poured another snifter of brandy, and after a moment, took the decanter of sherry and poured his sister a measure of it. At first he thought she would refuse the goblet, but then she accepted it with trembling fingers.

"Thank you." She didn't drink but just stared at her glass, her face slightly averted.

"In return tell me why we are here."

"They don't need to hear it."

"I assume you mean Carole and Betsy. . . . Why?"

Lily glanced up, her pallor noticeable. "You must be discreet because I have not been. My scandal was bad enough. They will not fare well in society if our family endures another one. If you haven't heard of it already, you will. They know some of it, of course, because everyone knows, but I am not sure if they understand how my notoriety will affect them."

What was so poignant, he discovered, was that she meant it. She was all of two and twenty. Did she not realize that at her age, all matters seemed catastrophic when in truth few were? Life went on. He might only be seven years older, but he'd learned that lesson.

"I am perishing from curiosity to discover," he said in lazy contemplation, "what a proper English lady like yourself might have done to supposedly humiliate her family."

There was only a minute's hesitation. "I spent the night with Viscount Sebring." Lily glanced up, her blue eyes dark but her gaze direct. Her chin lifted. "He refused to marry me."

Perhaps the most peculiar part of this conversation was that Jonathan experienced a murderous urge to make this heretofore unknown nobleman—though the man's nobility was questionable, considering the content of the current conversation—accountable for apparently ruining his sister's life. It wasn't pathos on her part either, for he'd been subjected to that before by emotional females and he could tell from the way Lily held herself that his help would not be welcomed. It was more just a curious sense of duty over what he'd previously thought would not engage him.

He was, he found, quite engaged. Involved. The look in her eyes alone would move any person with even a modicum of compassion, and he was her brother.

Good God, he was her *brother*. For his whole life that

had been an abstract concept, but at this moment, with her trembling body sitting on the edge of the chair in the room that used to belong to their father, the impact of his position was real. Lily had no one to protect her except him.

"He refused to marry the daughter of an earl? That is hard to believe. Tell me what happened." Jonathan sat down. His height was imposing and he knew it and he very much wanted his answer.

"It was an accident." Her voice was low.

"What you mean is he planned it and you accidentally fell into the trap. Go on."

"You don't know him." That brought her head up and her gaze was defiant. "Besides, as I understand it, you might have something in common with him. At least in our case there was no child."

She still defended this man. That was interesting. Jonathan ignored the jibe about the circumstances of his daughter's birth. He was aware of the rumor that he had not played the gentleman and had declined to marry Adela's mother. "He ruined you, and then refused to follow an honorable course. Is there something else I need to know?" His inquiry was polite but to the point. He was surprised to a certain extent that James hadn't told him, but his potentially lethal reaction might be just exactly why. It *did* anger him. "Introduce us so he and I can discuss this in person."

"There's no need for that."

"It seems to me there is."

"How do you know it was his fault?"

The question silenced him. She was right; he couldn't be sure. He didn't know her well enough to judge.

She went on coolly, "We are not talking about me, but about our sisters' upcoming season. All I wanted to say was that in light of my indiscretion, I feel it would be best if you didn't go beyond the pale in any way."

Considering her obvious dismay over his new role in her life, it certainly must have cost her to put it so plainly. Jonathan regarded her with ironic humor. "In short, I should keep my good intentions to myself and stay clear of champagne-soaked young ladies, is that it?"

She nodded. "People are watching you because you are . . ."

He waited, brows lifted.

". . . different," she finished, but had the grace to flush even though she'd managed to stay pale and resolute during her damning confession.

"Ah, yes, Earl Savage."

The color in her cheeks deepened. "I would never have said that."

His shrug was genuine. Even in his native country his mixed heritage was not without its drawbacks. Here in England, he was even more of an anomaly—only half the exalted earl and the other half a mix of the hated French and his mother's tribe. It was no wonder, he thought with philosophical contemplation, that he was viewed with dubious interest. "It doesn't concern me."

"But we *should* be concerned for Betsy and Carole."

He drank some brandy, but his casual pose was a bit deceptive. He wanted to return to America as soon as possible. The only way to do that was to marry his sisters off.

All three of them. As they were pretty and from a prestigious family and had good dowries, it had hardly seemed a difficult task before now, but even though Lily was probably the prettiest of the three, it seemed there was an obstacle he hadn't foreseen.

Damn Viscount Sebring. Damn one very enchanting

duke's daughter who had gotten him into trouble, and most of all damn the paradigm of the aristocracy that condemned a young woman to social ruin should she find herself compromised in the company of a male— who, since he was held to different standards, could just walk away.

This needed sorting out, and the sooner the better.

Lily's expression was stiff, but she managed to say evenly, "You have a child of your own. What of her?"

Jonathan inclined his head. "Yes, I have a daughter. She is very excited to meet her aunts."

"You must want to protect her from all the whispers."

"I am fairly sure she is young enough that she will not understand, and besides, I think she is going to have to become accustomed to whispers anyway." A truth that disturbed him, but it was what it was. "The circumstances of her birth aside, she looks very much like me."

"Yes." Lily's spoke slowly. "I suppose she will have much to overcome. Maybe you should have left her in America."

"That was something I considered but decided against." He said it coolly, because it was the perfect truth. "I'm her only parent and she needs me."

Just as I am your guardian and you need me also, whether you like the situation or not.

"I think," he said evenly, "you should tell me exactly what happened between you and Lord Sebring."

Lily stood and set aside her wine with a decisive click on the closest table. "Never," she said without equivocation.

And she meant it.

Interesting.

"Papa!"

The door opening without ceremony wasn't that

much of a surprise, as since their arrival Adela had been given free rein of the house. His daughter came dashing in, her dark hair in disarray, the ribbon that had neatly tied it back earlier long gone. In his admittedly biased opinion she was a beautiful child, with huge dark eyes and what was at times an almost exhausting vitality.

"You forgot to knock, Addie," he said mildly.

She stopped, momentarily arrested. "Oh, yes . . . sorry. Truly."

He smiled. Maybe it was a failing, but he rarely scolded her. He'd never looked upon it as being indulgent as much as that her infractions were usually the product of her ebullient personality and not actual misbehavior. "Before you tell me what is so important that you had to burst through the door, let me introduce you to your aunt Lillian."

Adela sketched a credible curtsy, her pink lace-trimmed dress showing suspicious smudges that told him she'd been out in the gardens again. "Pleased, ma'am."

To her credit, Lily, who had not yet done so in his presence, smiled. "I am also pleased to meet you, Adela."

"Papa calls me Addie." His daughter then whirled around, the formalities apparently dismissed, and said with all the earnest enthusiasm of a five-year-old, "In the stables there are *puppies*."

"What a miracle," he said dryly. "I take it you have already selected one."

She nodded, her dark eyes pleading. "Please. Oh . . . *please*."

What was one more complication in his already disordered life? And he'd certainly uprooted her and brought her to this foreign place. Jonathan said, "I have no objection, but it is not going to sleep in your room, so you must ask Cook if it can spend time in her kitchen. If she agrees, I—"

He stopped, for a small whirlwind exited the room at the same speed she'd entered it.

Then a remarkable thing happened. Lillian actually laughed.

Chapter 4

"It has been brought to my attention that perhaps I owe you an apology for my *outré* behavior."

Drat. No, double drat.

It was *him*.

Cecily pasted on her most gracious smile and plotted how to escape as soon as possible before turning around. That voice. She'd know it anywhere. The vowels were too rounded, the consonants not hollowed but somehow richer, and she caught a whiff of his cologne, which was also unfamiliar but intriguingly masculine.

Earl Savage.

She turned, looked up into velvet dark eyes, conscious of the crowded salon, the musicians on the dais tuning their instruments. The room was large, but it suddenly seemed very small, as if he was much, much too close, when in truth he was an appropriate distance away, standing by the chair next to hers.

Dissembling about the current furor wasn't a viable option. She wasn't very good at it anyway, and for moral reasons was opposed to lying, but she also found that even if you were able to convincingly submit a falsehood and have it accepted, more than half the time you were tripped up later, so what the point of it?

She opted for saying coolly, "There's no need for an apology, my lord."

"I'm told there is." He didn't precisely grin, but his mouth twitched suspiciously and he definitely did not look repentant as, to her chagrin, he chose the vacant seat next to her and sank into it in a graceful athletic movement, stretching out his long legs.

To her right, Eleanor gave what could only be interpreted as a gasp of dismay. Joining them without an invitation was hardly what a polite gentleman would do, but it appeared that didn't concern him.

Instead of apologetic, he looked quite . . . deliciously male. His dark coat was perfectly cut, and the contrast of his snowy cravat with his bronze skin dramatic. He would no doubt be that color all over, Cecily imagined involuntarily. Every inch of him, and . . .

That supremely unladylike thought came from nowhere. Never had she imagined any of the gentlemen of her acquaintance without their clothing. That she'd done so now was mortifying.

His regard was almost unsettlingly direct. "You haven't repeated what I said to you, which I suppose is just as well, but it has caused a great deal of speculation. I've heard there is actual wagering over what it might have been. Are all you aristocrats that bored and shallow?"

The insult stung, especially since he'd caused the problem in the first place. Though, if she admitted it, she secretly agreed with him. People were starving in the streets and wealthy young men were tossing money away on a single whispered sentence in a society ballroom. The frivolous waste bothered her more than the gossip.

"Lord Augustine, I hate to state the obvious, but *you* are a member of the class you just disparaged."

His teeth flashed dazzling white in a swift smile. "Am I? Oddly enough, I don't seem to quite fit in. At best I only half belong and I am perceptive enough to realize that the difference between myself and the lofty *ton* is not based on the color of my skin alone."

Since she had just been thinking the same thing—but with a different slant—to her chagrin, she blushed. She could feel the warm blood rise through her neck and heat her cheeks. She was rarely at a loss for words, but his bluntness robbed her of the ability to fling back a swift retort.

So did his overwhelming masculinity. The width of his shoulders was daunting; and even seated and seemingly relaxed he gave the impression of power. . . and maybe even danger.

He went on in a conversational tone as if they were discussing the weather. "My personal views on the attitudes of the English nobility aside, is there something I can do to repair the damage? You know better than I do, I'm sure."

To her surprise, he sounded sincere, though she would have sworn he was the kind of man who cared very little for convention.

At last she found her voice. "It *has* gotten to be ridiculous."

"Tell him not coming over and sitting next to you might help." Eleanor, who had been listening unabashedly to every word, hissed furiously in her ear. "People are staring again."

Cecily did her best to ignore her sister, but no doubt she was right. Unfortunately Lord Augustine proved to have extremely good hearing. He said mildly, "Your sister is probably correct, but I am not ravishing you on the floor in public. We are just having a conversation. How can there be any cause for alarm in that?"

"People will think you are paying attention to me,"

she explained, wondering if the room was really over-heated or if his proximity was the problem.

"I certainly hope I am as we are currently speaking to each other."

"I mean—"

"I know what you mean, Lady Cecily." The interruption was softened by a humorous quirk of his arched dark brows. "They will think I have a romantic interest."

Do you?

She almost said it out loud, partially because of the way he was looking at her, but maybe more because of how *she* was looking at *him*.

To her dismay the music was starting, which meant he had to leave now or it would be rude of him to get up and change seats during the performance. Not that she was positive it would deter him, but she sensed his disregard for society was based more on a lack of affectation than a lack of manners.

The soft sound of the violin began, the strains floating out and the murmured conversation fading.

Then he did it again. He leaned so close she could feel the warm whisper of his breath on her temple and he said so only she could hear, "You look very beautiful tonight, and while I admire that particular shade of rose on you, I am certain you would look even better unadorned. Can we continue this discussion later?"

So much for good intentions.

He entirely blamed the duke's beguiling daughter. Jonathan rose and went back to join his two sisters. Both Carole and Betsy, pretty and dressed in the new gowns he'd paid a fortune to the fashionable modiste to make up quickly for this event because Lillian had insisted that both their wardrobes were outdated and too girlish, cast him curious glances.

Maybe it wasn't entirely correct that what had just happened was Lady Cecily's fault. He shouldn't have confessed he was sitting next to her imagining her naked. Those sorts of fantasies were best left unsaid, but truthfully the sensual beauty of her bared shoulders and the hint of the upper swell of her luscious breasts distracted him from his original purpose, which had been to correct his earlier offense.

And then he had just compounded the problem.

If she hadn't blushed so becomingly earlier, maybe he would have been more circumspect.

Maybe.

He wasn't used to being less than himself at any time. The trouble was, as a man raised between two cultures, he just didn't worry about conformity because he didn't fit precisely into any part of his heritage.

Or that was *part* of the trouble. The other part was Lady Cecily's incomparable allure. He wasn't used to being so drawn to a female. Yes, he'd known many beautiful women—enjoyed them sexually on a mutually casual basis—but as James had pointed out, she wasn't available.

He was a warrior and the duke's daughter was a most delectable prize . . . except he was sitting in a very formal drawing room in one of the most civilized cities in the world and the object of all eyes.

Damn.

The only redeeming part of it all was that the music was actually performed with a modicum of talent, the musicians having been brought in from Vienna, and he enjoyed the performance enormously compared to the usual amateur recitals he'd been subjected to since his arrival in England.

Did the winsome Miss Francis play? he wondered, acutely aware of her across the room. Her head was slightly bent, her profile delicate, the languid wave of her fan sensual and tantalizing, and though he did his best to keep his attention on the string quartet, her presence was very distracting.

She hadn't answered his question.

What he couldn't precisely explain was how he needed to sweep the potential of any scandal under the proverbial rug as swiftly as possible for the sake of his sisters and daughter, or how anxious he was to return to his native country.

He hadn't told Lillian, Carole, or Betsy about his plans either. There was a certain legacy of guilt inherited with the title, for while he'd known his sisters existed, he really hadn't imagined having an actual relationship with any of them except of the most perfunctory kind. His father's visits to America had been frequent enough that they'd known each other well, and he had Adela to fill his life.

When the music was over, the general exodus of murmured polite greetings and farewells done, he dutifully delivered his sisters back to the town house in Mayfair. Lillian had declined to go out. Which, he was beginning to realize, was normal behavior for her. After briefly checking in on Addie, who was sleeping peacefully at this late hour, her nursemaid in the adjoining room, he headed for the club his cousin frequented—his own membership an inheritance from his father. Usually he found the smoky interior oppressive and the company pompous, but he'd received a note that James was back in town after a week's absence on business and hoped to catch him.

London society was so predictable, he thought as he walked in the door and was greeted by the steward. The men with their clubs, the women with their afternoon teas . . .

James was sitting at a table by himself, the newspaper neatly folded next to his glass of whiskey, and a quick grin lit his face as Jonathan approached. "How was the musicale?"

"Don't look so smug. It was not as insufferable as some," Jonathan said with a grimace, dropping into the opposite chair in a comfortable sprawl and nodding at the nearby waiter. "Though I do have to say playing duenna to young ladies is hardly my forte. Speaking of which, what happened with Lillian?"

James chuckled and shook his head. "I don't know if it's your mixed blood or that you are an American, but you have a habit of being disconcertingly direct. Do you know that?"

"I believe in stating what is on my mind." Jonathan ordered a brandy and settled lower in his chair. "Now, tell me about Lillian. All she will say is she is ruined and someone named Lord Sebring is responsible. At that point I was told to mind my own business in the clearest way possible, but may I evoke the argument that this *is* my business by default? Besides, if all of society knows, why is it I can't be privy to the same information?"

James considered him from across the table, his gaze somewhat wary. "I didn't mention it before because though she can be prickly, I am fond of Lily. I thought it better if the two of you got to know each other a little before any judgment was made."

"I'm not judging her, James. I'm no choirboy, as everyone is aware," Jonathan muttered in irritation. "I just need to know what happened."

An eruption of boisterous laughter from a nearby table prevented his cousin from answering right away, and in truth James looked reluctant anyway. In the subdued light his face was somber. "Actually, Jon, I am not sure exactly what happened either. I do know Sebring convinced her to elope four years ago, but in the end the marriage never happened. They made it halfway to Scotland and then came back to London, but not before staying in the same room overnight at some tawdry village inn. Had she not made such a successful debut that season, she might have escaped . . . well, not unscathed, but maybe with a good deal less notoriety. Sebring was quite the catch and it was immediately clear he was interested in her. There were enough jealous young ladies and their even more vindictive mamas that she was crucified socially over that night at the inn and their failed engagement. When the Incomparable of the season falls from grace, it is not an easy landing. She was torn apart in a very public manner. In my opinion she has never recovered from it and I am not sure I can blame her for being reclusive."

His brandy arrived and Jonathan took a small sip, the smoothness and fire easing down his throat. It bothered him to think Lily had suffered in such a manner. "Did she love him? Does she still?"

His cousin choked on a sip of whiskey, coughed, and then cleared his throat. "Love? *You* are asking about love?"

"I have a child. I understand the concept. You also know how fond I was of my father."

"We aren't talking at all about the same thing. I didn't realize you had a romantic soul, Jon."

Was he a romantic? Jonathan wasn't sure the word applied, but then again, he wasn't sure it *didn't* either. His possible romantic interest in the lovely Cecily was based on a more primitive inspiration: lust. Two brief encounters could not inspire a deeper emotion, but they certainly could cause sexual attraction. "Just answer the question, please."

"How would I know?" James retorted with asperity. "We're cousins, not confidants. Lily is the least likely person I know to reveal her personal thoughts. To me or to anyone else."

Jon smiled ruefully, sinking down a little more in his chair. "There you are wrong. She can be quite forthcoming. Case in point, my behavior has not met with her approval. I fear I didn't help it this evening either. The Duke of Eddington's daughter was at the performance. My attempt at an apology for the other evening and the resulting gossip wasn't all that successful. I'm going to guess just the two of us speaking tonight will raise more eyebrows."

"I am sure you are correct there." James looked amused and interested. "What did she say?"

"The beauteous Lady Cecily? She admitted the situation surrounding our brief first meeting is garnering a ridiculous amount of attention. I couldn't agree more."

"You are in accord? I see. Do I sense a covetous tone to your voice?"

Was *covetous* the right word? She intrigued him, and it was unexpected because he hadn't really ever imagined himself drawn to a haughty pale English beauty. But lust was an elemental emotion and it would pass. "She isn't an American," he said simply.

"Nor am I." James refuted the statement with inarguable logic. "Or Lily, or your other two sisters. Nor was your father. You are not *in* America. I think you need to accept that."

"I won't be in England long." His tone was just short of curt.

"Won't you?" James ran a finger around the rim of his glass, his expression thoughtful. "I admit I wondered how long you'd tolerate the strictures of the *haut ton*, but quite frankly, I also don't see how you can abandon your responsibilities anytime soon."

"I have no intention of abandoning anything. I just want to see it all settled quickly. I want to return myself and my daughter to our lives. To facilitate that process, I need make sure Lily is settled. What of Sebring? What happened to him?"

His cousin shrugged. "He married another. She's not half the beauty Lily is, but her father has powerful ties in Parliament and Sebring is unabashedly ambitious. It is common knowledge that it was a practical match based on gain on both their sides. His wife wanted a title."

The brandy in his glass was fragrant as he idly swirled the beverage. Though he didn't know Lily well, Jonathan found he was incensed on his sister's behalf. "The bastard destroyed her life *and* broke her heart?"

"You would have to ask her about the latter," James replied. "But, yes, the whole affair left her reputation in tatters."

"Or better yet," Jonathan said in a lethal voice, "I could ask him."

"With half of London proper circulating stories of your supposed bloodthirsty background, I think you should avoid both the innocent daughters of dukes and blackguard viscounts, Jon." James rubbed his forehead. "It will only resurrect what happened if you confront Sebring. Your father chose to leave it alone four years ago. Maybe you should follow his lead."

That was curious of itself. From what Jon knew of his father he would never have let one of his children be humiliated and the injury go unaddressed.

"Maybe," he said neutrally, but he wasn't sure he agreed.

There was more to the story.

Chapter 5

"When are you going to tell me?"

Cecily knew her sister wasn't going to just let it go, and she sighed, tying the sash of her dressing gown. Eleanor sat on the bed, her nightdress buttoned to her throat, her hands folded primly in her lap, her gaze inquiring.

Sharply inquiring.

That was Eleanor. Always straight to the point. But it wasn't as though Cecily was absolutely certain just what question was being asked. "About?" she asked cautiously, padding across the room to take a chair by the fireplace. The hope of a cozy read before bed seemed about to be dashed.

"Augustine."

Relief washed over her in a wave. Cecily was so happy they weren't discussing Lord Drury that she didn't even mind the intrusion ruining her nightly ritual. Usually she read at least a chapter each evening, and if it was a rainy day and she could indulge her passion in the library for hours, that was better yet. She knew she was a bit of a bluestocking, but so be it. She also liked to study the stars and her father's astrological maps, and as unfeminine as it might be, Eleanor had persuaded him to allow their brother's tutor to teach them both Latin and Greek.

A shrug lifted her shoulders. "There's nothing to tell."

"Tonight he attempted to apologize to you." Her sister seemed disinclined to accept the dismissal. "Up until then, I thought you were telling the truth. That he'd simply blundered with protocol like any colonial ignorant of proper behavior, but truthfully, he doesn't seem unintelligent and neither would I think him a man to bestir himself if there wasn't a need for it. Whatever he said to you at the ball was very *outré*, wasn't it? Otherwise I can't see him offering any kind of apology."

As usual, her sister was disconcertingly perceptive.

Evasively, Cecily murmured, "He seems to at least regret the resulting gossip."

"Which he did *no*t help this evening. If anything, he made it all worse."

No, Cecily acknowledged with an inner sigh, Lord Augustine hadn't helped matters in the least. When he'd sat next to her, she could feel his power, the heat from his body . . . and it was different. Intriguingly so. She wasn't used to having such a reaction to a man merely taking the adjoining chair, and his being the target of everyone's gaze made his every move even more conspicuous. Their brief conversation had been duly noted, and she'd been the recipient of curious stares for the rest of the evening, probably because of her telling blush.

"He obviously is still learning his way around London society."

"He's interested in you."

Eleanor had a unique way of stating her thoughts. Not that Cecily wasn't capable of speaking her mind also, but not with such forthright determination. She had opinions. Unlike her sister, she just exercised the option of keeping them to herself now and then.

"No doubt speculating on any interest he might or might not have is a waste of time. I am more debating just what he can do to make this all die down. I never answered his question. Truthfully, I wouldn't mind at all if people stopped whispering about it."

"I think the odds of society not noticing what Augustine does are fairly low."

That was true enough. His arrival in London had sparked an interest that splattered the scandal sheets almost on a daily basis, and somehow, through that chance encounter, she'd become embroiled in his mystique.

"Speaking of whispers, it appeared to me he whispered something else to you just before he left to go sit with his sisters. What was it?" Eleanor didn't dissemble. Ever.

However, Cecily hedged. "Do you feel obligated to repeat all your private conversations?"

Her sister tossed her long braid over her shoulder and gave her a very assessing look. "It was something very scandalous again, wasn't it? Even before he repeated his previous offense you had turned a very becoming shade of pink just from his arrival. Don't make the mistake of thinking I am the only one who noticed either. I sense the betting books at White's filling up again even as we speak. What did he say?"

. . . while I admire that particular shade of rose on you, I am certain you would look even better unadorned . . .

Had Cecily not had some very shocking thoughts of her own, she might be more outraged.

Good heavens, they had imagined each other naked. No wonder she had blushed. And it was not fair either, for while she only had a vague idea of what he might look like, he no doubt had done a much better job of picturing her without a stitch on.

At least *she* hadn't admitted it out loud.

"This evening he told me he liked the color of my gown," Cecily said, a half-truth at best. "But then intimated he might like me more without it."

Her sister's eyes widened slightly in shock, and she took a moment before she said, "Good heavens, Ci. What are you going to do about the deliciously handsome but not so predictable Lord Augustine? You cannot let him continue such behavior."

Cecily shrugged. "What is there to do? Two extremely brief conversations do not merit much contemplation. He's done nothing wrong and neither have I. Besides, I cannot keep him from doing as he pleases."

"Maybe not." Eleanor glanced down at her clasped hands, the movement brief but telling before her chin came up. "At least Lord Drury was not there this evening. I have a feeling he would have been most horribly jealous."

Precisely the subject Cecily didn't want to arise. Had Eleanor been a different kind of person, she might have been able to just ask her about her infatuation with the viscount, but her sister was guarded about her emotions, if not her opinions, and Cecily knew better than to intrude. It was touchy, also, because his lordship was openly courting *her* instead of her sister, never mind that she didn't reciprocate his interest. She wasn't even sure why she had no romantic inclinations for Lord Drury, for he was charming, well mannered, and quite witty— all good reasons for Eleanor to be so taken with him.

"I hardly think his lordship would notice my extremely brief and public conversation with Augustine."

"You are wrong. He's quite in love with you. One can hardly blame him, for you are the true beauty of the family."

Had she not known Eleanor so well, she would have interpreted her comment as self-pity, but that was not her sister. "How superficial you make it sound, but that aside, I don't agree with you over Drury's affection for me. How do you know? Did he say so?"

"To me? No, of course not." Eleanor drew herself up. "But Roderick told me some time ago the viscount was enamored of you, and I believe it is true."

"Why?" Almost as soon as she asked it, Cecily regretted it, for the answer was obvious. Because Eleanor watched him.

"I can tell."

"You can tell he admires my looks? While that is flattering, I suppose, it is hardly a basis for marriage."

Her sister had the grace to flush. "You have more to recommend you than just your looks. I'm sorry if it seemed I implied otherwise. You are very lovely, but also articulate and poised and demure. I am not surprised that men flock to you. He is only one of your many admirers. You've been a brilliant success this season. I was not in mine, and unfortunately I am not surprised at *that* either. I am neither demure nor poised."

"Elle." Impulsively, Cecily rose and went over to sit next to her sister on the bed, taking both her hands. "You are wonderful. Just because you did not find the right man your first season does not mean you were a failure. I count it as a success you did not settle for Lord Flannigan, who, if I recall correctly, was most determined to marry you."

"Marry my dowry." Eleanor gave a small, inelegant snort. "His intentions were no secret and I told him I knew well enough where his true interest lay. My marriage portion and my bosom. I don't believe the man could tell you the color of my eyes to this day, for his gaze was continuously focused below my neck."

There was no way to stifle a bout of laughter and Cecily didn't try. "Please tell me you did not accuse his lordship of staring at your bosom."

Eleanor shrugged and grinned. "I am afraid I did."

"Oh, Elle!" Cecily burst out in mirth again. "I confess I would have loved to be there for that moment."

"His lordship's expression was rather priceless. He decided then and there I would not be a suitable wife anyway. I think the words he used were 'unfashionably candid.'"

"I would call it splendidly honest," Cecily said loyally.

"But you are quite used to me." Her sister's fingers curled around hers tighter. Then the moment passed, for Eleanor was not one to wallow in sentiment. She let go and said crisply, "Rest assured, if Earl Savage has developed a penchant for you, I will keep an eye on him."

And I, Cecily thought, *will help you with your penchant for Lord Drury.*

It was very dark, a bit cold, and the thin sheets of rain felt good on his bare chest.

This—this—he understood. It wasn't at all the same, of course. For one thing, it was dank, the streets splashed with noxious mud, and the clatter of Seneca's hooves rang out through the night, but it still was what he craved.

A wild night ride, the wind in his hair, and if a footpad chose to accost him, Jonathan would welcome the encounter.

Maybe a part of him *was* barbaric. At least it was action, and in London he was . . . stifled. He wasn't one to court danger, but neither did he shy away from it. The country estate with its stately elms and lush green park was much more preferable, but even there the river bordering the gardens was wide and slow-moving, pretty but placid, unlike the rushing rivers of his native land. Everything in England, he'd decided, was settled, cultivated, cultured.

Except himself, of course, he thought wryly, pulling up his horse to a more reasonable pace and urging the animal toward the alley where the stables were maintained behind the fashionable town house. How many rich earls went out riding in the middle of a rainy night attired only in their breeches and not bothering to saddle their horses? But he'd be damned if he was going to wear a cravat for a midnight gallop, and the wet and cold never bothered him anyway. A ride had seemed the best course to soothe his current state of restlessness.

Perhaps he should have taken up the blatant offer from the very beautiful ebony-haired countess earlier in the evening. Lady Irving had not so subtly pressed into his hand a perfumed slip of vellum with an address and time written in a flowing script as he waited for his carriage to be brought around after the musicale. He hadn't been all that surprised because he'd been seated next to her at a dinner the week before and she had shamelessly flirted throughout the entire seven courses, to the point that even he had been taken aback—and he did not embarrass easily. Since the woman's husband had been at the table, Jonathan had done his best to stay polite and yet cool in the face of her heated pursuit.

As he'd mentioned to the duke's memorable young daughter, he didn't understand the aristocracy. To allow your wife to have clandestine—and not so clandestine—affairs simply because she'd already given you a son and therefore served her purpose, was far more barbaric in his eyes than the customs of his mother's people. To them, heritage was traced through the maternal side of the family. Though his aunt had raised him mostly in Boston—where his parents had met—she very firmly kept him in touch with his Iroquois legacy.

Something whizzed past, grazing his arm, and it broke his reverie, especially when there was a sound from the shadows and he was sure that even with the patter of the persistent rain he heard the scrape of running feet on the wet cobblestones.

In any other case he might even have given chase, but Seneca was winded from his run and Jonathan was soaked, and he had no illusions about the London streets at night. Even fashionable neighborhoods were unsafe.

He slid off Seneca, walked him around the small enclosure to cool him off, and then rubbed the big stallion down, enjoying the work, before putting him back in his stall. He let himself into the house through the back servants' entrance, careful to remove his muddy boots, and padded in bare feet through the dark hallway. At this hour it was quiet, shadowed, and he moved silently, going up the staircase to his suite of rooms. The earl's bedchamber was a bit grand for his tastes, but since he was in England to fulfill his duty and everyone expected he would take his father's rooms, he had moved in, albeit a little reluctantly.

So, he discovered when he opened the door, had someone else, but *reluctant* didn't apply to her presence. *Eager* was more applicable and *brazen* worked even better.

He stopped, arrested by this unexpected development to his evening, and uttered an inner curse.

From his bed, her lush nude body superimposed upon the linens, Valerie Dushane, Lady Irving, smiled. Her long dark hair was loose, her full breasts tipped with dusky nipples, and her legs just slightly, suggestively, parted. The neat triangle of dark hair at the apex of her thighs was trimmed close enough that he could see the definition of her sex. She murmured, "There you are, my lord. I was wondering if I was going to have to go looking for you."

Get yourself out of this . . . now.

"Your attire—or lack of—might have caused a bit of comment." He closed the door. Not because he wished to be alone with her, but what if the sound of their conversation carried and disturbed Lillian, for instance, whose bedroom was closest? He doubted they would be over-heard, but then again, the house was very quiet and Lady Irving was apparently quite determined. It didn't happen often, but occasionally Adela had a bad dream and he was needed, and he hardly wanted that scenario either.

Explanations at this hour in particular would be difficult at best, especially since he doubted anyone would believe the naked woman lounging against the pillows with her body in flagrant display was uninvited.

The countess's effrontery aside, he had to somehow deal with this in a diplomatic way and get her out of the house without anyone ever knowing she'd been there. Obviously Lady Irving was used to getting what she wanted. Jonathan was wet and chilled, and what mud the rain hadn't washed away still clung to his skin. He moved toward the screen in the corner where a basin and towel sat ready. "How the devil did you get in?"

He should probably be more polite, but the truth was, she shouldn't be lying naked in his bed without an invitation either. She had set the rules.

"It wasn't complicated. My maid had a few words with your valet and he let me in the house, very discreetly, of course. When you didn't arrive at the time specified on my invitation, I waited an hour and decided to change your mind. Oh . . . you're bleeding."

The breathy observation registered and Jonathan glanced down to note that indeed there was a fine line of red from a cut on his upper biceps, the seep of blood mingling with the water on his skin.

"It's nothing," he said, wondering now just what had been hurled his direction in the darkness. Whoever had run away had apparently not just flung a rock, which had been his first impression. "I should probably wash it."

"Don't be long, my lord." Valerie smiled and stretched

her body in a voluptuous arch designed to showcase her breasts—and they were spectacular, he had to admit. He ducked behind the screen to wash with the tepid water in the basin. He took his time, wondering just how to handle this less than ideal situation, tearing a small strip of cloth off his discarded cravat and wrapping it around his injured upper arm.

The cut stung, but the uninvited lady in his bed was a much larger dilemma.

He actually hadn't been with any woman since before his journey to London, but this wasn't how he had pictured ending his celibacy. As far as he was concerned, there was a strict line drawn over bedding another man's wife.

It was unconscionable. Rules existed in his world, no matter how much Lady Irving might feel like sampling the Savage Earl. Because, he thought sardonically, splashing water on his face and arms and reaching for a towel, that was the basis of this determined seduction. His unusual lineage titillated the sophisticated ladies of London society. He'd discovered that almost at once. Her taste for the exotic might be an amorous adventure for her, but for him it was crossing a self-imposed boundary.

As he swabbed his face and torso clean, he decided the English did not hold the standard of their self-proclaimed honor very high if infidelity was so acceptable. Still, his sisters need to be launched into society, and he hardly wanted to insult a very prominent hostess with ties to the royal family.

One devil of a problem.

When he emerged, she regarded him from across the room with a languid look. "Why don't you come here and demonstrate the wild edge everyone speaks of? I must admit that when you walked in, wet and only half clothed, I was more attracted to you than ever. Is that how you dress in your . . . native environment?"

"Native?" He repeated the word with full irony. "I take it we are not talking about the refined streets of Boston and New York but longhouses and birch canoes."

The furrow of her brow told him she wasn't quite sure, but she pictured him all too easily in an environment that was less civilized than the earl's suite that they currently occupied together.

His breeches were still soaked, but when he'd briefly debated removing them and putting on his dressing gown, he decided that it would be too intimate. Now, how to tactfully get rid of his unwanted visitor, though she'd surely been less than tactful with him and he wasn't sure she deserved his solicitude.

She ran her hand suggestively over the generous curve of her naked breast and shifted her hips just a little as she pinched her nipple. "Do not make me start without you, Augustine."

Displayed on the luxurious sheets, she resembled a courtesan, deliberately perfumed and ready, her nipples already peaked, her face flushed. He had to wonder if she hadn't started without him anyway, enjoying his bed in his absence and quite frankly, even if he didn't have scruples about her married state, the invasion of his privacy annoyed him. Still, he kept his tone modulated. "I'm sorry, Valerie, but without me it will have to be. I have a strict rule about married women. That aside, my daughter is just down the hall."

She rolled over to her stomach playfully. It presented the rounded curve of her bare bottom, which was, he had to admit, a sight any man would enjoy. The countess was extremely attractive physically, and he wished he could say nothing about her aroused him, but that aside, he wasn't going to touch her. "My husband doesn't mind," she murmured, crossing her ankles, her hair spilling in a dark wave over her back. "And aren't children asleep at this hour?"

She had several offspring of her own, if he wasn't mistaken, but undoubtedly they were taken care of by a retinue of servants.

"*I* mind." Jonathan ran his fingers through his damp hair and sighed. "Don't misunderstand, you're very tempting, I won't deny it. But I'm not interested in an affair, and I don't need the chance of another wave of whispers attached to my name."

"You mistake *me*, my lord." Her smile had a feline curve to it. "I don't want to have an affair. I want you to fuck me."

And here Jonathan had thought he was beyond the age and experience when he could be shocked. Even his considerable worldly psyche took issue with the bluntness of that declaration.

Then, suddenly, he understood. While the men placed public bets on everything from horseracing to the ridiculous obsession of speculating on what he might have said to Lady Cecily, women were no better. Plenty of them were inveterate gamblers. It was a fashionable pastime. "How much did you wager," he asked outright, not sure if he was insulted or just amused, "that you could get me to bed you first?"

She pouted with convincing drama, full red lips drawing into a playful moue. "That's remarkably arrogant. How could you even—"

"How much?" he interrupted, his voice mild but commanding. He crossed his arms over his bare chest and leaned a shoulder against one of the heavy carved bedposts, his brows lifted in inquiry. "What is the current prize for an interlude with Earl Savage?"

Lady Irving sat up in an indignant flurry of dark hair,

a faint scowl on her beautiful face. "That's none of your affair."

"Odd. Considering our circumstances, my lady, I think it very much my affair."

"You really aren't going to do this, are you?"

"Going to fuck you? Isn't that how you put it in your very genteel English way? No, I really am not."

She gave a small frustrated sigh at the definitive tone of his response, but then slid off the bed with pragmatic promptness, her heavy breasts swaying. She admitted grudgingly, "A thousand pounds to the first woman who piques your interest. And it isn't the profit as much as the *winning*."

"How flattering. And here I thought the purpose of a man and woman enjoying each other in a sexual way was something a bit deeper than a superficial competition. I can expect more midnight visits from your competitors, I take it? I'll start locking my door."

At least the countess proved to be a good sport, for she shot him an arch look and picked up her chemise. "It isn't just the wager." She deliberately ran her gaze over his bare chest. "You *are* somewhat of a novelty, my lord. Are all the men of your"—she obviously searched for a word that wouldn't offend him— "breed so barbarically handsome?"

In answer, he picked up her discarded gown. Any sense of affront had been blunted in his time at university, since his father had insisted he attend a prestigious school, and even back in America prejudice existed. He'd been insulted often enough before over his unusual bloodlines. "Let me help you dress."

"Does this refusal have anything to do with Eddington's daughter?" Lady Irving's voice was petulant.

For a moment he paused as he lifted the frothy volume of the fashionable garment, the lilac material spilling over his arm; the question was not all that surprising, he supposed, considering the gossip, but what took him aback was that he wondered for a glimmer of a moment if it just *might* have something to do with Cecily Francis.

Instead of answering, he said as neutrally as possible, "Allow me to play maid."

Obligingly, he fastened buttons and retrieved her slippers, grateful that she wasn't more vindictive over the rejection, and he even saw her safely outside, where her driver—no doubt used to his mistress and her nightly habits—waited down the street. Once they had rattled away, Jonathan went back up to his room and removed his wet breeches, donned his dressing gown, and poured a brandy.

A novelty. So far he wasn't having much success in fulfilling his quest to play the respectable earl in order to get his sisters settled and his affairs in order so he could return to his life in America. Though, he did remind himself as he wandered over and sat down by the remaining glow of the fire, *this* particular debacle had not been his fault.

What would I have done, he pondered in wayward contemplation, *if it had been the duke's glorious golden-haired daughter naked in my bed?*

Had that unlikely scenario been what he'd come home to from his midnight ride, he wasn't sure he would have played the gentleman no matter the consequences.

The realization was infinitely disturbing.

Chapter 6

Her father sat back in his chair and regarded her with a look that could only be described as ... as ...

Well, she couldn't describe it actually. It belonged to him alone and had certainly intimidated grown men. Roderick called it the "Eddington stare." Cecily, who had always basked in the warmth of her father's affection, was not sure how to handle the icy ducal disapproval.

He folded his hands on his desk. His hair was going from blond to gray gracefully, his attire, as always, was impeccably tailored, and the spectacles that he refused to wear in public rested on the pile of correspondence in front of him. "Explain to me why Viscount Drury would not make a suitable husband."

It was a relief to discover this summons had nothing to do with the unconventional Augustine and all the whispers, so she feigned nonchalance and shrugged. "I'm sure he would, just not for me."

"Why not?"

"He isn't my preference."

"I'm asking you again, why?"

"You wouldn't understand," she equivocated, unwilling to reveal Eleanor's hidden infatuation. It really wasn't her secret to tell, and truthfully, her sister hadn't admitted it to her either. If Cecily was wrong—yet she was certain she wasn't—it would be an unforgivable error. If she was right, still unforgivable. If Elle wanted to tell their father, that was entirely another matter.

"I beg to disagree. I am not unintelligent or lacking in understanding of this world. I might even venture to observe that my time in it far outweighs your own, so, out of respect for me as a parent and setting my rank aside, tell me why you would refuse such a very promising prospect if he offers marriage."

For a normally easygoing—if a bit distant—parent, he certainly was being uncharacteristically intent.

"Does it sound naive to point out I don't love him?" Cecily endeavored to seem as neutral as possible.

"Naive? I have no idea. Impractical, yes. A young woman should choose a husband based on qualities more important than whether or not he inspires some fleeting and hard-to-define emotion. In Lord Drury's case, he comes from a very highly regarded bloodline, has a solid fortune, and is considered to be respectable and even-tempered. What else could you ask for, pray tell?"

The resulting silence was uncomfortable as she weighed her answer. *How can silence be loud?* Cecily wondered, yet somehow the quiet rang in her ears. The ducal study was a little overpowering as well, with towering bookcases and dark, heavy furniture and paintings of her father's favorite horses lining the paneled walls.

To a certain extent her father was right. She knew that in his mind he *believed* he was right. He hadn't even mentioned that the viscount was also quite handsome—if you liked fair coloring and a pleasant smile, but she preferred men with long, dark hair and a dangerous reputation . . .

Goodness, this was *not* the time to think about the controversial Jonathan Bourne. She shouldn't think about the man at all.

Eventually, she said, "I find his lordship agreeable enough, I suppose, but—"

"Good, because I am very much in favor of this marriage. I wish for you to accept his proposal. Eleanor was remarkably stubborn her first season, and she is still unmarried as a result of it. I had several perfectly respectable offers for her hand, but she refused. I worry I'll be too lenient with you." He cleared his throat. "Especially considering the circumstances."

Oh, dear.

"What circumstances?"

"I'm told there are people talking about you, and not only do I not like it, but I will not sit by and let it affect your future. Drury is a good choice. I suggest you make it."

Damn, this *was* about the controversial Augustine.

Speechless, Cecily went very still in her chair. This was not like her father—or at least not the man she remembered as a little girl. Only, she acknowledged with wooden practicality as she tried to assimilate this new development, she wasn't a child any longer. The distance between them had lengthened as she grew older, and she hadn't thought too much about it because life had changed so quickly as she and Eleanor had entered society, not to mention that he was, as always, a busy man.

In retrospect, Roderick had tried to warn her, but it would have been better done stated bluntly that their father had this intention. Now she was off balance.

And what about Elle?

How do I handle this?

"I—I—" It wouldn't do to stammer. She took a deep breath and composed herself. "I don't *wish* to marry Lord Drury."

"I get that impression. Why?"

A vision of Jonathan Bourne came to mind, with his silky dark hair and a glint of wicked humor in his midnight eyes . . .

But she could hardly say so.

"The newly arrived Earl of Augustine has a less than perfect reputation."

Wonderful. Now her father could read her mind. Moreover, his steady gaze told her he'd specifically heard the details of the champagne incident. Not that she'd thought it would simply slide past him, but he did spend a lot of time taking care of his business ventures and she'd *hoped* it would. At least she could say in perfect truth, "I barely know him."

How true. Jonathan had never even asked to be formally introduced to her.

"As far as I can discern from the rumors, he rides the streets at all hours."

"Hardly a crime," she said, wondering if she should even be defending a man she didn't know all that well.

"But unusual, you must admit."

"Lord Augustine *is* quite unusual." She inclined her head. "I think he is used to a bit more freedom than London provides him."

Her father's gaze was steady and unrelenting. "Cecily, he has an illegitimate child he boldly brought into his household."

So that was the issue. Or part of it anyway.

"Good for him," she said recklessly. "At least he didn't tuck her away in some remote part of the country and pretend she didn't exist. I think it speaks well for his character rather than counting as a black mark against it. Shouldn't a father love his daughter?"

"Touché." Her own father had the grace to look faintly amused, but it faded almost at once. "That includes wanting what is best for her. Viscount Drury is a very well-placed young man. You have just acknowledged you find him pleasant."

"Pleasant is hardly enough for a marriage."

"It is a very good start, isn't it?"

As it wasn't a true question, she didn't answer, just sat stiffly in her chair.

"I think," her father said then with an exasperated sigh, his fingers skimming through his hair, "you and Eleanor are trying between you to test me beyond my capacity for tolerance. I am not interested in dissension. I want peace, and that includes having you both happy and settled. She refuses to be 'married off,' as she calls it, and as a result she is still waiting. You are apparently trying to follow in her footsteps, only you have somehow attracted the attention of all of the beau monde with your flirtation with Augustine."

"There hasn't been a flirtation." At least she could say that with conviction.

"No?" Her father frowned.

"No."

"Then Augustine isn't a true suitor? Because if so, I want you to realize I would have some measure of reservation."

She hesitated, but she couldn't honestly claim he even had any interest at all, and certainly no interest in courting her. Two scandalous compliments were hardly indicative of anything significant. And none of the other men who had claimed dances and brought flowers and called in the afternoons held more appeal than Lord Drury—some quite a bit less, in fact. No, she couldn't claim a sincere romance that would thwart a marriage to the viscount. "He hasn't given any indication of it," she admitted.

"Then why all the speculation about the two of you?"

"Without intending to be disrespectful, might I point out you already have claimed a greater knowledge of how society works than I have. It's gossip."

"Good, then." Her father's tone was lighter, but dismissive. "I want you to carefully consider Lord Drury's proposal when he arrives to make it. I'll give you three days and we will discuss this again. Keep in mind that this match would please me. The marriage contract is already with my solicitors."

That certainly sounded official.

An edict from the duke. Cecily found her palms were suddenly damp, in contrast to her dry mouth. Had it not been for her sister, she wouldn't have been so upset. She might even have agreed because it was expected of her, but she refused to go through the rest of her life awash in guilt for her sister's broken heart, especially when she wasn't enthusiastic about her potential bridegroom anyway.

Woodenly she rose, nodded, and left the room without even bidding her father a polite farewell. She thought maybe he said her name as she went through the door, but if so, she ignored it.

This was a catastrophe.

What should she do? She'd appealed once to Roderick and that had proved to be a futile attempt. The viscount had come to her father anyway to gain his permission, so she had to assume a certain amount of determination on his part.

She was without recourse.

That was patently unfair, wasn't it? Still, her brother should be able to relate to her what exactly Lord Drury had said to their father.

Roderick was in his rooms changing for dinner when she knocked on the door with not too gentle a fist. Her brother answered with his cravat still undone and an impatient look on his face that faded when he took in her expression. His voice was quiet. "I tried to tell you."

Cecily walked past him and sank into a chair, her legs a bit weak. "Did you not talk to Lord Drury?"

"Of course I did." Her brother sounded defensive,

but then he sighed. "He was more than willing to talk to me eagerly about you, but when I mentioned Eleanor, he changed the subject and brushed it off. It's fairly clear he's not just offering because of your suitability, but is truly infatuated."

Not precisely what she wanted to hear. And she disagreed. "We haven't known each other long enough for him to be infatuated," Cecily protested. "He knows Elle far better."

"Is there some time limit I don't know of for a man to be attracted to a woman?" Roderick narrowed his gaze. "Speaking of which, there's more talk about you and Augustine. Care to explain to me why?"

The earl again. Now *there* was a good argument for swift infatuation . . .

"Care to explain to me why you think I answer to you?" She and her brother were only six years apart in age and they rarely quarreled, but his presumption was irritating and in this case especially, the situation wasn't her fault.

Her brother rubbed his jaw, his mouth set. "It is if I am called upon to defend your honor. Is there some reason for me to speak to Augustine? Because I—"

"Don't be daft, Roddy. Have you seen the man? He is both older than you, and no doubt leagues more experienced. I understand he was in the war . . . so don't be a fool. He even *looks* dangerous and if only half of what they say about him is true, he is. I feel confident he is fully capable of defending himself."

"I'm a good shot." Roderick's face had reddened slightly.

Cecily probably should have known better than to prick his male pride, so she sighed inwardly and explained, "The earl approached me last night to apologize"—she left out the part where the man in question insulted the entire English aristocracy—"for what happened at the ball and the resulting gossip. Eleanor heard him. If there is more gossip, it isn't because of anything more than we briefly spoke for that purpose."

"I heard a slightly different version. I doubt our sister caught what he leaned in and whispered in your ear before he got up and rejoined his family," her brother said with sardonic inflection. "I hope you realize that if Father hears of all this, avoiding a possible scandal will make an engagement to Drury all the more appealing."

"He already has heard and there will be *no* scandal," Cecily said, exasperation with the entire situation—with men in general, including her father and brother—making her tone sharp. "I've had even less contact with Lord Augustine than Lord Drury. I would prefer if they would both leave me alone, to be frank."

"May I sit in?"

Jonathan glanced up, didn't recognize the individual addressing him, but was astute enough to know antagonism when he heard it. Tall and fair, the man was elegant and every inch the cool aristocrat, a very proper neck cloth at his throat, his face creased into an expression of overt disdain.

Still, no recognition, but Jonathan was no stranger to incipient dislike based on nothing but narrow-mindedness. He shrugged.

"Certainly," he said, indicating the empty chair next to him. "We've a spot."

Intuition had kept him alive more than once. Why had the table gone suddenly quiet? As a matter of fact, the room itself had quieted. Jonathan glanced at James, but his cousin's face didn't reveal much. Jonathan waited while Sir Wilfred, a portly man in his middle age with a ruddy face and usually gregarious manner dealt the cards without saying a word.

"You must be Augustine," the new arrival murmured, picking up his hand in a deceptively languid movement. "I don't believe we've met. Viscount Drury, at your service."

English protocol was a waste of time as far as he was concerned, so Jonathan just inclined his head slightly in acknowledgment of the introduction. "Yes, I'm Augustine. A pleasure." It still felt awkward using his title instead of his given name. In America, there were no titles, and just as well in his opinion. A man was what a man was, not a lord based on his lofty lineage.

. . . I hate to state the obvious, but you *are a member of the class you just disparaged.*

The beautiful Lady Cecily had a point, he decided wryly.

Drury was still an unfamiliar name and an unfamiliar face, so he wasn't sure why everyone at the table was slightly tense, but it seemed to be the case. Jonathan watched the other man seemingly peruse his cards and decide on a wager, all the while puzzled by the general air of taut anticipation.

They played the next round in near silence.

James laid down his hand on the baize covering the table. "My cards aren't good enough to toss my money away. I'm out."

Sir Wilfred similarly declined to bet, though the other two men in the game raised in cautious amounts. Jonathan had a good hand and he was bolder. Lord Drury, it seemed, also believed he could win, for he wagered aggressively and it took only a few more rounds— Jonathan taking four out of five hands but the other man never backing down—before Jonathan understood fully there was some sort of personal competition going on between them that had nothing to do with a simple game of cards.

What the devil is this all about?

It was uncomfortable enough that Jonathan finally rose, pocketed his winnings, and excused himself. As he turned to leave the table, Drury drawled with cool inflection, "Lady Cecily is going to be my fiancée."

That spun Jonathan around on his heel, the news not welcome on a level that had him confounded. He didn't want a wife—not yet anyway—and he certainly would not choose an English bride, but that was neither here nor there. At the moment, the trouble seemed to be an irate viscount and the interested audience of the entire gaming room. Aside from James, he didn't sense much support, so perhaps a confrontation was not in order.

This was exactly what his sisters did *not* need.

"Congratulations." Jonathan tried to sound bland. "She's undeniably lovely."

"I thought perhaps the information would be of interest to you."

Had it not been such a public forum and if Lily hadn't pointed out to him that a scandal would not help Carole and Betsy, who knows what he might have said. As it was, he kept his voice soft, but the lethal tone was still there. "I can't see why."

"Can't you?" Drury regarded him now with open, glittering enmity. "Considering your recent actions, I somehow doubt that. I've heard you are not all that well versed in our customs, and perhaps that is the excuse."

"*Your* customs?" A muscle tightened in Jonathan's cheek. "The implication being, of course, that I do not understand the protocol of polite society?"

"Or maybe you just deliberately disregard it."

That tone of insolence grated particularly. Jonathan tried to decide if the viscount merely had an impaired sense of self-preservation or if this was a way to make Earl Savage live up to his nickname and instigate a public brawl.

Sir Wilfred jumped up and moved to another table with a mumbled apology. Drury still sat, his gaze unflinching, his pose seemingly relaxed.

Had it not been for James, perhaps the discussion would have escalated, for certainly the pale Englishman didn't seem to have much regard for his personal safety, but Jonathan heard the scrape of a chair and a second later his cousin had clamped a hand around his forearm and was urging him out of the room. Once they were outside, Jonathan said in clipped tones, "If it were anyone else but you holding on to me, I might rip their hand off. There's no need for the not-so-subtle coercion. Feel free to let me go before I toss you halfway across the room."

James blew out a low humorless laugh and complied. "Just trying to keep it all civilized. Bloodshed in the card room always titillates the ladies but it disrupts the evening."

"I didn't start it."

"No," James agreed, edging past a group of matrons.

"*Was* there going to be bloodshed?" Jonathan adjusted his sleeve and surveyed the crowded ballroom with seeming detachment. "How serious was he? I know nothing about him."

"Let's just say the combination of your impatience with threats, a certain duke's daughter, and the viscount's misplaced sense of honor gave me twinges of alarm. You heard him—he has offered for the delectable Lady Cecily. Shall I find us some brandy?"

Jonathan wasn't sure whether to laugh or be offended at his cousin's pragmatic approach to the near confrontation. "I take it I am expected not to take offense at

Drury's obvious—and public—warning off? You have more faith than I do in my powers of forgiveness."

The ballroom was busy, the crowd milling, the dance floor full of swirling couples, the ladies in their brilliant gowns, the men in dark evening wear. Undoubtedly both Carole and Betsy were out there amid the bowing and bobbing partners. They'd both looked forward to this event, and Jonathan wanted them to enjoy themselves. James stopped for a moment and then he said quietly, "Yes. For the sake of your sisters you need to ignore his lordship's overbearing tactics, especially since you aren't serious about the young lady. Look, Jon, he's a favorite of the duke and word has it the marriage is a fait accompli. An altercation now would serve no purpose."

"I'm the one called a savage? He could use a lesson in manners."

"You have made his fiancée a subject of gossip. Do you blame him?"

Were he totally innocent, Jonathan could have protested with more vigor, but he wasn't—innocence was long past lost—and besides, he was a practical man at heart and wondered how much of his affront was the declaration that the lovely Cecily was apparently taken.

Not that he wanted her.

Well, he *wanted* her, but not in at all a polite way.

"I didn't even know who the devil he was until he joined us." It was impossible not to sound at least a little edgy.

"Therefore, since you have no quarrel with him, ignore what just happened."

It was sound advice and Jonathan would have wholeheartedly agreed despite his distaste for being summarily informed that he wasn't allowed to court a certain lady, but before he could speak, another hand—this one much less confining yet every bit as demanding—

fastened on his arm, slender fingers gripping with importunate force. A very soft, composed voice said succinctly, "May I have a few minutes of your time, my lord?"

It was Cecily, he saw, and it threw him decidedly off balance, considering he'd just been thinking about her. This evening she was more than dazzling in a nectarine gown of Lyon silk—he unfortunately knew a great deal about fabric, ribbons, buttons and the like after accompanying Carole and Betsy to the modiste recently—her blond hair upswept, but those tawny eyes he so admired shimmered with open distress.

He should say no.

"Alone," she added on a breath. "It's quite urgent I speak with you."

Chapter 7

S he'd actually grabbed his sleeve, and the moment Cecily realized what she'd done in front of most of fashionable London society, she dropped her hand.

Had she not been rather frantically looking for Jonathan, maybe she wouldn't have been so impulsive, but his sudden appearance as he emerged from one of the gaming rooms was such a relief she had simply reacted.

At least there was some reward for her impetuousness, for his face showed open surprise. So did that of his cousin, James, who despite their very dissimilar coloring bore a decided resemblance to the earl. It was in the shape of their mouths maybe, or the elegant arch of their brows, and both were dressed similarly in stark black evening wear and looked extraordinarily handsome. . . . Oh, devil take it, she didn't care who looked like whom, she needed to get Jonathan alone for a few moments.

"Of course," he said, staring down at her with those mesmerizing dark eyes, amusement replacing his startled expression. "Bloodshed be damned."

What does that mean? He shouldn't have sworn in front of her either, as it was highly impolite, but she was too distraught to care.

James Bourne said warningly, "Jon."

"What's wrong?" Jonathan pointedly ignored him.

His gaze was probing, inquiring, his dark brows drawing sharply together as he interpreted her current state of agitation with accurate comprehension.

"I'll explain, but . . . privacy would be best."

That he understood she was upset calmed her. In a quiet tone he asked, "Shall we step outside to the terrace or would you prefer we go out into the hallway?"

"Whatever is the most discreet."

"Neither one," Lord Augustine's cousin muttered. "And entirely unoriginal in the bargain. It's a warm night. If you want a private moment I do not recommend the gardens as other couples will have exactly the same idea, and the hallways are always busy with servants and guests in a crush like this. Is there any way to convince either of you to forgo this conversation?"

Cecily heard him, but the request was not an option.

Not after she'd seen Eleanor's reddened eyes and faced her sister's studied cheerfulness in the carriage on the way to the ball. Obviously the news of her impending betrothal had reached Eleanor's ears. It solidified Cecily's conviction about her sister's feelings for Lord Drury, and it would not be possible to live with herself if she didn't do something *now*. Her father had given her three days, but if the marriage settlement was already with his solicitors, coupled with her conversation with Roderick, it sounded as though she needed to do something quickly—now—before Viscount Drury had a chance to actually propose.

There was little question. She was . . . *desperate.*

Would Jonathan Bourne, the infamous Earl Savage, help her now that she'd risked this direct approach?

Jonathan glanced at the melee of fashionably dressed people around them. "James, will you dance attendance on Carole and Betsy, please?"

Relief flooded through her.

James Bourne said something under his breath, but sketched a small, polite bow and then nodded and moved away, shouldering into the crowd. Instead of leading her toward the doors to the outside, Jonathan told her in a low voice, "I will head toward the foyer. It is early yet, so a carriage should be easily summoned. I won't use the conveyance with the Augustine crest. I will actually be in James's smaller carriage, which is more nondescript. If you follow in a few minutes, we will not be seen leaving the house together and we can certainly talk privately if we go for a short drive. If we need to be alone, I'm afraid that is the best plan I can come up with at such short notice."

The suggestion was a little daring, but at this point, what was the difference between being seen in a secluded corner of the mansion with the earl or joining him in his carriage?

Not much, except the sacrifice of her reputation. But when she thought about Elle . . .

Potential scandal wasn't something she was going to worry over at this moment, even if she had assured her brother there wouldn't be one. The misery she'd seen on her sister's face was enough to spur her to action, however reckless it might seem, because truthfully, both their futures hung in the balance right now.

Was it wrong to fight what fate seemed to have crafted for her?

No. What was wrong was marrying the man her sister was desperately in love with when Cecily didn't even want him.

There was a bemusing touch to the melodrama of trying to secretly sneak off to meet with the notorious earl . . . at her own suggestion. Actually, she was slightly surprised he'd agreed so readily, but was glad he had. With luck, he'd be as amiable to the rest of her request.

This was a gamble. She wasn't at all sure she was doing the right thing, but she was taking action of *some* kind. If she didn't she might be dragooned into a disastrous arrangement.

A few minutes later, when she edged nervously out the doors of the mansion, she saw the carriage with the signature Augustine crest departing as if Jonathan was inside. Another, smaller vehicle sat down the curve of the drive, and at the sight of her a liveried servant opened the door.

Cecily hurried forward, saw a dark figure lounging negligently on one of the seats, and clambered in with such haste that her arrival was probably most unladylike. To her relief, Jonathan seemed to have the same urgent agenda, for he tapped on the panel and the vehicle lurched away the moment the door closed behind her.

And they were left alone, looking at each other.

This was the point at which she'd have to explain why she'd wanted to see him so urgently.

Awkward, that. Since she still didn't feel she could mention Eleanor, she needed to come up with a reasonable explanation for her somewhat *un*reasonable behavior.

"The footman won't say anything . . . or he shouldn't," Jonathan said, a slight smile curving his lips. "I gave him a little incentive to not mention a golden-haired young lady joining me. Now then, to what do I owe this pleasure?"

Sprawled on the seat in front of her, large and a bit formidable with his raven hair brushing his shoulders and his long legs extended, just his presence had her now—at the crucial moment—tongue-tied. What she wished to ask of him was a reach, a very long reach actually, for anyone, much less someone she didn't know well at all. So far all they had shared were two wicked whispered comments.

Both made by him. Maybe that gave her a little lever-
age, considering the gossip. But, how to do this . . .

Had she *really* just driven off with him? In close
quarters he seemed larger, more imposing, and unfortunately, even more attractive, which had been a problem
since the moment they'd met. Everything about him—
his unusual coloring, the vibrant masculinity that he
exuded, the sensual promise in his eyes—had intrigued
her since that first chance encounter. And now she was
about to ask him the unthinkable, but it was in a very
good cause.

With careful enunciation, she got right to the point. It
wouldn't do for her to be gone long. "I wondered if you
would consider an engagement."

"An engagement?" He didn't seem anything more
than mystified. The vehicle rocked around a corner and
she caught the strap to steady herself, but it did nothing for her frayed composure. How the devil did gentlemen do this? Proposing was an entirely nerve-racking
experience.

Even if it wasn't a sincere offer of marriage.

"Between us." She indicated him and then herself
with a nervous flick of her closed fan.

Lord Augustine considered her from across the small
space. "Forgive me for being obtuse, but what the hell
did you just say? You wish for me to marry you?"

Someone should really tell the man that profanity in
front of ladies was impolite. Apparently in the Americas
civility was optional, or maybe he was just independent
enough to ignore it. She suspected the latter. Cecily swallowed down the sudden lump in her throat and squared
her shoulders. To a certain extent, she didn't blame him
for his shock. She was somewhat shocked herself at her
own behavior. "No," she clarified hastily. Her voice was
faint. "I can explain."

"That," his lordship said, a mocking smile on his well-shaped mouth, "would be most welcome, Lady Cecily. I admit I am at a loss."

The cobbled street made the wheels of the carriage rumble, and she was reminded that she'd tossed the dice and left with him, and if her father found out—if society found out—she might be irrevocably ruined.

A small price to pay for Eleanor's happiness. Not that this rash move ensured her sister's future, but surely waiting for Cecily's engagement to Lord Drury to be set in stone was a lesson in torture. She refused to ever, *ever* do that to Elle.

With difficulty, she wondered just how to phrase this absurd proposition. Finally, she settled on, "I need to become engaged. I can't tell you why, but what I was thinking of was perhaps a temporary arrangement between us. Obviously I don't expect you to actually marry me."

Earl Savage blinked, settled back even more in his seat, and took his time answering. His handsome face took on a slightly sardonic expression. "If this is an oblique attempt to murder me, please be reminded I am not that easy to kill."

She had no idea what he was talking about. Perplexed, she frowned. "What?"

"Let us just say I am under the impression you are already engaged to a certain gentleman who made it quite clear just moments ago he thinks I should stay away from you."

"Already engaged?"

"Picture the antithesis of myself. Blond and very, very English."

Lord Drury had actually said something to him? She couldn't decide whether to be mortified or furious. Stiffly, she said, "I am not currently engaged to anyone, let me assure you."

"Well, everyone who was present in the card room thinks you are or certainly are about to be."

"I'm trying neither to murder nor to marry you, sir." She was proud of the crisp, pragmatic tone of her voice. "I merely wish to become your fiancée."

"Merely? Excuse me, but that does not seem to be a small decision. Why me, pray tell?"

He certainly had every right to ask. She clasped her hands and formulated a response—hopefully one that made sense. At the end, she said softly, "There is already gossip about the two of us, so it would be believable. I need the help of a true gentleman and I wasn't sure where else to turn."

Well, he wasn't sure he qualified as a true gentleman, especially considering the lascivious thoughts going through his head at the moment, but Jonathan was surprisingly willing to listen to the beautiful young woman sitting across from him. "Go on."

Her hesitation charmed him, but then again, unfortunately everything about her charmed him. From the tendrils of golden hair at her temples, the demure neckline of her gown over those oh-so-tempting breasts, the top of her glove on the supple muscles of her upper arm . . . to the way she tentatively bit her lower lip and regarded him from under the fringe of her lush lashes. "I don't *want* to get married quite yet," she said emphatically enough that he believed her conviction. "And I especially don't wish to marry just because my father has decided Lord Drury is his preferred son-in-law. I have other reasons, but I wondered if perhaps . . . Are the rumors that you wish to return to America in the fall true?"

What *other reasons* could a nineteen-year-old ingénue have for a false engagement?

It was his first thought, and a subversive one, for he found himself at once in the quandary of wanting to agree to—and to refuse—her request, all at the same time. To agree just because she had asked him and she looked so luscious in her soft orange gown that he wasn't sure a man on this green earth could refuse her, and to decline the honor because he had a sixth sense there was an inherent danger in accepting.

A man should always listen to his gods . . .

His aunt was been right, of course. Her gentle spirit embraced the idea of a higher power that served all men, not just those who believed in the strictures of organized religion. Intellectually, he agreed. If men took goodness as a sign of spirituality, then the world would be a better, more tolerant place.

But it wasn't that simple, an inner voice reminded him; Cecily's family might take issue with him as a potential son-in-law. The subject was carefully avoided in his presence, but he knew Adela's arrival in England with him had caused a great deal of speculation and disapproval. Not that it mattered to him what others thought of it—nothing would make him change his bond with his daughter—but he was pragmatic enough to have a realistic viewpoint.

"My intention is to return as soon as all is settled here," he admitted cautiously. "It is my true home. I realize I've inherited my father's title, but England is not where I was raised, after all."

"Why weren't you?"

The forthright question took him by surprise, but then again, at least she was interested enough to ask. Jonathan shrugged. "I was not quite two years of age when my mother died. My father didn't want me reared by nannies and governesses and tutors. He also wanted me to appreciate my heritage, and that would never happen in England. My mother's younger sister wanted me, and once he remarried, his new wife did not. He divided his time between his two families."

And having experienced the sting of rejection on that level, he vowed that Adela would not.

Ever.

"I understand." Cecily glanced down at her clasped hands. "I was also very young when my mother died. We have a lot in common."

A half-breed with an illegitimate daughter and a beautiful debutante who was the darling of the *ton*? He almost laughed, but stopped himself. It was odd, but he thought she seemed sincere. Then again, maybe he was blinded by her graceful, tempting form and those topaz eyes. That susceptibility was what had him in such a tenuous position in the first place. *A respectable earl should not abscond with a young lady during the middle of a ball*, he reminded himself; though respectability was a new concept. He had his own set of morals, of course, but his way of thinking did not adhere to the English system that applied to polite society.

If he didn't put too fine a point on it, he'd reacted in a visceral fashion when she approached him, not a logical one, and that was the power of just the touch of her gloved hand on his arm. He was not the one in charge, and it bothered him. He said in a level tone, "Thank you for the empathy, but I am still unclear as to why we are having this discussion."

She nodded as if the answer was what she wanted. "You are very eligible, my lord."

Jonathan had absolutely no answer for that frank declaration. He finally managed, "I don't think so."

"You are an earl."

To that he was able to give a brief nod. Whether he wanted to be or not, that was true. It wasn't that he was unaware that his title and fortune made some ladies of the *ton* overlook his mixed blood. He just had had no idea that Lady Cecily thought along those lines.

"So," the young lady across from him said as if addressing a courtroom, "I assume you must be under a great deal of duress to choose a wife? My brother is a ducal heir and a marquess, and I know he is being pressured already to find a suitable young lady and produce a son."

Not that Jonathan would mind going through the process required to conceive a child with the delectable woman currently racketing about the streets of London with him, but he had to admit he was unsettled by her matter-of-fact approach to what seemed to be a very outrageous proposal so far. He found his voice. "I am afraid I don't waste a lot of time worrying over other people's expectations of me, my lady."

"No." Her smile was faint and trembled a little. "I would guess you do not. But, still, hear me out, if you will, my lord."

"I admit I am fascinated by this conversation. It would be difficult to tear me away. Go on."

The carriage took a corner and she braced her hand on the seat. Jonathan did his best to ignore the subtle sway of her breasts under the bodice of her fashionable gown, but he didn't succeed very well.

"Is it possible we could invent an engagement and benefit both of us by having our families retreat in their quest to marry us off?" She added quietly, "This is very important to me."

Who knows what he might have said, but at that moment there was a horrible crack, the vehicle lurched sideways, and in an unconscious reaction, he lunged forward, caught her, and enfolded her in his arms before the carriage listed to its side and nearly toppled over.

Chapter 8

Eleanor Francis sat very upright, her hands properly locked in her lap, her expression hopefully composed.

There was nothing quite like being a wallflower, she decided, though truthfully, she knew part of her solitude was self-inflicted. No, she probably wasn't as pretty as her sister—this she acknowledged, though they did still look quite alike. To start with, she'd always been more ... buxom, but gentlemen actually seemed to appreciate that, and all along she'd recognized that neither her face nor her form was the problem. Almost from the beginning of her first season she'd realized the gentlemen who asked her to dance didn't often ask again. She'd done her best this year to stay poised and keep quiet, making only polite small talk, but it wasn't working.

Especially with the very handsome, elegant, intelligent, congenial—the list went on—Viscount Drury.

Oh, yes, he'd waltzed with her twice this evening, but she knew it was mainly to wheedle out of her information about Cecily, and quite frankly, that stung more than a little. He often played the gentleman and asked her to dance, which was kind of him, but his pity over her patent unpopularity wasn't at all what she wanted. Still, every time he asked she agreed because it was ... *something*. Not to mention he was a gifted dancer, whereas it wasn't her forte, so she managed to look acceptably graceful when they took the floor together.

He wasn't interested even though she was also the daughter of a duke and had exactly the same dowry. It was *her*. Not her looks, or her background—and that rankled more than anything. It was one matter to be disregarded because one was too stout, or too thin, or had an overlarge nose, but quite frankly, she found it even more mortifying to be perfectly acceptable as far as physical appearance went, but not desirable in other ways.

So, she decided as the slow swirl of dancers went by and laughter—from other people—rang in her ears, she was a pariah of her own making. What gentlemen found unattractive about her was her personality.

A humiliating reality.

She would suggest *social failure* as the epitaph to be engraved on her headstone, which might be needed quite soon, for if she had to stay in the corner with the dowagers for another moment, she'd just toss herself off the nearest convenient balcony. Eleanor rose, smiled as politely as possible at the assembled company, and excused herself, ignoring her grandmother's disapproving look over her leaving in the middle of a conversation.

There were times when a young lady just needed a stiff glass of tepid champagne.

Where the devil is Cecily anyway? she thought as she moved toward the drinks table. Being stuck in the Purgatory of this ball would be much, much easier if she could at least have someone to talk to. Later she would sneak away and then send the carriage back once she was home.

Snatching a drink from a footman passing by with a tray, she wondered how she was going to stand her sister's engagement party. Just the thought of that miserable upcoming event made her take a convulsive swallow from her glass. No doubt Lord Drury would be every inch the besotted fiancé and . . .

"Lady Eleanor."

The voice of the subject of her thoughts made her jump, and unforgivably, she spilled a dash of champagne on his shoe as she whirled around. As if to punctuate her faux pas, the music came to a theatrical halt just then and a throng of milling couples left the floor. "I'm—I'm terribly sorry," she stammered.

"I startled you. I beg your pardon. The fault is entirely mine." His smile was gracious and he didn't even glance downward at the now soiled toe of his formerly perfectly polished Hessian. "I was wondering if you had seen your sister."

"Yes, indeed. She's a little taller, her coloring fairer, though the family resemblance is definitely there between us, I'm told." The tart words came out before she could stop them . . . and it was *unfortunate*.

But really, having to sit most of the evening with her grandmother and her friends, and *then* the man she thought about almost every waking moment of the day—but who wanted to marry her sister—had materialized right in front of her. How poised was she expected to be?

The viscount merely laughed. The amusement lit his blue eyes and made him even more handsome—if that was possible. "You have a quick tongue and I sometimes forget it. Let me rephrase. Have you seen your sister recently, and if so, would you be so kind as to steer me in her direction?"

At least she could honestly say she had no idea of Cecily's whereabouts. "I'm sorry, but I have not seen her in a while, my lord."

He scanned the room, his affable smile fading. "How

interesting . . . I don't see Augustine either. He was just in the card room but seems to have disappeared."

At his height, he probably did have a decent view of the crowd, and Lord Augustine was maybe even a little taller, so he would be easy to spot. No, Eleanor told herself, taking another gulp of champagne, Cecily was anything but stupid and she would never leave with the earl and risk her reputation.

Would she?

Not normally, but her sister had been very quiet in the carriage ride to the ball.

Or had Eleanor been the brooding one? It was hard to say. She certainly had been miserable enough . . . and while she was happy to find she wasn't so selfish as to resent her sister receiving an offer of marriage from one of the most eligible bachelors of the *ton*, she hadn't noticed Cecily brimming over with joy at the prospect of becoming Lady Drury.

Why did life have to be so blasted *complicated*?

"I am sure she is just in the ladies' retiring room," she said, and then immediately wished she could take it back, because, really, she shouldn't have mentioned such an indelicate matter as having to relieve your bladder. It was a fact of life, but one never *talked* about it. She amended hastily, "I'll go look for her if you'd like."

"Thank you, but don't bother yourself, my lady." Viscount Drury's voice had taken on a telltale grimness in contrast with his usual glib good humor. "Perhaps you'd like to waltz with me again instead."

A third time? Well, she wasn't overrun with partners and it wasn't like she wanted to return to the dowagers, and besides, it might distract him from watching for Cecily, just in case her sister *had* done something reckless.

"It would be my pleasure, my lord."

Three waltzes. At least, she thought with an inner sigh

as she handed her glass off to a passing servant with a tray, the evening would not be a total loss.

She was sprawled like a common trollop on top of the Earl of Augustine. It was shocking to be resting on the hard plane of his chest, his arm like an iron band around her waist and his warm breath against her temple.

More disturbing than that realization, it felt rather nice, which was an odd sensation, since Cecily had no idea exactly what had just happened to put them in such a position.

It was clarified in the next moment when the man holding her against him said succinctly, "Broken wheel."

He somehow levered himself up against the slanted seat and, still holding her, with seeming effortless ease pushed open the door and climbed out. When he gently set her on her feet in the street, he peered down at her. "Are you injured?"

"No." She was slightly shaken, Cecily decided, standing by the side of the elegant equipage, which at the moment was listing dangerously to the side on the cobbled street, but her state had little to do with the accident. Wheels occasionally broke—it happened. However, it would have been best if it hadn't happened while she was clandestinely meeting with the infamous Earl Savage.

Life, Eleanor would have pointed out in her forthright manner, did not run along predictable lines and she would be a damned fool to expect it to.

"You are certain you are uninjured?" the earl demanded.

"I'm fine," she assured him.

The driver, a young man who looked much more upset than his lordship over the accident, said, "I swear, milord, Mr. Bourne likes things just so. I looked her over just this morning and there wasn't as much as a crack."

"It happens." Jonathan actually touched the man on the shoulder in a gesture of reassurance "Find someone to repair it and tell James to send me the bill."

Muttering, obviously chagrined, the young man nodded and crouched down to inspect the damage.

"You look a little pale."

"It's just the moonlight," Cecily reassured him, her voice sounding thin to her ears as she recalled how he'd caught her in his arms to protect her from the potential crash. In her life, she had never before been quite that close to a man. She cleared her throat. "But I am not sure our arrival back will be as unremarked as we hoped."

"Freddy could find a hack before he gets one of the other coachmen to help him repair the wheel." Casually in command, unruffled except for his cravat being slightly askew, he seemed every inch the aristocrat, no matter what he might think of his background. "Luckily, we haven't gone far. We could walk back, though an arrival in tandem will be noticed. However, it might take young Freddy some time to get back to us."

Either he was remarkably unfazed by their current predicament or he handled every situation with such an air of competent authority. "Which would not," Cecily pointed out, "be quite such a disaster if we were affianced. Let's walk. It's a pleasant evening and the longer we are gone, the more potential for disaster."

His disordered hair framed his face, emphasizing the stark masculine beauty of his bone structure, and thick lashes framed those dark, dark eyes as he stared down at her. Then he politely offered his arm. "You seem quite intently focused on this unorthodox proposition."

She'd done nothing but think about how she could possibly prevent her upcoming engagement since her meeting with her father, and yet she could come up with no other solution. He wanted her properly married, and Lord Drury was a bit more determined than she had first realized. She had denied to her father that Jonathan was really interested, but she thought she could get around that by explaining she hadn't known at the time how the Earl of Augustine felt about her. In light of the gossip surrounding them, she believed her family would not be all that surprised.

Actually, she *still* didn't know how he felt about her, or her idea, but if the way he was currently looking at her was any indication, he thought she had lost her mind. It was true, they didn't know each other well at all, but she hardly knew Lord Drury better.

And she certainly didn't sense the same pull of attraction toward him, which was unsettling. The man escorting her was a much better choice for this little deception than any of the other men she knew because he wasn't looking for a wife. She somehow doubted that he would drag her into the situation of what she considered a sometimes ridiculous set of rules when it came to aristocratic honor.

Cecily squared her shoulders. It was a sound plan. In the end, of course, she would have to deal with the whispers over her broken engagement and her fiancé's departure to America, but in her opinion that was infinitely better than a marriage without love. She was embarking on this charade not just for her sister's sake but also for her own. What joy would she find in her husband's life—in his bed—when she knew it hurt Eleanor? If the viscount never did show any interest in her sister, at least if he was married to someone else Eleanor would not have to endure his being her brother-in-law.

She said succinctly, "I am quite serious, my lord."

The street was a quiet one, residential and dimly lit by a scattering of stars above in the night sky, which made Jonathan's expression difficult to read. He asked softly, "And what, pray tell, is the benefit to me from a feigned engagement? I'm afraid you misunderstand my sense of duty when it comes to the title. James is my heir and perfectly capable of handling the earldom. He did so very well before my arrival and continues to manage some of the estate business. Other than making sure that my sisters are properly wed and settled, I have no intention of playing the English aristocrat any longer than necessary. You are right. Adela and I are sailing back to America as soon as possible."

"If you are already engaged, all those eager young ladies will turn their attention elsewhere."

"I don't notice them as it is." His voice definitely held a hint of cynical amusement.

That was unfortunately true. He rarely danced, he did not request introduction to any of the debutantes, nor had he expressed any intention of looking for a countess. Cecily's heart sank a bit, but she played what she knew was a trump card, hoping it would not backfire on her later. She lifted her chin. "My grandmother is the Dowager Duchess of Eddington. She has considerable influence. If you and I were betrothed, quite naturally she would take an interest in your family. If anyone could help arrange for your sisters to make brilliant matches, she could."

"Could she now?" He sounded skeptical.

"Oh, yes," Cecily said without pause.

"Ah, I see. That is quite a bribe." Walking along next to her, he gave a muffled laugh. "You are a talented negotiator, Lady Cecily. Now, tell me—if that persuades me to agree to this plan, what makes you think your father will even consider my offer?"

"You are an earl with a respectable fortune and if I explain to him that I prefer you over Lord Drury and want this engagement, I think he will agree."

"And taint the exalted Francis family bloodlines?"

She risked a sidelong glance up at him. "You are more sensitive than I would expect on that issue."

"I am well aware of my nickname." His response was dry. "For such a large city, there are very few secrets in London."

In their circles, that was correct. Except that Eleanor had a secret affection for Lord Drury. And hopefully Cecily and the Earl of Augustine would share one soon with their facade.

"But some can be kept if the parties involved are circumspect," she pointed out.

"Perhaps. But may I mention this is a somewhat unoriginal ploy. I don't know your father, but I assume he is an astute man. If he knows you are reluctant to marry Drury and you suddenly produce another suitable groom—and I am still unconvinced I will fall into that category—conveniently in time to foil the engagement, he will be suspicious. Let us not discount that it is, apparently, since you've heard it, common enough knowledge I have no intention of staying in England. I doubt he'd want you an ocean away. I have a daughter, and I certainly wouldn't."

Why his mentioning his child smote her so effectively she wasn't sure, but Cecily suddenly had visions of holding a beautiful dark-haired babe. She had to collect herself before she said in a tone more brittle than she intended, "Are you refusing to help me, my lord?"

"Use my first name. Such formalities make me feel even more a stranger."

"If you wish." She hadn't ever thought of how he felt

about being in England and of the aristocracy, but he was correct—he was not quite accepted.

"I didn't say I refused you." His voice had perceptively softened. "I simply think a better strategy could be employed."

They went on in silence for a short while except for the clatter of a passing carriage. At least the dim illumination would no doubt keep them from being recognized together.

Or so she hoped. This gamble had been reckless, for he still didn't seem inclined to give her a direct answer. In her inexperience, had she misjudged those two heated whispers as an indication of some interest when there was none? He'd also agreed with flattering alacrity to speak with her, though he had to know it wasn't without risk.

Cecily held her breath and said nothing. It was only two streets, maybe fewer, back to the mansion, and . . .

"I agree, but I have two conditions."

There was another party going on at a nearby town house across the street, lights and laughter spilling from the open windows. Jonathan stopped walking and urged her into the relative privacy of the shadows from an overhanging tree on the other side of an ornate iron fence.

His presence in the near dark was a little overwhelming. It evoked a sense of how small and slender she was next to his height and solid build, how vulnerable . . . and yet how safe, for though she would never walk a London street alone at this time of the evening no matter how fashionable the neighborhood, she hadn't even given safety a thought with Jonathan Bourne at her side.

Except she found that *he* might be a bit dangerous.

Long fingers brushed her throat and then tipped

her chin up as he lowered his head. The whisper of his breath touched her lips. "The first is I want to be able to do this whenever we are alone."

The touch of his mouth was at once hot and silky smooth. His lips molded slowly to hers, and Cecily caught her breath and slid her hand from where it had rested on his forearm to his biceps, the bulge of muscle hard under her clasping fingers. He kissed her slowly, and it wasn't at all as she'd imagined this moment; it was deeper, more earth-shattering, and when his hand at the small of her back urged her closer, she complied, her mind whirling as her breasts touched his chest. Even with the layers of clothing between them it was shockingly intimate.

But also tantalizing. His scent reminded her of country summers, fresh and clean, and the sensation of his tongue sweeping along her lower lip and eventually into her mouth caused a variety of responses, none of which she'd ever felt before but which seemed to be a diaphanous combination of wonder and exhilaration.

When he broke the kiss, she was breathing quickly, speechless, shaken. A part of her wondered if he felt the same, for he said nothing, and instead just looked at her as if he wasn't sure exactly what had just happened. Finally, he said huskily, "Do you agree?"

She had enough of her wits left to be able to ask, "What's the second condition?"

"I don't even recall," he muttered, and kissed her again.

Chapter 9

Jonathan was well aware of the shrouded night, the city street, the occupied houses all around them, but he registered the brush of the breeze and each nuance of the sounds of the city he so disdained with that part of him that contained elements of self-preservation.

A very different part of him that even now hardened in arousal begged to argue such practicality.

Practicality be damned.

Danger. His brain whispered the word even as he tasted and touched the woman in his arms, her scent intoxicating, like flowers after a spring rain. She tasted sweet too, of mint and wine, her lips dewy-soft and luscious against his. When he broke away for the second time, the luxurious length of her lashes stayed against the flush over her cheekbones, her quickened breathing evident by the lift of her breasts against his chest.

When she finally opened her eyes, he wished they were somewhere more lighted so he could see those tawny depths better. She'd responded, of that he had no doubt. He had enough experience to know when a woman participated with pliant, willing eagerness—and he had definitely enjoyed it too. His swift erection was proof of that, but that wasn't the point.

He shouldn't have done it. It was one matter to won-

der what it would be like to kiss the delectable Lady
Cecily, and quite another to *know*.

And yet, even knowing that he'd just made a grave
error, he only reluctantly let her go.

She stepped back a fraction, her delicate features
washed by insufficient light, and she spoke first. "What ...
what is our agreement then, my lord?"

Then and there he decided that British aristocrats
would never cease to amaze him. Flustered from her
first kiss—well, more than one extremely satisfying
kiss—she still managed a regal air that both amused and
impressed him. "I am not quite sure, but I have an idea,"
he said as he urged her back out onto the street to make
their way toward the mansion and the ball.

A very vague one at best ... Why am I agreeing?

Yet he just had.

When they were close enough that they could see the
lights, and the curving drive, he further compounded his
mistake of the evening. "If we do this, I will hold you to
your part of the bargain."

"My grandmother will sponsor your sisters, never
fear." Her profile was perfect and serene, her graceful
poise returned. The delicate orange of her skirts shimmered in the indistinct light.

"Hardly what I meant. I was referring to being able
to kiss you."

She compressed those soft lips he could still taste, and
who knows what she might have said, for at that moment
a male voice cut through their conversation like a slicing
blade. "Augustine, there had better be a damned fine explanation for why you disappeared with my sister."

No stranger to the nuances of a direct threat, Jonathan
saw Cecily's brother stalking toward them as they approached the drive, and relaxed a fraction. Not that the
young man did not look furious and outraged—he defi-

nitely did, the familial resemblance striking—but because he knew the difference between a tried warrior and untried bluster. Wealth and privilege were no advantage in hand-to-hand combat. Experience was everything.

Jonathan simply lifted his brows.

Cecily demanded, "Roddy, what are you doing here?"

"Trying to prevent a scandal, obviously." Slim, at guess not much older than his midtwenties, Roderick Francis moved forward with long strides as if he would take Cecily's arm and drag her away, but at the last moment he decided not to. Which was just as well. Jonathan was not that inclined to relinquish her.

Telling, that.

He'd have to think about it later, but right now he was faced with diplomatically quelling this awkward moment. He said calmly, "Why would there be a scandal? We took a short stroll, that's all. The ballroom was stuffy and I offered to escort Lady Cecily outside for fresh air."

"You've been gone a good while, sir." The young marquess's tone was scathing. "I should know, for I have been looking for you everywhere."

"Discreetly, I hope," Jonathan said sharply. It might be to his advantage if a connection to the illustrious Francis family really did help his sisters, but not if it was tainted by the implication that he'd compromised a young lady's reputation.

Even though he had...

"Of course," Roderick snapped back. "I'm trying to avoid more rumors over the two of you, not create another one. Unfortunately, I am not the only one who noticed your absence. It is only natural that Drury should expect some of your time this evening, Cecily. He's also been searching for you. Luckily, Eleanor came and told me. What were you thinking?"

"I was thinking it is *my* time and I can spend it with whom I wish." Her voice was cool and firm. "And I am not too pleased with Lord Drury at the moment, as it appears he is going about announcing an engagement that has not yet happened. The presumption is irritating."

Since she did seem willing to go to some length to thwart Lord Drury's determination to make her his wife, Jonathan didn't doubt her sincerity, but he also wondered if she understood the depths of male pride. The viscount was not going to be happy with this turn of events. That was hardly in question, considering his declaration in the card room.

"Why don't you return to the ball with your brother?" Jonathan suggested with quiet emphasis. "I will call on you tomorrow. In the meantime, I will enter the house through the terrace doors, as if I have been in the gardens."

"It is all walled," her brother muttered. "You can't get in from the street."

Jonathan just looked at him with a faintly derisive smile.

Cecily hesitated for a moment, but then nodded. "Thank you for the walk, my lord."

"It was my pleasure, I assure you."

Her heated blush at the reference to their embrace and those passionate kisses made her brother's eyes narrow in suspicion as he looked from Jonathan's bland expression to his sister's pink cheeks. But she defused any possible further confrontation by taking Roderick's arm and tugging him toward the marble steps into the mansion. Jonathan heard her brother say, "Augustine is going to actually call on you? Blast it, Cecily, this is deuced awkward. . . ."

She replied, but her words were lost as they moved away. At least, Jonathan thought as he skirted the edge of the formal front walk, Lord Drury hadn't been the one to spot their approach to the mansion. If he had been, Jonathan had the feeling there might have been a much more heated confrontation.

The gate into the back gardens was locked, and yes, the place was walled, but Jonathan scaled the brick barrier without much effort, landed on the other side, and dusted off his hands. Then he strolled back toward the house, passing, as James predicted, more than a few stray couples in the gardens, until he gained the veranda.

Even if the rest of the ball proved to be as dull as the beginning, this had turned out to be quite a memorable evening.

At least Roderick wasn't scowling at her the entire ride home—he chose to go off to White's instead of accompanying them, and while Lord Drury might have noticed her absence, it didn't seem that everyone else had, for her grandmother was in good spirits and chatting about who had attended and the quality of the food and the music.

Cecily must have given the appropriate responses, but she noticed that Eleanor replied in monosyllables, and instead of participating in the conversation, she eyed Cecily speculatively from across the carriage the entire short distance home.

Once we are alone, Elle is going to demand to know where I've been and why, and I can only tell her partial truths.

Damn it all, she thought, and then stifled an inner laugh, for she wondered if thinking in an unladylike curse might be the result of even a short time in Jonathan's company.

Once they reached the enormous house in Mayfair, built generations ago by some ostentatious Duke of Eddington, and alighted, Eleanor followed determinedly up the grand staircase behind her, her silk skirts gathered in her hands. Cecily knew better by this time than to try to escape the coming discussion. She opened the door to her bedroom with resignation, and saw that her maid had turned down the bed and left out her nightdress.

Though she and Eleanor didn't share a room, they did usually help each other unfasten their gowns enough so they could undress themselves and not keep their maids up to all hours waiting. Her sister shut the door firmly behind them, and said without preamble, "I think you need to explain to me what happened this evening."

Since Roderick could easily have already told her, Cecily pulled off a glove and tossed it on an embroidered Queen Anne chair, then replied, "I went for a short walk with Lord Augustine. Please don't tell me you didn't think the ballroom wasn't terribly stuffy."

"All ballrooms are stuffy. It has never made you leave alone with a gentleman before. Really, Cecily, quite honestly, I cannot believe you were led so easily. Yes, the earl is attractive in an overpowering kind of way, I'll grant you, but you are not a flighty miss, swayed by a few whispered words."

"He didn't lead me."

"Are you telling me this ill-advised walk was your idea, when you have so much to lose?"

Unfortunately, Cecily knew exactly what she meant. Lose Lord Drury as a husband. She and her sister had always been forthright with each other until this—until now—when the issue of romance had arisen.

How to diplomatically skirt this issue?

Perhaps to just tell the shocking truth. Cecily deliberately pulled off the other glove, kicked off her satin slippers, and sank down on the bed. She clasped her hands in her lap and confessed, "He kissed me."

Eleanor tripped over the hem of her gown and sat down hard in an opposite chair with an unladylike grunt. "He *what*?"

This evening Elle was particularly beautiful in a lemon yellow gown that set off her dark gold hair and, though tastefully modest, showcased the voluptuousness of her form. Her wide-set eyes were clear and very blue, and her skin was the color of new milk, without a single blemish. Why every man in the *haut ton* was not down on his knees was a mystery and nothing less. Besides her physical appeal she was also kind, intelligent, and insightful, which was sometimes unfortunate because of her candid nature.

"Twice." Cecily could vividly recall the way his mouth had slanted seductively over hers, the firm, unforgettable smoothness of his lips and the wicked brush of his tongue.

Her sister stared at her, and deduced the truth easily enough. "From the look on your face, it wasn't an unpleasant event."

"Far from it." She supposed she shouldn't have been so wanton as to openly enjoy it, but she *had* enjoyed it. "I don't know exactly how I imagined the experience. . . . I mean, I assumed kissing would be agreeable or people would not be so fond of doing it. But quite frankly, though I can't describe it really, it was . . . exhilarating, I suppose. It is the closest I can come."

"Was it really?" Her sister looked intrigued, effectively distracted from her disapproving lecture. "How did it come about?"

"We were walking along and he stopped in a shadowed spot . . . and, well . . ." Cecily felt a wash of heat into her face, not in true embarrassment, for this was just Elle and they had always confided in one another— apparently with the exception of her sister's feelings for

Lord Drury—but there was a surge of recollection of how Jonathan had pulled her possessively into his arms.

It had been unforgivably forward.

It had been unforgettably wonderful.

"And, well, what?" Eleanor prompted, leaning forward just a little, her blue eyes openly curious. "I've always wondered as well how it would be. What female doesn't, I would guess. A first kiss must be a turning point in a woman's life. Go on."

"It just happened." Cecily helplessly lifted her shoulders. "Of course, you are standing very close, so that of itself is quite startling, and he is quite tall and much larger and his arms very strong—"

"He didn't force himself on you, did he?"

"Of course not!" She responded to the interruption scathingly. "Good heavens, Elle, if he had would I be rhapsodizing over the experience? And secondly, Jonathan would never do such a thing."

"Jonathan?" Her sister's brows shot up at the use of his first name. "You know him so well?"

The skepticism irked her. "I know *that* about him. No force was needed, nor would he use it."

"I see." Eleanor sighed heavily. "I was afraid this would happen, Ci. You are becoming infatuated with Augustine. The other evening when he came and sat by you, I saw your face and wondered then if there wasn't a cauldron of trouble ahead. Couldn't you have chosen someone less scandalous?"

And I've seen your face when you look at Lord Drury. She almost said it out loud but stopped herself. The admission of her sister's feelings for the viscount had to come from Eleanor. If Cecily gave any hint of already knowing, her sister would suspect immediately that her refusal of his proposal had something to do with her.

It did, actually, but her opposition to the engagement

had become much more complicated after those two passionate, enlightening kisses with Lord Augustine.

Was she infatuated? Maybe she was, for her pulse quickened at the thought of seeing him again tomorrow.

And if there was the *slightest* opportunity, she would make sure they had a moment alone.

"Do we get a choice?" she asked lightly, lifting her skirts to unfasten a garter and roll down a stocking. "I'm beginning to believe that what happens is fickle fate choosing for us. I'm drawn to him, Elle. I have been from that first moment when I thought he was going to offer me his handkerchief and he did something else entirely."

"Yes, I remember it." Eleanor pursed her mouth, but there was a flash of amusement in her eyes. "The collective gasp from the ballroom was heard by all."

"He doesn't lack in audacity."

"No." Eleanor glanced away and then squared her shoulders. "I understand he has a child."

It wasn't as if she expected Eleanor, of all people, to skirt the subject. Cecily said neutrally, "So I've heard as well."

"Word has it he wouldn't marry her mother."

"I have no idea what happened between them." Although if she admitted it, Cecily *was* curious. Maybe— after those meltingly tender kisses, maybe even a bit envious of this mysterious woman who had enjoyed his passion . . . borne his child. . . . She needed to stop right there.

This was about her thwarted engagement to Lord Drury.

Wasn't it?

After that romantic walk, she wasn't as sure.

Chapter 10

Adela was sleeping soundly, small in the large bed because he'd refused to make her stay in the nursery on another floor. He wanted her close by, so she had a room in the family wing just down the hall from the earl's suite.

It wasn't how it was done, but then again, he wasn't exactly a proper English gentleman anyway, and when it came to his child, he was just a concerned father.

Her long dark hair was soft under his fingers as he sat in the chair at her bedside, a faint smile curving his mouth when he saw the doll clutched in her arms. His father had given it to her on his last visit, the delicate gift all porcelain pale face and golden curls, with an elaborate lace-trimmed gown and even a proper English parasol. Addie had been entirely too young at the time for such an expensive possession, but from the moment she saw it, she adored it and never slept without it.

Her nursemaid, clad in a robe, was used to his nightly visits and bobbed a curtsy from the doorway, evidently having heard him come in. Then she went back into the adjoining room.

He wanted more children.

Another serene sign?

Considering Cecily's proposal, perhaps it was.

It was a startling realization, but then again, it had

been an unusual day. Had that feeling always been there? he asked himself, staring at his sleeping little daughter. It was hard to sift out the complex reactions of being a parent from the equally perplexing emotions involved in any relationship between a man and a woman, but yes, as he bent over and lightly kissed his daughter's cheek, he knew without equivocation that he wanted more children. He needed an heir anyway, didn't he?

Jonathan rose and left, quietly closing the door behind him and heading down the hall toward his suite.

To his surprise Lillian was still awake. Jonathan could see the line of light under the door, which meant she was in her sitting room, no doubt reading again, for that seemed to be her favorite pastime. He walked by on the way to his own suite, stopped, hesitated, and then turned around to go and knock lightly.

It had been an evening of impulsive behavior already, he thought wryly. His half sister opened the door, clad in her nightdress and robe, her rich hair loose. She gazed at him in open question. "Oh, it's you. . . . It's rather late, my lord."

The prim edge in her voice didn't deter him. "Yet we are both still awake. May I come in?"

For a moment he thought maybe she would refuse, but she grudgingly inclined her head and stepped back. "It is your house, after all."

He was beginning to experience a certain level of irritation with her stubborn attitude over his new role as earl, though he did understand it to an extent.

Yet they had *both* lost their father, and he felt it keenly too, even though he had been far away at the time and wasn't now dependent on someone else. However, they needed a truce of some kind, and whether she liked it or not, Jonathan wasn't inclined to let her shut herself away. If she didn't wish to marry, he would support her comfortably, of course, but in his experience hiding from a problem usually made it worse, and he was beginning to think that was exactly what she was doing.

While Carole and Betsy were ingenuously open, chattering about the ball on the carriage ride home, laughing with the simple enjoyment of young ladies who were in the full flush of their debut, Lillian was a much more complicated proposition.

He was right about the books. They were scattered everywhere: on the marble-topped table, by a Queen Anne chair near the fireplace, on the mantel, the floor . . .

Jonathan picked up an open volume of Shakespearean sonnets on a settee and sat down opposite his sister, murmuring, "Are there any left in the library?"

That won him a smile—albeit a small one. Lillian regarded him with those crystalline blue eyes. "I think maybe a few are still on the shelves. Did you wish to talk to me about my reading habits at this hour? I thought you usually were out on that wild horse of yours."

"He's hardly wild. He lets Addie sit on his back and walks around as placid as a pony."

"I would never risk that."

"If it was a risk, neither would I." Jonathan stretched out his legs negligently and held her gaze. "Is there some new inventive reason you did not accompany us this evening?"

"I had a headache."

"Perhaps you should see a physician. It seems to be a persistent problem, Lily."

Her hair fell in a curtain across her face as she bowed her head and looked at her clasped hands, but the supplicant pose lasted only a moment. He'd already learned that Lady Lillian did not relish sympathy of any kind. Her chin came up, her gaze level. "I've already told you I am ruined. Why would I endure the sly looks and whispers if instead I can have a quiet evening at home and enjoy a good book?"

"I wonder if it would be as bad as you think. No one has said a word to me about whatever blemish you think is on your past."

Her brief laugh this time held derision. "Of course not. They are all afraid of you. Trust me, Jonathan, no one is going to insult me in your presence."

Earl Savage. He supposed he should be amused that his notoriety was actually useful in that aspect, but truthfully he sensed the hurt in the dignified way she held herself so upright in her chair. In the steadiness of how she met his eyes without flinching and, more than that, in the stubborn set of her mouth. She'd inherited that from their father. Jonathan remembered it very well. After a moment of careful consideration, he responded, "Then why not attend some social engagements with me? No one will slight you, and you might enjoy yourself."

Her dressing gown was a soft blue color that matched her eyes, and she gathered it around her and more tightly cinched the sash. "Because I will still know they are whispering."

"They whisper about me, apparently," he pointed out with prosaic firmness, "and it doesn't bother me enough to affect my life. Let them talk. If my heritage is offensive, then so be it. It doesn't offend *me*."

His sister's lips trembled. It was not much, almost unnoticeable, but he also caught the quiver of her slender shoulders. "You cannot help your parentage." She swallowed but didn't look away. "My disgrace is of my own making. It is not at all the same thing. So please, just respect my desire to stay out of the path of the gossips and let me be."

This was definitely not his area of expertise, but he

found himself oddly willing to try in spite of her resistance. "You've no dreams of a husband and a family? In my experience most women do."

"That's not fair." Her voice dropped a notch.

"Explain to me how I am not being fair by pointing out the obvious."

"I don't wish to discuss this."

"I do."

"And you always do as you please."

He really didn't want an argument. "No," he said after a moment. "I don't. I wish I could. But I have responsibilities, and those preclude self-indulgence. It isn't just that either. Happiness is a conscious choice. My aunt taught me long ago that spiritual gifts are accepted or refused by how we live our lives. The most impoverished peasant can be delighted by the opening of the first spring flower, and the most wealthy aristocrat can curse the day he was born because of some petty offense to his sensibilities. She is a very wise woman. To achieve serenity we have to view life not as it is measured by the world around us but as we ourselves measure it. We must accept that the scales are not at all equal."

"That is much easier to say," his sister informed him flatly, "as a privileged male."

"It wasn't at all easy to say," he responded, "when I knew it would be met with exactly that response. I am not trying to lecture you, just discussing the matter at hand. Are we at an impasse?"

Lillian finally looked away, staring at a portrait above the fireplace. The subject was a young woman, blond and lovely, with a spaniel at her feet, a smile on her perfect oval face.

He recognized the portrait. His father's second wife. The beautiful Lady Ruthanne had been every inch the

English countess. As Jonathan had sensed from a very early age that he was not precisely welcomed in his father's new household with open arms, he'd never known her well, and as a grown man he understood to a certain extent why. His mother had been first, and by his father's own admission, she was the love of his life.

Because of that, he could certainly afford to give Lillian some latitude, especially when he could only guess at what had happened in her past because he hadn't been there. His sister said quietly, "I don't know if it is an impasse exactly, but we don't see the matter in the same light."

A slight exhale preceded his response. "Lily, you don't make it easy to help you. I want to see to your future. It isn't just my duty; it has to do with my desire to see you happy. We don't know each other well, but we *are* brother and sister."

"We shared a father." She bristled.

"My point exactly," he said calmly, not willing to be provoked. She was younger, she was obviously deluded into thinking her future was over, and he wasn't about to argue about their disparate parentage, since neither of them had had a choice in the matter. "Now, tell me why you refuse to rejoin society. Leave out the gossipmongers. They aren't worthy of your—or my—attention."

Lillian stared at him, and then a small, brittle smile curved her mouth. "It is easy, my lord, to look down your nose at the workings of society when, as I pointed out, one is not only a male and an heir but also bound to a course which will take you away from the sphere. I am not so lucky. What happened, happened. It isn't forgotten, nor did I ever expect it to be."

"No," he agreed, crossing his booted feet. "Which is why I wonder who you deliberately sacrificed your future for, since I am willing to stake my life that you were never compromised."

There was one supreme disadvantage to having a brother from America with absolutely no sense of propriety and even less of an inclination to be a true gentleman.

He didn't tiptoe around asking questions but was instead disconcertingly forthright.

Damn him.

"What do you know of it?"

"Not enough. Care to enlighten me?"

Lily wasn't sure how to respond, so she settled for a frosty look of pure derision.

Unfortunately, he seemed unmoved. He lounged in the chair—her favorite chair, as it happened—long legs extended, his raven hair loose in careless disarray, his jacket and cravat discarded so the pristine white of his fine linen shirt emphasized his barbaric coloring and accented the imposing width of his shoulders. She hadn't been exaggerating when she'd said that most of society was reluctant to cross his path. His reputation fascinated the fine ladies and gave the gentlemen of the *ton* pause. Since she had to say something in the lengthening silence, she settled for "No."

"You are hiding something."

She was. The perceptive insight was disconcerting.

"You are entitled to your opinion."

"All I want is the truth."

Is that all *he wants?* a self-mocking voice in her head asked. *Just the truth?*

Instead of answering him, she looked at the empty hearth, the night too warm for a fire, her spine rigid.

"Stubborn wench," Jonathan muttered. More clearly, he told her, "Fine. If you refuse to explain to me what happened the night you were supposedly ruined, then I am going to consider the event so insignificant that we will act as if it never happened. From now on, you will attend these affairs with us, understand? Routs, balls, dinners, the whole lot of them. It is ridiculous for you to lock yourself away. From my understanding, your supposed lover has certainly done nothing of the kind but instead married another. If I thought it would do any good I would seek retribution on your behalf, but I suspect it would just make everyone remember the event."

Even the possibility of that horrified her and she shook her head. "Please . . . Jonathan . . . don't."

It was the first time she'd ever in her life used his given name—the same name as their grandfather, the fifth earl. He didn't miss it either, for his dark brows rose fractionally. "You care that much for the blackguard who by your own admission destroyed your reputation?"

How to answer such a loaded question? Her relationship with Arthur had been so complicated—and yet so simple—that she couldn't come up with a reasonable response.

"You do not discuss the mother of your daughter."

"Adela." Something flickered in his dark eyes. "My daughter's name is Adela. And no, I do not discuss Caroline."

That was more information than she'd had before. At least now she knew the woman's name. Her own disordered life aside, Lillian was curious. His open affection for his daughter had not gone unnoticed by the family or the staff, and truthfully, Addie was an engaging child. It wasn't deliberate, but Lillian had run into her because it seemed that the little girl was *everywhere*. The day before, they had nearly collided in the hallway and in her ingenuous way, her little niece had coaxed her into a walk in the garden, which had turned into a game of hide-and-seek.

So she did wonder how any woman would have abandoned such a lovely child. She cleared her throat. "You never married her."

"Just like Sebring never married you." Her brother smiled, but it was a mere thinning of his lips.

"True." Lillian could play fair. She exhaled and then said softly, "I would prefer you dropped the subject, and truly, approaching Arthur in any way would be a waste of your time. Just take my word that he regrets what happened as much as I do. But it *did* happen and all the beau monde remembers it. I think it best if I stay as unobtrusive as possible while Carole and Betsy are having their come-out."

"You do not strike me as a coward." Her brother's voice was even, but his dark eyes were very direct. "And your happiness is just as important as theirs. Never undervalue your worth, Lily."

"I'm doing what is best for my sisters," she insisted, but there was a tight knot in her stomach that said maybe he was right and she was simply avoiding her future.

Or lack of future. He was right about that as well. Spinsterhood didn't hold a great deal of appeal. She'd always wanted a husband—one that would adore her, naturally—and children. Having Adela underfoot was a special kind of torture, reminding her of what she was missing. It was a romantic view of marriage, but then again, she was a romantic at heart. Most of the books she devoured transported her to worlds where passion reigned and the heroines met the men of their dreams and their love conquered all the obstacles in their way . . .

But that was fiction, she reminded herself. She'd met her hero and the obstacles had been insurmountable. At the end of their story, they had both been left brokenhearted.

Not all fairy tales had a happy ending. That bitter realization haunted her every single day.

"Let me worry about Carole and Betsy. There's no reason for you to consider yourself on the shelf." There was an implacable edge to Jonathan's voice. "By my existence alone we already are a slightly unconventional family, so I see no benefit in you sitting alone night after night. As you pointed out, no one will get away with insulting you if I am present, so why not enjoy yourself? Men can be obtuse—I won't disagree with that—but with all our myriad flaws, some of us are not unintelligent. Perhaps you will meet the man who looks past one small incident and values you for the person you are." He paused. "Unless, of course, you tell me now that you absolutely have no desire to ever marry. In that case, I won't force you to return to society."

A part of her was taken aback. Even their father, who was kind and fair-minded, had not shown quite that level of benevolence.

She wanted to lie to Jonathan, to convincingly tell him that no, she didn't want to become a wife, a mother, and have her own family, her own life. *Happiness.* Yes, she wanted happiness. So she couldn't quite bring herself to do it. Stiffly, she said, "I doubt anyone truly wishes to live out their life alone."

His teeth were very white as he flashed a triumphant grin. "I was rather hoping you would say that." Jonathan rose to his feet in one lithe movement. "I am looking forward to escorting all three of my sisters to the next event, and perhaps you can assist Carole and Betsy with their many suitors. James is helpful, but truthfully, I don't have enough experience to know who is a possible fortune hunter and who might make a very respectable husband."

He was trying to make her feel useful, and Lily experienced an unwanted twinge of gratitude. Everything about him was foreign, from his deplorable accent to his dramatic dark coloring. For heaven's sake, the man didn't even drink tea. But maybe he was more tolerable than she had first imagined.

For instance, he very definitely had her father's smile.

And oh, how she missed her father.

Their father.

Her brother left the room and she sat there, quiet, contemplative, wondering if she had just made a grave error. Not for a moment did she think Jonathan's motives were strictly altruistic. He hadn't made a secret of the fact that he wished to return to America as soon as all was settled with his affairs in England. She was one of the details that needed to be tidied up, like a meeting with his solicitor, or a discontented tenant. If she married, he could abdicate responsibility for her future to some other male and walk away a free man.

On the other hand, he had proved to be surprisingly insightful, and it was clear that he would defend her honor in the most primitive way possible if need be, so perhaps . . . perhaps they could form some sort of truce.

She suddenly yawned, realizing she was extremely tired.

Maybe tonight she would sleep.

Chapter 11

"My driver said the wheel was perfectly fine when we left for the ball, but it clearly was damaged in some way. I suppose it's possible that we hit a hole, but I don't remember a jolt for the life of me, and he thinks it was deliberately tampered with—"

"I might marry her."

It was undoubtedly an unfair gambit, but Jonathan was still gratified to be able to startle James enough with the interruption that he dropped his forkful of eggs. "What? Marry who?"

"The duke's beauteous daughter."

That really sent James into a coughing fit. When he recovered, he asked, "Have you lost your mind or am I dreaming? I ask because I have a vested interest in the answer. If it is the former, I'll just take the steps to have you declared incompetent and take over your estate. If it is the latter, I'll have a good chuckle at my vivid imagination when I awake."

Jonathan had to laugh. He stirred his coffee, pondering what he would say next, but in the end it was simpler to just be honest. "It is a bit complicated, but be prepared for the announcement of a betrothal. I have contemplated the matter and wonder if it wouldn't be for the best for both of us if we marry."

"A marriage usually follows a betrothal, I believe."

James visibly hesitated, and then said, "Not to be argumentative, Jon, for the lady is both lovely and well-bred, but you are going to have to get her father's approval."

"I realize that, but Cecily evidently doesn't think it is going to be a difficulty."

"That's . . . interesting."

"Ah, you seem to disagree."

"I don't know the duke well enough to judge, but . . ."

When he trailed off, Jonathan supplied, "But I am not an English blueblood despite my rank and I happen to openly acknowledge my daughter, who was born out of wedlock."

His cousin muttered, "Yes, only I was not going to say it so bluntly. We are not just related, you and I, we are friends. If Lady Cecily is your choice in a wife, I applaud it. However, be prepared for an obstacle or two."

"I am going to call on the duke this afternoon."

James set aside his fork, folding his hands on the linen tablecloth. "Wait a moment. Does this mean you've changed your mind about your desire to return to America?"

"No."

His cousin frowned. "I am surprised that Lady Cecily has consented to leave England."

"She hasn't. I haven't even discussed that aspect of the arrangement with her yet."

"God forbid reason should enter into this, but I think perhaps you should."

"I've seen the way society works." Jonathan nodded at the footman offering more coffee. "Men and women often go their separate ways. I'll need to return to England quite often anyway."

From across the table James just stared at him. "You need to sire an heir. Rather difficult to do when apart."

"Does it bother you that I am thinking of marrying?"

That hadn't really occurred to him. James was such a fair-minded individual and, truthfully, had seemed relieved upon Jonathan's arrival to abdicate the responsibilities he had shouldered for nearly a year. He still managed some of the estate affairs but was not responsible for everything, as it had been.

"Of course not. I was thinking of logistics on your part, not my personal gain. Devil take it, Jon, you know that. I've never coveted the title. I'm just stating with all due logic that an ocean between you might be a problem."

Actually, he *did* know it. "I'll need to spend at least a few months a year here regardless."

"And that will be enough for your wife?"

"Why not?" he asked, reasonably enough he thought, for truly the English aristocracy had a habit of detaching passion from marriage. "I can let you and the solicitors manage the business and estates in general, and I can return to my own life between my visits."

James set his cup aside very carefully. His eyes, which were very blue, like Lillian's, held a certain hint of amusement. "Can I say first that I think you are mad? You truly believe it will work that way?"

He had no idea. But he did know he wasn't going to participate in a fake engagement. He desired Cecily—more than desired her—and if he needed a wife, she would be ideal. No, she would be *perfect*.

Besides, he wanted her in his arms and in his bed.

"Why wouldn't it?" He helped himself to a grilled tomato and some bacon. "Plenty of men enter into marriage in the same exact fashion. Sea captains, soldiers—"

"You are neither one," James interrupted without ceremony, picking up his cup. "I can't see you leaving your wife behind for months at a time either. If you know as much about society marriages as you claim, you will realize that once a woman has given her husband a male child, she enjoys a great deal of latitude. Affairs are the order of the day. Would you be willing to allow that?"

Never.

It was a primal reaction to the idea of Cecily with any other man. Jonathan shook his head. "I highly doubt she'd ever consider infidelity. That isn't her nature."

"How can you possibly know that?" James was, as ever, pragmatic and matter-of-fact. "You're infatuated, but let's look at this realistically. You aren't that well acquainted, Jon. You've been around her only a few times . . . enough for an indiscretion apparently, but—"

"I'm not infatuated," he said irritably.

"Aren't you? I believe you just told me you are going to marry the young woman."

A valid point. Jonathan took a moment, sipping his coffee, and then finally admitted, "Lust can be a powerful incentive. Fine, I concede the infatuation. Why not? She's bright and beautiful."

"I wasn't arguing that in the least. She's most definitely one of the most notable debutantes of this season and it will be a coup if you can convince her father to approve your suit."

That was the same argument he'd used to Cecily. She was remarkably without prejudice for a blue-blooded English lady. Perhaps she was naive enough to expect the same from her family. "Like I said, she seems to think he'll agree."

"That depends on how much the duke dotes on his lovely daughter. I'm going to guess he won't particularly approve without some coercion."

One of the attributes Jonathan had always appreciated in his cousin was that James had the ability to look at life in a straightforward fashion and didn't dissemble. With a cynical lift of a brow, he murmured, "I shouldn't expect a warm welcome then, when I call on His Grace, hat in hand?"

Across the polished mahogany of the breakfast table, James said mildly, "I'm going to venture a guess that it won't be a certainty that he'll approve." Then he elaborated. "I'm not telling you anything you don't know when I mention you are not a typical Englishman."

That was true enough. "No."

"You've caused a bit of gossip already over Lady Cecily. He won't be kindly disposed if he's heard any of it."

"True." It wasn't anything he hadn't already thought of himself.

"You do have a solid fortune."

"I do," Jonathan remarked with studied equanimity, sitting back and buttering a piece of toasted bread. "Not just the one my father left me but the one I made myself. But what does it matter? The Duke of Eddington doesn't need my money."

"Nor do you need his. That's a point in your favor."

"To offset my questionable background?"

"Maybe." James sent him a challenging look. "How much are you prepared to fight for her?"

"Should I have to? I don't know if you are informed or not, but a woman can make a thousand pounds should she coerce me into a compromising position."

"I've heard." James laughed. "Did you think I wouldn't? This is the *ton*, after all. You turned down Valerie Dushane. No one can quite believe it."

"Lady Irving is a bit forward for my tastes." That was putting it mildly. Since that incident when the lady had popped up in his bed, he'd fended off more than a few of her enthusiastic friends. Now that he knew the game, it was easy to spot those who were playing.

"You might have done yourself a favor and just bedded one of them." James picked up his coffee. "I know it sounds like licentious advice, but at least it would no longer be on the tip on everyone's tongue."

"Cecily might hear of it."

"So? You are not yet engaged."

His attempt at an uncaring shrug didn't work.

James set down his cup abruptly, his brow furrowed. "If her feelings concern you that much, you are in trouble, my friend."

Jonathan had the uncomfortable feeling that his cousin was absolutely correct.

The care with which she dressed gave away a good deal, she supposed. Eleanor's face said so, and truthfully, Cecily didn't particularly mind. She was pleased with the topaz lute-string gown that exactly matched the color of her eyes and her pale hair was caught up in an elegant coil a bit elaborate for midafternoon. Reaching for the crystal bottle holding her favorite perfume, she said lightly, "Will his lordship be impressed?"

"Remembering his remark on the night of the musicale, while he wasn't guilty of it then, he might just ravish you on the floor of the drawing room this time." Elle's voice was dry. "Which will still cause quite a sensation. Augustine must have truly impressed you to warrant all this concern with detail."

"It is just a day gown." Cecily shrugged.

"Your best. And all the attention to your hair and the fifteen minutes spent trying on different slippers have a unique significance. Usually you simply let your maid select a gown, Ci."

Since she had no idea of what alternate plan Jonathan might have, she said, "I am hoping perhaps he will offer for me."

Her sister's expression stayed neutral. Too carefully

neutral in her opinion. "I see. I was under the impression that Father rather favored Lord Drury's proposal."

What a perfect window of opportunity. Cecily dabbed a bit of perfume on her wrist and set the bottle aside, turning around on the small silk-covered bench before her dressing table. "If Augustine does come up to scratch, will you please take my side?" She searched for the right words that would tactfully explain why she didn't wish to marry Elijah Winters and yet not insult him in any way to the woman who she believed wanted desperately to become his wife. She clasped her hands together and sighed. "Lord Drury is a very nice man. He's quite handsome also, and has an attractive laugh, and as far as I can tell, he would never be unkind, or rude and abrasive, and there is no doubt his manners are impeccable, but truthfully, Elle, I am not romantically interested in him."

Her sister's lashes lowered a fraction. She was sitting comfortably on the bed, her ankles crossed, her gown a demure pale pink muslin that made her look young and fresh. "I confess I don't see why you'd prefer Augustine over his lordship."

Ah, that is at least close to an admission. Well, maybe not close, but a step closer.

"Do you not think the earl is handsome in a different, exotic sort of way?" Cecily asked. "I find myself quite breathless around him for some reason."

That might be a bit of exaggeration. Or it might not. When she thought about the way he'd kissed her . . .

He'd certainly left her breathless then.

"Perhaps he takes you by surprise with his unpredictable behavior." Eleanor softened the comment with a twitch of a smile. "He's dangerous, I'm sure, and not in the manner of the general perception. Whether or not he keeps a knife strapped in his boot and rides the streets of London at night, honestly—you know little about him. Certainly not enough to actually *marry* him."

"Because he's generally considered a heathen and a savage as well?"

It was odd, but the conversation suddenly shifted. Cecily hadn't realized how defensive she was on the subject.

"Of course not," Eleanor shot back. "I didn't say that at all. I've mentioned to you before I think he is a very attractive man. I just wonder how practical it is of you to expect a proposal of marriage from a person who has shown no inclination that he wishes to take a wife, much less an English one. Lord Drury is a much better prospect."

"Perhaps *you* think so."

Now *that* was quite a direct observation. A perfect opening if a confidence was forthcoming.

Instead of taking advantage of it, Eleanor said slowly, "I doubt my thoughts are all that relevant. We are speaking of your future, not mine."

This was getting tricky, but the timing did seem right. "Perhaps, but I am curious. Why would you marry Lord Drury instead of the infamous Earl Savage?"

Her sister was evidently at a loss for words—which for Eleanor was not a usual occurrence.

Cecily went on. "He's quite eligible, of course, but not wealthier. He's merely a viscount whereas Augustine is an earl, and I am going to guess they are quite close to the same age. I fail to see why Drury is the more promising prospect. You must admit Augustine is a bit more … dashing, maybe? No, for *dashing* implies deliberate charm and Jonathan doesn't set out to charm anyone. I'll settle for *exciting*. His less-polished edge means you can't quite know what to expect. You're correct—he's unpredictable."

"Whereas Lord Drury is *extremely* charming." Eleanor's jaw stuck out at a stubborn angle.

"Compared to Augustine's lesser finesse, I suppose that is true." Cecily held back a smile at the way her sister bristled over any criticism of the viscount. "But you have to admit he doesn't have the same brand of forceful masculinity."

"He's a gentleman."

"And Jonathan doesn't even pretend to that label."

"Not that I have noticed. He kissed you."

"Please don't tell me you think that even the finest gentleman would not kiss a lady given the opportunity." Cecily raised a brow.

"Lord Drury would not."

"What a disappointment."

"Ci!" Eleanor tried to sound scandalized, but she burst out laughing instead.

In answer, Cecily checked her appearance one more time, smoothed her golden skirts, and turned back. "Do you really think he will want to ravish me?"

"What I think is that you haven't paid this much attention to your wardrobe in a very long time, if ever." Eleanor's smile turned wistful. "I'm rather jealous, actually."

"Why?" The question was soft and had nothing to do with her new gown.

When Eleanor hesitated, Cecily wondered if her sister might actually confide in her, but in the end she merely shook her head. "Though I am not positive I agree with your choice, you are falling in love. That alone is to be celebrated, for as Shakespeare penned so eloquently, *O spirit of love, how quick and fresh art thou*. But keep in mind, once first flush of it passes, you will be tied to the man of your choosing forever."

"So will you, when you marry." *Tread cautiously*, Cecily reminded herself.

"I . . ." Eleanor began to say but faltered at the last instant.

There was a discreet knock on the door that interrupted the moment, and when Cecily moved to answer it, one of the maids stood there. "You have callers, my lady."

A ripple of anticipation moved through her, though the plural was a bit disconcerting. "I will be down directly, Mary."

Cecily glanced at where her sister perched on the bed. "Tell me you won't leave me to make conversation with both of them alone, Elle."

It was awkward as hell to arrive simultaneously with Lord Drury, but there wasn't much help for it, and as far as Jonathan could tell from what he'd heard, it happened often enough when two gentlemen were interested in the same young lady. Both stood in the grand ducal drawing room, the viscount aloof and tense, though Jonathan found he himself was personally more resigned than anything else to the unconcealed dislike in the other man's eyes.

He didn't actually blame him. The woman the viscount wanted had risked public censure to seek Jonathan out in an attempt to avoid a betrothal, and though Jonathan was still not quite sure of her entire motivation, he was sympathetic to a certain extent to the plight of his fellow male.

Drury had brought roses, the brilliant scarlet hue striking, all twelve perfect blossoms, no doubt from some glassed-in conservatory. Jonathan had ridden out early that morning and picked wildflowers from the banks of the Thames. Tiny pink ones, yellow blossoms with vivid violet centers, white blooms on a dark green vine, and tall stalks of leaves streaked with ivory that reminded him of home. The housekeeper had artfully put them in a crystal vase for him, and though the arrangement could probably be classified as a collection of weeds, he thought it was rather pretty.

If Lady Cecily preferred cultivated to wild, then she should look elsewhere anyway.

"I should not be surprised that you declined to heed my warning, Augustine." Drury's voice was cold and hard.

One brow inched upward and Jonathan drawled, "You suppose? You don't know me. Why should you be able to anticipate what I would do, one way or the other?"

There was a pause while they simply took measure of each other, the tick of the case clock quite loud in the silence.

"I suppose that is a valid point," Drury said grudgingly, straightening his cuffs, every inch the stiff British gentleman. "Let's just say I have heard a great deal about your possible interest in the woman I propose to marry, and you must admit your presence here at this moment seems to confirm those rumors."

Luckily, Jonathan was saved from commenting by the arrival of not just Cecily but also her sister, whom he had never met, both of them entering the room in a soft sweep of skirts, one clad in gold, the other in rose, the two of them indisputably lovely.

Being the son of an earl, even if Americans did not recognize English titles, Jonathan had been invited to more than a few rarefied drawing rooms back in Boston, so he knew what was the standard protocol of stilted polite conversation after the standard greetings were given. He really needed to talk to Cecily alone, and that now seemed quite impossible, which was irritating. However, upon bracing himself to the fact that he'd made this call for no reason—well, not entirely *no* reason, for Cecily was distractingly alluring in her golden gown—he heard Lord Drury ask her sister in his cool voice, "Would you perhaps like to walk in the garden, Lady Eleanor?"

It was hard to guess which of the three of them looked more surprised. Jonathan thought he was fairly adept at keeping on an inscrutable mask when it was necessary, and this certainly was one of those times. Lady Eleanor, who was somewhat of a provocative beauty if you liked lush, curvy women with dark gold hair and a standoffish manner, seemed the most stunned of all by the viscount's offer. A delicate wash of pink rose into her face, though Jonathan couldn't tell what reason there might be to blush. Then she said quite plainly, "It isn't me you wish to walk with."

"On the contrary. I just asked you." Drury didn't look the eager lover, but his voice held a certain hint of steel. "Shall we?"

"Go on, Elle," Cecily urged. "It's a lovely day."

Actually it was a bit overcast, but Jonathan wasn't about to point that out. He had no idea what his supposed rival's intentions were, but he wasn't going to argue with the opportunity being gifted to him. For a moment he thought maybe Cecily's older sister would refuse, but then she stood and nodded. "Of course."

When they exited the room, Eleanor's fingers lightly on the viscount's sleeve, Cecily gave Jonathan a dazzling smile. "Are those flowers for me?" She went unerringly to the vase he'd brought in. "They're lovely."

"How do you know I didn't bring the roses?" His

gaze lingered on the tempting smoothness of her slender neck as she bent to smell the bouquet.

She laughed and straightened, touching one of the delicate petals lightly with a fingertip. "Cultivated roses are not at all in keeping with your personality, my lord. Thank you. I am sure you picked these yourself, and that is more romantic than any flowery words on a card."

He hadn't endeavored to be romantic, or not consciously so, but she was right—he thought flowers from a hothouse duly ordered and delivered meant that very little personal effort was expended. "You are most welcome."

"You were very clever in how you handled Lord Drury." She turned and gazed at him with an almost poignant gratitude evident in her eyes.

The only clever thing he'd done as far as he could tell was to restrain himself from giving Lord Drury a swift punch in the jaw over his disdain, and that had nothing to do with his intellect but was a testament to his self-control. "How so?"

Her face was graced by a truly fascinating expression. Or at least he found it so. There seemed to be a lot about Lady Cecily he found entrancing. She murmured, "I don't know what you said to influence him, but my sister and Lord Drury just went off to walk together. I was puzzling over how to accomplish that when I realized you were both here, and you somehow did it for me."

"I did nothing." He inhaled a trace of the delicate scent of her perfume and his traitorous body remembered exactly what it was like to hold her in his arms. "He and I simply arrived at the same time, which, I might say, did not please him very much."

"Yet he still asked Elle to walk with him."

Jonathan was hardly astute when it came to young

ladies, but by necessity he was beginning to learn. His
gaze was sharp and searching. "You wish for your sister
and Lord Drury to become involved?"

"I absolutely wish exactly that very thing."

What Jonathan wished was that he wasn't so distracted by the gorgeous color of her eyes. The amber
hue reminded him of the stone he'd found in the river
as a boy. Warm despite the caress of the cool water,
the golden color unique, the surface smoothed by the
current passing over it for centuries. He kept it at all
times in his pocket, and it was with an enlightened reaction that he realized the spirits were speaking to him
again. It had always been one of his prized possessions,
a reminder of his youth, a magical charm that brought
him good luck, or so he'd always believed. Now, in this
moment, looking deep into Cecily's eyes, he knew why
he'd found it, and even more why he'd been so moved to
keep and cherish it.

She was *the* one.

With effort he centered his attention back on the
conversation. "Why?"

"Let's just say I think they would be very well suited."
Her lashes fluttered down a fraction. "And besides, they
have much more in common than they know. It would
be a good marriage."

She was young. Certainly younger than either of the
subjects of the conversation, and he couldn't help but
ask bluntly, "What makes you think it would be such a
stellar match?"

Her gaze flashed up with a touch of defiance. "Because I have considered it at length, my lord."

The last thing he wanted was to offend her. Jonathan offered, "I wasn't trying to be argumentative,
Cecily."

"Of course not. You can manage that without trying, Lord Augustine."

Had he not caught the hint of amusement in her voice, he might have truly taken offense. Instead he was intrigued. She had a habit of doing that to him. "Why do you want the ardent Drury to court your sister?"

Chapter 12

She had no illusions.

None.

Nevertheless, Eleanor still had a small sense of the surreal as she let Elijah Winters lead her down the garden path—but only literally speaking. He wasn't interested in her. If she even entertained the idea it made her a fool—and she might be outspoken, she might be less than fashionable, but she wasn't stupid.

Cecily had looked more stunning than ever this afternoon, her gown a perfect foil for her fair coloring, and both men in the drawing room had looked at her with clear admiration in their eyes.

Quite frankly, while she was happy for her sister, it was all very discouraging.

At least the afternoon was passable, though from the look of the clouds it might rain later, and she did prefer a stroll rather than sitting in a closed drawing room. The gardens behind the house were a bit formal and grand for her tastes, but then again, her father was a duke and grand was expected. This was not a place for children to run free and enjoy themselves, but a journey for ascetic pleasure—that is, if one liked bushes neatly trimmed and flowers in orderly rows and the paths carefully groomed and raked. Since the viscount didn't seem inclined to speak, she murmured, "I wish they didn't clip the roses. I know it sounds fanciful, but quite frankly, seeing the blooms wither and then gently lose themselves in a scatter of petals is part of a natural process. Our interference is an example of our need to control everything around us."

A true bluestocking observation, but so be it. They knew each other well enough that he would not be surprised.

Next to her, more handsome than ever in a dark blue coat and snowy cravat, his blond hair slightly ruffled by the breeze, Lord Drury shot her a quick, unreadable glance. "That is very introspective, Lady Eleanor."

"Just a stray thought, motivated, I'm afraid, by a personal distaste of how regimented English gardens are. I meant very little by it."

"Why do you always apologize for or try to conceal your intellect?"

That insightful comment caused her to glance up sharply. "What?"

"Never mind." His profile austere, he walked next to her, seemingly oblivious to the details of the park. "Please tell me, if you will, what is the status of your sister's relationship with Augustine? At first I thought he was just a mild flirtation, but now I am beginning to become alarmed. Surely she cannot be seriously considering someone who is . . . is . . ."

"A heathen?" Eleanor supplied ironically, her voice more dry than she intended. "From barbarian stock, not more than half noble, unless one counts noble savages as sound bloodstock. Then again, dark as he may look, let us face it, our fair coloring is no doubt Nordic in origin, based on when the brutal Saxons invaded England and perhaps . . . how shall I delicately put this? Um, enjoyed the bounty of their conquest?"

There. That would do it. What real lady would mention raping and pillaging in polite conversation? No one she could think of. Except her, of course.

As ever, she had an ability to be blunt to an indelicate extent.

But honestly, the past few weeks of studied, stilted conversation had made her want to scream, and since it was clear she wasn't going to impress Lord Drury anyway, why she should worry about it was a mystery. It wouldn't ruin a romance, as there *was* no romance. At one time she'd had the impression that perhaps he had considered courting her, but his normally friendly manner had turned distant, though she wasn't sure just what had happened to cool his interest.

Something she'd said, no doubt.

And now he was intent on Cecily, so she no longer had to guard every word coming out of her mouth.

It was actually a relief. Pretense had always come at a hard cost to her.

But to her surprise, he chuckled. It was low and almost inaudible, but he laughed. "I don't suppose I've ever thought of the Saxon invasion that way, but you do indeed have a point, my lady. I'll concede it is possible that our ancestry is no more noble than Augustine's."

There was nothing he would need to do to make her fall more in love with him. Still, being fair-minded was endearing. "It's possible," she agreed with a hidden smile, twirling her parasol. "I'm glad you are not one of those stiff-backed prigs who are insulted the moment a woman has an opinion."

"Of course not." He laughed again. "What a rare compliment. Imagine that. I am not a stiff-backed prig. You, as always, have a unique way with words, my lady."

He was right, of course. What a stupid comment. Quickly she tried to explain, "Don't sell British so-called gentlemen short, my lord. If a woman opens her mouth and something intelligent comes out, it is my experience that most of them turn and run like schoolboys. What they are so frightened of, I have never been sure."

The viscount walked beside her, his expression still amused—or maybe *bemused* would be a better way to describe it. "Your frankness never fails to amaze me."

"I am sure the gossips would agree."

"I don't listen—" he started to say.

"Yes, you do," she interrupted, her tone controlled, the moment poignant to her. "Of course you do. We all listen. If you do not put too fine a point on it, we are almost forced to listen. It isn't fashionable to disdain gossip nor, to be honest, is it human. But I do say we all are still able to use our functioning brains and decide for ourselves what might be worth hearing and what is just utter nonsense."

He looked startled, which didn't surprise her. After a moment, to her relief, he merely nodded. "I suppose that is true."

"Like whatever you've heard about my sister and the Earl of Augustine. There are no assurances any of it is true, so before you retract your offer, I think you should consider that aspect of it."

"I never said I was going to retract my offer."

Eleanor refused to be dismayed, partly for the sake of her own pride and also for Cecily, whom she wasn't sure was better off with the unconventional Earl Savage. Yes, love was *intoxicating*, but the very nature of the word involved impaired judgment. "Oh?"

Her handsome companion did look uncomfortable then, his polished boots scraping along the path as they walked.

Now we are getting to it.

"I called today to ask the favor of an intimate conversation on the matter. Who would imagine he would arrive at the same time?"

"Who would imagine he would arrive at all? He isn't in the habit of calling on young ladies."

"Yet he made an exception for Lady Cecily. You and your sister are close, or so it is said. Has she mentioned her feelings for Augustine?"

Eleanor's conflicted personal angle on the situation aside, this was treading very close to waters that were of unsure depth. On the one side of it, she wasn't at liberty to speak for her sister. Not when she wasn't objective, and certainly not when it involved Cecily's entire future.

On the other hand, she knew her sister had developed a penchant for the raven-haired half-foreign heir to the Augustine title. That dreamy-eyed look when she described his kiss was evidence enough, and Eleanor was alarmed on her sister's behalf.

Earl Savage might, or might not, be interested in Cecily.

No, not true. From the glimmer in his dark eyes, he was definitely interested, but the level of that pursuit had to combat his reputed disdain for a permanent tie to his English roots, and an aristocratic wife would be a problem in that regard. It was all too likely that he was just dallying with her and nothing would come of it except one young woman's disappointment and possible broken heart.

She knew about *that* from personal experience.

One of Eleanor's worst faults was her inability to lie. Actually, maybe that wasn't a fault, but it was inconvenient now and then—like at this moment. Elijah Winters was still looking at her expectantly, and she needed to come up with a reasonable answer. "She finds him intriguing, my lord." She chose her words carefully. "You have to admit he is not your average English gentleman. However, whether it is anything more than that is not a question I can answer, for I truly don't know."

That was extremely diplomatic for her. Perhaps she was getting better at not being so unfashionably frank after all.

"I see." Next to her, the viscount wore a faint scowl, staring straight ahead as they walked. "I suppose his background might seem romantic in some way to a young woman who has led a sheltered life."

"And he is very handsome."

Well, that was much more her usual style and *not* very diplomatic. She hastily amended, "If you prefer your men dark and a bit out of the ordinary."

"I will have to take your word for it, Lady Eleanor, because I don't prefer men at all myself." A hint of wry amusement infused his voice. In the late-afternoon sun his hair was lit with chestnut glints among the gold.

She had a longing—a very secret and shameless longing—to touch his hair. To run her fingers through it, and if Cecily's reaction was any indication of how much she had enjoyed the scandalous Augustine's kiss, Eleanor wanted to experience that same exciting, forbidden moment, but with the man strolling next to her.

The irony of it always struck her, and never more so than at this moment. "No, it is clear Cecily is who you fancy."

Maybe it was something in her tone—she was so abysmal at being subtle—but he turned to look at her then, his pace never faltering but his eyes narrowing just a fraction as if he suddenly really *saw* her.

Now I've done it.

Could she save face? Maybe, though heat rose into her cheeks, which was probably betrayal enough. She babbled, "Why . . . why wouldn't you? She's lovely, intelligent, gifted with charm and poise and tact, and really, since I adore her also, I don't blame you."

"Don't blame me?" he repeated, a slight question in his voice.

It was no illusion. He truly was staring at her now, as if the words struck him.

As if he *knew*.

The birds were twittering, the air was fragrant with flowers, and the clouds had broken momentarily, so the sun was warm on her shoulders. He just looked at her. Oh, dear Lord, she was making everything quite worse by the passing second. That last bit gave away entirely too much. A surge of panic gripped her, as if she had stripped her soul bare accidentally and wasn't ready for it. Which she most definitely wasn't.

If they kept on walking she would say something else unfortunate. It was bound to happen, and she didn't know if she could bear the humiliation of his knowing of her secret passion for him and the inevitable rebuff.

So she took the only reasonable course and caught her skirts in her hands. "Excuse me."

And with unforgivable rudeness she left him there as she all but ran like a coward back toward the house.

Cecily decided to simply tell the truth. "My sister is in love with Lord Drury. I am not. How could I possibly marry him?"

Jonathan's smile was enigmatic. "I see. That explains quite a lot."

"I've told *no one* else," she said with firm inflection. "Well, no one but Roddy because I hoped he could get a sense of whether or not Lord Drury might in some measure return her interest."

"The secret is quite safe with me, rest assured."

She believed him. Maybe that was what it was about

him that drew her. Oh, yes, there was a physical attraction she could not deny, but while she doubted that the rules of gentlemanly conduct mattered much to him, she had the impression of an underlying strict moral code of his own making, and she was certain enough of his word to trust him. "Thank you."

Jonathan nodded once. "I've considered the engagement."

Cecily was annoyed with herself for having a light, rapid heartbeat, damp palms, and generally a very ingénue reaction to just being in the same room with the man who had so often occupied her thoughts in the past days. She hoped she managed some semblance of aplomb when she less than brilliantly said, "Oh?"

His face was not the easiest to read. The corner of his mouth quirked, and his expression could only be explained as completely impassive. This afternoon he was more striking than ever in fawn breeches and a dark brown coat, his sleek hair neatly tied back. He hadn't sat, but stood by a small table that held a miniature of her great-great-grandmother, ruff and all, painted two hundred years ago.

It was rather incongruous—tall, exotic, powerful male beside petite, pinch-faced woman in a small gilt frame superimposed on the overly decorous room. The contrast was striking both culturally and in a symbolic sense. Cecily merely looked at him, as it was his turn to speak.

"As a ruse, it is a very thin method of deception. I've already pointed that out, I believe."

She blew out a short breath. "No one can prove we don't mean to marry."

"But neither can we prove our intentions are so serious."

"I suppose not. . . . No one can until we actually don't

go through with the ceremony." Still pleased about Lord Drury's departure with Eleanor, she refused to let anything ruin her elation. "A long engagement is not unusual. We needn't make this complicated."

"It's already complicated."

He had a point. She smiled; pleased with the way he looked at her, as if the trappings of the dress, the fine furnishings, her carefully ordered hair, didn't matter because he was looking into her eyes. "How so?"

He moved across the room toward her. The door was open, of course, since she would never be allowed alone with a gentleman in private—in particular with Jonathan Bourne. There was probably a servant hovering in the corridor.

"Because of you," he said, not doing anything but just giving her a fascinating masculine grin. "Because of me. Because I kissed you. Because you kissed me back. If you think this is going to be simple, you're wrong. First we have to consider the matter of your father's approval of me."

Cecily tried to ignore her fluttering pulse and the physical reaction due to his proximity. "You have an English father and a very significant title. But you also have an American mother who was unconventional by the standards of all the classing of rank I've ever heard of, and so therefore, my lord, I agree, this will not be an effortless deception."

She sounded fairly composed at least.

"My sister Lillian will never be fooled, and I do not want to earn her mistrust."

That was enlightening information. Not hearing that Lady Lillian would know what they were about, but that he cared about his sister's feelings. Cecily had been dealing with masculine privilege her entire life. For instance, she knew her father loved her, but he would also have no qualms about forcing her into a marriage if he felt it was best for her, her protestations aside. In contrast, Roderick, of course, could do as he pleased.

It wasn't fair, but it was life.

Standing there, she experienced a small, singular moment in which she wondered what it would be like if she truly did marry Jonathan Bourne. They didn't know each other well enough for her to be sure, but she thought he seemed like the type of man who would give his wife a great deal of freedom. Would he be possessive, she wondered as they gazed at each other in an ever-lengthening silence. Maybe—not because he considered her a possession but because he wouldn't want to share her attention. Life would never be tame; the edge of wildness about him was exciting, fascinating, and it might even last a lifetime. . . .

Quickly, Cecily shook off that impractical fantasy. She cleared her throat. "I think it is admirable you don't wish to lie to her, my lord."

"I don't lie to anyone as a rule, and am pointing out that is somewhat of a problem if we wish to do this. The entire premise is based on a falsehood."

The sight of Eleanor leaving on Lord Drury's arm was fresh in her mind. Impulsively, Cecily took a step forward. Close enough that if she wished to reach out and touch him, she could.

An interesting concept. Especially since she found she absolutely did wish to touch him. "Please."

His lashes drifted down a fraction, and she realized his attention had shifted to her mouth. He said nothing, but his lingering smile was intriguing and seductive.

She tilted her face up, aware that she stood only a scant, scandalous distance away, her senses on the alert because he was so close. The tantalizing hint of his cologne, the warmth from his tall body, the flare of something primal in his dark eyes, the small sound of his exhaled breath . . .

He let out a muttered expletive as he caught her waist and pulled her into his arms. "This," he said succinctly, "is what is going to be the problem, damn you."

Chapter 13

It was one matter to be very attracted to a beautiful young woman and agree to help her, especially if she dangled in front of him the hope of freedom in the guise of aid for his sisters—not that he even needed that incentive, though. She was dangerous enough as it stood. It was another matter to realize that by its very nature, the attraction could be a trap.

A delicious one, certainly, Jonathan acknowledged with Cecily nestled against him, his mouth seeking the delicious softness of her lips, but a trap nonetheless. He intended their marriage be based on the practical aspects of the arrangement.

However, he was feeling most impractical at the moment.

Beware.

But his brain ignored the warning from a cautious inner voice and instead insisted on focusing on the soft pressure of her breasts against his chest and the evocative scent of her hair. Right there in the ducal drawing room he kissed her, in sight of whoever might come to the doorway, and God knew if the duke had been informed that the half-breed Lord Augustine was calling on his daughter, some attention would be paid to how they were chaperoned.

Jonathan needed to explain his stipulation to agreeing to an engagement.

Right after he finished this intriguing kiss. One slim arm came up to circle his neck, and she sighed into his mouth and parted her lips for the brush of his tongue, participating with the same shy and yet eager enthusiasm that had so entranced him the last time he'd held her in his arms.

In bed she would no doubt have the identical bewitching effect, but magnified, if he could lie with her naked and willing beneath him, her breath warm against his cheek as he moved inside her bewitching body. . . .

It was a very enticing fantasy that just might become a reality if he could only convince her to agree.

He pulled her in closer, and his hand flattened at the small of her back and then drifted downward over the perfect curve of her bottom through the fabric of her dress. She didn't object; instead her fingers slid into his hair, loosening it. He stifled a groan and arousal flared through him, primal and fierce. The kiss turned molten as he slanted his mouth over hers and wickedly used his tongue to tease and then withdraw.

Like the first time, she was an apt pupil, learning the erotic dance quickly, her fingertips tracing his cheek. The catch of her quickened breathing was arousing, and he hardly needed that, for he was already stifling the urge to pick her up and carry her to the closest level surface where they could finish this in the most pleasurable way possible. . . .

"That is quite enough."

The frosty voice broke into his haze of arousal, and he realized belatedly that someone had come into the room, cynical amusement at war with lust. As a trained soldier, he was usually more alert than this, but at the moment he was admittedly distracted. With some reluctance, he broke the kiss, let Cecily go, and turned.

The woman glaring at him could only be the formidable Dowager Duchess of Eddington, for if one looked past the imperious expression of glowering disapproval and the inevitable lines of age, the resemblance to Cecily was actually quite remarkable. Though he very rarely indulged in formalities, perhaps now was the time to conform to politesse. He bowed. "Your Grace."

"You must be Augustine." The hauteur in her voice held a scathing edge. "I've heard you described a time or two. It appears that for once the gossip is accurate." Small and regal, with iron gray hair, her gown an uncompromising fashion that even Jonathan's untrained eye recognized as severely outdated, the duchess openly inspected his appearance from the polish on his Hessians to his face. The ribbon that had held his hair lay on the floor now, and he was aware that he no doubt looked every inch his American heritage with his loose hair brushing his shoulders. "I am he."

He was also aware of Cecily moving to sink down on a nearby settee. A swift sidelong glance showed that her cheeks were a brilliant scarlet.

"I do not see how, considering your coloring, but you do resemble your father." The duchess walked past him and chose a chair by the grandiose fireplace, whose intricately carved Italian marble mantel was unlike any he'd ever seen before. "You have the look of him. Maybe it is the nose. Whatever you may be, *that* is an English nose."

The implied insult that he wasn't an aristocrat in her eyes didn't bother him. He'd certainly endured worse. "You knew my father, then?"

"Of course."

"He was an admirable man." He could say this with studied assurance and moved across to lean against the mantel, giving him a better view of both Cecily and her grandmother. "I would prefer he still held the title. Not because of any selfish motivation except that I miss him."

The dowager duchess blinked and then narrowed her eyes. "Well said."

"Well meant," he countered, because honestly it was. "He was my father and I loved him."

"I see you are not of a retiring nature, Lord Augustine." Eugenia Francis leaned back in her chair and her gaze was challenging.

"No." He couldn't help but smile.

"I just caught you in a compromising embrace with my granddaughter."

Cecily made an inarticulate sound of what he could only interpret as mortification.

"Your arrival, Your Grace, was most ill-timed, I admit."

"Are your intentions honorable?"

"Would I admit it if they were not?" He was more than a little curious to hear how she would respond.

"Yes." Her eyes were assessing. "I think you would."

A grudging compliment if ever there was one. "I don't know if I adhere to your standards, ma'am, but I am truthful," he admitted.

"You wish to court my granddaughter."

This wasn't precisely how he wanted to approach it, so he equivocated. A more private conversation was his preference. "We've discussed it."

"Hardly an answer."

She was right. So he nodded. "I want her as my wife."

The dowager duchess switched her gaze to Cecily's face. "What about you?"

It seemed that his potential fiancée also did not like to tell lies despite that the feigned engagement was her idea in the first place. She bit her lip, but then raised her chin and said quietly, "I will marry him if his lordship offers."

"Harrumph."

Well, Cecily had just said it, and as they hadn't gotten quite that far in their discussion yet, Jonathan didn't think he could be blamed for offering nothing but a bland smile. "I offer," he said with lazy insouciance, but he was actually tense, which surprised him. Her agreement was important, damn it all. James was right—he *was* in trouble. "Though I should speak with her father first."

"Absolutely correct, Lord Augustine." The dowager duchess sat very rigid and upright. "My son is in his study. Have the footman right outside the door show you the way. After what I just witnessed, I'm guessing the sooner you speak with him the better."

As a dismissal it was effectively done, but he still hesitated. All along Jonathan had thought the pretense a bad idea, though he understood now why Cecily had instigated it. It made much more sense to him now that he knew she was protecting her sister. That kind of loyalty was admirable and spoke to him about her character.

As if she needed to be even more tempting.

If he truly married her, that was different. He wasn't at all sure how she'd feel about having a husband who eschewed living in England, and they did need to discuss that aspect of their life together. However, he himself was more and more convinced that their paths were meant to be one.

Cecily's beauty had struck him from that first moment when he'd seen her splash half a glass of champagne on her undeniably lovely bosom, but as he grew to know her better, he found her delightful in other ways.

Will she love Adela?

He thought she would. No, somehow he *knew* she would. Cecily had an open mind and a giving spirit.

Still, he wished to have a chance to tell her that he intended the engagement to be real before he actually approached her father.

"Are you certain?" he asked her, after deciding it would be impossible to request even just a moment in private with her. The duchess didn't seem the compromising sort, and what she had seen was not exactly a chaste kiss.

Cecily nodded, her lovely topaz eyes clear and direct, her hands folded very ladylike in her lap. "Yes."

He couldn't really do less for his sisters than follow through with this, especially now. If he was going to change his mind, kissing his future wife in the duke's drawing room had been a bit reckless.

He really couldn't see a way to do anything but see her father, as he'd been ordered to do just that.

With a nod, he left the room.

"Do you want my opinion?"

Even though she was still embarrassed at being interrupted at such a personal moment, Cecily still had to stifle a laugh. "Do I actually have a choice, Grandmama?"

"No."

"As I thought."

"I think Augustine is intemperate and not the least respectable."

That description of Jonathan didn't precisely surprise her. On the other hand, Cecily knew her grandmother well enough to sense that the stated disapproval was not entirely heartfelt. From the moment when Jonathan had disappeared through the doorway to go meet with her father, she'd waited for the scolding she knew was coming for her wayward conduct with the notorious Augustine.

"He is all that and more, I suspect." Cecily adjusted her skirts and smiled blandly, though her heart was still pounding from that scandalous kiss. "Respectability is an abstract concept to him."

"Very handsome," her grandmother said gruffly. "I don't dispute he's attractive. But so was his father. I remember David Bourne."

"Oh?" Cecily asked, not just politely but because she wanted to know more about the adventurous earl who went to America and married a native chieftain's daughter. "What was he like?"

"What was he like?" Her grandmother looked taken aback by the candid question.

Cecily nodded, sitting back. "I'm very curious to know everything I can about Jonathan, and his father would be a good starting point. What can you tell me?"

In a gray silk gown, her hair tightly coiled, her grandmother looked down her nose from across the elegant inlaid table between them—though how she was able to do so was a mystery, as she was considerably shorter. "Tall, blond, effusive, charming . . . not quite the traits I see in his son."

True enough. Jonathan was neither effusive nor blond. "He's quite tall," she pointed out, "and he *can* be charming, though I admit it is a rather different sort of charm than I am used to."

"That," her grandmother said acerbically, "must be true, for otherwise I would not have found you so . . . occupied."

Occupied. That was one way of putting it, she supposed. That passionate kiss was ill-timed, but really, any drawing room kiss was going to be inadvisable. The surroundings were much more suitable for formal afternoon tea and stilted conversations. Cecily still wasn't sure why it had happened. "I'm a bit bemused around him, I admit. I assume that is how it is supposed to be."

"Supposed to be?"

"When one falls in love," she clarified.

It wasn't often she confounded her grandmother twice in one conversation—in fact, in her recollection it had never happened before this moment.

Her grandmother was even silenced momentarily, no small feat. Then she said gruffly, "There is no set of rules."

"I thought there was nothing *but* rules," Cecily responded, her tone polite and quiet.

That caused another telling pause, before her grandmother finally gave a small sniff. "If you are enamored of that young man, I suppose I can understand it, but I am also concerned. His family is unconventional at best."

"Because his father married a woman not considered suitable?"

"Not suitable? That is a kind way of putting it. A foreign woman of mixed descent. What could be less suitable?"

Thinking it was better to be forthcoming than to wait, Cecily simply said, "And of course, though he has never been married, he has a daughter whom he openly acknowledges."

"So I hear."

The audible sniff was not surprising, as she didn't really expect her grandmother to approve.

"His sister isn't even received by some of society. She has a very tarnished reputation."

That was interesting news. There were certain topics that no one discussed with ingénues. True, his oldest sister did not attend any social functions, but Cecily had assumed it was because she was already two and twenty and perhaps had tired of the endless rounds of parties since she was, by virtue of her age, considered to be on the shelf. After all, this was just Eleanor's second season, and there was already a noticeable difference in how she was regarded next to the crop of young ladies making their initial debut.

Cecily knew better than to try to pry the specifics of Lady Lillian's disgrace out of her grandmother. Besides, it didn't really matter. No wonder Jonathan had agreed to the betrothal. It lent them a sense of camaraderie, for it seemed each of them was trying to help a sister who sorely needed it. "Can you repair it?"

"I beg your pardon?" Her grandmother stared at her as if her face had just turned a spectacular shade of blue.

"Lady Lillian's reputation." Weighing her words, as it was important that she be able to fulfill her promise to Jonathan, Cecily said carefully, "I expect I will be marrying Lord Augustine, so it would be best, don't you agree, if his sisters were properly settled."

There. That was an admirable challenge.

And while she wasn't sure of many things in this world, she did know her grandmother fairly well. Her father had come by his autocratic ways quite naturally. The word *failure* did not exist to the Dowager Duchess of Eddington. Had her grandmother known of Eleanor's penchant for Viscount Drury last season, a match between them would have been a much better possibility. Had she been at liberty to tell her, Cecily would have gone that route rather than this drastic one, but Elle wouldn't even confide in *her*, so this was the best she could do.

When she thought about Jonathan's kiss, it wasn't that bad of a choice either. The feel of his hands, sliding erotically downward, the sensation of his tall body pressed against hers . . . and her unladylike response.

She would have to set that aside for future contemplation.

"I am sure you could help her overcome her dilemma," Cecily continued with what she hoped was perfect equanimity. "Couldn't you?"

A toss of a second gauntlet.

"I have no idea."

"We both know you could. With your consequence, you could gain anyone entrance back into society. Whatever gaffe she committed, she is still the daughter of an earl."

"It was hardly a mere 'gaffe.'" Her grandmother sniffed. "And do not practice that winsome smile on me. I am not your susceptible Earl Savage."

"Mine? I am not so sure he's mine quite yet. And I don't think he's all that susceptible either," Cecily declared, pleased that she sensed a victory. "The two of you will no doubt get along famously. His spirit is as independent as yours."

That did stir a laugh—albeit a small one. "Upon first impression, I can't say I'm flattered. As far as his sister goes . . . I think you are asking a bit much of me. My influence would help Lady Lillian, of course, but so far as actually garnering her attention from respectable gentlemen, that I cannot promise."

That admission was a coup in itself.

"But you are willing to try?"

"I disavow giving a direct promise until your engagement to that roguish young man is officially announced."

Yet Cecily saw an interested gleam in her grandmother's eye. Grandmama was a bit of a dragon now and then, but at heart she was a kind woman under the regal exterior, and she did pride herself on her influence with the *ton*.

Cecily rose and went over to kiss her cheek. "Thank you."

A thin hand lifted to touch her face in an uncharacteristic affectionate gesture. Faded blue eyes held a concerned question. "He is truly what you want, child?"

Cecily knew she was being asked in terms of commitment and marriage, but if *want* included the frisson of excitement that she felt every time Jonathan looked at her, then she wasn't telling a falsehood when she replied, "Yes. He is everything I want."

Chapter 14

To his mind, the informal setting of the study was vastly more preferable for an interrogation than the stuffy confines of the vast drawing room, but it would have been better had Jonathan actually known the Duke of Eddington before he had to petition him for his daughter's hand in marriage. They'd seen each other, of course. The *ton* was not such a large circle that they would not run into one another, and besides, Jonathan knew his father had counted the duke as a friend, but a brief introduction at their club hardly helped him to take the measure of the man.

How far that past friendship with his parent extended might be tested in the next few moments, along with the elasticity of the ducal lack of prejudice. Upon the announcement of his presence by the very august butler, Jonathan adjusted his cuffs with seeming nonchalance. "Your Grace."

The man in question glanced up, showed no real surprise—no doubt Jonathan's arrival had been duly reported—and nodded at a chair. "Augustine. Sit down."

The phrase "better than nothing" came to mind and Jonathan selected a captain's chair that might have, from the wear and tear, come from a real ship, and sank into it. It was comfortable, which, coupled with its appearance, said something he liked about his host. It had to have some sort of sentimental value or it would not be there among the polished bookcases and expensive paintings.

Cecily might come by her sensitivity naturally. A good sign.

"Brandy?"

"No, thank you." He wasn't on a social call.

It was new to him, this begging the custodial permission. With Carole and Betsy on the marriage mart, he might as well get used to the process—though in their cases he would not be the petitioner. And Lillian . . . an entirely different story. He was determined she would not be left to languish unwedded for whatever innocent—and he was convinced the more he got to know her that it *was* innocent—mistake she'd made with Sebring.

"Don't thank me yet." The exalted Duke of Eddington sat back and eyed him with assessment. He was not particularly impressive physically; of medium height, with thinning fair hair going gray and patrician features, but his air of power was there in the aura of the confidence of complete privilege. "You are here about my daughter."

True enough. "And I'm not the first," Jonathan said with equanimity, also taking the older man's measure. In his culture, warriors were weighed not on their background but on what they had earned. "I know Drury wants her."

The duke raised his brows over how that was phrased, but his gaze sharpened. "An interesting and somewhat barbaric way of putting it, to be sure. Shall I assume what I've heard about you is true?"

"That depends on what you've heard." Jonathan kept his voice even. "I doubt much of it is in my favor, but might I point out that very few in society truly know me?"

The Duke of Eddington leaned back a fraction more. Jonathan was attuned to the reactions of his enemies, and in this case he recognized that his adversary had relaxed.

A good sign.

"Go on. Make your case."

"I wish to marry Lady Cecily." Jonathan smiled negligently. "I could point out my title, my wealth—which might not be as princely as yours but is certainly substantial—and a family lineage that is traced back to early British kings, but truthfully, I am certain enough you know all that. If you can overlook what some think of as mixed blood, I am in a practical sense a better match than Drury."

That drew a lifted brow. "How do *you* think of it?"

An interesting question.

"My heritage?" It was going to be only one of several stumbling blocks—he'd known it all along. What was amazing was how it mattered not at all to Cecily. Her confidence in his desirability as a son-in-law to such a prominent man and her lack of personal prejudice were endearing. "With all due respect, keep in mind we are all a whole of two different parts, Your Grace. Almost all the monarchy of the world is bred with other cultures. Isn't that how dynastic marriages work? For the sake of alliances, a king marries his daughter to the prince of another country. In that sense, there is no such thing as a pure bloodline."

The duke at least looked amused. "That's a valid argument, true, but I have no need for an alliance with the Iroquois Nation."

"Nor could I give you one," Jonathan said dryly. "In their eyes I am half English. Snobbery is not limited to these shores."

A glimmer of respect shown in the duke's eyes. "Point taken."

"If so, then can we dismiss my father's first marriage and move on to the other issues between us?"

"At least you acknowledge other issues exist."

He did, but it still chafed him to have to excuse his relationship to members of his family who had little or nothing to do with the scandal surrounding them. "My sister and my daughter." Jonathan's voice took on a certain hard edge that he could not suppress. "Lillian might have made a mistake, but let's give Lord Sebring full measure of responsibility also, and as I understand it, he is received everywhere. As for Adela, she had absolutely nothing to do with the circumstances of her birth and I refuse to apologize for her existence in any way. She brings light and joy to my life."

That impassioned declaration made the duke raise his brows. "I see. Yet I understand you refused to wed the child's mother."

"That is between her and myself."

If he had just made a grave error, so be it, Jonathan decided as he sat there, because while his growing passion for the lovely Cecily was alarmingly intense, he could never betray his daughter—or even the prickly Lily—by acting as if either of them embarrassed him.

And they didn't. Life was imperfect, but as his aunt had told him often during his youth, if the spirits didn't challenge men and women, it would be a dull existence.

"Fair enough. I respect that, but it hardly makes you a better prospective son-in-law. If you were in my position, what would you do, Lord Augustine?" His Grace reached over, picked up the decanter, and poured himself a measure of gold liquid into a fat-bottomed glass.

"As you pointed out, you are not the only man with an interest in my daughter."

Jonathan regarded the duke evenly. "At the risk of sounding arrogant, I will say Cecily *wishes* to marry me. So since you pose the question, my answer is I would take my daughter's preference into account. After all, it is her life. She is as intelligent as she is beautiful. Let her choose."

For a moment they measured each other, equally assessing. Then the duke said, "You are quite certain, Lord Augustine?"

He thought about Cecily's unorthodox proposal, the carriage's broken wheel, and then that intoxicating first kiss. He couldn't wait to introduce her to the other pursuits men and women could enjoy together. Not that he was at all certain she would wish to actually marry him, but it was an educated guess convincing her would be his pleasure. "She has already told me she would accept my proposal."

"You discussed it with her first?" The duke's brows elevated fractionally at Jonathan's assured tone.

"The subject has arisen between us, yes." He wasn't about to explain that the engagement was her idea because that would prompt her father to ask questions and he'd already given his word he would not reveal Lady Eleanor's affection for the viscount.

The real question now, of course, was how interested the duke was in his daughter's happiness.

And sitting there in her father's study, he wondered if their children would be dark or have her delicate fair coloring. The vision of her heavy with his babe invaded his mind and took his soul prisoner.

"You and Cecily are very different." The Duke of Eddington sipped his brandy before continuing. "You were raised in different worlds, in a literal sense. And word has it you have no intention of staying in England. I hope you both have thought this through in a clear-minded way. I would miss my daughter and have never heard that she has a desire to immigrate to America."

It was gratifying to find that he was at least taken at his word about Cecily's feelings. Jonathan hesitated, and then said quietly, "I promise that we will thoroughly discuss the arrangements of our marriage before the ceremony takes place." It was a pledge not just to her father but, though she didn't realize it, to her as well.

He didn't make promises lightly. When he did make them, they were kept.

"I hope you are sincere, for with Cecily, you had better reconcile that you must follow through."

There was no stifling his involuntary laugh. "Yes, I've met her. She can be a very determined young woman."

"Neither of my daughters is particularly compromising. They take after their mother."

This time Jonathan smiled in spite of himself, for the duke's voice held a certain dry edge. "I believe you, Your Grace. I have three younger sisters and a daughter I am responsible for. It gives one perspective."

"I suppose it would." Cecily's father smiled for the first time. "If you'd like advice on how to handle them, look elsewhere. So far I am personally stymied." He paused, and his fingers toyed with his glass. "So that you know, I liked your father."

"So did I."

"We have that in common then." The duke eyed him from across the desk, his graying hair neat in the shining late-afternoon illumination, his eyes speculative. "I also like Drury. I know him far better than I know you, and this is my child we are discussing."

"I will care for her; do not worry."

The Duke of Eddington looked at him steadily. "Rest

assured, should this marriage take place, that is precisely what I expect from you."

The summons had come as she had expected, right after Jonathan's departure. Somehow, this afternoon, her father seemed a little less intimidating. Maybe it was that he rarely appeared without his coat, but it now was folded neatly over the back of his chair. The air was redolent with the masculine aroma of brandy and tobacco.

"This is what you wish, then?" he said without preamble when she chose a seat and he sat back down.

There was that question again. Cecily nodded, wondering if all potential brides—not that she actually was one—were so interrogated.

Maybe only if they were marrying the roguish Earl Savage. Or pretending to marry him, anyway. She nodded. "It is precisely what I wish."

Her father looked at her gravely and then sighed. "I don't suppose pointing out that Lord Drury is a more conventional choice would do any good, would it? I've seen that stubborn tilt to your chin before."

He could point it out to Eleanor, who might or might not care about his conventionality but was in love with him regardless. Cecily smiled. "Jonathan is actually quite civilized."

Or is he? From that audacious kiss they had just shared in the drawing room she had the distinct impression that he could be very uncivilized indeed.

"Your children—"

"Would be beautiful," she interrupted, because truly, any child of Jonathan's would no doubt be as perfect physically as he was. She caught herself and corrected her statement. "*Will* be beautiful."

"What of the one he already has? Can you live with that? From my conversation with him, I think you will be expected to not just tolerate her presence in the household but to accept her."

As they weren't actually marrying, the question was just philosophical for her. "I love children, and truly, how can her birth possibly be held against her?"

"Echoes of Augustine's own words."

"I'm not surprised. Despite our different upbringings in many ways, we do seem to think in a similar fashion. That is why it will be a good match."

And we both love our sisters.

"You sound so sure of my agreement." Her father reclined behind his desk, every inch the regal duke. "I have not yet given my approval. And let us recall that after my meeting with him, Lord Drury has certain expectations."

"But you haven't given *him* your approval either," she said quickly. "Quite frankly, with or without Jonathan's suit, I would not consider the viscount."

"Yes, I get that impression." He rubbed his forehead, his expression resigned. "Augustine won't be the easiest choice. What of his desire to return to America?"

She'd thought of how she would answer that question. "His family is here, and quite naturally, his business affairs will require he spend time in England. And you are right about not being the easiest choice. He already has the ability to annoy me, but then again, Grandmama tells me the men you care about always do. I am convinced he can be redeemed, given the right direction."

He laughed. He didn't often. . . . She'd never thought about it, but his life must be very serious, for in front of his children at least, laughter was rare.

How odd. What else did she not know about him? A disconcerting thought. It prompted her to ask impulsively, "How did you meet Maman?"

Her father looked surprised at the very personal

question. It was not something she'd ever inquired about before, and truly, considering that she was now discussing her own possible engagement, maybe it was time she did. Why was it she'd never known about her parents' romance? Was there even a romance to discuss? Maybe there had never been one. Cecily wondered. Maybe it had been arranged; much like how he had wanted her to simply accept Lord Drury's offer and be done with it.

"We were introduced when we were very young."

She looked at him, so familiar in the setting of masculine paintings of horses and hounds, his brandy glass on his desk, and correspondence piled on the blotter. "Introduced how and when?"

"Our parents were friends. The betrothal was signed before I was ten." The snifter sat on his desk and he took a sip. "I was a ducal heir. It isn't unusual to settle such matters early."

Cecily murmured, "That hardly seems fair."

"I found her attractive enough."

"Shouldn't there be more to it?"

"Are we back to the subject of emotional attachment again?"

"It appears we are, though I am glad you were pleased or I wouldn't exist."

He looked disconcerted at such a frank statement. "I don't know if you are being deliberately provoking just to irritate me, but I'm willing to overlook it so we can continue. This discussion is about *your* engagement. If you wish to marry the Earl of Augustine, I will consider it."

She recognized that austere tone. Her father rarely argued. He considered it beneath him. If she wanted to know more about the circumstances of her parents' marriage—and to her surprise she did—she would have to look elsewhere. The importance of the moment was that whatever Jonathan had said to him was obviously convincing and for that she was grateful.

"Yes, I want to marry him."

One brow raised, her father gazed at her across his desk. "Very well. You seem quite determined. I'll inform Viscount Drury that other arrangements have been made and talk to Augustine again tomorrow."

"You have another daughter," she suggested, arranging her skirts with a careless motion of her hand. "It isn't like the viscount and Elle haven't met. Perhaps they would be a more suitable match anyway—and I don't think she'd be adverse to the suggestion."

Did that sound casual enough?

"A more suitable match? How so?" Whatever he was, her father was no fool. She'd gotten his attention. His gaze was speculative.

"They are just so much more . . . compatible."

"Are they now? Is there something I should know?"

Cecily rose, smiling. This was turning out perfectly, from the inquiring look on her father's usually impassive face to his acquiescence over her engagement. "It was just an observation."

"Was it now?" he asked dryly. "Why is it I sense I have just been manipulated?"

Chapter 15

"Watch me!"

Next to her, Lillian saw Carole hide a smile. Betsy didn't even bother to try, her grin open as they all observed their precocious niece attempting a clumsy tumble across the small inner square of grass in the garden and leap up in triumph.

Perhaps in the midst of disgrace, in the middle of the blow of her parents' untimely deaths, in the chaos of being forced into self-imposed seclusion, Lillian had forgotten about the joys life had to offer, among them a child's exuberance over such a simple pleasure as a sunny afternoon and a patch of grass. Had four years really passed her by?

"Lovely." Lily applauded, her neglected parasol leaning against the marble bench where they sat. Since her complexion hardly mattered, what did she care? "Addie, do it again."

"Don't encourage her." Carole gently elbowed her in the ribs. "Her gown is already getting quite dusty."

The late-afternoon sun slanted across the flowers, the soothing low drone of a bee intent on a nearby bush soporific. Betsy brushed back a chestnut curl and laughed. "I have to admit Addie is delightful. I was startled when she first called me Auntie Bets, for I felt like a veritable fossil, but frankly, her sunny disposition is quite captivating."

And Jonathan clearly adored his little daughter. No one could deny that. The unconditional acceptance of a child born on the wrong side of the blanket was unusual, but then again, their brother was not a typical aristocrat either. His eclectic habit of late-night rides aside, he read to Adela in the evenings, closely supervised her care, and whenever possible, took her with him. Childish laughter was no longer a surprise in the household, but an expected sound.

It was odd, but since his arrival, which she had so dreaded, Lily was finding life . . . interesting for the first time since her debacle with Arthur four years ago, and she had her unpredictable brother to thank for it.

While Addie executed another less than perfect somersault, Lily murmured to her sisters, "So tell me, how is it all progressing?"

Why was it she felt so old when she really wasn't more than a few years their senior? Maybe it was the unwelcome reality of making a grievous error and having to live with the consequences.

Carole and Betsy glanced at each other and smiled.

"What?" she demanded. "Good heavens, you can't keep it from me if there is something to tell."

Betsy waved a hand. "There are a few promising prospects out there."

"As in?"

"The Lane brothers perhaps."

For a moment Lily had no idea who that might be, as she was so out of touch, but then she understood. "The twin sons of Lord Stonevale?"

It was Carole who nodded, looking demure in her ruffled day gown. "For a moment we thought we were interested in the same man, but then it turned out there were two of them. Imagine."

"Two sisters and two brothers . . . that is interesting."

"Come join us at the next gathering and we will all compare our thoughts on the subject." Betsy's eyes grew suspiciously bright and she reached over to clasp her hand. "We have quite missed you, you know."

Add guilt to her list of myriad emotions. . . .

Luckily Addie dashed up, her dark hair in disarray, and extended one decidedly grubby hand. Unfortunately the new addition to the household, a puppy of questionable lineage that seemed to consist of a great deal of fuzzy hair, clumsily followed along and decided to sit on the hem of Lily's new gown.

"What am I looking at?" Lily inquired, lifting the wiggling little dog up and gently setting it aside. "Let me see."

"Magic." Addie's little face was adorably sincere, her eyes fastened on her palm as she unfurled her fingers.

It was a rock, small and gold, polished in some way by the elements so that the surface was smooth and rich. Lily picked it up and examined it by turning it over in her fingers. "It's lovely, Addie."

"It was on the floor. It fell out of Papa's pocket."

There was enough of an anxious look in the child's eyes that Lily said reassuringly, "I am sure he won't mind you are keeping it for him."

"I had to. I told you. It's magic."

"How so?"

"He said so." Adela's dark eyes were wide. "What if I lose it?"

Lily looked at the gleaming stone in her palm. "Shall I return it to him?"

A vigorous nod was the response, and the child took off scampering down the path, her nursemaid hovering, the small puppy running along in pursuit.

"It's a rock," Betsy said, her expression skeptical.

"Rather pretty, though," Carole added, but she also looked unimpressed. "But why would he carry it about with him?"

"I've no idea." Lily closed her fingers around it. Jonathan was not the easiest person to understand, but she could at least say with some certainty that they were getting to know one another. She smiled. "Maybe because it's magic?"

"Congratulations."

The throaty tone alone would give him pause, not to mention the provocative sway of the body in his arms. Jonathan snapped back to attention because he was truthfully watching for Cecily's entrance anyway. "For what?"

"Your engagement."

He didn't even know if he had the Duke of Eddington's approval yet. How the devil could Lucille Blackwood get the news before *he* did? "Pardon?" he asked cautiously, sweeping her into the next turn of the waltz.

"You called on Eddington's young daughter and spoke to her father this afternoon."

His eyes narrowed a fraction. "How do you know that?"

"Oh, darling." She laughed. "You truly are quite . . . colonial. News travels quickly in London. Didn't you know? Everyone is agog over it."

He wasn't her darling, but that was hardly the issue. Even as she suggestively trailed a finger across his jaw, he wondered how the devil he could find James. While he was still a novice in English society, his cousin knew everything.

Well, *just* about everything.

"No, I didn't know, but I'm learning."

"I hope so."

He wasn't going to rise to that baited inference.

"Agog why?"

"Not quite the match anyone expected."

"And here I thought the *ton* was whispering about us constantly."

"No wonder. You're delightfully . . . smooth, my lord," Mrs. Blackwood murmured, her skirts swirling across his legs, her fingertip now drifting across his lower lip.

"I shave," he replied, knowing that wasn't what she meant, maybe more terse than he should have been, but then again, he hadn't expected this rumor to surface before he'd had a chance to discuss it with his family. It had been only hours since he'd met with the duke.

Actually, considering that it was nearly midnight, eight good hours, maybe more, and she was right—this was the *ton*.

"The impending loss of bachelorhood surely is a landmark in a man's life."

At the sultry tone of his dance partner's voice, he understood. A voluptuous brunette with blue-green eyes and a seductive smile *and* a contemporary of the persistent Lady Irving, she'd been even more flirtatious than usual this evening.

He was getting tired of this game.

Ah, that damned bet. One thousand pounds riding on being the first to lure him into a tryst. He'd all but forgotten about it. "If my impending engagement were true, I would hope so," he said dryly. "Marriage is hardly to be taken lightly, don't you agree?"

"It's a bit boring, actually," she told him with a slight shrug. "My husband and I barely see each other. Our *interests* are so different."

The implication that she was free this evening didn't escape him. Apparently all those jaded aristocratic ladies worried his possible betrothal might thwart their purposes. Or maybe it added more spice to the challenge, he thought in the next moment as she leaned in closer and her lavish breasts pressed against his chest.

"Perhaps the two of you should strive to make more time for each other." He eased her backward enough for some sense of propriety.

"All he likes are his horses, his club, and his mistress."

"In that order?"

She laughed. "If I were pressed to guess, I would say so. He likes racing, his likes his drink, and maybe after those two pastimes grow tiresome, he visits his paramour."

"It does not trouble you?" He was genuinely curious.

"No."

Jonathan raised his brows at her frankness, still swirling her among the dancers. "I find it hard to believe that you couldn't distract him with a little effort."

"Why would I want to, Lord Augustine?" Her reply was breathy and deliberately soft.

"Because you are married? As you mentioned, I am a quaint colonial in some ways, but loyalty and vows are significant in my world."

The music ended a moment later and he gratefully extracted himself from her clinging hands and set off to find his cousin. James actually found him first, on his way to the drinks table, and because they knew each other well, he handed over a glass of champagne—he had two—and said, "I'd venture a guess you could use a little sustenance now that you found an avenue of escape."

"I've always thought you much more intelligent than you appear to be." Jonathan was able to grin, which after that excruciating waltz, was saying something. "How pained did I look?"

"Very," James acknowledged. "I'd suggest the smoking room, but you always prefer outside."

"Always."

"I was afraid you'd say that. It's raining." James sounded resigned, glancing at the nearby moisture-streaked window.

The warm day had produced a drizzly evening and the air was damp and heavy. Jonathan chuckled involuntarily. "Think of the practicalities. We'll be able to converse freely, for we will be alone."

"That's because no one with any sense wishes to stand outside in full evening kit in the damp," James grumbled.

That was probably true. The rain against the tall windows was not hard, but it was steady.

"What the devil happened to your face?" Distracted for a moment from the conversation, Jonathan saw a large dark bruise just below his cousin's left temple with a glimmer of concern.

James reached up and touched it with a small wince. "Damned footpad accosted me the other night as I walked out of our club. I'm not sure what he hit me with, but I went sprawling into the street and if it wasn't for the steward at the door who shouted and ran to my aid, I'm sure I would have been robbed. I never saw it coming. I had a nasty headache the next day, let me assure you."

"It looks like it."

Jonathan might have said more, but at that moment a young baronet he'd met several times walked past and clapped him on the shoulder, an affable smile on his face. "Felicitations, Augustine, on your engagement."

As the man walked away, Jonathan muttered, "How the devil does everyone *know*? *I* don't even know, damn it."

"Can I ask what exactly we're discussing?" There was

a degree of caution in his cousin's tone. "Did your meeting with the duke not go well after all?"

"I think it went very well indeed, but I can't be sure. For what he is, he seems decent enough."

"For what he is?" James was openly amused. "I suppose that is a not so oblique reference to his position in the hierarchy of the British aristocracy. May I point out, Jon, that our family—"

"No, you may not," Jonathan interrupted curtly. "And that really is not what I meant anyway. Yes, he's an exalted duke, but I am glad that first of all he is a father, and he *should* take his daughter's future into consideration with due weight—I know I'll do so for mine, so I cannot blame him for not giving me a direct answer. I'd think less of him if he blithely agreed to my proposal and didn't discuss it with her." Jonathan took a solid swallow of tepid champagne.

"Maybe you need to define that actual problem, then. As far as I can tell, she wishes to marry you and you wish to marry her."

This wasn't the moment to mention that Cecily had no real desire to actually marry him. "I haven't told Carole or Betsy, much less Lillian, yet. I thought I would wait until arrangements were made. I can't believe that this would spread so quickly. Luckily Lily declined to attend because she says she needs some new gowns."

That translated to acknowledging the need to actually discuss the particulars with his intended bride as soon as possible. If, that is, her father even decided Earl Savage would make a suitable husband.

"As for the circulation of the rumor of the engagement, believe it." James's voice held considerable cynicism. "The duke does not clear his throat and his entire household not know it. Let's admit also that you are quite the noticeable visitor. Every servant from the footman who opened the door for you, to the butler, to the—"

Jonathan interrupted again, which he wouldn't normally do, but he caught a glimpse of hair of a certain pale shade that seemed permanently etched in his brain, and even from across the crowded ballroom and with her back turned, he recognized the smoothness of her slender shoulders and the elegant length of her neck. "How long has she been here?"

"She?" James failed completely in his attempt to look puzzled as he also gazed in the open terrace doors.

"Cecily, for God's sake."

"If you are asking if she saw you waltzing with the overtly friendly Mrs. Blackwood, I am going to say yes, she did." His tall cousin grinned. "Your disordered life is making mine a lot more amusing, I admit."

"Glad I can be a source of entertainment," Jonathan muttered and strode off through the crowd.

She didn't see him coming, but sensed it from the sudden glances of the people standing around her. It was a small ripple in the crowd, as if they parted naturally, and really, from the interest in her arrival, Cecily had gathered that the denizens of London's elite circles already knew Lord Augustine had offered for her hand in marriage.

Even though he was walking up behind her and wasn't in direct view, the looks on the faces of the women alone would have announced his arrival.

Jealousy was a new emotion and not a particularly welcome one. When she'd entered the ballroom in the wake of her grandmother and seen Jonathan on the dance floor with a very beautiful woman pressed suggestively against him, she had experienced a definite pang.

Mrs. Blackwood had actually reached up and touched his face, and even from a considerable distance there had been no mistaking the flirtatious gesture. Cecily's reaction had been a white-hot flash of resentment.

It would not do to become possessive of a man who had made it clear he had no intention of staying in England.

But when she heard his voice, the foreign inflection something she found familiar now, Cecily experienced another pang, this one of something deeper, something tumultuous and, she feared, extremely naive.

She wanted to see him. No, she *desperately* wanted to see him. The second emotion was quite different from the first.

"I've been waiting."

She turned, the small group of people around her having fallen silent anyway, and summoned a smile. Jonathan bowed, his evening attire impeccable, his hair once again held back, this time, she noted as he took her hand and bent over it, with a strip of what looked like tanned leather laced through with shining black beads. Treacherously, that brought back memories of their shared kiss that afternoon and how she'd picked up that stray piece of ebony satin from the floor after he'd left, taking it upstairs to put it in her jewelry case as if it was something precious. When he straightened, without doing much than giving a cursory nod at her small group of friends, he murmured, "Dance with me."

"Excuse us," she barely managed to say before he tugged her away by the hand toward the marble dance floor, the clasp of his fingers firm. She said breathlessly as she caught up her skirts to keep up with his long strides, "Are we in some sort of hurry?"

He set his hand at her waist when they stopped, his smile so beautiful that it had a most peculiar effect on her stomach. "I wish I could say I was a patient man, but I'm not. We are the center of the attention of anyone who can see us in this throng, and before our engagement becomes even more public I would very much like to talk to you about our . . . arrangement. I think a waltz is about as much privacy as we are going to manage this evening. Do you mind?"

"N-no . . . of course not."

He didn't seem to notice the slight stammer. "We definitely need to make sure we want the same result from this engagement."

A twinge of panic assailed her. Was he going to back out *now*? Cecily tilted her face up, doing her best not to let anything but cool composure show. "How so, my lord? Have you decided you prefer Mrs. Blackwood instead?"

"What?" He genuinely looked blank for a moment and then his dark eyes narrowed. "Oh . . . hell, Cecily, trust me, no."

Maybe it was his signature lack of careful, polite speech, but she believed him, especially as he tugged her closer and took her hand.

The music started then, and at least she was a little more relaxed as they began to dance, for he sounded sincere, though under his skin there was a hint of a deeper color. Jonathan informed her, "That's not even worth discussing. I want to talk about the end of our bargain."

He waltzed quite well for someone who presumably was more at home in the forest than on a dance floor, which further dispelled some of the myths about him but didn't really surprise her, for he had the muscled body of a true athlete. "Already? It hasn't even officially begun yet."

"Did your father speak with you?" He swung her into a turn with lithe grace.

"Yes."

"And?"

The intensity in his dark eyes made her forget her pique over the forward Mrs. Blackwood, and truthfully, his dismissal of the woman had sounded genuine. She smiled. "Expect a ducal summons tomorrow. He is amenable to your proposal."

"I'll respond, but only if the situation is settled between us."

What the devil did that mean? Her brow knitted. "I thought it *was* settled."

The sinewy hand holding hers tightened. "Not quite. If you remember the first time I kissed you—and I certainly hope you do—I said I agreed to an engagement on two conditions, but I only gave you one of them. I never told you the second condition on which I accept our bargain."

He hadn't, true. And as if she could forget that first tender, and most enlightening, kiss. Or the second. And the third one, that afternoon, had been quite different and infinitely intriguing. "What is it?"

"I want you to marry me."

At first she wasn't sure she quite understood. The music and the crowd were both loud, and he'd said the words quietly. Cecily stared up at him. "What?"

"Marry me."

Was he really proposing or was this part of the play-acting they'd agreed upon? Uncertain, a little shaken, she was lucky his hold was secure and his footing sure as they moved among the throng of other dancers, for otherwise she would have stumbled.

At her silence, Jonathan clarified in a calm, decisive voice: "Become my wife in truth so we are not perpetrating a farce of an engagement on both our families, so neither of us is perjuring ourself to society—not that I care about that aspect of it for myself, but your reputation *does* matter to me—and for the sake of my sisters, I do not want to cause further whispers. Let's be practical—if we break our engagement one of us will have to take the blame. I would shoulder it without qualms if it wasn't for the other people it would injure. If we do this, I want it to be real."

Marry him?

Truly?

Trying to define the rush of her response to that question as she registered his sincerity was difficult. Myriad emotions swept through her. Exhilaration, doubt, joy, fear, excitement, more joy, which surprised her, because . . .

No, it didn't surprise her, she had to acknowledge, because his potent male beauty was addictive, heady, and she also liked his complete lack of affectation, his clear intelligence . . . everything. She even liked his deplorable habit of swearing in front of her.

Jonathan leaned closer to whisper, "Besides what I just said, I have another compelling, less honorable reason, my lovely English lady. I do not trust myself much longer to not seduce you."

Her heart had started to pound. He had that unfortunate effect on her. Because she was so off balance, she said tartly, "What if I said I fully trust my ability to resist your charms, Augustine?"

"Then you'd be lying."

"You are so sure?" She trembled just a fraction and no doubt, as close as he held her—scandalously close—he could feel it.

His smile was slow and arrogant and wicked. *Extremely* wicked. "Positive."

Recklessly—but then, he made her reckless; he had from the moment they'd met—she whispered back, "I think you'd have to prove that to me, my lord."

Chapter 16

They were very beautiful together as they danced, her sister and her fiancé, he so dark and male, she so blond and feminine. Though, Eleanor noted, Lord Augustine was as usual flaunting propriety by holding Cecily entirely too close, and yet again had whispered something in her ear in front of everyone. The engagement was the talk of the evening, but at least in this case his forward behavior would be excused, for he was willing to pay the ultimate price a bachelor could offer.

Marriage.

"What do you think?" Roderick's voice was diffident, as if the question was abstract, though Eleanor knew her brother usually was fairly straightforward. He'd sought her out and actually taken a chair next to her, where she'd been doing her best to hide in a corner of the room.

"About Cecily and her unusual choice in a husband?" She pretended to need her fan, though the evening had turned cool and damp. "I am not surprised. From the moment they met there has been a flirtation with scandal, so maybe this is best. I'm glad he is willing to come up to scratch, because goodness knows he has already—"

She stopped just short of saying bluntly that she wasn't at all sure Jonathan Bourne couldn't steal more than just a kiss or two from their sister. Though Cecily was normally levelheaded, she hadn't shown a lot of good judgment when it came to the earl.

"Goodness knows he has already what?" Roderick asked, stylish in his evening wear, his face drawn into a glower. "All along I wondered if I should have had a word or two with his lordship over—"

"They're engaged," she interrupted. "Perhaps not formally yet, but they will be."

"It sounds to me like they *need* to be," he muttered. "Has the bastard touched her?"

"Actually, I believe he is quite legally the earl or he wouldn't have gained an audience with Father this afternoon."

"Devil take it, Elle, I wasn't being literal. You know what I meant."

Luckily she was able to avoid commenting because of the imminent approach of a small group of young ladies, who were seemingly just chatting and laughing, but had a singular intent, and that was to catch the attention of the heir of the Duke of Eddington. She knew better than to suppose that this secluded corner held any other allure, and so did Roderick. Alarm replaced suspicion, and as far as Eleanor could tell Cecily's coming marriage was dismissed for the greater need of self-preservation, and her older brother scrambled to his feet with a muttered excuse and fled in the direction of the smoking room.

Had she been in the mood for it, she would have found it humorous, but truly, she now wished she'd just begged off attending this evening, because even as Roderick beat a hasty retreat, Lord Drury approached in the wake of the bevy of disappointed debutantes.

No. Sitting there, trying to hide in her corner, she thought emphatically, *no*. She'd already humiliated herself in front of the man earlier that afternoon. She did not want to discuss that, or her sister's reputed engagement to someone else when he was undoubtedly disappointed, and maybe a little embarrassed in his own right at not quite being jilted but at least being passed over when all of London knew of his interest.

But she'd run away already once today, and doing it again . . . well, that was quite unforgivable. Besides, there was really nowhere to go.

So she stayed, her bottom planted firmly in the chair, and wished herself just about anywhere else.

"Is it true?" he asked without preamble, coming to stand next to her chair, his moody gaze on the dance floor. "With your forthright nature, I knew you would tell me."

Well, she *had* left him adrift in the gardens, so she could hardly fault his manners in failing to offer a proper greeting. This evening he wore a fawn coat and white breeches, the pale colors suiting his fair coloring. The slight froth of lace at his sleeves was indicative of his usual elegance without being overdone, and his cravat was intricately tied. His hair was usually immaculate, but now it was slightly ruffled, as if he might have run his hand through it, no doubt in agitation over the whispers about the woman he wanted to marry choosing someone else.

It reminded Eleanor of the first time she'd seen him, last season on her debut. Love at first sight? It had certainly seemed like the way the experience was described. Because he knew Roderick, he was one of the first gentlemen introduced to her, and she'd gone home that evening with stars in her eyes because the viscount had danced with her.

Later, of course, she realized that it was a courtesy to her status as the daughter of a duke and his friend's sister, but Lord Drury had been charming and if he'd found her awkward and nervous, he'd shown no sign of it. Neither did he avoid her later, unlike some of the men who had initially shown interest but because she wasn't a simpering idiot in their presence changed their minds about her possible desirability as a wife. Throughout that increasingly grueling social whirl last year, Elijah Winters had continued to dutifully ask for a waltz now and again, so at least while she might have been one of the biggest failures of the debutantes, she didn't look like a complete wallflower.

So she owed him the truth. "Yes. It's true."

"Ah."

"I'm sorry," she murmured, clasping her hands together.

"Don't be. In a philosophical sense, I suppose this is a better course of events than if she had married me. What if she had later met Augustine and regretted her choice?" His voice held a tinge of irony. "I don't think of myself as a man who has an overabundance of pride, but I do wish for a faithful wife."

"Cecily would never stray." Eleanor stood abruptly, facing him, her objection vehement, her arms stiff at her sides. Whatever her feelings about the situation, she could not tolerate criticism of her sister. Had Cecily deserved the doubts about her character, Eleanor would still defend her, but she absolutely didn't deserve them. "You are understandably disappointed, my lord, but her loyalty is not in question."

"Neither, apparently, is yours." He looked down at her undoubtedly flushed face. "Don't take offense. I wasn't criticizing her or casting aspersions, but merely intimating that from what I just witnessed of their first public dance, her heart seems to be involved. That's all. I've no choice but to concede the field."

To her surprise he smiled after that little speech. It wasn't much, and there was still a grim glint in his eyes, but he gazed at her and smiled.

She was such an utter, besotted fool. *This*, she thought, *is why I'm in love with him. Because he isn't just handsome and titled and has other assets any young woman would value, but because ultimately, he is a decent man.*

"If you are wondering why she is more drawn to Augustine than you, I confess I don't understand it either."

Oh, dear. This time it wasn't so much what she said, but the *way* she'd said it.

There was a slight pause and then he said slowly, "That is a very generous compliment, my lady. Thank you."

It was tempting . . . very tempting, to just ask him candidly why he had at one time seemed to be leaning toward a possible courtship between them but then changed his mind. It wasn't an overwhelming desire for Cecily; his reaction to her engagement to another man bore out that assumption.

But she was afraid of the answer.

Until something interesting happened. Never once, in all the time they'd known each other, passed pleasantries at different events, even gone riding alone at the ducal country estate, had he ever looked at her except with polite attention. But for a moment, just a fleeting moment, his gaze flickered to her décolletage, then immediately returned to her face.

He was hardly the first man to admire her bosom, but it was the first time she didn't mind at all. At least he knew her as a person as well. Flustered, she murmured ridiculously, "I think I see my grandmother. She specifically said she wanted to leave early this evening."

He recognized a dismissal when he heard one. "A pleasure to see you as always, Lady Eleanor."

Then Lord Drury bowed and walked away.

It was a late hour to have a caller. Lillian had already donned her nightdress and was half asleep when the maid knocked on her door to announce who was downstairs, asking for an audience.

Needless to say, she dressed as quickly as possible, slipping into a floral day gown, because she was not going to put on an outdated ball gown at this hour or for this visit, running a brush through her hair and twisting it into a careless chignon. She checked her appearance in the glass just to make sure it was acceptable and then reminded herself wryly that her visitor wouldn't care. It wasn't that she wasn't pretty; she knew she was in the way of having nice bones, chestnut hair and blue eyes and clear, unblemished skin, but it didn't matter. At one time her heart had fluttered each time he called, but truly, now, and back then also, though she didn't know it, what she looked like was not something he cared about one way or the other. They had been friends, nothing more. *She* was the one who had misread his intentions.

What did Arthur Kerr, otherwise known as Lord Sebring, want?

There was only one way to find out.

Taking a deep breath and moving at a deliberately sedate pace, she went downstairs.

He was in the informal drawing room at her request, the dimensions not so shadowed and overpowering as the main public drawing room used to receive guests. The light tap of the rain at the windows made a soothing background sound. The maid had heeded her request and brought a bottle of claret on a tray with two glasses, and also lit several lamps, so the space was cozy enough with its brocade-covered sofas and intimate seating groups. She stopped in the doorway, admiring the clean line of Arthur's profile with a pang as he stood and stared at one of the portraits over the unlit fireplace, his expression remote, his shoulders set.

The sight of him was so achingly familiar; yet again he was like a distant figure in a dream.

Once, she'd loved him. Not lightly, but completely, with all the passion a young woman could feel.

But she hadn't known him, not the real man, and it made her distrustful that her judgment was sound, not to mention that men in general were honest. Even if it weren't for her disgrace in the eyes of society, she was resistant to the idea of ever embarking on another romance. Spinsterhood was not completely without its merits.

She hadn't seen him since his marriage, so it took some courage to square her shoulders, walk into the room, and say calmly, "You look well, Arthur."

He turned, his gaze skimming her casual mode of dress, and a well-remembered smile graced his finely modeled mouth. "So do you, Lily. As beautiful as ever."

Was he telling the truth? It was hard to say. A multitude of lies lay between them. *She* wasn't being sincere. He looked tired, maybe even a little haggard. Still strikingly handsome, of course; not as tall as Jonathan, but well built, with even features and expressive brown eyes, his hair always a little long, his dress impeccable at all times, the height of fashion in the line of his dark coat, embroidered waistcoat, fitted breeches, and Hessians. His neck cloth was a spill of linen edged with lace, and the ruby stickpin nestled in the snowy folds the epitome of elegance. It was unfortunate, but she still experienced a pang in his presence, when she had been so sure she was done with the regrets.

It still hung there in her past—her disastrous elopement and what had happened between them that night at the inn. There was no question of it—whatever Jonathan thought, she *had* lost her innocence that night because of Arthur, and it had changed her world forever.

"Thank you." Her voice was, thankfully, tranquil. She moved into the room, outwardly serene. "Would you like a glass of wine while you tell me why you're here?"

"No." His breath hissed outward in an agitated exhalation. "I mean, yes."

Lillian glanced up, about to pick up the antique crystal decanter.

"Yes to the wine," he said in a subdued voice. "But I confess I don't know quite why I'm here."

"I don't either." She carefully poured wine into their glasses. "But let me venture a guess. Because you need to talk to someone who knows you."

He moved to take the proffered glass, his smile rueful and holding a hint of regret. "You are right, of course. We always did talk, didn't we?"

Yes, they had. And laughed. It was why she'd fallen in love with him in the first place, for however charming her other suitors were, she'd been very comfortable with him from their first introduction.

The settee by the small polished table in the middle of the room was too close, so she chose a chair nearby and balanced her glass of wine in her palms. "What has happened?"

Arthur took a gulp from his glass and sat down. When he swallowed, his face was averted. He spoke abruptly. "The doctors think Penelope might be barren."

Now she understood, or least had a fair idea, of why he had called.

It was a bitter bit of news, she knew, for he'd married his wife for two reasons: her father's connections and to beget an heir. Though the former was the advantage he'd hoped it would be if his ascent in Parliament was an indication, she knew the latter was important to him as well. Lillian looked at the ruby liquid in her glass. "I see."

"She desperately wants a child."

Must I really endure this conversation?

"That does not surprise me." She still cradled her wine, but didn't drink, watching his face. At best his expression could be described as . . . tortured. And as much as she wanted to, she couldn't hate him for what had happened between them. "Most women do."

"For that matter *I* want a child. We've been trying." Arthur was not quite able to meet her eyes, staring at a small figurine on the table instead. "But in three years it hasn't happened."

"I'm sorry."

His gaze finally came up to meet hers. "Yes, I believe you are. One of the many things I admire about you is the generosity of your spirit."

She finally lifted her glass to her lips. It was something to do rather than look into his eyes and mutter another platitude. The rain in the background did not help lighten the mood either.

"We just returned from Vienna. . . . There's a doctor there who is said to work miracles, but he didn't have any particular words of wisdom we hadn't already heard. It was a disappointing venture."

She could say she was sorry again—but she needed to manage more than another two-word response. In truth she *was* sorry, but generous spirit or not, this was not the easiest topic for her to discuss with the man she was once convinced she would marry. "I can understand how you might be disappointed."

"Yes." He looked at her intently. "You do. Perhaps that is why I am here. Because you do understand, Lily."

"Not entirely." Her smile was forced. "Knowing something and understanding it are two different matters."

"I suppose that's true."

There was enough desolation in his voice that she winced. Still, after all that had happened, she couldn't bear hurting him. "Tell me, did you ever consider talking to your wife about…your feelings?"

The sound of moisture dripping from the eaves and tapping against the glass was suddenly loud in the resulting quiet between them. He finally shook his head. "No."

"Is she that . . ." She wasn't sure how to finish the sentence. It was no small part of the reason she'd distanced herself from even the remotest fashionable circle—she had no desire to meet Lady Sebring, for reasons both complicated and emotional.

". . . blind?" he finished for her, his voice gentle and despondent. "Willfully so, if I had to guess, but in answer to your almost question, no, I would never trust her to try and find a glimpse of sensitivity if I confessed that the reason I didn't marry you was more out of love than anything else. As it is, she's horribly jealous and your name has been thrown in my face more than once."

"I can't see she has reason to be jealous of me. I am, after all, the jilted fiancée."

Arthur gazed at her. "She has reason. You are the only woman I have ever loved."

But never loved in the way that she had thought he did.

She set aside her wine, for truly she had no desire for it. "What will you do?"

"If she never gets pregnant?" His laugh was mirthless. "I don't know. Truly, Lily, I don't know." He stopped, and then shook his head and exhaled heavily. "Going to her bed is so distasteful to me I am not sure I can continue the pretense. She will hate me if I decline to continue to try, and she will hate me even more if she discovers why. I shouldn't have married her."

Was it vindictive of her to agree? Perhaps—and she'd had four years to forgive him. She couldn't imagine how his wife would feel about this conversation. "You shouldn't have married *anyone*."

"I have a title and a fortune, Lily. It was my duty. My father expected it."

She had a dozen arguments against that. Honesty. Integrity. The vows he'd taken . . . but she also knew the strict standards of their class, and as much as she could, she understood his reasons. "I suppose it would have taken a great deal of courage to not take the accepted path."

A humorless smile curved his mouth, but to give him credit, he did not avoid her gaze. "For what it is worth, it took a great deal of courage to tell you the truth."

"Maybe you should lend your wife the same consideration."

"And explain to her that my preference is not women? That the nights when I declined to bed her because I claimed to be too tired, or too foxed, really were because I had no desire for her? No. I have lived with her now for three years and can say with some measure of certainty that she is not compassionate enough to understand."

"But I am?"

"Yes," he said gently. He stood then, his expression bereft. "I should not have come here, should I?"

After his departure Lily sat, staring at their two wineglasses, one on each end of the table.

Both were half empty, which was rather symbolic.

She was tired of her life being that way.

Chapter 17

Perhaps it was the rain.

Perhaps it was the challenge.

Perhaps it was the woman.

The last, Jonathan decided as he contemplated exactly how to accomplish his mission. One part of it was simple. The back garden wall was nothing he couldn't circumvent with ease—and he had, so easily done and not a problem. It was more a matter of how to find Cecily's bedroom, and then, of course, how to get to it.

Actually, considering the English habit of letting foliage grow up the walls of their homes, that was hardly going to be an issue either, but he certainly did not want to burst in on the duke, or her brother, who barely hid his antagonism as it was, or Lady Eleanor.

So he stood there in the dark garden, more at home than he had ever been in the crowded ballroom earlier, the smell of wet earth and damp foliage more pleasant than any delicate perfume.

Cecily had never answered his question. And having asked it, he *needed* an answer.

I want you to marry me.

Perhaps that wasn't a question after all. A declaration was more like it. A statement of what he wanted, but what Cecily wanted had not yet been established.

So he waited, soaked but ignoring the discomfort,

because waiting was part of any warrior's game. He considered the weather balmy compared to that of New England, and despite his sodden clothing he was in good spirits. After all, he thought, crouched behind a drenched yew that lifted its dripping branches, she had not said no. Quite the opposite. She'd dared him to seduce her.

He certainly hoped his future wife understood he wasn't one to deny a contest, especially not one with such a tantalizing prize in the balance.

Actually, he thought she'd known exactly what she was doing.

A part of him sensed he'd already won her, and another, more primitive part wished to claim his prize at once. That single waltz had been a lesson in restraint as he'd taken Cecily in his arms for the first time in public.

The duke had deigned to attend the festivities, so it was a fairly educated guess that he'd retired first or was still at his club. Roderick Francis hadn't come home yet, which wasn't surprising, for most young noblemen with too much privilege and youthful inclinations toward the dissolute pleasures offered to those of their class and wealth did not return home until dawn. So, the two windows with lights made perfect sense because both Cecily and her sister were home. All he had to do was decide which one might be which. Entering the bedroom of the wrong unmarried young lady was not a mistake a man wished to make.

Every good scout could reconnoiter, and he set his hand and tested the strength of the ivy on the house before he began to scale the wall. He climbed with ease, the brick facade giving easy footholds, the old vines in places as thick as his wrist. Moments later he was balanced on the ledge outside the first window, peering in through the lacy curtain. The room was quiet, empty as far as he could see from the light of one lamp on a small table by the bed. He slipped a long, thin knife from his boot, inserted the blade between the window panels and flipped the latch up in a deft movement.

The moment he slid his legs over the sill, he knew it was Cecily's bedroom. Her scent was familiar now and it drifted to him, evocative and tantalizing, like an intimate touch. He tugged off his boots and set them outside on the ledge in the rain—they'd be less than comfortable, if not ruined later, but he didn't care— and in bare feet he prowled across the soft carpeting. The bed was hung with pale yellow and the coverlet was a matching shade, the effect feminine and dainty. A dressing table with several crystal bottles, an armoire in the corner in a light wood that was indistinct in the muted light, and several wing chairs covered in a silk to match the bed curtains completed the room. A painting of a small child with blond curls hung over the mantel of the fireplace and Jonathan studied it, wondering once again if their children would be fair or unfashionably dark like him.

How far he'd come from the reluctant earl who'd arrived only a few months ago to assume the responsibilities of his father's legacy. There was no denying that once he'd offered his assistance due to an unexpected champagne accident in a scandalous way to the lovely daughter of the Duke of Eddington, he'd experienced a change of heart over his forced tenure in England.

Not that he'd changed his mind about leaving. That needed to be addressed between them. Adela's American heritage was an integral part of her life, and just as Jonathan's father had wanted for him to experience that side of his background, he wished that for his own daughter. He also hoped that by being given the choice of two cultures, she could control her own life. That meant Cecily would have to accept living between two worlds as well, and he wasn't sure his proper English lady was agreeable to such a drastic change in her life.

Quite a *lot* needed to be discussed. It was why he'd scaled the wall and invaded her bedroom.

From his experience with his sisters, he now understood that young ladies liked to chat with each other after the evening was over, much, if he was honest, as gentlemen liked to have a drink together at their exclusive clubs. He entirely doubted the conversations were at all the same, but call it what you will, a bit of gossip was a bit of gossip. Since the rest of the house was dark, he assumed Cecily was with her sister.

He chose to lean against the wall in the corner—since his breeches were soaked he hardly wanted to ruin any of the fine upholstery by sitting down. As it was, a moment later he decided to peel off his sodden shirt to protect the floral wallpaper, draping the offending garment over the porcelain washbasin. Then he returned to his shadowed spot and waited. He'd told Cecily he was impatient, and that was true in certain ways, but also false. If the reward was in his grasp, he could bide his time.

Some things were well worth waiting for.

Cecily moved into her bedroom, still restive, not sure she was going to be able to sleep, but Eleanor had made it clear she wasn't in the mood, yet again, for confidences, so there seemed little point in attempting a tête-à-tête.

Despite her own eventful evening, Cecily had seen her sister speaking in the corner with Lord Drury. Even if she hadn't, she would have heard about it. She did understand how it might not be exactly the right time for confidences between them, but she was also hurt that though they had always been close, Elle still kept this one secret from her.

Men complicated everything, she decided in patent disgust, shedding her dressing gown and dropping it on the floor. It was a toss of the dice as to which one annoyed her more at the moment, Jonathan or Lord Drury.

"We never finished our discussion."

She whirled, a gasp escaping at the sound of the deep voice in the confines of her bedroom, no less.

Jonathan, she decided in the next dizzying second as she caught her breath. That solved the puzzle. *He* annoyed her more, for what the devil was he doing there?

He stood in the corner, his brawny arms crossed over his bare chest, barefoot, wearing nothing but a pair of damp breeches that clung to him in what she perceived to be an indecent manner. In the darkness he loomed taller, his hair was wet and loose, and there was no possible way he could adequately explain his presence. Needless to say, having an almost completely undressed man in her bedchamber was an unprecedented occurrence, not to mention the repercussions of what this meant to her life if they were discovered.

Except, of course, if she married him . . .

Even then, it would cause a furor.

"How did you get in?" She stalled for time, suddenly aware of her nakedness under her simple nightdress. She gathered it around her, crossing her arms over her chest.

He'd noticed, too, his gaze lazily skimming her bodice. "Window."

It *was* open. She could smell the chimney smoke and the damp, clean scent of the rain. The one-word response was typically Jonathan. "You climbed up the side of the house?"

"Not difficult to do."

"I'll keep that in mind." She moved to close the window, pulling it shut with a soft thud. "Do you mind," she asked in a low voice as she turned around, the breath of light rain having dampened her gown, "telling me why you are here, my lord?"

"I would think that would be obvious, *my lady*." There was just a hint of mockery in his tone. "As I said, our conversation on the dance floor has not been finished."

Had he been fully dressed, she might have formulated a glib answer. As it was, she couldn't help how her gaze fastened on the bronzed planes of his bare chest. The defined musculature was . . . fascinating. "This is a bit dramatic, isn't it?"

"I was not going to be granted entrance at the front door for this conversation at this hour, was I?"

"You could call at a more reasonable time—"

"But what if I'm not inclined to wait?" He unfolded his arms and took a step toward her, coming a little out of the shadows.

She'd set this in motion. She'd known it the minute she looked into the depths of his eyes and practically dared him to seduce her. He smiled, but it was a predatory curve of his lips as his gaze traveled over her. Looking at his sleek damp dark hair and half-dressed state, she suddenly thought Earl Savage a most appropriate nickname. "Jonathan." She took a cautionary step backward in response to his advance.

"Yes?"

"This is . . . is unthinkable." She almost took another step backward, but there was really nowhere to go, and besides, she wasn't afraid of him as much as she was afraid of herself.

One of his dark brows arched upward. "What are you thinking about, my beautiful English lady? If the answer is how it feels when I kiss you, then I confess I've been thinking about that quite a bit myself."

"I'll be ruined." It was the merest whisper, and if she was truthful, just words to say while she desperately scrambled for her reason.

"Only if we're discovered."

"My father is home."

"I can be quiet." He advanced another step, more primal than ever, a tall, bare-chested, elemental presence in her bedroom, and while she should have been alarmed, instead she was filled with a delicious sense of anticipation.

Ever since his proposal during their waltz earlier, she had done nothing but think about what it would be like to accept. Not in terms of being the Countess of Augustine. Not in terms of his reputed wealth. Not in terms of his background or his barbaric nickname either. But with the concept of being his *wife* swirling through her head.

He smiled in that singular way. "Can you?"

"Can I what?" She stared at him, so conscious of his closeness that it affected her breathing.

"Be quiet." His smile was a swift flash and his voice soft.

She had no idea what he meant precisely, but there was a dangerous gleam in his eyes that made her pulse race. Heart pounding, no breath left in her lungs; no wonder she was a bit dizzy. "Jonathan, I—"

"Let's find out." He came forward then, so swiftly she didn't even have a chance to react, and he swept her against him and kissed her.

And it was oh so different this time. Hungry. He de-

voured her, hot, a little wild, demanding, his arms unrelenting and hard, and the sweep of his tongue into
her mouth caused a shiver of anticipation. The moment
she'd seen him there, so tall and dark in the shadows,
she'd known he was intent on claiming not just her acquiescence to the marriage, but *her*.

Maybe it was what she wanted. The decision not given
to her, but taken away, for God help her, she was only
too willing and wasn't sure what that made her. Ladies
did not countenance men invading their bedchambers,
but then again, they did not hare off in carriages with
them either, nor did they propose false engagements.

Duke's daughter or not, maybe she wasn't a lady.

He doesn't want to live in England, a sensible voice
whispered in her rational mind. *You need to think about
that . . . and his daughter and the woman he refused to
marry. What happened? It does not seem likely that Jonathan would so shirk his responsibilities . . .*

But this wasn't a contemplative moment.

This—*this*—was a passionate, captivating kiss, and
as close to him as she was, she could feel the hardened
state of his arousal, which filled her with some trepidation, but also with a sense of overwhelming excitement.
It was elemental, but then again, that described the Earl
of Augustine very well. He smelled of rain and the night
breezes she so missed from the country.

It was a long, determined kiss, and she might be
young, naive and in the flush of her first love affair, but
she still recognized that it was designed to vanquish, to
rule, to dominate. The play of his tongue was wicked,
ungovernable, invading, taunting, and then tender and
slow, as he changed the angle and sensually wooed her
with his mouth.

When he lifted her in his arms as easily as one might

sweep up a small child, she understood that the bed was their destination, and the question of their future might be answered in the most definitive way possible.

Clinging to him, she registered the softness of the mattress at her back as he deposited her on the silky sheets, her respiration uneven. He was half naked, his skin damp, his ebony hair swinging forward as he followed her down and kissed her throat, his long, powerful body overshadowing hers. "If you wish to stop me," he murmured against her skin, "you can."

"You know I don't." Her voice was hushed.

He touched his lips to hers again, softly, gently, at odds with the fiery purpose in his eyes when he lifted his head and gazed at her. "I was hoping you would say that."

Chapter 18

Seduction. Yes, he'd done it before. In lighthearted ways when failure didn't matter in the fabric of his life—not that he'd failed ever in this game, but this was the first time the lady's capitulation had ever meant so much. His usual conquests were women who wished a dalliance with him for any number of reasons, including his looks, his aristocratic status, his fortune . . . his reputed skill in the bedroom.

This encounter was nothing like any of those past liaisons.

Beneath him, so soft and beguiling, Cecily wore nothing but a white gown that did little to hide the curves of her breasts or the neat triangle between her thighs. Her long, pale hair spilled around her slim shoulders, framing her delicate face, and he possessively ran his fingers through those silky strands, reveling in the fine texture, the warmth, the entrancing scent. Her eyes, framed by lush lashes, at the moment poignantly held a look of both adorable confusion and what he recognized as feminine desire.

All along he'd known his cool English miss had an innate sensuality that merely needed to be encouraged and nurtured. He wanted her and she wanted him.

The perfect equation. With a questing finger he traced

her lower lip with a light seductive touch, following the sensual curve.

Jonathan's erect cock advocated urgency while his brain advised caution. She'd just given him her acquiescence. He needed to give something back and assure her this wasn't only sexual. His breath brushing her ear, his aroused body tense, he whispered, "I've imagined this since the first moment we met." That was a declaration of soul-shattering honesty.

That was why he'd scaled the ivy-covered wall, why he was willing to give up part of his life to marriage. It wasn't all of it, no, but he could at least tell her that with self-effacing honesty.

Cecily touched his cheek. "I would not welcome you if I hadn't also."

She had? It moved him. He was getting in deeper by the moment.

"There's more." His mouth touched hers, teased, tasted, and then lifted. "I've pictured our children."

A confession of such a magnitude he couldn't quite believe he'd said it out loud, but then again, it was true. She was going to be his wife. He would settle for nothing else, and though physical desire was important between a man and a woman, it was only a fraction of a life made up of many parts.

The communion of their souls was just as important.

Her eyes were suddenly luminous and her voice hushed. "Jonathan."

"I think," he said with remarkable control in his opinion since his body was going up in flames, "this discussion ends here. We can talk later."

The cup of his palm around her breast stopped whatever words of prudence she might have uttered. Cecily gasped as his thumb circled her nipple through the fine material of her nightdress and she arched in artless enjoyment even at that simple caress.

Good. He liked his bed partners enthusiastic and had known from the first time he took her in his arms that she was not just beautiful but beautifully responsive. "This first." He pulled the ribbon on her bodice free and eased the garment over her shoulders, revealing creamy skin and full, firm breasts, his breath catching in his throat at her beauty even though he'd known all along it would be exactly this way. The lift of her hips to allow him to completely slide the fine lawn over the length of her legs and toss it aside implied a trust that humbled him, reflected also in her unusual tawny eyes as she watched him in a mixture of shyness and female triumph, as he stared at her unveiled body.

Woman incarnate. Supple limbs, soft curves, unbound golden hair ...

He was lost, but he'd *been* lost since that initial champagne spill and his less than gentlemanly rescue, and he was no longer fighting it.

With a fingertip, he touched one taut nipple. "You are exquisite."

"I haven't seen *you*." Though her hands clenched in the bed linens, she didn't move to cover herself. He didn't have to be particularly insightful to know from the bright color in her cheeks that she wanted to tug the sheet up. A blush of pink infused her skin from head to toe, actually, and the delectable heated scent of woman and roses made his erection surge.

As if he needed more encouragement. Jonathan eased off the bed and fought the fastenings over the prominent bulge in his breeches, well aware of her watching the movement of his fingers. He shoved the material down his hips and impatiently stepped free. Then he joined her again, covering her lightly before the flare of alarm in her eyes became fear over his aroused state, his kisses gentle on her mouth, her eyelids, at the hollow beneath her ear. "Now you've seen me," he whispered. "You've seen my desire for you. I want you eager, sweetheart, not afraid."

Slim fingers ran down his back. "I'm not afraid of you," she told him haltingly between soft, sweet kisses, "but I have no idea what to do."

His inner smile was heartfelt. "You don't have to know what to do. Nature did that for us. Don't you trust in your instincts?"

Languid beneath him, her eyes soft as honey, Cecily shook her head, but she gasped as he stroked his hand up her rib cage to touch her bare breast. "I'm not a . . ."

"Heathen?" he supplied ironically, not inclined to debate their disparate heritage when what he wanted most in his life was in his grasp—literally, his fingers cupping her resilient flesh.

"Not the word I'd have selected . . . oh, Jonathan . . ." She arched her back at his touch, which was as arousing as hell.

When he bent his head to her breast, she stopped speaking, but as he began to lick and tease her erect nipples, first one and then the other, it struck him that he knew she was telling the truth.

She would *never* have chosen the word *heathen*.

It didn't exist in her to hold his mixed blood against him, and maybe that was one of the reasons, besides her incomparable allure, that he'd fallen in love with her so easily.

Was he in love? By the gods—his included—yes, he was coming to the conclusion that was what had happened. Their chance meeting in the crowded ballroom, those fiery kisses, the amber stone . . .

He loved her. His mind tried to put together some coherent thought as he savored the soft sweetness of her skin, because he'd invited himself like an invading warrior. But he would have to worry about that later. Much, much later . . .

This conquest would be done properly.

"There's nothing you can do wrong, trust me." His fingers slid downward over the curve of her hip, his mouth warm against her nipple, his tongue tracing a ring around the taut pink crest. "I'm like a man starved for a meal and you are so very . . . *delicious*."

Her fingers ran into his hair, lifting the strands, her body shivering under his ministrations. "Oh."

"Let me handle everything." The double entendre was smoothly said, but it was *his* breathing that was uneven as he kissed a seductive path down her stomach. He gently urged her legs apart and contemplated the fastest path to make sure a female found sexual satisfaction. It was a simple enough method if he could gain her cooperation. Her innocence was an issue, and from the sudden tension in her slender body just from his hands on her inner thighs, this might not be easily done.

"You'll like this," he assured her, kissing the satin skin of her inner thigh. "Relax. You do understand you are going to have to trust me? Lovers trust each other, and wives especially must have faith in their husbands."

"I haven't said I'll marry you, Lord Augustine."

That was the crux of the matter, but Jonathan knew enough about her to assure himself that they would not be naked in bed together if she didn't intend to marry him. He grinned. "Haven't you?" His thumb traced the seam of her labia and she quivered again.

Perfect. Every delectable inch of her.

"No." A whisper.

"Is it arrogant of me to believe I can convince you?" He dropped a light kiss on the dainty patch of her pubic hair and parted the folds of her sex with his fingertips very delicately. The small sensitive bud that he knew would stimulate her to climax was pink and exposed, and she did her best to turn away, but he caught her hip and held her still. "Don't panic now." He licked the luscious curve of the back of her knee. "I'm just beginning."

It was incomprehensible, but Jonathan's intent seemed quite clear, and Cecily let out a small cry of protest when he put his mouth wickedly between her trembling thighs.

She'd never been so shocked in her life.

It was infinitely sinful.

Completely indecent.

Terribly wonderful.

Sensation rippled through her body, the simple word *pleasure* taking on a whole new meaning. She wasn't quite sure what was happening to her body, but it was irresistible, confounding, and as her eyes drifted shut, she wondered how she could possibly let him do something so outrageous and simultaneously begged him silently not to stop. The ebony silk of his hair against her skin, the clasp of his hands against her hips, the erotic teasing of his tongue . . .

Rapture thrummed through her in small, wild pulses and she couldn't help but clutch his wide shoulders, wanting to protest the intimate contact but unable to speak. Instead her breath came in small panting bursts, which would normally embarrass her, but that was hardly foremost in her mind.

The culmination was intemperate, brought on as the tension built, like adding layer upon layer, and Cecily vaguely knew she'd shed all modesty and opened her legs wider, inviting the scandalous contact. When the firestorm finally burst, she melted in a shower of sparks and bright lights, the wash of physical joy a miracle, a revelation in the definition of idyllic, a crescendo of pure rapture like she'd never imagined existed.

Life would never be the same.

"Shhh." Jonathan kissed her. Lost, drifting, she didn't really realize he'd moved until his mouth touched hers, his tall body propped above her, his hair brushing her cheek. "You promised to be quiet, love."

The slight lilt of laughter in his voice registered, but she was too sated to resent it.

Had she made a sound? She certainly didn't know, but what she did come to realize was that he'd adjusted himself between her thighs, and there was a pressure as he positioned his rigid cock at her female entrance and began to enter her.

Maybe if she hadn't been so overcome by just his presence, by the ramifications of having him in her bedroom at this hour, of being alone with him, being entirely nude in his arms, she might have been more afraid. But as he slowly invaded her body inch by inch, Cecily instead tightened her arms around his neck and did her best not to resist the inexorable possession, her face pressed to his brawny shoulder.

He spoke to her then. In little phrases that meant nothing because the lyrical language was so different from any she'd ever been taught or heard, and she clung to him and tried to assimilate both the experience and the captivating sound of his voice. There was a sting of pain that made her stiffen as her virginity was lost, but it passed as quickly as a summer cloudburst, to be replaced by the experience of him embedded in her body, joining them fully.

It was hot, inflaming, and as much as she knew he should not be there in her bed, the part of her mind that was capable of reason reminded her that he wished to marry her—he'd petitioned to her father, no less—and so, in light of that commitment, they could do this.

This.

This glorious primitive act that she hadn't quite imagined, even as he slid backward, and then penetrated her again, deeply and powerfully, his hips flexing against her thighs, was beyond comprehension, she decided. Not just the sensation of bare skin to bare skin, the clasp of his arms, the look in his dark eyes, but . . . Jonathan's breath hissed out, and for the first time since she'd met him at that fateful ball, his face held a singular vulnerability.

"Cecily. . . ." His features were drawn and tight, as were the muscles under her hands. "This needs to be for the both of us. Tell me I'm not hurting you."

"No." She reveled in the taut hardness of his back, of the way he moved in her, the slick friction unique. "No," she repeated, the word barely audible. It wasn't quite comfortable yet, but he definitely wasn't hurting her and it was getting better by the moment.

"Good." His smile was an elusive ghost, barely glossing his mouth, his dark hair loose and touching her face as he moved. "For I don't think I could stop now if the north wind whispered in my ear."

She had no idea what he meant, but she discovered it moments later as she began to experience that same unique excitement, the shuddering prelude to that tumultuous joy. It came as a flicker first, like the initial streak of the rising sun at dawn, and built, growing as Jonathan thrust and retreated, his movements increasing subtly in speed, his half-closed eyes watching her face.

"Ohh . . ." Cecily held on to the hard bulge of his biceps and trembled into the next glide of sex into sex, wondering how this glorious act could be such a well-kept secret, for surely, if everyone knew . . . there would be no virgins left in England.

It came in a burst of brilliant color, so persuasive that she was lost in the blissful peaking event, only barely cognizant that Jonathan held her closer and went very still, the pulse of his sex within her accompanied by a low groan.

In the aftermath, she lay limp and breathless beneath him, not quite sure how to interpret the experience. Pleasure, some pain—thankfully only fleeting—and an emphasis on how large he was to her slender form, but also how tender and considerate a man could be when he took care with his lover.

And he *had* taken care with her. She was aware of the gentle drift of his long fingers through her hair and he lifted his head, smiling down at her with lazy male confidence. "Will you?"

"What?" She wasn't quite capable of forming a coherent thought. Damp, breathless, skin to skin with none other than Earl Savage . . .

"Marry me."

She blinked.

His brows quirked upward. "You'd forgotten the reason for my visit?" Well, if she had, it was entirely his fault. For seducing her.

Absolutely she had to marry him. No doubt about it, and even if he wasn't braced above her on his elbows, giving her that slow, evocative smile, she would have agreed.

"You don't want to live here." Her voice was hushed,

for truly she was still bereft of breath, her entire being tingling.

"We can discuss it later."

No. She should never agree to postpone such an important conversation , and she knew it. Her father's strictures came to mind, as if men normally cared about what women wanted. "Not later," she managed to say, liberality important to her. "I am *not* going to marry someone who simply wants to own me and issue dictates."

Jonathan undid her then. It was as easy as a small smile and a sentence. He said softly, "You aren't a possession; you're a gift from the gods. And I will not force you to go to America if you don't wish it."

That was a relief. Now that she had lain with him, if he went to her father and told the truth, all choice would be taken from her. "Thank you." She watched his expression very carefully. "What of your daughter?"

Their bodies were still intimately joined, and her hands on his back felt the immediate tension in the muscles under her fingertips. "Adela? What specifically is the question?"

"I don't know much about children. Will she like me?"

"*That* is your concern?" He kissed her temple and his voice was audibly thicker when he spoke again. "Whether or not a five-year-old child will like you? No wonder you bewitch me, my lady. In answer, yes, she will adore you."

"Why didn't you marry her mother?"

There. I asked it.

For their future, she very much wanted to know.

An undefined emotion glimmered in his dark eyes and then he eased free of her body, much to her disappointment. He settled next to her, long, lean, and unabashedly nude, his breath going out in a lengthy sigh as he ran his fingers through his hair in a swift, masculine mannerism that she was coming to know. "I suppose it's only fair that I explain to you. I don't usually. I haven't even told James."

It was common knowledge he and his cousin were close friends, and not just because of the familial relationship either. Cecily waited, her body still tingling. She did not want to distract him if he was going to reveal a story he obviously kept closely guarded, and at this point shyness was ridiculous when he'd seen—and touched and tasted—every intimate part of her; still, she wanted to inch the sheet up to cover herself.

"I was twenty-three when Adela was conceived. Boston may not be Mayfair, but there is still an elitist mentality. My status as the son of a wealthy English earl won me some attention. I won't lie—there were women." His smile was ironic. "You'll hear that anyway, no doubt, and you might as well hear it from me, though please take my word, normally I am a careful man."

"Careful?" Cecily's brow furrowed. "What do you mean?"

"Not to impregnate a lover."

"Oh. How?" It was slightly off the topic, but she was intrigued. This entire evening had been a revelation.

He laughed softly. "You are endearingly innocent, my sweet, but I'll save that explanation for another time, if I may. When Caroline contacted me to tell me she was pregnant, she swore she was sure it was mine. She was correct, of course. I knew it was possible . . . but we had been together only one night. I had no idea what to do, but when she told me her husband would never allow her to keep a child that looked so little like him, what choice did I have? I received my daughter the night she was born and have thanked all gods, mine and yours, for Addie ever since. I don't defend myself, since I despise the uninformed gossip anyway, but now perhaps you see why I don't explain the situation. No, I did not marry my child's mother. It wasn't an option. In retrospect, that is just as well. She gave up Addie to me very easily. I think at that moment I changed from a boy into a man. I would alter nothing. I celebrate my child's existence every single day."

That revealed quite a lot, both about the man, and the reason he kept his daughter so close and did not apologize for it.

"I cannot wait to meet her," Cecily whispered, moved. Raking her fingers through his raven hair, she smiled tremulously. "And in answer to your proposal . . . yes. Yes."

Chapter 19

She'd lain awake for over an hour, restless, unhappy about avoiding the conversation with Cecily. The stillness of the house was oppressive, her inner turbulence even more disquieting. In the end, Eleanor gave up trying to obliterate her problem in slumber, as that cowardly tactic clearly wasn't working anyway. She was a great believer in speaking her mind—wasn't she was infamous for it?—and she was ready to confess everything, for she had an uneasy feeling that Cecily already knew her secret anyway.

It had better *not* be why her sister had declined Lord Drury.

The war between conscience and good sense was always a difficult one, and Eleanor engaged in the battle, her hand lifted to knock on her sister's door.

Then she froze.

What the devil?

The hushed sound of a man's voice carried enough that she heard the muted tones, and then Cecily's breathless laugh. Then silence as Eleanor stood there with her mouth no doubt hanging open, followed by a sound that only could be described as a low moan.

Though she was taken aback a bit, she could not say with definite clarity that she was stunned. Her quest to apologize for being so standoffish and cold had yielded an eye-opening realization of a different kind.

The Earl of Augustine was in her sister's bedroom. No other man would be met with enthusiasm, and from the sound of it, he was most welcome.

Oh, bloody hell.

The sound of unsteady footsteps on the staircase made her turn, alarm shooting through every nerve ending. Roderick's return at this moment was not opportune, and she also should not be in the hallway of the family apartments clad only in her nightdress and hovering outside her sister's door unless she had a good explanation. Certainly the truth would never do. Briefly she considered a mad dash toward her own suite, but then loyalty asserted itself and Eleanor understood well enough that her brother's at the moment maybe enhanced sense of male affront over what might be happening behind that closed door could cause a catastrophe.

Jonathan Bourne didn't need to be protected, for he was more than able to take care of himself. Neither was his presence in the ducal mansion—though scandalous and unorthodox—that much of a surprise if given some thought—but it was still dangerous to the extent that she knew Roderick would take offense.

By the gentlemen's code, so he should.

In her mind, by all laws of practicality, if Augustine and Cecily were destined to be together and they hadn't waited to share a bed . . . well, they would not be the first couple to take that route. In this case, avoiding a confrontation seemed to be the best of all possible ideas.

That the earl could defeat her brother in a confrontation, with either fists or weapons, was not a difficult conclusion to draw.

Quickly she walked forward, her expression deliberately sleepy. When her brother reached the top of the stairs, she murmured, "Roddy?"

"Oh . . . sorry." He was obviously a bit foxed, for he stumbled slightly as he gained the upper hall. "Didn't expect you here, Elle."

"Couldn't sleep." She smiled.

"Just getting in," he countered, his own smile lopsided.

Like she couldn't tell *that* from his undone cravat and the cloying odor of perfume and brandy. Eleanor linked her arm through his. "Let's get something to eat, shall we? Raid the kitchen like we used to do when we were young. Do you think Cook has any meat pies left?"

"We didn't have meat pies for dinner," he protested, but let her persuasively coax him back toward the staircase.

"She always makes them." It was true. The cook, who could produce sumptuous seven-course dinners, was from Wales and she liked meat pies. Roasted salmon and duckling in cherry sauce and all the other fancy dishes a duke should be served aside—she truly did make a very delicious, moist meat pasty.

And if they went downstairs, crept into the kitchen, and ate a few of those flaky, delicious treats, maybe it would give Lord Augustine enough time to slip away unobserved. In the morning, along with her apology and confession, Eleanor planned on delivering a stern lecture on the merits of prudence to her beautiful younger sister.

"I could probably use a little food," her brother confessed, his blond hair mussed, his speech only slightly slurred. "Helps in the morning, you know."

"I'll have to accept your word on it. Proper highborn ladies don't get foxed," she said primly, but her mouth twitched.

"A lot you know," her brother muttered with a grin. "Is Ci still awake? Maybe she'd like to come with—"

"No, she's sound asleep," Eleanor said firmly. Keeping Roderick alive was paramount, so the lie was justified. He wasn't so drunk he would not understand the implications if he heard the sound of a male voice beyond that closed door. Eleanor told herself her sister was due to be properly betrothed to her earl anyway—savage or not—and Eleanor really had only barely managed a few mouthfuls at the most earlier at dinner and so was surprisingly hungry. She led the way, Roderick tottering a little next to her, down the darkened stairs and through the main hall to the servants' entrance and then finally into the recesses of the kitchen. As a child, she'd always loved it, for it smelled comforting, like salted hams and freshly baked bread, and a dozen other delectable treats.

"Just sit down." She fairly shoved her brother into one of the sturdy chairs at the big, well-scrubbed table. "I'll see what I can find."

She foraged through the pantry, to her delight discovering a fig pudding glazed with sugar on the sideboard, a nice wedge of cheese, and sure enough, the promised pasties. She brought it all to the table along with some ale. Settling down, she took a bite of the meat pie, decided it truly was bliss on earth, and washed it down with a small drink from her cup.

Roderick also ate with obvious appreciation, his fine-featured face shadowed by the one lamp they'd lit, which barely illuminated the huge space of the mansion's kitchen. At the end, he licked his fingers in a most inelegant way for a marquess and ducal heir, and smiled. "Quite a brilliant idea, Elle."

She wished she were full of brilliant ideas, including what to do about her own situation with Lord Drury. After this evening, she knew he had resigned himself to

Cecily's decision. That meant if he was truly looking for a wife, then he would direct his interest elsewhere.

Naturally, to one of the demure, lovely young debutantes who did not have a reputation of being unforgivably blunt.

How entirely depressing. Taking one last morsel of cheese, she wiped her hands, and knowing Roderick's close friendship with the viscount, asked outright, "Was Lord Drury among your cohorts this evening?"

"Elijah?" He contemplated his mug of ale and then rubbed the back of his neck. "Yes, he was there. It was my usual set."

"He must be devastated over Cecily's engagement to Augustine." Her voice was very carefully neutral. It was only natural that she should ask, she told herself, for the viscount's intentions were no secret.

Speaking of the earl, she certainly hoped he was decamping from her sister's bedroom as she spoke, with as much stealth as had allowed him to arrive undetected in the first place.

To her surprise, Roderick shook his head. "Not quite as much as you'd think, seeing as Drury seemed dead set on her."

"Ah." Not a particularly glib response, but it was late, she was unsettled, and though the impromptu meal helped, she still wasn't positive she could sleep.

Her brother regarded her across the table. "He's a good catch."

Oh, Lord. A flush touched her skin. *Does everyone know?* Her voice was brittle. "I'm sure he is."

"Nice enough, too. A capital fellow, if you ask me."

No one had, but it would be rude to point it out. "Seems to be," she acknowledged with a light shrug.

And then the first promising thing that had happened since she'd started this second somewhat miserable season occurred. Roderick said in an offhand voice, "He asked about you."

It hadn't been a dream after all.

Cecily rolled over, realized she was nude under the sheets, and sat up in a flurry of loose hair and chagrin, wondering what had become of her nightdress. Either Jonathan had managed to toss it neatly over the chair at the far corner of the room or her maid had already come in. The latter was much more probable.

That was hardly perfect.

An indiscretion was one matter, rumors of that same fall from grace another. It was probably a good thing, she decided, that she was about to become engaged.

You could even now carry my child, Jonathan had whispered to her after he'd made love to her a second time, both of them replete in each other's arms, pleasantly exhausted, the novelty of her first sexual experience leaving her without words to express how she felt about that possibility.

Instead she'd kissed him gently without the fervor of their earlier joining, and that was the last part of it she remembered because she'd evidently drifted off to sleep.

How audaciously sure he'd been of his welcome, she thought, feeling a few twinges of evidence as to what had transpired as she slid out of bed and went looking for her dressing gown. She found it and slipped it on, and even as she tied the sash a knock on her door made her whirl around.

A guilty start if there ever was one.

Did she even look the same? Cecily wondered, not sure how everyone that saw her now couldn't *know*, for certainly she did not feel the same as the girl who had entered her bedchamber last evening. She was different, her entire life was different, and it wasn't just that Jonathan had effectively seduced her body, but more that she had realized she was not a girl at all but a woman in love.

Of course it was supposed to be a life-altering moment. She knew that; she just hadn't expected it to be so . . . so . . .

Eleanor let herself in quietly and shut the door. This morning her sister was very pretty in a white gown with pale green eyelet trim, her dark gold hair drawn neatly back in a sleek chignon, her blue eyes—the ones Cecily had somehow not inherited from their father—direct. "Good morning."

It was absurdly normal. Yes, it was a good morning. It was a glorious morning actually, never matter that it was cloudy, though the drizzle had seemed to stop. "What time is it?" Cecily glanced at the clock on the mantel. It was a pretty piece that their grandmother had given her, antique and reputedly from the palace at Versailles, with gold filigree hands and delicate flowers painted on the porcelain face. It was late, she saw, much later than she usually slept. Never had anything like a simple white nightdress hanging over the arm of a chair seemed so conspicuous.

Like a white flag of surrender. And surrender she certainly had the night before, if innocence counted as a prize.

"I'm guessing Augustine did not break his neck descending the wall," Eleanor murmured, gazing pointedly at the damning nightrail and settling gracefully into a chair. "A nice feat and quite polite of him. Having a deceased earl in one's garden is never socially acceptable."

Cecily went very still and stared at her sister. For a moment she considered a vehement denial, but decided it was pointless. She took in a deep breath, exhaled, and asked, "How did you know?"

"I couldn't sleep."

Since this was her sister, since it was undoubtedly obvious she wore nothing under her dressing gown, and since it also seemed that they'd been heard—Cecily tried to ignore the heat in her face and didn't bother to try to brazen it out. "I would never call him prudent," she said with a small, rueful laugh. "But yes, he arrived and departed in a relatively anonymous manner. Or at least I thought so. I certainly hope you're the only one who knows he was here."

"If I hadn't been unable to sleep and come to your door to apologize for being so brusque earlier, I would never have heard anything." Eleanor folded her hands in her lap and seemed fascinated with her intertwined fingers. "It was quite . . . enlightening, really."

Could this get more embarrassing? "How much did you hear exactly?"

"Not *that*," her sister said, her face also taking on a peculiar shade of pink. "I meant that I truly do believe you prefer Lord Augustine to Lord Drury. You might have refused an engagement with the latter for my sake, but you never would have bedded the former without deeper feeling on your part."

The confession at last. Knees weak, Cecily sank down on the bed. She opened her mouth to explain that she hadn't bedded so much as she'd *been* bedded, but she decided the fine distinction was unimportant and nodded. "True."

"It made me feel considerably better," her sister told her, looking much like someone who might be in front of a tribunal of the Inquisition. Then, being typically Elle, she glanced up and said frankly, "Because I know you know."

"About your feelings for Lord Drury?" Cecily nodded. "Yes. Or I suspected anyway."

How nice it would be to get this out in the open.

Her sister toyed with a bit of green trim at the edge of her sleeve, and then sighed with obvious resignation. "Goodness, Ci, when did this get all so complicated?"

"Love just seems to be."

"Yes, I agree. When I met Elijah Winters last season, he showed no sign of looking for a wife. As it turned out, I hardly attracted a host of suitors anyway, so when the season was over and we returned to the country, I wasn't all that disheartened over my lack of popularity. His friendship with Roddy meant he visited us now and then, so it wasn't as if I didn't get to see him." Eleanor lifted her chin, her gaze level. "I was even misguided enough to think maybe he'd came to Eddington Hall so often because of me. Then the minute you make your debut, he's passionately on his knees."

"Figuratively on his knees," Cecily corrected. "And it has occurred to me that he might be more interested in you than even *he* realizes. All I know is he makes more attempts to get you alone than he ever has done with me."

"To talk about you."

"To talk *with* you," she countered. "What if I am just the excuse? I've never sensed a real interest. He certainly did not invite me on a morning ride when at Eddington."

"Ci, we happened to be at the stables at the same time. I am sure that as a gentleman, he felt he had no choice but to suggest we ride together. And that aside, if what you are saying is in the least true, why wouldn't he just approach *me*?" her sister asked in a very small voice.

It was a bit difficult to articulate her theory, but then again, she'd been thinking about it for quite a while. "Perhaps you intimidate his lordship. I don't think you'd deny, Elle, that you are not the average retiring miss.

Last season you won a reputation for being excruci-
atingly sharp-tongued, and since he is a gentleman of
some reserve, maybe it made him wary. Still, perhaps he
couldn't keep from thinking about you. Talking about
his courtship of me was a good excuse." Cecily paused
and smiled wryly. "It wasn't much of a courtship, actually. Aside from the flowers he has sent, he has probably waltzed with you more than he has with me. One
of the reasons I was opposed to an engagement is that I
don't really know him. That means, of course, he doesn't
know me either, so what he thought he wanted might
not be the wanton young woman who is now irrevocably
compromised."

Eleanor replied stoutly, "Compromised? Nonsense.
If you don't want Augustine, no one needs to know it
ever happened. I would never tell anyone."

Her sister's loyalty was moving, but she *did* want him.
She wanted nothing more. Cecily murmured, "I think
matters are settled between Jonathan and me, so do not
worry on that point, but what I am saying is that you
and Lord Drury are much more in accord than he and I
would ever have been. Goodness, Elle, he turns to you
for advice. That shows a level of respect a man rarely
gives a woman."

"Respect is nice but not especially romantic." Her
sister rose, paced over to the window, and put a palm
against the glass, staring outside at the dreary day. "Do
you think there is actually a chance? What should I do?"

Eleanor, as an older sibling, was much more likely to
deliver advice than ask for it. Cecily weighed her words.
"I think there is a very good chance. He is looking for a
wife and he admires you. Three waltzes in one evening,
walks in the garden . . . I'm not the only one to notice. If
he's blind to it, you need to awaken him to the fact it is
you he wants, not me."

"How on earth do I do that?"

Emboldened by her newfound experience, Cecily let her mouth curve into a smile as she surveyed her sister's lush beauty in her becoming gown. "I haven't much direct advice, but I suspect you'll find a way."

Chapter 20

He rode Seneca out every day, rain or shine, and this particular morning had neither. The rain had cleared off, but the leaden skies remained, though they didn't alter Jonathan's good mood—which had nothing to do with the weather and everything to do with a certain golden-haired young woman he'd left sleeping peacefully just before dawn.

But he had to admit his fine spirits were tempered by curiosity. Lily had been waiting for him right after breakfast, looking young and pretty in a light blue riding habit, and to his surprise she had actually suggested they ride together.

How could he refuse such a proverbial olive branch? Besides, he needed to discuss his engagement with her anyway, as he suspected Carole and Betsy had already at the least heard the rumors.

But he discovered as they walked their horses sedately through the park, the leaves of the trees still dripping and the path sodden, it wasn't his upcoming marriage she wanted to discuss, but her aborted betrothal.

His sister, her gloved hands lightly holding the reins of her mare, said quietly, "Lord Sebring came to see me last night."

Seneca splashed through a puddle. Jonathan processed that revelation. "I wasn't home. I hope you didn't receive him without a chaperone present."

For that he received a stony look. "He already ruined me, remember? Why should I refuse?"

A valid point. "I do remember," he said coolly. "Though, as you are about to reenter society, perhaps you should be more discreet. I believe you were the one to inform me that I should do nothing that might reflect badly on our family at this crucial time for Betsy and Carole."

"I was somewhat startled," she admitted after a moment, looking straight ahead, her expression somber. "It was quite late. I doubt anyone saw him arrive. I assume that he was careful, since otherwise his wife might hear of the visit."

Jonathan had also paid an unorthodox visit last evening, so it would be hypocritical to criticize Lord Sebring, but at least he didn't already have a wife and he had every intention of marrying Cecily. "Let's hope he was."

They rode in silence for a few minutes and he waited, for he now understood that the ride had a purpose, and while Lillian could be prickly and disapproving, he did wish for more understanding between them.

When the clouds parted for a moment and a brief ray of sunshine came down, she said, "His marriage is pretty wretched for him."

"As I understand it, he's to blame for his choice." The words were neutral. He didn't know Sebring and he didn't care too much about his miserable marriage, not if the man had been the source of such pain for Lillian.

"From how *I* understand it . . . not entirely."

"If you refer to what James claims to be Sebring's aspirations to advancement in English politics, I am sorry,

Lily. That still is his choice. By marrying to further himself, he needs to pay the price if she is not the woman he really wanted." He consciously loosened his jaw. "He left you to suffer the consequences of the failed elopement in a very public way that has hurt you. I find it inordinately hard to forgive."

"He did it because in his own way, he loves me."

That admittedly made no sense whatsoever to him. Jonathan leveled a hard stare in his sister's direction, their horses moving along the path, the slight splash of their passage nearly the only sound on this damp morning. "Female logic tends to escape me. I'm finding that more and more. How does a man show his love for a woman by persuading her to run off with him, spending the night at an inn and thereby destroying her reputation, and then blithely refusing to marry her?"

She bit her lower lip, white teeth digging into the tender flesh, and then she returned his look in fair measure. "Your word this is between us."

That sounded serious enough. In exasperation, he said, "As if I would ever reveal a confidence, Lily. We may not have a lifetime of acquaintance, but surely you know that much about me. Of course."

"I'm not worried for myself. I am worried for Arthur's sake."

What the devil is going on? Why would she worry about the blackguard?

Haltingly, she continued. "It wasn't blithely at all that he changed his mind and brought me back to London. We intended to marry . . . but he had second thoughts. In the end, he didn't marry me because our friendship was deep enough he couldn't do that to me."

This was about as clear as a thick London morning fog. Jonathan asked bluntly, "Do what to you? What is worse than ruining and then jilting you?"

There was a slight pause and the expression on her face was strained. "That night at the inn . . . he told me finally . . . he confessed he doesn't really like women . . . *that* way."

Jonathan was hardly unworldly, and he understood at last what she meant. There were men who preferred men. It wasn't as unusual as most people pretended, but certainly not a usual topic of conversation, and he just didn't know what to say to his younger sister. Picturing such a disillusioning disclosure when she had sacrificed so much was difficult. Whatever he'd expected, it wasn't quite that particular explanation. "I'm sorry," he finally murmured.

"So was I," she responded, her voice muted, "especially after I'd agreed to elope with him. I think he believed that because we'd become such good friends, it could perhaps work. The belated fit of conscience, however, is still appreciated and probably only happened because we genuinely liked each other. What if I'd married him—which I would have—and found out later about his . . . inclinations? I'd rather be ruined."

"Which," Jonathan said slowly, "you are not in a literal sense, I take it, in light of this new information."

"No. He didn't touch me. From the way I understand it, he didn't even want to."

Surely a devastating realization for a young woman in love. Jonathan felt a fresh surge of anger wash over him at the bleak tone of her voice. "You've taken the brunt of this."

"No." She shook her head, her expression drawn but not angry. "Jonathan, think about it. He could have never told me and married me. Yes, it took some courage to face that my life had changed forever, but not nearly as much as it took for him to tell me the truth before it was too late. He gave me a choice. I chose infamy rather than living with a man who would never love or desire me except as a friend."

He tried to imagine marrying a woman who did not want his attentions, and a bit of his anger eased as he saw her point. Still, his voice was terse. "He married anyway."

"A completely different arrangement. She coveted his title."

"That excuses it?" He guided Seneca around a dripping oak.

"I'm not sure." Lillian's mouth tightened. "How can I judge either of them? But this I do know—he *thought* he was giving her what she wanted. I desired something far different from him than just becoming Lady Sebring. I wanted a husband who loved me in a romantic way, and he knew I would be devastated when I sensed the truth."

Now that the picture had gone from blurry into crystal clear focus, Jonathan did think he understood her decision and her insistence that they keep the family name off the forked tongues of the gossips. Not to mention her reluctance to rejoin society.

She didn't trust men.

He didn't blame her. First her would-be fiancé had betrayed her, and then her father had died and left her future in the hands of a half brother she barely knew who lived an ocean away. "You must have told Father the truth."

"Yes." The answer was very quiet. "I had no choice, for he insisted that I marry Arthur and I had to give the reason for my refusal. In the end, he agreed with me. I suppose to a certain extent it was because he'd been so very in love with your mother and then experienced a much less happy existence with my mother, who married him for much the same reason Arthur's wife became Lady Sebring."

Unfortunately, that was true as far as Jonathan knew. His stepmother had been beautiful, sophisticated, and extremely accepting of her husband's long absences when he visited America. His father had never said much, but Jonathan always had the impression that except for his three daughters, his father regretted his loveless second marriage.

This was the point—as her guardian, Jonathan should reassure Lillian that all would be well and that she would fall passionately in love again, but both of those were out of his control. What he could do is promise to do his best to see to her future.

The sun peeked out from behind the clouds again, sending gilded light down onto the path and illuminating the droplets of rain like tiny crystals in the clipped grass. He asked, "What is it you want, Lily? Tell me."

"Someone," she said on an audible exhale, "with no secrets."

He laughed, but it was with sympathy. "A male who has no indiscretions he doesn't care to disclose? I'm afraid that is probably close to impossible, but there are secrets and then there are secrets like Lord Sebring's. Considering his position and title, I can see why he strives to make sure no one knows. He's hardly alone in his inclinations, as you put it, but let me assure you most men are interested only in women. I am not judging him, simply stating the truth. Obviously you still value him as a friend, and he must also think of you in the same way or he wouldn't have come to see you last evening."

She nodded, but her blue eyes, so like their father's, were haunted. "His wife might be barren."

"Ah, I see. The English nobility and their everlasting quest for a direct line of succession." He couldn't help the slight sardonic tone of his voice. "I am going to guess his enthusiasm for the task of impregnating his wife was

low to begin with, so continued failure brought along
with it considerable personal unhappiness."

"Can you see," Lillian said with perfect pragmatic
emphasis, "why I am glad I am not her?"

He could. His past with Caroline had also been less
than perfect. What had started out as a lighthearted evening of seduction with no plans for any future had resulted in a child. Once she'd delivered Adela, his former
lover had also never once asked about their daughter's
well-being nor had she contacted him. She hadn't even
inquired as to what he would name her.

For himself he didn't care so much. For Addie, who
would one day have questions, he wasn't quite sure what
he felt, but he did know at least one of the emotions was
outrage on her behalf. At least he'd had loving parents.
Both of them.

"I had an unsatisfactory experience when it came to
Addie's mother," he admitted.

"As awful as mine?" Lillian sent him a wry sidelong
glance.

"The story is not the same, but I would say it certainly
could compare when you consider the ramifications."

It had been a relief to tell the truth.

Lillian wasn't even sure what had prompted her to
confide in her brother except maybe that though it startled her, she was coming to like him. After a lifetime of
resenting his very existence, it was oddly comforting to
come to the realization that he was not just the foreign
heir, the beloved son from the beloved marriage, but
maybe also a person she could both like and trust.

She needed to talk to someone and she'd chosen Jonathan. That of itself was enough to give her pause and
reassess some parts of her life, but he'd also not been
horrified or disgusted. Instead he simply rode next to

her, so comfortable on his big horse that he looked a part of the animal, his dark hair loose on his shoulders this damp morning, his face thoughtful.

"I do now understand your choice," he said slowly, his long-fingered hands unmoving on the pommel of his saddle, since his well-trained horse never visibly needed direction. "Thank you for telling me."

Four years ago she'd decided she did not need another male besides her father to direct her life—not when the one she'd chosen had bungled it so badly, but there was a measure of relief in shifting a little of the burden to her brother's broad shoulders. Lillian merely watched the slight movement of the wet leaves in the breeze as they rode past a copse of trees. "I am not certain why I just did it, but perhaps I needed to tell someone."

"You do not need to be so rigidly independent."

"Don't I?' she countered. "Were you betrayed by your fiancée and then left orphaned?"

"I lost my mother at a very early age," he replied in an offhand voice, "and have experienced my entire life the stigma of belonging only halfway to two very different cultures, not entirely accepted by either. I can say with fair certainty that I understand being ostracized."

It was a valid enough argument she had no retort, witty and flippant or otherwise.

Jonathan said nothing as they approached the river path. Then, as if all he wished to do was confound her this dreary morning, he said quietly, "I wish we'd known each other earlier in our lives. It's entirely my fault, I'm afraid. I refused to come to England to visit more than once or twice. Father requested it often, but I was obstinate in the face of his patience, and to his credit, he didn't ever chastise me for my opposition. I hope it is not too late to admit to you I regret it now."

As hard as it had been to confess her past, it was

much easier to accept his apology. She'd not been exactly gracious upon his arrival either, and he'd overlooked the animosity. Dryly, Lillian said, "I understand being obstinate. We do not look alike, but we are obviously related."

"Obviously." His laugh was soft.

"Betsy told me there are whispers that you are going to be betrothed to the Duke of Eddington's youngest daughter." She sent him a swift sidelong glance to try to gauge his expression.

"It's true."

"That's unexpected."

"I agree." His handsome face was impassive. "My plans were quite different."

"What changed them?"

"I can't say anything with confidence that would be the right answer. She caught my attention—how's that?"

Lillian hadn't met the beautiful Lady Cecily, but even if she no longer went about in society, she still read the gossip columns. "I understand she is very blond and very lovely."

"I agree with both descriptions."

"Are you going to tell me *anything*?"

"No." A faint smile graced his mouth. "Except that this will not be a long engagement."

Which actually told her quite a lot. It made her slightly ashamed she'd never considered his happiness at all. It seemed an abstract concept—she'd just assumed that being the Earl of Augustine, inheriting a fortune, and having every male privilege, would make anyone happy.

Except that title and wealth had certainly not made Arthur happy. Nor, when he'd arrived in England, had it made her brother happy either judging from his initial demeanor and impatience. It had taken a woman to achieve that change.

So money and status were not everything. . . . She already had learned that lesson as the disgraced daughter of an earl. One could be rich and miserable. One could be beautiful and shunned. It hadn't been the easiest journey, but she had reconciled the reality. "Congratulations."

"Thank you."

Had it not been for her own harsh experience she would have berated him for his silence on this courtship, but she could hardly fault him.

Instead she could be quietly happy for him . . . and she was. She nudged her horse closer and reached into her pocket. "I think this belongs to you. Addie found it and was anxious you should have it back."

He looked at the stone in her gloved palm. "I had wondered what had happened to it."

"Addie says it is magic." She sent him a mischievous smile.

"I can attest it is." In contrast, his response seemed quite sincere.

"Then how did you lose it?"

"I'm not sure how I dropped it. Perhaps the spirits felt their work was done with me. They must have wanted you to have it. Please keep it, Lily."

Her fingers curled back around the small polished stone even as she reminded herself she didn't believe in whatever spirits he was referring too.

Jonathan said quietly, "I'm serious. Keep it with you and fate may surprise you."

It was an interesting idea, certainly, and even though she hardly credited a bit of stone with the same power he did, it was thoughtful of him. "Thank you." With a sudden mischievous smile, she said, "I hadn't quite imagined Earl Savage marrying a proper English lady."

Jonathan grinned back, his dark eyes gleaming. "She might not be as proper as you think."

"Haven't you colonials heard? Many of us English ladies are not," she replied with a laugh and a lofty lift of her brows. "I'll race you to the river." And then she kicked her mare into a gallop regardless of the wet path, swerving in front of his horse, intent on winning this impromptu challenge.

For the sake of English ladies everywhere, if for nothing else. And perhaps the absurd gift worked, for regardless of his horse's superior size, she made it to the Serpentine a nose ahead.

Chapter 21

"For a man who just discovered that an entire portion of his mining operation has been shut down due to deliberate sabotage, not to mention who is about to have what I suspect will be a difficult interview with the father of the woman he hopes will be his intended bride, you are remarkably cheerful."

Jonathan gave his cousin an ironic look. "On the opposite side of the equation, may I point out that Cecily has accepted my proposal of marriage, and as far as the mining problem goes, like most minor disasters, it can be repaired and remarkably no one was hurt. It is not a significant amount of my wealth anyway."

"Browne threatened me when I dismissed him. I admit I was a bit surprised. He's a quiet and self-effacing man upon first impression and I'd been dealing with him for nearly a year."

It did seem logical enough that the former business manager might be responsible for the fire and the damaged equipment, but they had no proof. "Would he go so far?"

James frowned, sprawled on the opposite seat of the carriage. "I wouldn't have thought so, but we know for certain he was embezzling and your father had left in his notes that he was beginning to suspect him as well. He was certainly the first person the foreman for the mine named in the missive he sent me."

It was irritating to imagine deliberate malice, but at that moment they pulled up to the ducal mansion and Jonathan's attention was diverted to what might be one of the most important interviews of his life. "Send a note," he said as a footman opened the door of the carriage, "and post several guards at the mine to make sure the repairs aren't sabotaged." Then he grinned. "And wish me luck."

Moments later he was being shown once more into the Duke of Eddington's study and offered a drink and a chair with polite chilliness.

"Our solicitors will contact each other then." The Duke of Eddington said the words without any audible emotion and regarded him with heavy-lidded eyes, his face revealing neither satisfaction nor disapproval. "Once the details of the marriage agreement are settled, we can discuss a date for the wedding."

This time Jonathan had accepted a brandy and he swirled the gold liquid in an idle movement, choosing his words carefully. "There's no need to wait. I have no intention of bargaining over something as personal as my marriage. I don't need your money, and whatever Cecily wants she can have. I'm a rich man. The contract can be done this afternoon in the time it takes for your solicitors to draw it up and us to sign it."

"You don't even know the amount of her dowry, Augustine. Keep in mind a man can never be too rich," his future father-in-law said with cool intonation.

Having Cecily as his wife would be more than enough compensation for giving up his life as an unattached male. Moreover, now that he'd bedded her, he knew he would be scaling the wall of the ducal mansion on a constant basis if forced to wait months for a formal wedding ceremony. And who was to say she couldn't be pregnant already? One night was more than enough to conceive a child. Adela's existence was proof enough of that.

"Perhaps not, but nothing about my wanting to marry your daughter is about wealth or position."

"Very diplomatically said."

"The honest truth." Jonathan met his gaze squarely. "With your permission granted, we were hoping for a quiet wedding within the next few weeks. I'll obtain a special license." With a possible pregnancy looming, he felt his future wife would agree. He smiled to ease the moment. "I have already admitted to Cecily I am not a very patient man."

Behind his desk, the duke sighed and rubbed his temple. "And according to my son, my normally levelheaded daughter is inclined to less than prudent behavior when it comes to you. As in leaving a social event alone with a young man without a chaperone and being gone a conspicuous length of time. I am informed that from the moment the two of you met there has been a flirtation with scandal."

Had Jonathan been able to deny it, he might have, but the man was perfectly right. "I would never purposely damage her reputation, Your Grace."

"Is that a warning or an observation, Lord Augustine?" The duke lifted a hand, palm out. "You do not have to answer the question. Her grandmother will not approve if I agree to this, but I think I should. I would like to state here and now that I firmly believe arranged marriages are much simpler than the kind where feelings are involved."

"Your position on the matter is duly noted." Jonathan did his best not to look triumphant, for truly he'd thought he would have a much harder time persuading Cecily's father to agree to a swift wedding.

He finished his brandy and rose. "I won't take up any

more of your time, Your Grace. When the papers are ready, send them over."

"It will be taken care of. Oh, yes—" The duke picked up a thick cream-colored envelope. "I am instructed to give this to you. It is from my mother. An invitation to a country party, I believe, for your entire family. Poetic justice, if you ask me, for if the dowager duchess is displeased with you over your haste to wed her granddaughter, she can express it to you in person. And if I know my mother, she will."

For his entire family? That sounded promising. While Carole and Betsy seemed to be doing well enough as far as attentive young gentlemen, he was most concerned about Lily. Jonathan said, "We accept, of course, with pleasure."

"Tell me if you still feel that way after the experience. I myself will not be going." The duke paused, lifting his brandy glass. "And by the way, Augustine, my bedroom faces the gardens and I rise very early. I thank you for not landing on my prize rosebushes upon your departure this morning. The gardener tells me there were no footprints either. Someday you must tell me how you accomplished it."

At a moment like this, silence certainly seemed to be the best course. With an inner curse, Jonathan reminded himself he'd known he should have left right after Cecily had drifted to sleep. But he'd enjoyed holding her, the lissome weight of her body in his arms, the light caress of her breath across his bare chest. Instead of speaking, he simply lifted his brows in an acknowledgment that was best left unsaid.

"If you weren't so intent on marrying her, I would have taken much greater offense, I assure you." Cecily's father's voice was lethally soft. "I've no doubt she welcomed you, and that also kept me from requesting a meeting at dawn on the field instead of this one. If you make her happy, that is atonement enough, but I do expect it."

Being fairly caught out rankled, but Jonathan gave a short bow. "You have my word that is my intention."

"I'll hold you to it," the Duke of Eddington said without equivocation. "I love my daughter."

"So do I." With that, Jonathan left the duke's study.

It was far more than he had intended to say.

He was afraid it was the perfect truth.

Her fiancé's entrance into the drawing room resembled a predatory tiger strolling in, but then again, she'd never seen that, so Cecily could only make the comparison based on a vague idea of what it would be like to have a large, dangerous animal come toward her.

Surely it was similar. He looked too tall for the space, entirely too wild for the sophisticated surroundings, and his exotic beauty was a contrast to the pale satin-lined walls and elegant furniture. Jonathan stepped toward her, took into account her grandmother and sister, and then halted, his mouth twitching in a rueful smile. "Good afternoon, ladies."

He had a mesmerizing mouth. She could remember it warm against her lips . . . and in other places that elicited a less than ladylike response, but if she thought of that now, she'd blush furiously and that would never do. Cecily rose and formally offered her hand. "Good afternoon, my lord."

Jonathan bent over her fingers in perfect politesse, but as usual he never quite managed to look entirely civilized. He straightened and looked into her eyes in that unique intense way he had. The way that made something interesting happen to the pit of her stomach. "I believe, Lady Cecily, we are now officially betrothed."

"I assume, then," her grandmother said in her most commanding voice, "that you will be joining us this weekend?"

Only her grandmother would think her potential guests would drop everything to whisk off to the countryside at such short notice—though, Cecily had to concede, several acceptances had already arrived that very morning. When the Duchess of Eddington summoned, society answered.

Jonathan bowed as gracefully as any court sycophant, but his dark eyes held a hint of cynical amusement over the regal delivery of the question. "We will most definitely attend, Your Grace."

"We will expect Lady Lillian, you understand."

There was *definitely* a glint of humor in his dark eyes over the outright order. "I am sure she will be delighted to be your guest."

"At least I will not be the only spinster there," Eleanor said with her usual candor. "Tell her Grandmama's edicts aside, she must come so we can keep each other company."

It was clear that Jonathan had no idea what to say to that remark, and truly, Cecily knew it wasn't self-pity at all; it was just how Elle saw the situation. Coming to his rescue, she said, "Shall we take a short walk in the garden? Now that the sun has come out, it is a lovely day."

"We do have a few matters to discuss." He offered his arm.

"A short walk," her grandmother emphasized, upright in her chair, "as you are not yet married."

But Cecily saw a telltale shimmer in the older woman's eyes that belied the scolding tone of her voice and yielded to impulse and went over to give her a hug. "We will be the model of discretion; do not worry, Grandmama."

"Humph."

As they exited the room, she saw out of the corner of her eye her grandmother tug a handkerchief from her sleeve.

"Model of discretion?" Jonathan repeated with lifted brows as they went down the long, polished hallway to where French doors opened to the formal back garden. "I am not sure, my lady, that is possible." His voice dropped in timbre. "Last evening comes to mind. That is why I petitioned your father to agree to a very short engagement and a special license. I realize if we choose that course, it will keep you from planning an elaborate celebration."

He opened the door and she stepped out into the warm afternoon air, her emotions wavering from elation to trepidation. Things were moving very fast as it was, and she'd just adjusted to the idea of actually marrying him. When she'd initiated this plan to prevent an engagement to Lord Drury, she hadn't quite anticipated the recent turn in events. It wasn't as if she didn't *wish* to marry him, but the notion of doing it so soon was a bit startling. Then again, he was correct. They'd not been discreet, and she doubted the word was actually in her volatile husband-to-be's vocabulary.

The sky above was clear blue with just a few wispy clouds, and though the leaves of the bushes still glistened with moisture, the air was light and warm. Cecily took a moment before she answered, and Jonathan let her have it, saying nothing more, the only sound their footsteps on the flagstone path and the twitter of the birds. The fragrance of blooming flowers was heady, the brilliant blossoms still beaded with jeweled droplets of rain. Then she nodded. "I have never harbored dreams of a grandiose wedding. I know some women do, but quite honestly I do not like being the center of attention, so a small intimate ceremony is more to my taste anyway."

"We are in accord then. For my part, expeditious holds a very potent appeal."

The husky note in his voice brought a blush of warmth to her skin, as if he'd touched her, though their only contact at the moment was the light resting of her fingers on his coat sleeve. "After last night . . ."

When she trailed off, he sent her a heated glance. "A night that will be enshrined in my memory forever. After last night, what?"

Dare she really be so bold? She was not nearly as outspoken as Eleanor, but maybe part of what appealed to her so much about Jonathan was that because he didn't hold so tightly to convention and strict protocol, she could just be herself. "After last night I don't want to wait either. Does that make me wanton?"

"No." His smile was slow and sure and purely masculine. "It makes you more desirable than ever, which is going quite a distance. How the devil am I going to survive this weekend? Please tell me your bedroom will be easily accessible and not involve ivy-covered walls."

Her skirts brushed a low-hanging rosebush and sent a flurry of droplets across the silk, but she didn't care. "I am sure we can work out a very *discreet* arrangement, my lord."

"Or a very indiscreet one," he said wryly. "Your father apparently glimpsed me departing this morning."

That was unsettling. Cecily had no idea how to feel about her august father knowing she'd had a gentleman—if Jonathan even qualified—in her bedroom until dawn. "My sister knows, too," she informed him. "She came to the door. . . . She evidently heard your voice."

"I believe it is expedient that we marry then, since we cannot seem to meet secretly." He stopped by a sheltering rhododendron and pulled her into his arms. The kiss was tantalizing, long, and evoked memories of forbidden pleasure.

No, he did not bring the traditional posies or write poems, nor would she ever picture him doing so, but there was *sentimentally* romantic, she was discovering, and *sensually* romantic, and the two were not at all the same.

He was not a smooth, polished aristocrat, and she doubted he ever would be.

It seemed she didn't want an urbane, sophisticated English gentleman.

She wanted *him*.

She kissed him back. When their mouths parted, she murmured, "I was not the one who snuck into my bedroom."

"You were the one who moaned when I—"

"That's enough," she interrupted and kissed him again, this time with her own urgency.

"I disagree," he murmured against her lips. "It isn't enough. With you, will it ever be enough?"

As his arms tightened around her, Cecily couldn't help but press closer, moved by the emotion in his voice, her body intimately enough against his that she could feel his growing arousal. "I believe I just promised my grandmother we would be the soul of propriety. Hopefully none of the gardening staff are anywhere nearby."

"*I* didn't promise her anything," he said and kissed her again with unmistakable hunger.

But the realities were what they were. Making love in the ducal garden was not an option, so now that it was all settled, when a few heated moments later she suggested they go back inside, with obvious reluctance, he agreed.

After all, the weekend looked to be quite interesting.

Chapter 22

It was absurd, but he might actually be . . . nervous.

The realization hit Jonathan with a mixture of amusement and self-derision, but in his defense, it was important that his daughter and the woman who had consented to become his wife like each other. Addie had never had a mother, and he did not know whether the idea of sharing his usually undivided attention for the first time would please her or shake her small world. There was little question that to compensate for Caroline's complete absence in his child's life, he'd done his best to offer her everything he could.

Cecily, also, was going to have to accept his daughter unconditionally, and that was asking quite a lot.

Add to the weekend the plethora of females that he had to deal with, including one grandiose duchess, three sisters, and a soon-to-be sister-in-law . . .

That was enough to fray any man's nerves, he consoled to himself as the carriage rolled to a halt.

He opened the door—he rarely waited for the footman; he knew he should, but then again, his consequence was a position that held only superficial meaning to him, not a conscious state of mind—and he lifted Addie out, her face alight with joy at both the end of the journey and the rather awe-inspiring and stately facade of Eddington Manor. It was one of those sprawling Elizabethan country houses built of gray stone, with a series of fountains bordering the steps, the park huge and immaculately kept, the drive a graceful sweep under an arched portico carved with the family coat of arms.

"Our house is big, Papa," his daughter whispered confidentially, "but I am not sure it is *this* big."

She was more than pretty in a small dainty gown Lily had selected in a girlish shade of pink, her dark hair tied back neatly, her eyes wide.

"I am not sure the royal palace is this big," he said with a wry smile, taking her small hand. "But houses are only stones and bits of wood. It is the people inside that matter."

As if to punctuate his words, Cecily came out the front door then, a slender figure in ivory muslin trimmed with blue satin ribbon, her hair in a simple chignon.

She's been waiting for me. . . .

The realization made him smile, a rush of emotion tightening his throat as he watched her rapidly descend the steps, her skirts lifted slightly, the sun gilding her hair. "I was concerned," she said a little breathlessly, her gaze riveted not on him but on Addie. "Your sisters arrived an hour ago."

"Yes, well, we had to stop more frequently, which is why I sent them on in a separate carriage." He took her hand and kissed it, his mouth lingering a moment too long for propriety, and then turned. "Lady Cecily, may I present Lady Adela."

Addie did a fair curtsy and Cecily said softly, "I am very glad to meet you."

The look in her eyes asked if he'd told Addie yet about their engagement, and he slightly shook his head before reaching into the carriage, scooping up a small ball of fur curled on the seat as the dratted dog had been a bundle of energy the entire journey and then had the nerve to fall asleep when they rumbled into the driveway. "This," he said dryly, "is why we had to stop so often."

The puppy gave out an excited little bark and Addie laughed with delight as he scrambled around her feet in wide circles. "His name is Adonis," she told Cecily with a dimpled smile.

"I . . . see." Cecily obviously was stifling laughter as she assessed his less than perfect pedigree, which no doubt included a motley crew of ancestors.

"He was a Greek god." Addie had all the earnestness of a five-year-old. "Aunt Lily and I have been reading stories."

"Indeed." Though her mouth twitched, Cecily added, "He's very handsome, so it is appropriate. Shall we take him for a walk in the gardens before we go inside?"

"Papa said he has to stay in the stables."

Jonathan ignored the imploring look sent his way, for as far as he was concerned, after that carriage ride, he'd suffered a great deal more than Adonis would for having to nap on a bed of straw. "We agreed the only way he could come along was if he was kept out of the house. I doubt the duke would approve of him napping on a silk-covered settee or an expensive rug, and though he is improving, I do not want to be constantly apologizing for his little mishaps."

"Perhaps a compromise can be worked out." Cecily extended her hand. "Shall we?"

She and Jonathan exchanged a look then, poignant with emotion, and as he watched his daughter and future wife walk away together, the ridiculous little dog scampering between them, he decided this gathering might just be a grand success after all.

What a dismal failure.

Or rather *she* was a dismal failure. A much more accurate observation.

It wasn't like she'd really had grandiose illusions of what the weekend party would bring—Eleanor had been disabused of those last season as she'd watched with almost detached enlightenment as her social star—which had launched nicely—sank lower and lower in the brilliant sky, but if she was willing to admit it, deep down in her cursed romantic soul, she'd rather hoped this event might go better.

So far it could be termed, at least for her, a disaster.

For one thing, she decided as she sat in a chair sipping lemonade on the back terrace of Eddington Hall, it was clear that Elijah Winters wasn't going to attend the party. Carriages had begun to roll in just before luncheon and it was now late afternoon. She didn't really blame him, and she hadn't been able to think of a way to ask her grandmother if he'd even been invited. Her one attempt to casually bring up the guest list had been met with the cryptic reply that anyone her grandmother deemed important had been included.

It was all somewhat disheartening, but then again, Cecily was happy—of that there was no doubt—so Eleanor's personal disquiet was not as important. The morning had been spent debating over what gown Cecily would wear for her fiancé's arrival and Eleanor had offered advice with good-natured sisterly wisdom and found it amusing to see her sibling, who was usually the modicum of poise and self-reserve, in such a fluster. Personally Eleanor doubted the earl cared one way or the other what her sister wore, he was so smitten.

No, *smitten* didn't really fit the untamable Augustine. He was so . . . so . . .

"Would you mind if I join you?"

Her gaze swerved up.

It seemed Lord Drury had decided to make an appearance after all.

Blond hair waved back from a face that might be considered austere except for the almost always evident good humor in his blue eyes. His cravat was perfectly tied, his coat a dark brown in contrast to his fawn breeches, polished Hessians hugging muscular calves. To her dismay, Eleanor sat up so quickly she splashed some lemonade on the hem of her gown.

She had an embarrassing habit of doing that in his presence, but at least this time she'd done it to herself. "Oh."

"I'm rather late." Lord Drury indicated a nearby chair and pretended not to notice her clumsiness. "May I sit? Everyone else, it seems, is either napping, participating in archery, or out for an afternoon ride."

He also had a glass of lemonade, though his held a suspicious brown tinge as if maybe it had been spiked with a bit of whiskey.

Her grandmother *was* the consummate hostess.

"Of course, I do not mind." Had she refused any eligible bachelor the adjoining chair, her grandmother would have had her head.

And *him* . . . well, there was the small matter of how her heart had begun a quick, treacherous pounding.

"I loathe archery." He sank down in an opposite chair by a small glass-topped table and crossed his elegantly booted ankles. "I can't stand to waste away my afternoon sleeping, and neither was I in the mood for a cross-country amble."

"I didn't know you'd arrived."

His smile was wry. "I was delayed by business. I debated over coming at all, I confess."

"I understand very well." She stared out at the massive park, the stately trees and clipped grass a sight she well remembered from her childhood. "Country parties are a bore, aren't they?"

There was a brilliant line. He would fall instantly in love with her over that one.

His good-looking face was bland. "They can be. But we both know that is not what I meant."

"Yes."

Lord . . . surely she could do better . . . except, in her case, she was much better off not saying anything at all.

Or was she? Eleanor took some heart in that he'd come and joined her. For that matter, that he'd bothered to come to the gathering at all, for while it was hosted by her grandmother and was a coveted invitation, there was surely a bitter edge to it for him, since everyone in attendance knew Cecily had accepted Jonathan Bourne instead of him.

Maybe all he wanted was a sympathetic ear. She said frankly, "I don't think I would have attended were I in your position. I'm surprised you did."

Elijah's brows went up. "And I'm surprised it took you so long to voice that surprise. How long have I been here?" He pulled out his watch and theatrically looked at it. "A minute? Why the delay?"

Was that an insult? She couldn't be sure. No, she decided, he would never insult her, and besides, there was just the smallest tilt to the corner of his lips. "I'm not being critical, I just—"

"You are too kind to be critical," he interrupted, relaxed in his chair, his hands resting on the arms and his gaze on the trees in the park, their shadows oblong on the mown grass. "You are honest. It is different, Eleanor."

No, not an insult; a compliment. She should be beyond maidenly blushes, but her cheeks held a sudden, peculiar warmth at his use of her first name so informally. "Thank you."

He didn't look at her, seemingly intent on the peaceful vista stretched out before them. The archery tournament was on the west lawn, far enough away that the participants were mere figures in the distance. "I don't suppose it will sound very logical, but I think your sister represented to me an ideal that doesn't exactly exist, which she proved to be true."

Though normally she would have asked him what he meant, Eleanor with effort refrained, because with a brother and a father, she'd at least learned that when men wished to discuss their feelings—which did not happen often—it was best not to intrude on the moment. The less said, the better.

"Cecily is undeniably beautiful, but also I found her understated manner to be what I thought I might like in a wife."

There truly was no reply to that statement, so she didn't try. In fact, despite the glass of lemonade she'd been sipping, Eleanor found her mouth was quite dry.

"But," Lord Drury said with equanimity, his face bland, "perhaps I was wrong. It's clear she isn't nearly as reserved as I believed, so maybe my approach to all this is flawed. I am obviously not as astute as I thought I was."

If he wanted reserved, he didn't want her, so Eleanor also just pretended interest in the amateur archery competition. "I think, my lord, that often what we perceive as an ideal might be more fantasy than reality. Human beings are in general flawed, but when you contemplate the matter, it is part of our capricious charm. If someone is predictable, are they not by the very definition of that term dull? I do understand a gentleman wanting decorum in his wife, but asking for predictability is sentencing oneself to a life of complete boredom."

A long-winded speech, but she felt better for delivering it.

For she meant every emphatic word of it.

Out in the grass, a small bird fluttered down, hopped about, and then flew off. They both watched it as if it were a fascinating feat of nature. "You have a point," he finally drawled in his cultured voice. "I rarely view introspection as a good idea, but lately I have been asking myself a few pertinent questions."

"Such as?" Maybe she shouldn't have asked, but after all, she'd been sitting by herself and *he'd* joined *her*.

Elijah looked at her. Directly. Actually, *very* directly. "I suppose I wondered how important the impressions of society were to my own. Propriety is all well and good, but ultimately, surely a satisfactory relationship is between the two people involved and no one else. Deferring to popular opinion is tempting, of course, since it takes courage to do otherwise."

It would be best if at this point she kept her opinion to herself, but she had never done all that well with that course of action. "I agree with that view."

"It made me ponder that I've maybe taken the wrong road this season. Perhaps last season as well."

Dare she ask it? Last season. Did he mean her? Dare she inquire why though she'd felt their friendship growing, he had suddenly cooled in his attentions and backed away?

No. She didn't have enough courage.

Or did she?

What was there to lose anyway?

"What did I say to offend you last year?" She paused and took a breath before she rushed on. "I might be wrong and you never felt any interest in me at all, but I thought maybe you did. . . . I hoped. Then suddenly you no longer spoke to me except with excruciating politeness. Something happened, and truthfully, I have thought about it almost every single day and am still mystified."

He didn't answer at once, and Eleanor stilled her now trembling hands against her skirts, reminding herself that in the end it didn't matter what he said. In some measure she'd given him a disgust of her, and so be it. Knowing exactly how she'd come about doing it might be enlightening, but it repaired nothing.

Lord Drury took a sip of lemonade and cleared his throat. "I am ashamed to say it out loud."

Ashamed? The oddness of that declaration made her simply stare at him.

"You conversed about Miss Austen's novel with a depth of understanding about how it so skillfully represented English society one evening and then debated the new Corn Laws in the same conversation with a fluent ease and expertise that made me wonder if my modest interests in literature and politics would bore you."

Whatever she'd expected him to say, it wasn't *that*.

"So you see, maybe I am one of the grievous dullards you so disdain."

Before she thought, Eleanor said, "Cecily disdains them too."

"Thank you for reminding me. She is marrying someone else, so you are no doubt telling the truth." His smile held cynical humor. "I think this entire endeavor has forced me to examine my life a little closer."

"And what did you come up with, my lord?"

"How is it I knew you would ask me that?"

"Because you are acquainted with my tendency to speak my mind." There was a hint of rueful honesty in her reply, but then again, it was the truth.

Yet he answered. "I suppose I am." He paused. "I believe women find me pleasant. I know I try to be. Physically I am not repulsive—"

"Far from it." She said it with too much conviction and, as a result, blushed.

He smiled at the vehement interruption. "Thank you. In any case, it is all very well to be well mannered and pleasing to look at, but I am conservative to a fault, and my interests, if I look closely at them, are superficial at best. I am passionate about nothing."

"Whereas I am passionate about everything." Eleanor grimaced. "One is no doubt as bad as the other."

"Indeed. I agree. So I've come to the conclusion that perhaps I have been going about all of this the wrong way."

"All of what?"

"What I thought was a reasonable approach to a sensible marriage."

His reply made her look at him, raising her gaze from where it had fastened on the tips of her slippers. There was still telltale warmth in her cheeks. "Is there such a thing as a sensible marriage, my lord? By virtue of the intrinsic meaning of the phrase, it seems impossible. Romance cannot be sensible, for that takes any semblance of romance out of it."

"I wasn't speaking of romance." He took a hearty sip from his glass of lemonade and muttered, "I was talking about a suitable arrangement between a man and a woman, and that *is* possible, or at least in the world I thought I lived in it was."

"You thought you lived in?" Eleanor elevated her brows.

"The one in which a man reached a certain age and decided it was time to select a wife and set up his nursery because he has an obligation to his title and family name to do so."

"I am perishing to know the criteria males have established to define *suitable*, for considering *my* unmarried status, it is obvious I am lacking in some way."

It happened again. His gaze strayed downward, just

briefly, a flicker of a glance. "You are not lacking, Lady Eleanor."

"I wasn't talking about my bosom."

Amazingly enough, he laughed at her frankness. "Neither was I, but do I have to beg forgiveness for noticing you are particularly fetching in that shade of blue?"

It took some effort to avoid pointing out that she doubted he'd really been admiring her gown, but she *did* refrain. "No forgiveness required, but I am finding this conversation fascinating. So, since you stated you think you've been going about finding a wife the wrong way with the sensible approach; may I ask how you are going to solve this thorny problem?"

He looked into her eyes. "If, as you say, there is no such thing as a sensible romance, perhaps I am going to toss logic to the four winds and court a woman who amuses me, whom I find physically attractive, and with whom I can converse freely, never mind whether or not she is a model of decorum. One who might even be able to teach me something about . . . passion. Do you have any suggestions as to whom I might choose, Lady Eleanor?"

Being an engaged lady had its merits, that was for certain, and the provincial lifestyle of the countryside also had an appeal. Not the least of which was that when she and Jonathan went for a late-afternoon ride, they were truly alone.

How delightful it was going to be, Cecily mused, taking in the sunshine, the sweet fragrance of the clean air, the bucolic setting of pasture and woodlands, to have a new freedom that had been denied her all her life. First nannies, and then a succession of governesses, to be replaced with chaperones; she'd been shadowed her entire existence. "This is lovely."

"*You* are certainly lovely," her companion murmured,

his glossy dark hair gleaming under the sun, his coat casually draped over his saddle, his cravat discarded, a glimpse of a bronzed chest visible through the neck of his partially unbuttoned shirt. Their horses walked side by side down a wide path usually taken by the cows grazing in the pasture beyond.

"Thank you. However, I was referring to the freedom."

"I dislike the city as well."

"That isn't what I meant."

His quizzical sidelong glance clearly stated he did not quite understand.

Familiar with how males took for granted the privilege they enjoyed, she clarified. "I could not normally ride alone with you."

His dark eyes took on a singular sensual glimmer. "For fear I might take unforgivable liberties?"

"But as you are going to soon be my husband—"

"Very soon."

"It is allowed," she finished her sentence.

"I interpret that as being given oblique permission to take said liberties."

"I think your misspent youth is asserting itself, Lord Augustine," she replied, her tone teasing. "That was not implied at all. What was implied was that you are honorable enough to be trusted to ride out with me without a chaperone because you have already offered to wed me."

"*Honor* is a flexible term, isn't it? The English sense of it isn't quite the same as mine, I'm afraid." He moved his horse close enough that his leg brushed her skirts as he gazed at the lazy bend of the river ahead of them, the water slow and clear.

Yes, he *was* honorable. A man who would never neglect his daughter, no matter the circumstances of her birth. He clearly adored her. She said, "Addie is delightful."

"Most of the time." His smile was indulgent. "Even the most doting father cannot say she is perfect. But she does have a glowing outlook on life that is contagious. That mongrel she has adopted is proof that she looks at the world with a predisposition toward benevolence. I think he was not only the smallest of the litter, but the least attractive specimen. It was love at first sight."

As lightly as possible, Cecily said, "I don't doubt the existence of that phenomenon."

Instead of addressing the comment, he gazed at the clear water. "Tell me, do you swim?"

How could he even ask that question? Proper young ladies were not supposed to learn how to swim, mostly because they were not allowed to shed enough clothing that they could get into the water and not drown themselves.

As ever, her future husband was extraordinarily unversed in proper behavior.

Cecily took a moment and decided that since he wasn't particular about propriety, he wouldn't be scandalized. "I would not ordinarily confess this, but Roddy taught me. Eleanor bullied him into teaching both of us. When she is determined to learn something, she is quite intimidating."

His smile was a slow, attractive curve of his lips, the sinful arc beguiling and seductive. "Then perhaps we should find a sheltered spot. It's warm, and I can't tell you how much I have missed the water. At home I swim every day if possible. Have I told you about the lakes near where I was raised? They are crystal clear and deep."

"My hair," she said ridiculously, for while she might not be deeply experienced, she already recognized the hungry look in his eyes. "I cannot return to the house disheveled. My grandmother would go into an apoplexy at any time, but with a house full of guests, she'd be furious with me."

No exaggeration there. So why was she tempted?

"I'll make sure it doesn't get wet."

She protested one last time. "Jonathan . . . we . . . we can't. It's light out."

He stopped his horse along the bank and slipped out of the saddle in one of those lithe, athletic movements that she found so fascinating. "Light," he informed her as he took the reins of her horse, "makes it all the more interesting."

Chapter 23

Was he tempting fate? Jonathan wondered as he lifted Cecily from her mount, his hands spanning her slender waist, his mood restive. It seemed now that the decision was made in his mind to marry her, he considered it over and done with.

It *was* simple enough. She was his. He'd claimed her. She'd lain with him, and he'd given her his seed without any of the precautions he normally took. Addie's birth had had a profound effect on any reckless sexual tendencies, but with Cecily it hadn't even occurred to him to try to prevent the conception of a child.

In his eyes—in the eyes of *his* God—he and Cecily were already joined. Whatever ceremony followed was in his opinion insignificant compared to the commitment they'd already made to each other.

He ran a fingertip over the curve of her smooth cheek. "You belong to me."

"Spoken like some imperious chieftain," she informed him tartly, though she began to unfasten her riding habit. "But if you are determined to swim, my lord, I've already proven myself unable to resist your persuasion."

His fondness for spirited English ladies was growing by the moment. "It's a warm day and no one is about." He also began to undress, unbuttoning his shirt. "Besides, not all the persuasion has been mine alone if memory serves. The night of our carriage mishap I believe *you* approached *me*."

Her tawny eyes held a hint of playfulness as she shed her tailored dark blue jacket. "That was the night you first kissed me, so I make no apology."

"As I recall, against my cousin's advice, I tossed all caution to the wind and accepted your desire for a private conversation with alacrity." His shirt landed on the grass.

"We have a mutual recklessness then." Her skirt slipped off and she bent to remove her half-boots.

When she smiled that way . . . it undid him.

And she was perfectly correct. They did have a common bond of less than demure behavior when around each other, and to his mind, nothing could be more indicative of a love affair.

Perhaps he was a romantic after all, for he found her inability to resist him to be highly arousing.

Though the scenery might lack the drama of the more rugged terrain of mountains and valleys, England held its own charm, especially on a day such as this. The sky was blue, the pastures green, and the river moved slowly past, the water silently beckoning. This corner of the park was far enough away from the house that even with guests he wasn't worried about them being discovered. He sat down on a rock to tug off his boots with impatience, tossing them both carelessly aside. Their horses were already grazing on the soft grass of the riverbank, reins dangling.

He needed her. Wanted her. "Cecily," he murmured, the sight of her in her chemise so enticing he almost didn't catch himself just before he disordered her neat chignon despite his promise, self-control just an abstract concept in a moment like this one. He craved the tactile sensation of her hair spilling over his hands, the silken softness of it against his skin, the scent of it against his face. But, for the sake of propriety, they needed to be careful.

Unrestrained passion had its merits, but she was undoubtedly right about her grandmother, and the last person he wanted to antagonize was the dowager duchess.

Slow . . .

He didn't question Cecily's capitulation. He was ten years older, infinitely more experienced, and she responded to him so sweetly he knew she was not going to resist this seduction.

"Let me," he urged, his voice going low, his hands sliding over her slim shoulders, along the lacy neckline of her shift to the ribbon holding the bodice together. He slipped it free and the material parted, revealing the rounded curves of her breasts—not overly large but beautifully feminine, with those blush-tinted nipples he'd tasted and teased to taut peaks the night when they'd first explored passion together.

The night that had irrevocably changed his life.

Jonathan cupped her, his fingers dark against the ivory of her skin, his arousal already so pronounced that the material of his breeches was uncomfortable. "You terrify me, Lady Cecily."

That statement, said so matter-of-factly, startled her, bringing her gaze to his, her eyes widening in obvious question.

In answer he slid the chemise from her shoulders, making her gasp and frantically try to snatch it back up. "Jonathan!"

He just grinned. "Have you never gone swimming naked?"

"No, of course not!"

Before she could retrieve the discarded garment he

lifted her, wading into the river with her in his arms, still clad in his breeches, her nude body warm against him, the slight sound she uttered as the cool water made contact with her skin just as intoxicating as her perfect pale beauty.

He'd just told her the truth. It always frightened him to have this depth of feeling for another human being. Adela had now and again the usual aliments of childhood, and each time she became fevered or showed signs of illness, he had to conquer an inner panic.

Love was risky. He'd lost his mother very young and that had been difficult enough, but he'd been a man when his father died and maturity had done nothing to lessen the pain of the loss. Holding Cecily close, he understood the fragility of bone and flesh, the comprehension unwelcome, for what he wanted most in his life was to protect her and keep her safe.

They were going to be a family. He cherished the idea of it, and yes, it terrified him as well.

"Jonathan, I—"

This was not the time to explain. He was only slowly getting used to the notion of being deeply in love himself, and above them the sky was an azure arch, the water was soothing, and they were alone and skin to skin. Making love held a greater appeal than discussing his feelings, which he didn't do often anyway. "Prove to me you can actually swim." He interrupted whatever she was going to say, his tone deliberately teasing as he lowered her into the water, still carefully holding on to her even though where he stood it was only about waistdeep. "I have my doubts about proper English ladies actually having that skill."

If looks could kill, he might be dead and gone, but she was so enchanting, the pale globes of her breasts lapped by the water, her hair still neatly coiffed—even if he would prefer it loose—that he smothered a laugh.

"I think you might be disabused of that notion, my lord."

Cecily struck out, the cool water streaming over her shoulders, memories of childhood flooding back—she and Roderick and Eleanor sneaking off to swim, which was decidedly against the rules.

So was this. Especially when she turned to see that Jonathan had stepped out of the river to shed his breeches and cut the water in a clean dive, surfacing so close to her she caught her breath.

His sleek dark head rose from the water, and he shook the hair out of his eyes, his teeth gleaming in a boyish grin. "Ahh, if this is what English house parties consist of, I am going to accept every single invitation that comes my way. Delicious wet naked ladies on warm summer afternoons are a definite incentive."

Treading water, Cecily gave him a mock glare. "Only one wet naked lady, I hope."

"Only one," he agreed softly.

And she believed him. Part of it was the sudden seriousness in his eyes. Part of it was how he reached for her to draw her close. He was tall enough that he could stand, and she drifted willingly into the circle of his arms, his strength holding her easily. "Just me?"

"Just you," he agreed and kissed her.

She was new to this. To the sublime power of heady desire, to the freedom of sharing with another person after being raised with the stricture that one must not touch or be touched, that concealing clothing was a must, that any hint of indiscretion should be abruptly stifled and hidden. Here she was, in the afternoon sun no less, in the arms of her lover, and from the hard length of his erection against her stomach, she gathered that this forbidden interlude was going to proceed very pleasurably.

And she had never been so right.

When he cupped her bottom and adjusted her position, she closed her eyes as he seemed to be able to precisely gauge the right angle to hold her for his heated entry between her parted thighs, the contrast of the cool water and his importunate need both stark and exciting.

All coherent thought stopped at that moment.

He moved inside her, she moved at his urging in response; his hands on her hips, holding, supporting ... Cecily arched back, the pleasure enfolding her with an insidious grasp at the penetration. It went without saying that she'd never made love in the water before because her only experience had been with him that night in her bedroom.

This was different. Of course it was. No closely drawn drapes. No shrouded interiors. No rules. Just her and her untamed lover Lord Augustine in the river in the late afternoon, naked and entwined.

If she thought about it too much it would ruin the glory of the moment, and as he moved in a subtle dance of invasion and retreat, Cecily decided it was indeed glorious.

Pleasurable.

Maybe even primal, but then again Jonathan wasn't exactly governable under any circumstances and certainly this didn't qualify. His lips feathered across her temple even as he took her. "I need you."

She ran her fingers through his damp hair. "So you've said."

"You aren't aware of it now?" His erection was deep inside her, so he had a point.

Close, clinging to him, Cecily exhaled. Every nerve ending was on fire, her entire body tingling. "I'm not aware of anything in particular right now ... Jonathan, can you ... please ... help me?"

He could, she discovered several drowning moments later, the pleasure a combination of the soft evening, his touch, their joining, and the passive glide of the river. He held her close, she shuddered in rapture in his embrace, and the pleasure peaked so vividly she lost the breath from her lungs.

It made her want to cry with joy.

It made her want to admit that she was in love. But as they trembled together, she bit her lip and pressed her face into his throat and thought about being a dutiful wife.

A countess. A mother.

Lady Augustine.

Maybe she'd rather be Lady Savage.

The moment lingered, the smooth sensation of the water caressing her back, the hold of his arms. . . . It was inevitable that eventually he shifted, his muscular body hard against hers, and then withdrew from her body, though with a smile he still gently supported her in the water. "Now do you see why I am such an advocate of making love in the daylight?"

"How often have you done so?" While she'd been struck with jealousy when she'd seen Mrs. Blackwood shamelessly throwing herself at him, she was more curious about his past than she was possessive of it now that they were engaged. It was also difficult to be petulant in the aftermath of such heated pleasure, especially when he was smiling, the sun shining on his raven hair, and there was patent amusement in the depths of his dark eyes.

"This is the first time."

She didn't quite believe that declaration and it showed.

"Making love," he clarified softly, the clasp of his hands sure and strong. "No, I was hardly without experience when I met you, but still, the term *virgin* can be applied to not just a woman's physical innocence. I make *love* to you. It's different. It is certainly new to me."

Not quite the declaration she wanted, but close.

The breeze ruffled the river and brushed her face. While a part of her couldn't believe she'd been so brazen as to embrace an afternoon dalliance, another part knew that this—*this*—was why she'd fallen in love with Jonathan in the first place. A predictable life was all well and good, but maybe she was more well suited for a less traditional marriage.

To the wickedly attractive man of her dreams.

Though they needed to at least pretend to be circumspect. "We should go back." She artlessly kissed his jaw, relaxed and happy in the moment, her arms twined around his neck, their bodies buoyed by the water.

"We should," he agreed, his lips warm against her temple. "Addie will be looking for me."

"And I'm sure Adonis misses you," she teased. "Addie told me he sat on your lap a good deal of the journey here."

"That creature is a menace." He drew his brows into a frown, but didn't quite succeed in concealing a rueful laugh. "But overzealous mongrels aside, my sisters might also notice our prolonged absence. Not to mention your grandmother."

"I can't find the strength to get out of the water."

"I'll carry you."

"Is this love?"

Should she have said it? Probably not. But after all, they were engaged, they were lovers, and the idyllic afternoon was like a scene from a romantic novel. The sun, the water, the pleasure . . .

"I was hoping you'd define it for me." Jonathan still held her, and his face had taken on a serious cast, his mouth curving as he waded through the river. "I know it's unique in my experience."

Which was much more vast than hers. "As in mine."

"It had better be." His voice was gruff with displeasure, his jaw instantly displaying a militant tightness. "You're mine."

"So you've said." It wasn't like she was arguing the point, but at least his possessiveness indicated deeper feeling.

He climbed up the bank easily, carrying her as if she were nothing. He did have enough of a sense of humor to laugh then. "That sounded entirely too autocratic. Let me put it this way: I'm not interested in killing anyone this weekend."

"Much less barbaric." She managed to keep a straight face only with effort. "Think of how that would irritate my grandmother. Blood on the ducal rugs and all."

"Not precisely what I meant, but yes, I imagine it would." He set her on her feet on the grass, his lean body streaming water, and reached for his shirt. "Use this to dry off. I'll wear my coat over it and no one will know."

They would know. Not because of his wet shirt, but because she couldn't believe either of them could help that meaningful glance, the inhaled breath at the merest touch of their hands . . .

Yes, this is love.

And she was naked with the Earl of Augustine, who was soon to be her husband, as the beginning of the sunset sent glimmers of crimson across the horizon. She took the fine linen garment from his hand and bent to draw it up her calf, playful and yet serious. "You are very gallant, my lord."

"I don't know if that term applies." Nude and unself-conscious, his chest glistening, he waited for her to return the garment, tugging on his breeches, his gaze fastened on her swaying breasts "Proper gentlemen don't lure their fiancées out for an afternoon tryst."

"For any tryst at all," she corrected.

"Your hair is undisturbed." His dark coloring stark in the fading sunlight, he didn't look in the least repentant, but instead grinned. "I would like some credit for that feat."

Cecily's spontaneous mirth helped a bit with her discomfort over being naked in broad daylight, even if it was beginning to ebb. She picked up her discarded chemise. "I'll try to remember it."

"Could you ever forget this afternoon?" His voice was low, all levity gone.

She answered quietly and in perfect truth. "Never."

Chapter 24

"An earldom is a cachet, after all."

Lillian looked at her cousin. "Is it?"

James, also sitting on the terrace in the blush of the setting sun, did his best to be nonchalant, but she really wasn't fooled. "That is hardly new information."

"No."

"But it isn't like that between them."

"You mean she isn't marrying him for his fortune or his title."

They'd been friends since childhood and knew each other well. James was her father's younger brother's son; they'd been raised in the same house, shared a common heritage, and though he was a few years older, they had always been close. He shook his head. "A love match if there ever was one. I would not have thought Jonathan susceptible, but then again, she's quite a lovely girl, not to mention her bloodlines are as blue as the sky above."

"Whereas his . . ."

". . . are somewhat mixed, but Lady Cecily does not seem to care, and apparently neither does her father, for he agreed to the match."

"He must love his daughter enough to realize she has made up her mind. If Jonathan is what she wants, he is what she must have." Lillian looked the other way, to where the trees held a deepening color as evening approached, remembering her own father, who had loved her without reservation. Loved her enough to understand about Arthur. To not a force a marriage to save his pride and her reputation at the cost of her happiness. She'd cried in his arms after her supposed elopement, and then he'd given her the choice about her future.

Long shadows fell across the grass and insects had begun to chirp. She said very quietly, "I did not expect to like him."

James didn't misunderstand the subject of that observation. "Jon is a unique individual, as we all are, I suppose, but I understand. I had a barely veiled prejudice against him as well, I admit, until we came to know each other years ago. I still do not understand his spirituality, but then again, he doesn't require me to understand it either. If he never becomes a convert of the Church of England, so be it. One of the traits I admire is his ability to separate his self-worth from the opinions or habits of others. He is what he *is*."

She thought about the polished stone he'd given her, even now tucked into a pocket in her day gown. Though she didn't normally succumb to superstition, in this case she'd decided it could hardly hurt to carry it around.

Her problems with her brother had nothing to do with religion or politics, or anything else besides how their father had *loved* his mother. An English earl had defied convention and married a woman who was half-French and half-Indian, and maybe Lillian needed to admit she'd been a bit poisoned by her mother's scathing opinion on the matter. "When he arrived I was prepared to deal with a barbarian."

James laughed, his good-natured face holding amusement. "Oh, don't mistake me—your brother can be decidedly lacking in manners if he deems it appropriate to the situation. I remember once . . ."

When he trailed off, Lillian looked at him in open inquiry.

"Never mind," her cousin equivocated, lounging in his chair, his expression chastened. "That story isn't for your ears, but regardless, I am glad if the two of you are finding common ground. He is truly concerned for your future, Lily."

"I know he is." She could say that with a dry finality, for why otherwise would she find herself under the wing of the formidable Dowager Duchess of Eddington? "So far this afternoon I have been introduced to a number of eligible gentlemen, all of whom are either titled or rich, but none of them holding both virtues, which tells me the duchess is trying to angle for the most amiable suitor for a young lady with a questionable reputation. Will he want my dowry, or just a wife from an aristocratic family, even if her shine is slightly tarnished?"

"Jon is trying to help you."

"I know."

She almost—*almost*—found it humorous.

"You *aren't* tarnished, for God's sake," James muttered and reached for his glass of wine, his long legs crossed casually. "Anyone who thinks so is a fool. Whatever happened with Sebring is long past, and quite frankly, men aren't nearly as snobbish over scandal as women are."

She disagreed—or at least she partially disagreed. One of the reasons she'd declined a reentry into society was not just that women snubbed her but also that men now looked at her in a different way. Maybe James was correct and the perception was different, but it was still snobbery. The assumption that she was now no longer an innocent made her a target in a game she did not know how to play, no matter what everyone thought.

"You are being diplomatic, but I thank you." She

actually was more relaxed than she had imagined she would be in this setting, with the pomp of a formal dinner ahead of her—and all those attentive but speculative gentlemen.

"There's no need to thank me. I was telling the perfect truth."

"Not everyone, man or woman, is as kind as you are, James." So true. After her father had died, he'd stepped in until Jonathan could arrive, and it had taken months for her brother to receive the news and make arrangements to come to England. Had she not had her cousin . . .

Well, it had been bad enough to suffer through the pain and loss. It would have been much worse without James. They were as close as a brother and sister.

"Lillian, don't undervalue yourself or others will also." His voice was very quiet. "I wish life wasn't like this, but sometimes we are forced to deal with the small-minded constrictions of those around us."

No one understood that better than she did, but maybe he was correct. "If there is one lesson I've learned, please trust that I *know* that one."

"If anyone dares to insult you, they will answer to me or Jon."

"Thank you."

"Then you'll have an open mind during this event? I know most of the gentlemen here. If there is one that captures your attention, I will tell you everything I know of him."

"I will try." She sent her cousin a curious glance. He was undeniably handsome, and while not titled—and since Jonathan was getting married, nor was he likely to remain an heir apparent—he was still a Bourne and while their family name was perhaps not without a blemish or two, it was still well respected. "What of you?"

"What of me in what context?" He looked puzzled.

"Are you looking for a wife?"

She might have suggested he jump off of one of the ramparts of the Tower of London, he looked so horrified. "No. No. Of course not. No."

"One 'no' would do," she responded mildly, still teasing him. "I just wondered if as you scour the legions of your acquaintances for me, I should start doing the same for you. There are undoubtedly a lot of lovely ladies waiting out there for the perfect man. The duchess has invited some of them here, in fact."

"I'm hardly scouring."

"Aren't you?"

James was James, after all, and he ended up just giving her an amused smile. "No. If you'd like I'll take an eternal vow to not scour, but I can't answer for anyone else. The dowager duchess is quite formidable."

Yes, she was.

Lillian wasn't sure if she could hold up again under the caustic regard of the beau monde, especially given the unpleasantness of her previous experience. "I don't know if I can do this," she confessed, her voice small but the trepidation real, the negligent cross of her ankles beneath her elegant new gown a contrast to her tension. "James, how am I supposed to float back into the most fashionable circles as if nothing ever happened?"

He smiled in an irritating way only a male could achieve. "Apparently with the help of the extremely influential Dowager Duchess of Eddington."

Lily smiled sweetly back, seeking retribution. "I would not count on walking away from this weekend unscathed yourself. There are a good number of young women present, so we will suffer together."

He groaned in open masculine dismay, which gave her some measure of satisfaction.

* * *

Dinner had been sumptuous, and in the aftermath the group had broken into various groups—charades on the terrace, an impromptu concert in the music room by a young lady who played a series of Scottish tunes with a surprisingly adept touch on the pianoforte; the requisite port for the gentlemen and sherry for the ladies ...

"May I have a word, Lady Cecily?"

She glanced up from where she was sitting on the edge of a group of ladies, startled. "Lord Drury." It was all she could do to keep from stammering.

"All I wish is to have a brief conversation. Unless you think your fiancé will take offense and attempt to behead me in the rose garden, in which case I can understand your refusal."

Everyone around her laughed, but she had to give him credit for having the perfect amused expression on his face, and truly, it was very gracious the way he approached her with open friendliness to defuse the gossip.

She actually didn't know how Jonathan might feel about it, but then again, a certain level of trust was needed in every relationship, in her opinion, and males did not own an exclusive right on granting it or not, and the viscount's easy smile indicated he was simply being humorous about the possibility of violence.

His lordship's voice was low as she rose to accept the invitation. "This will take only a moment, but I do prefer privacy."

He knew about the engagement. Her grandmother had formally announced it at dinner, so what point was there in refusing? Cecily allowed him to escort her to the doors opening to the terrace, and though their departure was no doubt noted by everyone in the room, it was less conspicuous than it would have been in London.

"We'll stand in full sight of the gaping crowd," he told her wryly, stopping just outside, the dark gardens in the background, the country air tangy with summer. Lanterns had been lit all around the flagstone area, so they were no doubt very visible. "Do not worry. I just wanted a few moments of your time."

"I'm getting used to the extra attention." She smiled at him uncertainly. "Jonathan does not go unnoticed. If we are going to be married . . ."

"And it appears you are," he finished for her. "Then yes, I think you will need to adjust to the interest. I wanted to offer my congratulations. You seem very happy."

He gazed at her with visible sincerity and it seemed, though it was ironic, for the first time since their introduction they actually understood one another. She could pursue the veneer of a polite acquaintance, but she was hopeful he had not drawn her out to discuss her upcoming wedding.

She was, in fact, sure he hadn't.

"I *am* happy." Then she went on, though she wasn't sure she should. "Eleanor said you had a lovely chat this afternoon." That was rather pointed, but she could swear progress was being made. The comment had been casual, but as they'd dressed for dinner, her sister had been not precisely jubilant but certainly lighter-spirited than in the past weeks, and she'd even allowed herself to be persuaded to wear an emerald gown that she usually disdained because she claimed the neckline was too revealing. Cecily had received an accusing look for having her maid pack it, but it was worth it, for Elle had been the recipient of more than one admiring perusal from the males in attendance.

Viscount Drury took in a deep breath and appeared to make some inner decision. "I have wondered if I've been reading more into the recent conversations between your sister and me than I should."

This was progress indeed.

She was an extremely amateur matchmaker, but so far so good. Cecily did her best to avoid looking openly jubilant. "Eleanor is quite stunning this evening, isn't she?"

"Yes," he agreed, elegant and nonchalant in his formal kit, his blond hair in perfect order.

"She's also intelligent."

"Yet again I agree with you."

"Kindhearted."

Now he started to smile. "I sense your affection for her, Lady Cecily."

"I was simply pointing out that while she has a few flaws, as we all do, she would make any man an admirable wife."

"I take it that means I am not getting the wrong impression?"

Now that Eleanor had admitted it to her, the quandary of how to answer that oblique question was much easier. "I think you are very intuitive, my lord," she informed him with a serene smile.

"I have not been accused of *that* very often," he said in a droll voice. "I'd more think I am cursed with being singularly obtuse. But may I thank you for being so frank with me? Shall we go back inside?"

"Indeed we should."

When Jonathan joined her a few moments later, his desire to behead her former would-be suitor in check, it seemed, he drawled, "You look extremely complacent, my dear. I think you should at least try to control that particular smug glow."

She looked up at him from under the fringe of her lashes and did try to assume a more demure expression. "His lordship wanted to offer his congratulations on my engagement."

"Did he? I saw the two of you talking most earnestly out there. And?"

Was he jealous? He didn't seem to be, but then again, after that interlude in the river, he had every reason to be secure enough about her affections.

"To ask about Eleanor."

"A coup then?" His smile was genial, his dark hair loose for a summer country party, brushing his shoulders. His less-formal clothing suited him, his manner more easy when he wasn't trussed up in a formal cravat; her grandmother knew young men well enough to make sure that by this time in the evening her guests understood they could embrace informality.

If only she knew just how informal they'd been earlier in the river.

Heaven forbid.

"I don't know if I would view it as a fait accompli quite yet, but a very good start."

"I rather thought the conversation had run along those lines."

"Now you are omniscient, Lord Augustine?" she teased, aware of the people around them no doubt listening to every word they could catch.

He looked at her and leaned down. His breath warmed her temple. "Maybe I am. I knew the instant I saw you that we were meant to join our souls."

Suddenly they'd shifted out of a refined English drawing room without moving a muscle.

He could do that to her.

With just a whisper.

Chapter 25

At dinner she'd been seated next to a baronet named Sir Norman on one side who talked of nothing but horses and on the other a young man who constantly cleared his throat and refused to look at her as he ate his way through all six courses with his nose pointed to his plate. Eleanor was confident that her grandmother hadn't planned to seat her in such an unattractive spot, but considered the arrangement suitable for a young woman who was past her first blush as an ingénue.

In contrast, Lord Drury was seated down the table between two attractive females, one a shy debutante and the other a young, pretty widow with striking ivory skin and auburn hair who was openly flirtatious to an extent that Eleanor wanted to excuse herself from dinner with as much dignity as possible and go upstairs to cry.

No, not cry, she decided. Like anyone else, she had moments when it happened, but she really wasn't the weepy kind. Maybe go upstairs and give the wall a swift kick, which would undoubtedly bruise her toe and accomplish nothing, but it was excruciating to sit and watch him smile and laugh with another woman.

However, this seemed like a poor time to give up, no matter how charmed he seemed to be by the lovely Mrs. Kirkpatrick.

That was why when they finally retired, Eleanor

found herself in her sister's bedchamber, restlessly pacing, the hem of her dressing gown trailing behind her as she related the full details of the conversation between her and the viscount that afternoon.

Cecily smiled at the end of the recital, her eyes alight. "He actually asked you whom he should court? Did you mention yourself perhaps?"

Eleanor whirled around. "As if I could say that, Ci."

Her sister's amber eyes were reflective. "I suppose it would be a little forward, but still, I think he was inferring something. It isn't so bad to be a little forward, trust me. I was the one who essentially proposed to Jonathan."

And all the *ton* thought her sister was the demure one. Eleanor had to admit she was a bit taken aback. "You did?"

Perched on the edge of the seat at her dressing table, her long hair loose and a smile gracing her mouth, Cecily nodded. "Need I say it worked out quite well?"

If glowing happiness was any indication, no, it didn't need to be articulated, but still . . . Eleanor couldn't go to Lord Drury—or maybe she should think of him as Elijah, as that made him a little more approachable—and suggest that if he had romantic inclinations she would be amiable.

No. Out of the question.

It was too outrageous to contemplate. Unladylike. Maybe it worked with the somewhat unusual Augustine, but Elijah was a traditional English gentleman. He may have misjudged Cecily in some ways and mistaken her usual demure poise to mean she was a compliant, malleable young lady—when she really wasn't either of those—who would make a perfect wife, but that had been what he *wanted*.

Except . . . well, he had said that afternoon that he had changed his mind.

. . . someone who amuses me . . . with whom I can speak freely . . .

"Maybe I *should* talk to him." The words tumbled out in a rush, but the very thought of it caused her pulse to flutter. "But I have truly no idea what to say."

"You?" Cecily looked amused. "That would be a unique moment."

Eleanor gave her sister a quelling glare. "You are not being helpful, Ci. I can hardly tell him that I've harbored a secret infatuation for him ever since the day we first met."

"Why not? Besides, I think he has already come to that conclusion anyway." Cecily went on as if what she'd just said was perfectly reasonable. "And please, be yourself. He is intrigued by you, not the quiet persona you've tried to adopt this season."

"I frightened him off the first time." Eleanor pointed it out with all due practicality.

Cecily just smiled and lifted her brows. "I think his lordship has gotten past that. Besides, from what you told me he said, he frightened himself off. Quite different. The issue was not with his perception of you, but with his own self-doubt."

Put that way, it was much better. Eleanor took in a deep, calming breath. "Maybe you are right."

The knock was so quiet he wasn't sure his imagination hadn't produced it. Elijah Winters glanced at the clock and frowned when the light rap was repeated. He was only half dressed because he'd dismissed his valet earlier and sat on the balcony off his room sipping the duke's excellent brandy and contemplating the rising moon. Contemplating why he'd accepted this invitation at all. Contemplating the luscious Lady Eleanor and the paradox of being attracted to a woman who had all the attributes he normally avoided in a female.

However, as he'd stated just that afternoon, he wasn't sure what he wanted.

When he was finally foxed enough that he was sure he could sleep, he'd started to prepare for bed, and at the moment he wore only his breeches.

Who the devil was at his door?

Normally he would have put on his dressing gown, but the garment was not in sight and he had no idea where Bosco might have put it, and quite frankly, he'd had enough to drink he didn't care much, because if propriety was an issue, no one would be knocking at this late hour.

When he jerked open the door, he had to admit he wasn't prepared to see the subject of his thoughts standing there, her hair loose in a dark gold fall over her slender shoulders, clad in a robe of some ivory material that made her look very pretty and very young ...

Which exactly matched the uncertain look in her eyes.

"What are you doing?" he rasped out, knowing Eleanor had to have come from the part of the manor house with the family apartments to the guest wing and anyone might have seen her.

"I need to talk to—"

Elijah caught her arm and ignored her startled gasp as he tugged her into the room so anyone coming out into the hall wouldn't discover them conversing at his door at this hour. "Have you lost your senses?"

"I'm pretty certain I have," she muttered with endearing irritation, "or else I would not be knocking on your door."

Two points came clearly into focus at that moment.

He was barely dressed.

She was barely dressed.

And they had *both* lost their minds, since she'd come

to him and he'd dragged her inside his room. In retrospect all that brandy had been a poor idea. Instead of thinking about the scandalous implications of her presence in his bedchamber, he found his gaze traveling over her tempting form, the folds of her nightclothes not quite concealing enough to eradicate the memory of how that dazzling emerald gown she'd worn earlier had showcased her spectacular breasts and slender waist, not to mention the gentle flare of her hips.

It wasn't that Eleanor hadn't always been alluring, it was more that he'd never been quite sure how to handle his reaction to her. Cecily was different. He'd felt comfortable from their first introduction. A liking, albeit nothing soul-stirring—and there was no doubt that Eleanor's serene sister was very beautiful . . .

Yet still nothing like her unpredictable sibling, who right at the moment stood barefoot and clad in her nightclothes in his bedchamber. "Why are you here?" he asked, his voice thick from the brandy. "You do realize this is beyond foolish."

Or maybe it wasn't *just* the liquor he'd consumed. She was beguilingly close. There was only one lamp left burning, quite low, and her hair was the color of warm honey. Though normally he would never have imagined himself being so bold, he wished to run his fingers through the silky length of it.

In fact, he had quite a few improper thoughts at the moment.

"I need to speak with you." She took in a deep breath and her breasts, he could not help but notice, quivered in a very tantalizing sway. By the same token, her gaze was riveted on his bare chest.

Turnabout being fair play and all, he didn't mind in the least her staring at him, if she didn't take offense at him staring right back.

He somehow managed to find something reasonable to say. "What can't hold until morning and the proper confines of the breakfast room?"

"I . . ." She faltered, and looked away for a moment, but then squared her shoulders. "I waited for you."

Speechless, Elijah stared at her, wondering if this was all some kind of bizarre hallucination. "Waited for me?"

Though her cheeks were now scarlet, Eleanor lifted her chin. "I suppose I could have more finesse in saying it, but that is about it. I waited all through last season for you to notice me and—"

"I noticed you," he interrupted harshly, which he would not normally have done with a well-bred lady under any circumstances. "Take my word. I noticed."

"If so, you are not easy to read, my lord."

It had been a rather difficult past few days, and maybe it was the brandy, maybe it was just that she was there, like a barefoot goddess in his bedchamber where she absolutely should never have come at this hour—or any other hour actually—and maybe it was the revelation he'd experienced that afternoon when he'd walked out onto the terrace and seen her sitting there, alone and pensive and undeniably beautiful in the afternoon sun.

He wanted her. She wasn't all that fashionable with her outspoken views, and certainly she hadn't married her first year out . . .

Because she'd waited. For him. What more could a man ask?

"Is this clear enough?" he asked as he covered the two strides separating them.

He kissed her. There was no misinterpreting the way he pulled her into his arms and lowered his head to take her mouth. Eleanor stiffened in surprise, but to his gratification, she immediately melted against him.

He might not be Earl Savage, but there was definitely

a primal edge to the long, intense embrace, and when he finally lifted his head, he discovered a shocking truth.

It was more satisfying than he had realized to not always be perfectly polite.

Eleanor, who had very cooperatively slipped her arms around his neck, gazed into his eyes and said in her direct way, "I think I understood you perfectly just now, my lord. But explain it to me again."

Chapter 26

Morning. Not yet. Almost dawn, with reddish streaks in the sky, and he'd woken because he'd spent most of his life out of doors essentially and he was aware of the cycles of the moon and sun at all times.

Jonathan slipped the halter on Seneca, and not bothering with a saddle, he vaulted onto his back. The big horse had been in the city too long; it was there in his eager sidelong dance as Jonathan settled into place, in the toss of his head at the single rein.

They both needed a wild run.

All around them were gentle pastures and lanes and meandering streams. So he let the stallion have his way and they raced down the long drive, scattering small stones, the brush of the cool air a rush against his skin.

So this is happiness, he thought as the stallion took a low stone fence with muscular ease, imagining his lovely fiancée still in her bed, her skin warm and smooth, her hair spread over the pillow in silky disarray as she slept. More than that, imagining the swift charm of her smile, the musical sound of her laugh, the way her eyes softened when she looked at him . . .

He hadn't come to England to fall in love. He hadn't come to England to form more than a dutiful acquaintance with family. How ironic that he had, in fact, not come to England willingly at all, but only because he had loved his father and knew it was expected of him and now his life was different.

Entirely different. It was a readjustment in thinking, for he'd promised Cecily he wouldn't force her to go with him to America, but then again, he wasn't at all sure she'd want to leave the island that had been her home her entire existence. He couldn't blame her if she didn't. His desire to return home was based on the same principle of wanting to continue the life he'd always known.

What if, he wondered as his horse picked up speed along a straight stretch and Jonathan's hair whipped back as he crouched lower, he couldn't convince her to leave with him?

Could he still go?

He doubted it.

What a sobering acknowledgment.

The countryside tore by and the dawn blushed into true daylight, and eventually, splashing through the same river where he'd made love to Cecily, Jonathan guided his mount back toward the ducal estate at a sedate walk to cool him off.

Then the beautiful morning changed.

The first bullet caught him squarely in the shoulder, the impact of it taking him by surprise since it was the last thing he expected, the telltale crack registering only as he realized what had happened by the slashing pain. Only by a miracle did he keep his seat as his startled horse lunged forward, and that was short-lived when Seneca swerved wildly at the sound of a second retort.

Hit twice, Jonathan thought, the pain now blossoming lower also, spreading like a slow tide, the force of hitting the ground jarring, knocking the breath from his lungs. He lay there a moment, his brain signaling the need to move, to find cover, but his body not responding. He finally took in a shuddering breath and managed to roll to his knees. There was blood everywhere, his shirt was already soaked with it, which told him the second bullet had also hit him in the torso, but he really couldn't tell where because it seemed like his entire body was on fire. There was a thicket of bushes and a small copse of trees to his right, but how to get there was a problem.

Bad. This is bad. He'd been wounded in the war twice, but this was worse.

The attempt to get to his feet was unsuccessful, the weakness infuriating, and he tried again only to be shoved down violently by a booted foot that connected with his wounded shoulder with agonizing accuracy and thrust him onto his back. The world spun.

"You heathen bastard."

Through an ever-growing haze, Jonathan looked up at his assailant. There was little doubt of it, for the man carried a gun in the crook of his arm. He was ordinary enough: once-fashionable clothes a little worn, his face weathered to a dark tan, a shock of black hair above features at the moment drawn into a scowl. Eyes as dark as Jonathan's own stared at him with unmistakable hatred, though he didn't recognize the face.

"I finally got you, Augustine."

Twice shot, he found it difficult to respond. As far as he could tell he was bleeding . . . everywhere.

"I've been laying for you. Waiting. Your cousin, too, so high and mighty. Letting me go after years of service. Telling me he thought I was stealing. Did you think I would just walk away?"

Letting me go . . . what the devil did that mean? It took his foggy brain a moment to process that statement but then it slowly crystallized. Browne. The former manager he'd instructed James to dismiss. The one looming over him at the moment and still holding a gun.

*   *   *

The man leaned forward and Jonathan could smell not just the coppery blood leaking from his wounds at what seemed an alarming rate, but the scent of burnt powder as well. "I followed you here for the grand party after I missed you that night back in London. Hoped it would be easier here to stay out of sight. In London there's always people about. I knew you'd go riding alone." His smile was chilling. "Not yesterday, though. Weren't alone at all, were you? You defiled the daughter of a duke like she was some whore, not a proper lady. Stripped her bare and dragged her into the water and had your way with her, you did. He'll pay me money to keep that quiet, especially once you're dead and not able to be taken to task for it."

If the man hadn't viciously kicked him in the side, Jonathan would have pointed out that he wished to marry Cecily, that the duke had agreed to his offer of marriage, so he certainly didn't have this level of objection, and while His Grace might not be happy over the indiscretion, the lady had clearly been a willing participant.

And that Jonathan loved her.

So deeply that as he knew consciousness was only barely in his grasp all he could think of was how to stay alive. Cecily, his daughter, his sisters, James . . . he had a lot to live for.

"I am . . . " He fought to gasp the words, because he was fairly sure he could now add broken ribs to his ever-growing list of injuries. "The Earl of Augustine. I'll—"

"Look at you. You aren't no bloody English lord," the man argued contemptuously. "And you're worth more to me dead. I brought two guns. Didn't want to chance a miss. Your cousin will no doubt come looking for you. I can't wait to see him face-to-face again. Told the smug bastard I'd get even."

James had been attacked back in London also, and

then there was the cracked wheel of his carriage that the driver swore had been deliberate. . . . They'd just never connected the events.

A mistake, Jonathan realized through the haze of pain.

The next kick caught him in the temple.

The world went black.

Being late for luncheon was not the way to win her grandmother's affection. Cecily glanced at the clock again and decided that trying to apologize on her fiancé's behalf was a futile endeavor. He'd gone out riding early, according to a stable lad, declining to saddle his horse and simply jumping on the animal and departing at a speed that impressed the boy if his gamin grin was taken into consideration, but truly, he was *late*.

So they went ahead and ate, the guests pointedly ignoring Lord Augustine's absence, but it was duly noted, and she had to admit several hours later, when James Bourne took her aside from a lawn game that she wasn't really participating in anyway, his face showing true concern, she shared it.

"Jon wouldn't do this," he said succinctly. "It's time to go looking for him. He might depart on a long ride, but not for over half a day, and certainly not when he was someone else's guest, and most of all he wouldn't do it because of you and Adela. He wouldn't embarrass you and he never misses breakfast with his daughter."

"You think there's been an accident?" Her chest constricted because she'd been telling herself for hours that, no, nothing bad had happened.

"Absolutely. Don't you?'

"Perhaps he got lost."

"Jon?" He looked at her incredulously. "He can navigate the wilderness blindfolded. No. I have no idea where he might be, but he isn't lost, my lady."

She hadn't really thought so either, but if she accepted that, then she also had to accept that something was truly wrong.

"Even if there was an emergency and he was called away suddenly, he'd hardly just leave all his belongings and his child and sisters behind without a word to anyone." James ran his fingers through his hair in an agitated movement. "I do not want to alarm you without cause, but I think there *is* cause."

Cecily agreed. Her mouth was dry. "Where could he be?"

"Let me take a couple of the footmen and we'll start looking. I don't want to stir up alarm up unless it is necessary."

She nodded resolutely. Anything was better than just sitting and waiting. "Give me a moment to change and I will come with you."

"My lady, I—"

"I'm coming," she interrupted with finality, and James smiled slightly in surrender.

"You are going to be a good match for him." He inclined his head. "Fine, then. I'll have your horse saddled as well."

He turned toward the stables, and she made a brief excuse to her grandmother, who was watching the game from a chair in the shade of a spreading elm, and hurried toward the house at an unladylike run. She changed swiftly, her fingers slightly shaking, not bothering to ring for her maid as there wasn't time. James was waiting for her in the circle of the drive, her mare ready.

As he helped her mount, he said, "I've already sent several of the servants out on foot into the grounds of the park to search the wooded areas. We'll ride south first, toward the village. Maybe he's been seen."

Someone groaned.

He might have even made that low sound of pain, Jonathan realized. He fought to open his eyes, failed on the first attempt and wondered if consciousness was even a good idea, and finally succeeded.

Sky. Blue.

The smell of crushed grass, birds twittering in the trees, the gentle rush somewhere of water . . .

Where the devil was he? What happened?

His head ached incessantly, as did the rest of him, and the searing pain when he went to lift his arm was enough to make the world fade away again for a moment.

In the world between light and dark, he drifted, aware of the agony but not connected to it.

Then it came back to him. The shots, the vindictive Browne, the blow that had sent him into oblivion . . .

In an abstract way, he knew the lassitude was a true danger, for if he did nothing and just lay there, bruised and bleeding, he would die, and if at any time of his life he had ever wanted to live, this was it.

Get up, Jon. Don't let the bastard win. Think of Addie. Think of Cecily.

A shadow fell over him and he realized that it was Seneca, who blew out a restless snort and nudged his leg. He wasn't surprised the big horse hadn't left him; he'd had the stallion since he was a colt and trained him by himself. It was obvious, though, that the animal disliked the smell of blood.

The miracle was the lead rope hanging from his halter.

"Closer," Jon managed to croak around the metallic

taste in his mouth, trying to reach for the dangling lead and wondering if he would faint again in the attempt.

And though he wasn't at all sure if Seneca could understand him or if it was merely luck, the horse did swing his head just enough that the rope brushed his hand and he managed to catch it. With gritted teeth, he used the support to rise, swaying and cursing softly in what choice words he knew of his mother's native tongue, which included a few phrases that would have made the average Englishman blanch.

But he gained his feet, now wishing he'd bothered to use a saddle, for getting on his horse in his weakened condition was going to be an interesting feat. Leaning against Seneca's solid weight, he slowly turned, spied a fallen tree and wondered if that might serve . . . if he could get to it.

Twenty steps, which he could have sprinted in seconds that morning, took five grueling minutes to complete. His shirt, stiff with blood, was also damp with sweat by the time he made it, and he wasn't at all sure he could accomplish what would normally be the simple task of climbing up on the log to give himself the advantage of being closer to Seneca's back.

Somehow, in the twilight of increasing weakness, he managed to plant his foot on the fallen elm, balance his weight with his fist in the stallion's mane and his old friend stood extremely still, patient when he was usually restive and eager to run, and Jonathan eventually slid into a halfway-mounted position, the lead still trailing, no way to give the animal direction except with the pressure of his knees and the subtle nudge of a heel, neither of which he was very capable of at the moment.

"Back," he whispered.

Maybe it was the instruction, maybe it was a gift from

the gods, or maybe now that his master was on his back the horse understood he was free to head back to the stable where he knew oats, water, and a comfortable stall awaited him after his morning run and vigil—whatever it was, Seneca swung around in the right direction.

Barely holding on, Jonathan slumped over his mount's neck, the mist of consciousness floating over his senses like an elusive ghost.

Chapter 27

Lily did her best to look enthusiastic at Sir Norman's offer of a stroll through the park. She smiled as graciously as possible, but before she could even answer, both of them poised on the steps, she spotted the horse moving slowly up the drive.

It was not hard to identify her brother's large, sleek black stallion. She'd been wondering why Jonathan felt it appropriate to absent himself all day, but as the horse got closer, his gait considerably slower than his usual spirited pace, she realized there was no rider.

Or was there?

Horror hit her as she saw that someone—and no one but her brother could even think of riding the intractable animal—was astride, collapsed forward, one arm dangling.

"Help me." She unceremoniously grabbed her companion's arm, practically dragging him down the steps. "Hurry!"

"My dear lady," Sir Norman sputtered, but then he too seemed to catch sight of what had her sprinting down the long drive, for she heard him mutter, "Dear Lord. Oh, dear Lord."

At least her would-be suitor—one of the ones who was obviously poor but eligible—was young and reasonably well built, for her brother was a tall man.

If she still had a brother.

Blood. It was everywhere—on the horse's side in a dripping stream, and Jonathan's shirt was dark crimson with it, his right shoulder lodged against the horse's withers. Though normally no one could approach Seneca, much less a female in swirling skirts at a full run, now he came to a halt and merely watched her with liquid eyes, his stance tense but unmoving.

"What happened? Dear Lord . . . I don't . . . oh, dear . . . I . . ."

If Sir Norman continued to babble, Lily might ruin the vestiges of whatever reputation she had left by murdering a baronet in the prestigious driveway of a duke. "Help me get him down," she ordered, heedless of her new day gown of sprigged muslin that she thought rather fetching. She doubted Jonathan would mind her ruining it under the circumstances. "Gently. He's hurt badly."

An understatement, if his gory appearance was any indication. Luckily, one of the footmen had seen either the horse or her frantic dash, because he came running up then, and the three of them were able to ease Jonathan off the back of his horse.

Under the bronze of his skin he was deathly pale as they laid him down. His long raven hair was disordered and even his lips were colorless. Lily could not repress a sob, and if she hadn't glimpsed the slight flutter of his eyelids, she might have become hysterical, but it was not the time to dwell on how much she would miss him now that they knew each other at long last. If this was as bad as it seemed . . .

"Bloody hell." Sir Norman had gone green. "He's . . . he's shot."

The footman, a young Scot, looked rather pale himself at the sight of all the blood, but at least he didn't seem as if he was going to faint dead away and so was deemed the best choice for decisive action. She said sharply, "Go to the house and tell the duchess Lord Augustine is severely injured. Obviously a physician is needed. And send help for us to get him up to the house. Now!"

The young man nodded and set off at a pace that satisfied her that he understood haste was needed. Sir Norman, on the other hand, took out a handkerchief and started to act as if he would wipe his brow, but Lily reached out for it. "Give me that, if you please."

She knew next to nothing about patching up a wound, but it was obvious enough that Jonathan needed to stop bleeding and so she folded the white square and pressed it to her brother's shoulder. It was rewarding when he groaned.

Not dead yet.

Hurry.

"Give me your cravat. And take off your shirt." She glanced up at Sir Norman. "Be smart about it, please. We need to make some bandages and I want to have enough."

To his credit he did start to remove his coat, but then he mumbled, "Can't take my shirt off in front of a lady."

"My sensibilities are not that delicate, remember?"

At the reference to her supposedly tarnished past, he flushed, but it worked. He handed her his cravat before he shrugged out of his coat and unbuttoned his shirt.

She was almost afraid to see what had happened, but it did appear that perhaps the assumption that Jonathan had been shot was correct. Besides the shoulder, there was a hole visible in the blood-soaked material near his waist, as if something had torn through the fabric. She gingerly tugged the shirt free from his breeches and placed the cloth over what seemed to be a jagged and ugly wound in his side that caused her stomach to lurch as she saw the lacerated flesh.

How this had all occurred, she was not sure, but what she was sure of was that he needed help immediately.

"Jonathan." It was a helpless whisper. She had no knowledge at all to help him other than to try to stop the blood still seeping from the wounds, and tears she did not know she was shedding fell on his ashen face in small crystal splashes as she spoke to him.

He heard her, which was encouraging, because his eyes opened briefly, but they drifted shut almost immediately, and all she could do was take his limp hand and kneel there beside him in the grass and pray.

They weren't more than halfway up the long drive before Cecily realized that something was gravely wrong. It wasn't that the knot in her stomach hadn't already grown tighter and tighter on the ride back from the village but there were at least a dozen of the guests in a cluster near the front of the house, including her grandmother, who broke away from the crowd and in an unprecedented event, walked out to meet them rather than letting them come to her.

Everyone, she saw, was staring at her and all conversation had stopped.

"James," she said, the tremor in her voice evident.

"I know," he replied grimly, kicking his horse into a canter. "Something's happened. We should hurry."

The dowager duchess stood resolute by the big fountain as they rode up, a small, regal figure in her signature gray, her face set. Cecily had seen that expression once before. When her grandmother had imparted the news to her, Roderick, and Eleanor that their mother had "passed on," as she called it.

A chill ran through Cecily and she didn't bother to wait for James to help her dismount but slid off her horse instantly. "Grandmama?"

"There's been a terrible accident."

Though she knew he would normally have shown more deference to the duchess, James, who had practically flung himself off his mount, said harshly, "What kind of accident? Where's Jon?"

"Mrs. Hawkins is with him now, but the physician has been sent for, I assure you, Mr. Bourne, and I gave clear instructions that he is to get here with all due speed." Her grandmother paused and refused to look at her. "Lord Augustine has been severely injured, I'm afraid."

All due speed. That had an ominous ring to it, and judging by the gravity of the tone in which the news was delivered, the cold fear that seemed to have clenched around Cecily's heart was warranted. Her tongue was unwieldy, as if she'd forgotten how to talk. "I need to see him."

If her grandmother replied she didn't hear it, for she went past her toward the house, up the steps without regard for the sympathetic looks of the gathered group of guests, though if it hadn't been for James's supportive hold on her elbow, she would have stumbled. He looked every bit as shaken as she did and they didn't exchange a word. During their fruitless ride, they'd both agreed that they'd had a feeling of growing foreboding all day and now there seemed nothing left to say.

Two of Jonathan's sisters were in the upper hallway outside the door of the room he'd been given, and it helped not at all to see their tear-streaked faces. At the sight of James, the youngest, Carole, jumped up and ran to him, and he put his arms around her.

Whatever had happened was bad indeed. Cecily opened the door without knocking and stepped inside, the rest of the elegant bedroom a blur, her gaze focused on the tall form lying on the bed.

Jonathan. *Her* Jonathan, though at the moment he

didn't much resemble the wickedly attractive lover she knew. His bare chest was swathed in bloody cloth and his skin did not have the usual bronzed tone but was almost a grayish hue. The side of his face that she could see sported an enormous bruise from his hairline to his cheekbone, and his features were drawn. It was obvious that he was unconscious, as his body lay lax and unmoving.

Lady Lillian was sitting by the bed and she looked up at Cecily's entrance, her demeanor calm but her own face ghostly pale. She said with no inflection at all, "Please do not take offense, but I was hoping you were the physician."

"I did as well." Mrs. Hawkins, the housekeeper, rinsed out a bloody cloth. "I kin patch up a scrape here and there, but this is too much for me." Then her face softened. "But don't worry about your young man, my lady. He's strong as an ox."

Perhaps he had been, but it was a little hard to believe at the moment.

Cecily's hands were trembling and she clenched them into fists to try to stop it as she approached the bed: fearful, desolate, and a whole gamut of emotions between. His hair was starkly black against the white of the pillowcase, and she bent and touched the dark silk of it, uncaring about the intimate gesture, even though by now James had also come into the hushed room and stood silent behind her, and both Lily and Mrs. Hawkins were watching.

"What happened?" James demanded in a low voice, as if speaking too loudly would make the injuries worse. "The duchess said there was an accident."

Lily said, "He was shot. Twice. *That* is no accident."

Cecily froze, her fingers smoothing back a lock from Jonathan's brow.

"Shot?" James's question reflected her sense of shock and outrage. "Lily, by whom?"

"No one knows." Jonathan's sister's tone was bleak.

"Do you have any idea why?"

Roderick. Cecily's first thought was that her brother might have acted after all on his sense of outrage over a possible indiscretion, but she dismissed it as fast as it came, for two reasons: the bruising on Jonathan's face and that he'd been shot twice. Her brother would never have shot a wounded man a second time, *if*—and it was doubtful—he could have bested her fiancé in the first place. Besides, why would he challenge a man who wished to marry her when their father approved the match?

He wouldn't.

Who else?

"Where was Drury?" James's voice was tight and even through her distress Cecily registered the implied accusation.

The viscount was no more guilty than Roderick, but before Cecily could say so, the arrival of the physician stopped the conversation. The man, small, neat, and dapper, came into the room, took one look at the patient on the bed, and banished all of them. "Out, please. All of you except Mrs. Hawkins."

Had she not known Dr. Gilchrist since she was a young child, she might have obeyed, but Cecily straightened. "No. Please. Lord Augustine and I are to be married. I want to help, even if it is to carry linens."

The physician looked at her set face and then nodded. "Everyone else leave the room."

They looked mutinous, but Cecily caught James's arm in a familiarity brought on by tragedy. She said fiercely, "If you can think clearly, you have more motive than Lord Drury does. If Jonathan dies, you would be earl.

The viscount has nothing to gain, as he was never in love with me anyway and my engagement is settled and official. If you want to help, find out who did this. Look elsewhere, but *look*. Surely you have more information than anyone. And make sure no one tells Addie. I am not an expert, but I do remember that when my mother was ill I was so very frightened. Lily can stay with her."

For a moment, it seemed that he might argue.

She was too shaken to care about who might be listening, too aware of the doctor already giving quiet orders and removing instruments from his bag. "I'm staying. I love him."

A bit more than she'd meant to admit, especially when she hadn't yet told Jonathan, but then again, she didn't care.

James did not seem surprised.

Instead he took her hand, raised it to his lips briefly, and whispered, "Don't leave him. He needs you."

Then he spun around, herded Lily out of the room, and shut the door.

"One shot went clear through his side," Dr. Gilchrist muttered. "I doubt it did much damage. That shoulder is another issue. We need to take out the bullet. If you faint on me, Lady Cecily, we won't have free hands to catch you."

"I won't faint," she promised.

Just don't let him die.

Chapter 28

There was nothing like attempted murder to ruin a house party, Eleanor thought wryly, watching another carriage roll away. London would soon be agog over the newly engaged Lord Augustine's brush with death, but at least the doctor now cautiously predicted that he would survive. Since neither wound was fatal, the loss of blood was the main issue, and it appeared he'd also been beaten in some way and had some broken bones.

"I see Sir Norman has decamped."

The calm, deep voice made her turn. Elijah joined her on the front steps, dressed for riding, his appearance as immaculate as ever. She said with what she thought was admirable poise, "I assume you are departing also."

"That depends." He looked at her intently. "Your grandmother suggested that as a family friend, perhaps I could stay a few more days to keep you and Augustine's younger sisters company. Between Roderick, James Bourne, and myself, that is one gentleman for every unattached female. I hope my presence appeals to you."

"I think you know full well it does," she answered, an inner joy blossoming, though it was difficult to be jubilant when her sister's fiancé was at death's door.

Those two kisses the other evening had been the very epitome of her fantasies, and the usually pleasant

and reserved gentleman she knew had been not polite
in the least. She'd tasted the brandy on his breath and
wondered in the chaos of the events that had transpired
since then if he was going to excuse himself on the basis
of too much drink for their impetuous embrace.

It seemed he wasn't.

Elijah smiled, but it was brief. "Under the circumstances,
it isn't much of an occasion for trivial festivities any longer,
but at least we can occupy ourselves while we wait for Augustine to recover enough that he can travel again."

"It might be a while." Eleanor felt her face tighten, remembering her sister's exhaustion that morning. She had
insisted on staying in his room all night, and not even their
grandmother had contradicted her. Quite frankly, propriety aside, if Jonathan Bourne hadn't already compromised
Cecily, he was certainly not in any shape to do so at the moment. "I still do not understand how it happened. None of
the guests would ever do such a horrible thing, and it isn't
as if he knows anyone else nearby. Why?"

"I have asked myself the same question, I assure
you." Lord Drury added dryly, "Though I understand I
was the first suspect."

"No one truly thought so."

His smile was rueful. "I admit I was a little annoyed
with Augustine once I understood I had a rival, but that
was the extent of it, and as you know full well, my feelings were not engaged. At least not where your sister is
concerned."

The weighted meaning in that last comment was like
being given a secret to keep and hold close. "I know," Eleanor said softly, looking into his eyes. If the venue had
been less public, she would have said more, but at that
moment two footmen came out carrying a trunk past
them to the last waiting vehicle.

They were still standing on the steps and the sky

above was dismal with the threat of rain, so perhaps it was best if the guests departed anyway.

"I hope you do not intend to go riding alone," Eleanor said, eyeing his riding breeches and the quirt in his hand.

"Actually, once James Bourne dismissed me as the possible culprit, he asked me if I would help him investigate what might have happened. As I understand it, the earl has a head injury in addition to his wounds, and the doctor predicts he might not precisely remember the incident. We are meeting at the stables. Roderick is going with us."

"I don't think Lord Augustine has been awake enough to really articulate what happened. Cecily said he has drifted into consciousness several times, but now they think he might be sleeping instead of insensible."

"It's good he's a healthy male with athletic tendencies to begin with." Elijah quirked a brow. "I can't really think he'd be easy to kill if he saw it coming. An ambush is a bit of a different matter if one doesn't know the enemy is out there. I agree with you—no one around here would have cause to hate him. He's been in England barely three months. I know your sister has had other suitors, but none that were serious or I would have heard about it through the inimitable gossip chain of the *ton*."

"I agree." She took in a breath. "May I go with you? I would like to help."

It looked as if his first reaction was to object, and maybe even point out that she was a female, and therefore not useful, but instead he ended up giving her a brief smile. "I cannot see why not. I know I, for one, would enjoy your company."

There was light, warmth, and a beautiful woman.

Perhaps this was heaven.

Except, Jonathan had to acknowledge a moment later, his side ached, and his shoulder hurt like the very

devil. Surely heaven didn't involve this level of pain, but
at least he could open his eyes this time and not see two
of everything. A headache lurked in the background,
but it wasn't overpowering.

A cool hand touched his brow. "Are you awake?"

Guest room at the ducal mansion. He recognized the
fine furnishings and pale green draperies, and the doors
to the balcony were open to the late-afternoon sunshine;
he could tell by the way the light slanted across the floor.
Cecily sat next to him, her blond hair gathered back
from her face, wearing a somewhat wrinkled pink gown,
her tawny eyes full of concern. Once again her fingers
feathered across his skin. "We've been so worried."

He would answer her if his mouth wasn't so parched.
He croaked out, "Water?"

She hastened to bring a small cup to his lips and he
sat up at great personal cost, and held it himself with the
hand opposite of the shoulder that now throbbed with
the beat of his heart, devouring the liquid quickly. She
brought him another cup right away, and even as con-
fused as he was over what might have happened, Jonathan found he enjoyed the gentle sway of her hips as she
moved across the room to the pitcher.

Not dead quite yet.

He drank that one too. It seemed to help, and slowly
he sank back against the pillows. The weakness was infuriating, but then again, an extremely beautiful young
woman was hovering over him, so the situation was not
as dire as it could have been.

"Where's Addie?" The concern homed in, sharp and
intense as his head cleared a little.

"With Lily." Cecily smiled uncertainly. "They seem to
be growing very fond of each other. No one has told her
precisely what happened. We didn't want her to worry.
She's safe. I give my word."

He relaxed a fraction. "Thank you."

"Cook sent up some broth. Can you take some?" Her face was drawn into an anxious—charming—frown.

Was she just beautiful all the time? Even when rumpled and obviously tired?

Yes, she was.

Jonathan at least attempted a smile. "In a bit, yes, I think so."

He'd been here before ... in the aftermath of a serious wound, but this was far superior to the army form of nursing offered to him then. Those were usually overworked women who administered tender care on a severe time limit in the middle of a war. He far preferred gazing at his lovely intended bride, but he did note the slight dark circles under her eyes. The way he felt, he'd been ill for some time ...

Try to remember.

It was just flashes. The coolness of the morning. The reckless ride. Seneca splashing through the river ...

Some of it came back. The crack of gunfire, which he certainly hadn't expected in the quiet of the English countryside and certainly not on the ducal estate. Then a second shot ... and he'd fallen ...

Jonathan said slowly, "Someone shot me."

She nodded, a delectable golden curl that was loose from her chignon brushing the graceful column of her neck. "What else do you recall?"

"Not much," he admitted. The second bullet must have grazed his side, for he noted that besides his shoulder, there was a swath of bandages around his waist as well. That could have been bad, he realized grimly—being gut-shot was usually a death sentence. "The shots. Seneca was spooked and I was surprised and I fell...."

There was more. He knew there was more, but he just couldn't quite bring it into focus.

"You must have hit your head on something. Dr. Gilchrist thinks you have some broken ribs as well."

No wonder it hurt to even breathe in. "Sounds lovely," he said ironically. Then his voice softened. "You are as beautiful as ever, but you look tired. I am not going to ask, because I know you've been here the entire time. The spirits tell me it's true. When did this happen?"

"Two days ago." She smiled and took his hand, twining their fingers, her slender hand much smaller than his larger one, but the joining perfect just the same. "What would make you think I'd ever leave you? I am just grateful *you* didn't leave *me.*"

His delicate English lady had an inner strength of purpose that he was fairly sure had brought him back from the brink of death.

And the spirits approved enough to not topple him over the edge.

"I'm rather grateful myself." It took some effort to tighten the grip on her hand, and as a man who wasn't easily moved to tears, he hastily attributed the burning in his eyes to his injured state. Even when he'd received word his father had died, he hadn't cried, but now . . .

"I hadn't yet told you that I love you." She leaned closer, her floral feminine scent an intoxicant and her words even more so. "It was all I could think about. I'd never *told* you."

"Nor I you." His voice was barely audible.

"There's nothing stopping us from doing so now."

"I'll go first," he murmured, watching her from under half-lowered lids, knowing that in his entire life he would never take for granted her beauty, the inner even more than the outer. She was without guile, and had always, from the moment they encountered each other that fateful night of the ball, looked at him as a man, not a half-breed earl, and she *loved* him.

"I love you." Pain was an abstract concept that had nothing to do with the joy in his heart, so he smiled as he spoke the words, no reluctance, her presence a balm more effective than any medication. Serenity filled his soul. He'd been spared for a reason, and that reason was even now smiling back at him, her eyes misty.

"I love *you*." Cecily touched his bruised cheek. "So much it frightens me, and I know quite a bit about fear from these past few days."

"I'm sorry, my lady." The quiet voice interrupted before he could say anything. Jonathan very much wanted to explain that romantic love was different and he'd never loved a woman this way before, but maybe it was for the best to save that impassioned speech for another time, as he was not certain that eloquence and acute pain went hand in hand very well.

Cecily turned. "What is it, Mrs. Hawkins?"

"The duke has arrived and is downstairs requesting your presence. I'm to sit with his lordship in your place, my lady."

She blinked. "My father is here?"

"The duchess sent for him. They are in the private salon."

Had Jonathan had the strength to object at the interruption at such a poignant moment in their lives, he might have, but truthfully he was weaker than he had imagined, so he simply nodded when Cecily made her excuses and left the room in a flurry of rose perfume.

Mrs. Hawkins, who was tall and angular, with a pronounced Scots accent, said pragmatically, "It's time to change the dressings anyway, your lordship, and the lassie can't be here for that."

Thankfully he was already half asleep when the woman pulled down the sheet.

Chapter 29

No one spoke as she entered the room, and while she normally would have gone to greet her father, Cecily instead registered the disparate presence of not only her parent, her grandmother, James Bourne, and Eleanor, but also William Shakes, the gamekeeper, dressed in his usual worn breeches and dusty coat, sitting awkwardly on the edge of an embroidered chair as if he might soil it. He jumped to his feet when he saw her, looking relieved not to be sitting in the presence of the regal company of the duke and the dowager duchess. He continually turned his hat in his hands in an obvious nervous mannerism. Thickset and soft-spoken, with dark hair now shot with silver and skin weathered into an oak mask, he had been a fixture on the estate as long as Cecily could remember.

She said nothing, simply smoothed her skirts and hesitated because the tension in the room was palpable.

"William," her grandmother said in a chilly voice by way of greeting, "saw the man who attacked Lord Augustine. He heard the gunfire and he followed the culprit."

"Thought he was a poacher," William muttered, shifting his weight uncomfortably. "He had all the signs. Several guns, blood on his boots; what else was I to think, I ask you. A nuisance, the lot of them. So I shot the bugger." Immediately he directed a guilty look at her grandmother for his language. "My apologies, Your Grace."

Cecily's elation over Jonathan's move toward recovery and their tender words vanished, replaced by confusion. William was one of the nicest, most gentle men she knew. "You'd never—" she began to say.

"He did." Her father cut her off, his expression rigid. Elegant as usual in his severe formal dress, he stood stiff-backed by a settee, his features cold and his hands laced behind his back.

"He did," James Bourne agreed, his expression neutral. "Drury and I have been trying to piece together what happened for the past few days, and we found a shallow grave on a remote part of the estate. The man buried there is named Josiah Browne. He used to be an estate manager for our family, until we discovered he was embezzling funds and terminated his employment. I suspect he was behind several suspicious accidents that have happened lately, such as tampering with the wheel of my carriage and an attack I thought was merely an attempt to steal my purse. He definitely had a grudge against both me and Jonathan. He must have followed us here."

The broken wheel was certainly an event she'd never forget, but still, William would never deliberately kill someone.

"Why didn't you tell us?"

William's jaw jutted out at a stubborn angle. "Just a poacher."

"When Elijah told me where they found the grave," Eleanor said quietly, "I thought maybe they should talk to William. Very little happens on the grounds that he doesn't know about."

Elijah? The first-name usage was encouraging, but Cecily was still so bewildered by this turn of events that she only barely registered it.

Her father said grimly, "I came from London to deal with this, as the Shakes family has worked for ours for generations. As your grandmother just said, William has admitted to killing the man and burying the body. Our problem now is what to do about this. A magistrate might hang him."

For all his austere ways, her father was a kindhearted person. It didn't surprise Cecily that he would travel for hours for the gamekeeper on one of his estates.

"'Twas for no reason other than what I said." William refused to back down, but his face took on a dusky hue. "Let them hang me."

"Everyone leave us, please, so I can have a word with William alone." When her father spoke in that autocratic tone, no one argued, not even her grandmother. He turned to Cecily. "As this directly concerns your fiancé, you stay."

"As far as I am concerned, Shakes did us a favor," James said as he rose to leave the room, his eyes somber. "Whatever happened to Browne was no less than he deserved."

Once the room was cleared and the door closed, her father nodded at her. "Cecily, sit down."

She sank obediently into a silk-covered chair while William still stood with a hint of defiance that she didn't at all understand, the two men facing each other, lord and servant, but also of an age, and though her father was duke and William a mere gamekeeper, they'd been raised on the estate at the same time. Her father rubbed his jaw and said with weary familiarity, "Will, please, for the love of God, will you simply tell me the truth? When a man is nearly killed, and another found buried on my property, I am ultimately responsible. We need a better story than you thought he was a poacher. You've caught many a poacher before without killing them, much less not bothering to inform anyone of the not-so-insignificant event of a man's death."

"The likes of him won't be missed."

"No, I am guessing you are correct in that assumption, but for the sake of my personal edification, I would like to know what happened. If I must explain this event—and enough people know that I must, not to mention he should be buried properly—I don't want to sound like a fool who employs a murderous gamekeeper. There must have been just cause or you would not have taken such a drastic course. Just tell me."

With obvious reluctance William said, "I heard shots. Saw him riding away. So I stopped him and told him he was going straight to the authorities for trespassing on the property of the Duke of Eddington. He was a nasty fellow. As I said, he had a gun and there was the blood. One thing led to another."

"It was self-defense?"

Had at that moment William not glanced at her for the first time, his already ruddy skin taking on a deeper color, Cecily would not have made the connection.

Nasty fellow.

Oh, God. The world stopped. She suddenly saw in her memory the slow-moving beauty of the river, the water sliding past, her and Jonathan shedding their clothes, frantic for each other, him sweeping her into his arms . . . and then they'd made love.

She'd not thought about anyone seeing them in that remote corner, but that was possible if what James claimed was true and this Josiah Browne had followed them to the estate from London and was prowling the grounds. . . .

The words came involuntarily from her mouth. "What did he say? Oh, God in heaven, William . . . he saw us, didn't he? If you took him to the magistrate he would tell the court everything. . . . You were trying to protect me, weren't you?" It was so mortifying, yet she was sure she was right.

"I've no idea what you are talking about, milady. I saw him riding about in the early hours and I shot him. That's the extent of it." William's rough voice was bereft of excuse. "I had no idea his lordship was what he was hunting, but I figure that's worse than any hart or hare anyway. Did the world a favor, I did."

Her father muttered something she didn't catch.

It was a bit difficult to reconcile that maybe they'd been watched during the magical interlude in the river, and that the murderous Browne would have used that to try to escape penance for his attack on Jonathan, but cool logic told her that was what had happened.

Despite the audience of her now frigidly disapproving father, Cecily rose and went over and took William's rough hand in hers. "You tried to protect me, and as he shot Jonathan in a very cowardly way, I believe you are right, he was a very nasty fellow. Now, let my father help you."

William looked at her for a moment, and then nodded once. "He was a murdering swine, not to mention a trespasser. I'd kill him again, I would."

"So you had a murderous confrontation with a poacher," her father interjected into the conversation, his voice cool. "Is that correct, Shakes?"

"That's right, Your Grace."

"I believe I understand now what happened. You are dismissed. Do not worry—I think I can ensure that no charges will be taken to the local court. Go back to your duties."

William awkwardly tipped his hat and left.

When she turned around, Cecily found she was grateful for not having a larger audience, for truly, the glare of the patrician disapproval of her father was unnerving enough.

Her feelings at this point were divided, Cecily decided, flushed but her stance erect. She wasn't inclined to apologize for the interlude in the river—because it would no doubt always be one of the most cherished afternoons of her life, and while Jonathan had lain there between life and death, she had consoled herself with the knowledge that she would always hold those tender moments in her heart.

Still, it was all rather mortifying.

"And here I thought Eleanor was the daughter that would give me the most sleepless nights." Her father sighed. "At least no one is any longer trying to murder the man you apparently need to marry with all due speed. I wish you joy of each other, for you seem well suited if mutual recklessness is a measure of compatibility."

"This is my fault."

"No, my dear, it isn't." Her father's voice was surprisingly gentle. "I forbid you to feel that way."

When she started to say more, he held up a hand, palm outward, to stop her. "Did you invite the odious man to the estate and ask him to shoot Lord Augustine from the cover of the bushes and then do his best to beat him to death? No, of course you didn't. Nor was Augustine unjustified in letting go a man who was openly stealing from him, according to James Bourne, so there you have it. Perhaps more discretion would be wise, but that is hardly a crime.

"There's no question that this Browne was a villain who deserved what form of rustic justice was bestowed upon him. William is not by nature a violent man, so the provocation must have been extreme. Besides, we know Browne was armed and willing to use his weapon, so perhaps it is just as well that we will never know exactly what happened. I am certain enough justice prevailed, with or without the due process of our tedious legal avenues, that my conscience does not bother me. It sounds to me as though I might have been moved to violence myself."

Cecily faced her father, a bit bemused by his attitude. "So that is the end of it?"

"No."

"No?"

He smiled. It was slight, but definitely there. "I think you have a wedding to plan for when Augustine can stand upright long enough to recite his vows."

She could have sworn that when she nodded and went to leave the room, her father added under his breath, "Which had better be soon."

She couldn't have agreed more.

"Papa!"

His daughter threw her arms around him with such enthusiasm that he stifled a flinch, but Jonathan pulled her close and dropped a kiss on the top of her shining head, pressing his cheek against her silky hair. With a great deal of effort and some help from James, he'd managed to don a pair of breeches and halfway put on a shirt, though one arm was in a sling to keep him from using his shoulder and so the latter garment was not buttoned enough to conceal the bandages, not to mention that the bruises on his face were not something he could hide.

"You've been sleeping," Addie said accusingly as he lifted her onto his lap with his good arm despite his cracked ribs. The pain was acute, but the reward worth it. She snuggled against his chest. "For ever so long."

"I was tired." He'd tried to come up with an excuse a five-year-old would accept, but he wasn't exactly brilliant at the moment, so he'd decided to just tell as much of the truth as possible. "I had an accident. Like when you slipped on the stairs and broke your arm."

"It hurt," she acknowledged, her small face drawn into a frown.

"Yes," he agreed wryly. *Like hell*, an inner voice added.

"Aunt Lily said you fell from your horse, but I said no. You never fall."

Good for Lily. The aunt in question stood nearby in the doorway of the small sitting room off his bedroom, a slight smile on her face. "I did this time," Jonathan said, catching his sister's eye and hopefully conveying an unspoken thank-you. "It hurt too."

"Did you cry like me?"

He wasn't sure how to answer that earnest question, so instead he stroked Adela's cheek with a fingertip. "Can I tell you a secret?"

His daughter's small face lit with delight and she sat up. "Yes! I love secrets!"

"I'm going to marry Lady Cecily."

Whatever he expected, it wasn't the scornful female look he received. "*That's* not a secret, Papa," Adela informed him, slipping off his lap with childish impatience. "Nanny told me. Cook told me. Aunt Betsy and Aunt Carole told me. Cousin James—"

Apparently he was related to a multitude of conspirators. With a suppressed laugh, Jonathan interrupted her. "I apologize, then. I'll try for a better secret next time."

"Treasure?"

"What?"

"Buried treasure. With curses on it."

He glanced sharply at his sister, who shrugged, but her lips compressed in undisguised mirth. "We've been reading together. She has an adventurous spirit."

"Now, that's a surprise," he murmured. To Addie he said, "You do like Lady Cecily, don't you?"

His daughter nodded, and said ingenuously, "She's nice. And pretty. And her eyes are magic."

"I couldn't agree more."

At that moment, he noticed something else. A slender form in the doorway, familiar, evocative of delicious memories even in his weakened state. Lily noticed Cecily's arrival also, for she promptly took Adela's hand and said, "Perhaps we should go looking for treasure along the river."

When they left, Cecily chose a nearby chair, her smile warming the room. "You look better."

"James just told me less than an hour ago I look like hell."

"But as I said, better than the past few days. Has no one ever told you that cursing in front of a lady is rude?" She lifted a brow.

He attempted to shrug, but it was a poor idea with his injured shoulder. "I do think I have been lectured before on the subject. I must not have been listening."

Cecily laughed, the musical sound spontaneous. Then his wife-to-be, lovely in a simple white muslin gown, with a ribbon holding her pale hair back, gazed at him and said, "My eyes are magic? What does that mean?"

"Come kiss me and I'll explain."

"You are hardly in any condition, my lord, for—"

"Kissing? I assure you my lips are completely uninjured."

Though he was fairly sure she called him intractable so quietly he barely caught it, Cecily did come forward and placed a chaste, cool kiss on his mouth.

"A real kiss, if you please." His grin was teasing. Yes, he ached, and the pain was distracting, but not nearly as distracting as the lovely young woman bent over him, her hands braced on the arms of his chair, those magical eyes so close.

The second try was much, much better.

So he relented and told her about the magic.

And then managed to coax out a third kiss.

Epilogue

The sound of labored breathing matched perfectly with the rising wind rattling the pane of the window.

"It's going to storm." Cecily smoothed a lock of hair from her husband's brow, not sure in the aftermath of such acute pleasure whether she was able to do more than lazily let her lashes drift down.

She *was* tired.

Pleasantly so.

His erection still impressively rigid inside her, Jonathan kissed one brow, then the other, and murmured softly. "I think the storm has passed, but perhaps it will resurface again."

"It sounds to me like it is approaching," she said dubiously, the thunder getting louder.

He nibbled on her earlobe. "I meant here in our bed."

How could she not laugh? And shiver. He was above her, *in* her, and their physical union aside, such a part of her that she couldn't imagine life without him.

She looked into his dark eyes. "Promise me again that you do not regret not returning to America as you planned."

"We'll go there soon enough." His mouth did beguiling things to the pulse point at the hollow of her throat. "After our child is born. I have matters to bring to a conclusion here, and trust me, I am content. The definition of *home* has taken on a new meaning, my love. I thought it was a place. I was wrong."

"How so?" Languid against him, she touched his hair, those ebony strands decadently long and brushing his shoulders.

"If you and Addie and our coming child are safe and with me, *that* is home."

It wasn't as if she disagreed. Her pregnancy was now confirmed. And at this moment, in the tangled linens of their bed, with streaks of lightning in the distance, she wanted to be nowhere else but in his arms, whether in England or America.

"She's excited about the baby."

"Addie? Yes, she is. She wants a baby brother. She asks me every day when *he* will get here."

"And you?"

"Give me a healthy child and a safe delivery and I will be a happy man."

"Are you worried about Lily?" she asked as his mouth brushed over the tip of her right breast, causing a tingle she well remembered.

"Can we talk about my *sister* some other time?" He moved up to kiss her, his tongue invading, conquering, distracting her even as he claimed her in a more primal way. When he lifted his head, he smiled wickedly. "We have some unfinished business, I believe."

Mystified, she looked up at him and then gasped when he took a glass from the bedside table and splashed cool wine over her bare breasts. His voice held a sultry roughness. "As I said then, I wanted to do this the first time I saw you and now seems an opportune time. Do not worry—I will lick it away."

As his tongue teased and tasted every curve and leisurely explored each hollow and valley, she decided that this was *exactly* the right time.

Sometime later, when they rested together again after the acute peak of pleasure, the softly spoken words, the heated sighs, he laughed.

"What is so amusing?" She was more tired than usual with the pregnancy, though everyone promised her the fatigue passed eventually.

"Your sister's wedding is tomorrow."

"Elle's wedding is entertaining?"

Jonathan laughed again in a swift exhale. "I can't wait to witness Drury getting leg-shackled to your sister."

On the edge of sleep, Cecily murmured, "I agree. Both Carole and Betsy also have serious suitors, but what of Lily?"

His fingers sifted through her hair, his lean body propped above her, comfortably pinning her to the bed. "The spirits tell me she will find the right one eventually."

"Your spirits? I wished they talked to me."

"They will." He smoothed his hand over the slight swell of her stomach. "We are one."

"I am still worried about her."

He laughed. "Your grandmother is in charge of her future, and the determination there intimidates even me. I think we can rest assured that she is being managed quite well. The Dowager Duchess of Eddington is a formidable force when she takes on such a challenge."

"Lily will never forgive you for that." Cecily summoned the strength to smile at him. He truly was the most handsome man ever—if one favored them a bit uncivilized, with delicious exotic coloring and midnight eyes.

"Probably not." His voice held a hint of amusement.

"Families," Cecily said as if it was a new observation, "are quite complicated."

"Is that why we are starting one?" His breath whispered against her ear. "To complicate our lives? I thought between England, America, my daughter, four sisters between us, and a brother and cousin, not to mention all the assorted other family members, we were already in a complicated enough situation."

"I cannot wait to hold our child." Her hands smoothed his bare back. He was leaner than before his injuries, but she still reveled in his strength "It is how life continues."

"It is how *love* continues." Her Earl Savage looked into her eyes and said the words softly, only for her.

And like the first time they met, with one whisper, she was swept away.

Read on for a look at

TWICE FALLEN,

Emma Wildes's next book in
the Ladies in Waiting series

Coming in December 2011
from Signet Eclipse.

Summer 1815
The Battle of Waterloo

The battle was over, but his troubles were not.

Damn.

Damien Northfield shifted his weight and did his best to ignore the dizzying weakness that made it almost impossible to move. It wasn't that he'd never been wounded before, but this was different. His mouth tasted like sawdust—it felt as if he'd swallowed an entire cartload of it—and all around him was a sea of battered, bloodied bodies. If it were not for the occasional eerie moan, he might have thought himself entirely alone, the single ghost among the dead.

His left leg, he discovered, was useless.

Each time he attempted to lever himself up, the pain was enough to make him grit his teeth and fight to remain conscious. There was no doubt that there was a certain attraction to the state of insensibility, especially when dealing with the agonizing repercussions of trying to stand, but the truth was, he didn't have the luxury of being able to lie down and die.

This could not be it. The end of all of these past years and the effort he'd put into his duties? No, not here, like this, now.

He had his whole life ahead of him.
Didn't he?

London, 1816

A library, she'd learned, was a delightful place to sit during a formal ball.

First of all it was blissfully quiet, Lady Lillian Bourne
thought, settling back against the comfortable cushions.
The music was barely audible in the background, and
Lily was grateful she was not assaulted by noise from all
sides. If she were daring she might be able to stretch the
respite to twenty minutes.

Even as she reflected on how she despised the press
of so much noise and too many people, the library suddenly lost its status as a solitary refuge.

The door opened, it closed, and then it opened again
almost at once.

Lily could have sworn she heard a deep male voice
mutter a curse that contained an intriguing word she
didn't recognize.

"*This* is where you were going, my lord?"

The second speaker was a woman and the question
held a sultry female intonation. Lily had to resist the
urge to sit up and see who had entered the room, but
she wasn't all that anxious to be discovered herself, so
she remained hidden, propped carelessly on the velvet-
covered settee in an unladylike pose with her ankles
crossed.

"Yes, for just a few minutes of *solitude*."

The weighted emphasis on that last word was lost
on his companion. The woman's laugh was musical and
light. "You are always so droll."

"Am I?" Lord Whoever's voice was dry but not offensive, just offhand. "I wasn't aware. Can I help you, Lady Piedmont?"

Lady Piedmont? As in the wife of the man some speculated might become the next prime minister? That was interesting. Lily didn't merely follow the society papers; she was also careful to pay attention to the political machinations of the English system of government, and she knew the name well.

"I think you know why I followed you."

Lily might not be as sophisticated as rumor had it, but that murmured inflection was hard to miss. Low, with a heated note that told her she definitely did not now want to make her presence known, and the lack of a response indicated that perhaps some sort of physical contact might just be occurring.

How the devil *did* she get herself into these situations? she wondered with a mixture of irritation and chagrin. All she'd wanted was a few minutes of peace and quiet before having to face all of society gawping at her and not succeeding in concealing their avid interest in her every move, lest she fall from grace again.

Once had been entirely too much.

"Miriam," the unknown man said, his voice a notch deeper, "don't. I refuse to cooperate."

"Ah, but there is evidence to the contrary. Your cock is getting hard, darling."

"A beautiful woman is endeavoring to unbutton my breeches. I think with most males there would be a predictable physical reaction, but that does not mean I want this to go any further."

"No? Rumor has it you are remarkably well endowed. I am rather eager to verify that for myself." The words were said in a low, persuasive purr.

"Good Lord, don't you females have anything better

to discuss? I'm sorry, but I am uninterested in assuaging your curiosity."

Lady Piedmont was undeterred. She said quite breathlessly, "Kiss me again."

"I didn't kiss you the first time," he argued. "*You* kissed *me*. It's quite different, my dear."

Lily could no longer contain the impulse, easing up to take a quick glimpse over the top of the settee. It was a large, long room, and she was in the shadows at the far end. The beleaguered but as yet unidentified lord was no doubt busy enough fending off his determined seductress, and certainly Lady Piedmont's attention was focused on her quarry, so she doubted they would see her.

Sure enough, there were the very lovely Lady Piedmont, who might not have been in the first bloom of youth but could still put most ingénues to shame with her flaming-red hair and generous figure, and a well-dressed man whose hands at the moment shackled her wrists, obviously to keep her from her pursuit to unfasten his clothing. The lady in question was still pressed suggestively against him, his back to one of the bookcases. Had it been a reluctant young lady being accosted by a male, Lily would have grabbed a handy weapon, such as the heavy Chinese vase sitting on the table to her right, and come to her rescue, but from what she could see, the object of Lady Piedmont's desire was tall and wide-shouldered and looked entirely capable of taking care of himself.

"I'm flattered," he said with a hint of humor, "at your interest, but our mutual absence from the ballroom will be noted. I think it is more than prudent for you to return as soon as possible."

"Prudence has never been my main virtue."

Lily could believe that, especially the way the woman had plastered herself against him. Virtue didn't apply. The word *shameless* came to mind.

"Do you really want to become the target for a barrage of backhanded whispers?"

No, Lily thought from firsthand experience. *Trust me, you don't.*

"Can we discuss this . . . later then? Someplace more discreet?"

"No."

"Darling, I—"

"No." His tone was gentle, maybe even indulgent, but there was an undercurrent that implacably supported his denial.

"Why not?" There was a definite pout in the question, but at least it indicated she finally understood he meant his refusal.

"For a myriad of reasons."

Lily felt a flicker of admiration. After all, it wasn't as if most men in society didn't indulge themselves in casual affairs. Yet this man declined the beautiful Lady Piedmont's aggressive offer. And his rejection wasn't tempered with a variety of explanations. *No* was *no.*

Good for him.

Then he dropped Lady Piedmont's wrists, and despite her outraged gasp, somehow he deftly opened the door and deposited her outside. He was back inside, with the door closed and locked, before Lily could register the impressive maneuver.

Lily ducked back down before he turned, hearing him mutter, "By the devil, there had better be brandy in here somewhere."

There was. The tray with the decanter and glasses rested on a small polished desk very close to where she sat wondering how fate could be so wily as to conjure a scenario in which she, who meticulously strived to avoid any situation that might be even mildly indiscreet, suddenly found herself locked in a room with a strange gentleman.

Her reputation could not survive another scandal.

If there had been a way to decamp out the window, or maybe scamper under a convenient chair, she would have taken it, but he moved purposefully in her direction and her breath caught in her throat.

Damnation, as her older brother, Jonathan, might have said. This was awkward.

Then again, it wasn't as if she'd done anything wrong. She'd merely done exactly what the man who had intruded claimed to do: sought a bit of a reprieve from the ball. It was not her fault he'd attracted the importunate Lady Piedmont.

There was nothing to do but brazen it out.

The faint hint of violets when he'd entered the room had been the first clue that someone else was present as well. The sweet scent was more subtle than the overwhelming gardenia perfume Lady Piedmont wore, but definitely there and, in a library full of the smell of dusty leather and gently decaying paper, out of place.

Then had come the subtle rustle of silk as she moved, giving away her location, which happened to be a settee in a small grouping by the tall windows at the back of the room, where he imagined a lovely view of the garden awaited anyone who sat in the daylight for a quiet afternoon read.

Just the spot he would have chosen. Already, Lord Damien Northfield thought, he was intrigued by the mysterious lady he imagined was in a slight state of panic over her inevitable discovery. That he could tell also, for while the sound of the orchestra in the ballroom still came faintly, her quickened breathing was audible to someone who had spent a great deal of the Peninsular War using all five of his senses to keep himself alive.

He could understand why she might not have announced her presence when he arrived with the rabid Lady Piedmont on his heels, but the real question was, why had she been hiding in the library in the first place?

As he needed that brandy, and he was interested in the answer to that question, he walked down the length of the room, his damned leg aching every step of the way, and said in a neutral voice without even glancing at the settee, "Good evening."

There was a short silence, punctuated only by the clink as he removed the top of the decanter, and then the splash as he poured some of the liquor into a small crystal snifter.

"You knew I was here?"

Damien liked the sound of her voice. A lovely contralto, carefully modulated, and though it was tempting to turn around and see what she looked like, he denied himself, taking a sip from his glass. The brandy, he was happy to discover, was the best France had to offer and very smooth. "Yes."

She sat up. He knew it because of the sound of her feet touching the floor and the slight—almost inaudible—creak of the settee's springs. "Why didn't you say anything?"

"Why didn't *you*?" The brandy was heady and he swirled the liquid once before taking a second sip and slowly turning around.

His first impression was that his quiet spy was striking. No, not beautiful—at least not like Lady Piedmont with her generous breasts and flaming hair—but . . . different. Pretty. Memorable even. Her hair was a rich color that in the insufficient light looked light brown with a few golden glints, and her figure was slender, not overly curvaceous, which was pleasing enough, and her skin pale and smooth. Her gown wasn't beribboned and festooned with lace, but instead simple and yet fashionable, the neckline emphasizing the gentle curves of her breasts, the rose color offsetting the creaminess of her complexion.

She had a very defiant tilt to her shapely chin.

It must have been a personal flaw in his intellectual composition, but he found that militant air fascinating.

"I was here first."

It was a valid argument, so he shrugged, but he was *watching* her. Would he ever rid himself of the habit? God, he hoped so. He was always watching. It was not an option in the existence he'd just shed, and he was uneasily settling into this new one. But he didn't wish to go through his entire life vigilant and on guard.

"Yes, you were." Damien took another drink. He'd done countless interrogations, and word had it he was very, very good at it. In fact, he knew he was. "Since there is no one to introduce us, and you just witnessed a rather personal scene, I think informality is in order." He bowed slightly. "Lord Damien Northfield, at your service."

There was a perceptible hesitation, and then she said coolly, "Lady Lillian Bourne."

He hadn't been back in society long enough to really know any of the current gossip, not that he cared all that much about the generally superficial sins of the aristocracy anyway after so many bloody years in Portugal and Spain, but there was something in her voice that told him she thought the name might mean something to him.

It did actually. It belonged to her. Lillian. He liked it. It was elegant and yet not too prim.

"May I offer my apologies for what you overheard?" It was the least he could do, for if she was an unmarried young lady—and he would stake his life on it—that hadn't been the most appropriate of dialogue.

"It seems to me you were not the one being improper, my lord."

Lovely *and* intelligent, the dry note in her observation duly noted. "I was doing my best to dissuade her," he agreed with a slight, hopefully disarming smile.

"She's very beautiful."

He was a little surprised at the directness. "Yes." He swirled the liquid in the glass, took a sip, and then expounded, "But unabashed pursuit is not appealing to me. I've been hunted enough."

The lighting was dim, but he still caught the flicker of surprise in her eyes. "That is an interesting statement. Are we still discussing eager women throwing themselves into your arms?"

"No."

"I thought not."

Anyone else would ask her why she wasn't in the ballroom, but he rarely inquired directly to gain information. His methods were much more subtle. "Though I confess I am no longer accustomed to the workings of the *ton*."

Lady Lillian, he discovered then, was not predictable. He anticipated that she would either comment that she'd heard of him or ask him why he'd been absent from the exalted circle he mentioned, but she did neither. Instead she rose in a flurry of rose silk and violet perfume.

"I need to get back to the ball and cannot be seen leaving the same room as you. As unlikely as it would be that anyone would be observing the library, will you still please do me the favor of waiting a decent interval before rejoining the party?"

And here the evening had just taken on a warm new glow and she wished to leave.

Fortunately he was a master at negotiation.

His smile was affable. "Of course." He paused. "If you will tell me why you prefer this dark library to the festivities."

"You set *conditions* on being a gentleman?"

Damien didn't blink an eye. "Absolutely. I think you will find I set conditions on everything."

Strategy was a simple matter usually. Judge your opponent and react accordingly.

"I will find?" she repeated delicately, and truthfully, he found the phrasing odd himself.

Damien Northfield, who once might have been more important to the campaign on the Iberian Peninsula than even the Duke of Wellington, was not sure how to respond.

"Should we meet again," he equivocated, glad now for the brandy in his hand. He took a solid sip and watched her give a nod and move gracefully toward the door.

He liked the sway of her hips.

He also admired the curve of her spine, and the soft color of her hair in the lamplight.

Oh, yes, he vowed silently, *we will meet again.*

For she had not answered his question.